Collected Stories and Sketches: 3
Ice House of the Mind

Etching by William Strang, 1898

R.B. Cunninghame Graham

Collected Stories and Sketches

Volume 3

Ice House of the Mind

Edited by Alan MacGillivray and John C. McIntyre

K&B

Kennedy & Boyd
an imprint of
Zeticula
57 St Vincent Crescent
Glasgow
G3 8NQ
Scotland
http://www.kennedyandboyd.co.uk
admin@kennedyandboyd.co.uk

His People originally published in 1906
Faith originally published in 1909
Hope originally published in 1910
This edition copyright © Zeticula 2011
Frontispiece from *Etchings of William Strang* by Frank Newbolt, Newnes, 1907.

Contributors:
R. B. Cunninghame Graham: The Life and *The Writings*
© Alan MacGillivray 2011
Introduction to *His People* © Alan MacGillivray 2011
Introduction to *Faith* © Alan MacGillivray 2011
Introduction to *Hope* © Alan MacGillivray 2011
Four Women in *Faith* and *Hope* © John C. McIntyre 2011
Cunninghame Graham: Editing His Spanish © John C. McIntyre 2011

Cover photograph © Jessica Greaves 2011
Cover design by Felicity Wild
Book design by Catherine E. Smith

ISBN 978-1-84921-102-4

"All that we write is but a bringing forth again of something we have seen or heard about. What makes it art is but the handling of it, and the imagination that is brought to bear upon the theme out of the writer's brain. It follows therefore that all writing, as I said before, brings sorrow in its train.....To record, even to record emotions, is to store up a fund of sadness, and that is why all writing is a sort of icehouse of the mind....

(*Faith*, Preface).

Contents

Preface to the Collection

Robert Bontine Cunninghame Graham first came to public attention as a Radical Liberal Member of Parliament in the 1880s, when he was in his thirties. The apparent contradiction between his Scottish aristocratic family background and his vigorous attachment to the causes of Socialism, the Labour movement, anti-Imperialism and Scottish Home Rule ensured that he remained a controversial figure for many years right up to his death in the 1930s. Through his father's family of Cunninghame Graham, descended from King Robert II of Scotland and the Earls of Menteith, he had a strong territorial connection with the West of Scotland. On his mother's side, he had significant Hispanic ties through his Spanish grandmother and a naval grandfather who took part in the South American Wars of Liberation. His own world-wide travels, particularly in the Americas, Spain and North Africa, and his amazingly wide circle of friends and acquaintances in many countries and different walks of life gave him a cosmopolitan breadth of experience and a depth of insight into human nature and behaviour that would be the envy of any writer.

And it is as a writer that we now have primarily to remember Graham. His lasting political monuments are the Labour Party and the Scottish National Party, both of which he was deeply involved in founding. Yet he has to share that credit with others. His literary works are his alone. He wrote books of history, travel and biography which were extensively researched but very personal in tone, so that, although highly readable, they might not easily withstand the objective scrutiny of modern scholarship. Rather it is in his favoured literary forms of the short story, sketch and meditative essay, forms often tending to merge into one another, that Graham excels. Over forty years, between 1896 and 1936, he published fourteen collections of such short pieces, ranging over many subjects and lands. With such a wealth of life experience behind him, Graham did not have to dig deep for inspiration. Probably no other Scottish writer of any age brings such a knowledge and awareness of life's diversity to the endeavour of literary creation. However, the quality of his achievement has not as yet been fully assessed. One reason is not hard to find. There has never yet been a proper bringing together of Graham's separate collections into a manageable edition to provide the essential tools for critical study. Consequently literary attention has never been really focused on him, something for which the climate of twentieth-century Scottish, and British, critical fashion is partly responsible. Neither the Modernist movement nor the Scottish Renaissance seems to be an appropriate pigeonhole for Graham to inhabit. He has instead had to suffer the consequences of being too readily stereotyped. Perhaps entranced by the glamour of his apparent flamboyant persona of 'Don Roberto', the Spanish hidalgo, the Argentine gaucho, the Scottish laird, the horseman-adventurer, a succession of editors have republished incomplete collections of stories and sketches selected more to reinforce an image of Graham as larger-than-life legend rather than as the serious literary man he worked hard to be.

The purpose of this series is to make Graham's literary corpus available in a convenient format to modern readers as he originally intended it. Each collection of stories is kept intact, and they appear in chronological order with Graham's own footnotes, and retaining his personal idiosyncrasies and eccentricities of language and style. It is not the intention of the editors to make magisterial judgements of quality or to present a fully annotated critical edition of the stories. These purposes would go far beyond the bounds of this series in space and time, and must remain as tasks for future scholars. We merely hope that a new generation of general readers will discover Graham's short stories and sketches to be interesting and stimulating for their own sake and in their own right, diverse and revealing of a strong and generally sympathetic personality, a richly-stocked original mind and an ironic, realistic yet sensitive observer of the amazing variety of life in a very wide world.

Alan MacGillivray
John C. McIntyre

Robert Bontine Cunninghame Graham

The Life

Robert Bontine Cunninghame Graham belonged to the old-established family of Cunninghame Graham, which had its ancestral territory in the District of Menteith lying between Stirling and Loch Lomond. The family had at one time held the earldom of Menteith and could trace its ancestry back to King Robert II of Scotland in the fourteenth century. The title had been dormant since the seventeenth century, and the Cunninghame Grahams showed no real interest in reviving it. In fact, Graham passed his childhood officially bearing the surname of Bontine, because, during his youth, owing to a strange legal quirk relating to the entailing of estates and conditions of inheritance, the name 'Graham' could only be borne by Robert's grandfather who held the main Graham estate of Gartmore. Robert's father, William, an army officer, had to take another family surname, Bontine, until he inherited Gartmore in 1863. As a young man thereafter, Robert does not seem to have bothered which name he used, and when he in his turn inherited Gartmore, he kept Bontine as a middle name.

Graham was born in London in 1852. His half-Spanish mother preferred the social life of London, while his father had his responsibilities as a Scottish landowner. Accordingly, Graham's boyhood years were spent moving between the south of England and the family's Scottish houses at Gartmore in Menteith, Ardoch in Dunbartonshire and Finlaystone in Renfrewshire. Before going to preparatory school, he spent a lot of time with his Spanish grandmother, Doña Catalina, at her home in the Isle of Wight and accompanied her to Spain on a number of visits. This was his introduction to the Spanish way of life and the Spanish language, in which he became proficient. At the age of eleven he went to a prep school in Warwickshire, before going to Harrow public school for two years. He apparently disliked Harrow intensely and in 1866 was taken from it and sent to a Brussels private school which was much more to his taste. It was during his year there that he learned French and had instruction in fencing. After a year in Brussels, Graham's formal education ended and he spent the next two years until he was seventeen between his homes in Britain and his grandmother's family in Spain, developing along the way his passion for horses and his considerable riding skills.

Graham's adult life began when in 1870, with the support and financial encouragement of his parents, he took ship from Liverpool by way of Corunna and Lisbon for Argentina. The primary motivation was to make money by learning the business of ranching and going into partnership on a Scottish-owned estancia, or ranch. This was seen as a necessity, given that the Graham family had fallen into serious financial difficulties. Graham's father, Major William Bontine, had sunk into madness, the final consequence of a severe head injury in a riding accident, and had engaged in wild speculation with the family assets. Consequently, the estates were encumbered with debts and the Major's affairs had been placed under the supervision of an agent of the Court of Session. As the eldest of three sons, Robert had to find his own fortune and eventually pay off his father's debts. Much of his travelling in the following decades, both alone and later with his wife, Gabriela, had the search for profitable business openings at its heart.

Between 1870 and 1877, Graham undertook three ventures in South America. The ranching on the first visit came to nothing, although, being already an accomplished horseman and speaker of Spanish, he very quickly adapted to the life of the gauchos, or cowboys. He also observed at first hand some of the violence and anarchy of the early 1870s in Argentina and Uruguay; he contracted and recovered from typhus; and finally he undertook an overland horse-droving venture before returning to Britain in 1872. The following year he returned to South America, this time to Paraguay with a view to obtaining concessions for cultivating and selling the yerba mate plant, the source of the widely drunk mate infusion. In his search for possible plantation sites, Graham rode deep into the interior and came across the surviving traces of the original seventeenth and eighteenth century Jesuit settlements, the subject, many years later, for one of his best books. He had little success in his efforts and returned to Britain in 1874. After a couple of years travelling, mainly in Europe, but also to Iceland and down the coast of West Africa, Graham set out again, this time with a business partner, bound for Uruguay, where he contemplated ranching but actually set up in the horse trading business, buying horses in Uruguay with a view to driving them into Brazil to be sold to the Brazilian army. This (again) unsuccessful adventure was later described in the novella, "Cruz Alta"

(1900). Graham again returned to Britain and took up residence at his mother's house in London, becoming a familiar man about town and a frequenter of Mrs Bontine's literary and artistic salon, where he began to develop his wide circle of friends and acquaintances in the literary and cultural fields. It was his experiences in South America in the 1870s that formed his passion for the continent and directed so much of his later literary work. Out of this came the appellation of 'Don Roberto', which is now inescapably part of his personal and literary image.

Paris was another of Graham's favourite places, and it was there in 1878 that he met the woman whom he very rapidly made his wife, much to the apparent hostile concern of his family, particularly his mother. The mystery and (probably deliberate) uncertainty surrounding the circumstances of his marriage cry out for proper research among surviving family documents. One can only sketch in the few known facts and legends. Graham met a young woman who was known as Gabriela de la Balmondière. By one account she had been born in Chile with a father of French descent and a Spanish mother. She had been orphaned and brought up in Paris by an aunt, who may or may not have had her educated in a convent. By another account, she was making a living in Paris as an actress.

After a brief acquaintanceship, she and Graham lived together before coming to London and being married in a registry office in October, 1878, without family approval. In time everybody came to accept her as an exotic new member of the family, although there seems to have been some mutual hostility for several years between her and Graham's mother. It was not until the 1980s that the discovery of Gabriela's birth certificate showed that she was in fact English, the daughter of a Yorkshire doctor, and her real name was Caroline, or Carrie, Horsfall. Why Graham, and indeed the whole Graham family, should have gone on through the whole of his and her lives, and beyond, sustaining this myth of Gabriela's origins invites speculations of several kinds that may never be resolved.

After a few months of marriage, Robert and Gabriela set out for the New World, first to New Orleans, and then to Texas with the intention of going into the mule-breeding business. Over the next two years they earned a precarious living by various means both in Texas and Mexico, until the final disaster when a Texas ranch newly acquired by Graham and a business partner was raided and destroyed by Apaches. The Grahams finally returned to Britain in 1881 with substantial debts, and lived quietly in Spain and Hampshire. The death of Graham's father in 1883, however, meant that Robert finally inherited the main family estate of Gartmore with all its debts and problems, and had to live the life of a Scottish laird with all its local and social responsibilities.

The restrictions placed upon Graham by his new role could not confine such a restless spirit for long, and in 1885 he stood unsuccessfully for Parliament as a Liberal. The following year he was elected the MP for North-West Lanark, the beginning of an active and highly-coloured political career that continued in one form or another for the rest of his life. He spent only six years actually in Parliament, a period in which he soon revealed himself as more a Socialist than a Liberal, espousing a number of Radical causes and becoming deeply involved and influential in the early years of the Labour movement, being, along with Keir Hardie, one of the co-founders of the Labour Party. The high point of his time in Parliament was when he was arrested and committed to prison, accused of assaulting a policeman during the 'Bloody Sunday' demonstration in Trafalgar Square on 13th November, 1887. From his maiden speech onwards, he wrote and spoke out forcefully on behalf of Labour causes and finally in 1892 stood unsuccessfully for Parliament directly as a Labour candidate. Even out of Parliament Graham continued to be active politically. Although he gradually ceased to be a leading figure in the new Labour Party, his new-found talent as a polemical journalist, in great demand in the serious papers and journals of the day, enabled him to remain in the public eye with his concern about social conditions and his unfashionable anti-Imperial attitudes. He was opposed to the Boer Wars, as he was also to the new imperialism of the USA, shown during the Spanish-American War of 1898, which affronted his strong attachment to Spain and Latin America. His commitment to Scottish Home Rule led him in his later years to find a new role as a founder of the Scottish National Party.

After leaving Parliament in 1892, Graham and his wife were free to travel more frequently, sometimes together but more often pursuing their diverging interests apart, and always on the look-out for possibilities of improving their finances. Spain and Morocco were the main areas of their travel. Graham also began to diversify in his new-found interest in writing into the prolific production of travel books and collections of short stories and sketches. Yet nothing could stave off for ever the inevitable consequences of his father's irresponsibility. The debt-ridden estate of Gartmore had eventually to be sold, and the Grahams settled for financial security on the smaller family estate of Ardoch on the northern side of the Firth of Clyde. Even so, a worse blow was to befall Graham. Gabriela had never been physically strong and was prone to pleurisy (not helped by her chain-smoking habit). She died in 1906 on the way back from one of her many visits to the drier warmth of Spain. Her marriage with Robert of more than a quarter of a century had been childless, but they were a close couple and Robert missed her greatly.

As his life advanced into late middle age and old age through the new century, Graham developed his writing with more collections of short stories and works of biography centred on Mexican and South American history. His astonishingly wide circle of friends in all fields of society and his continuing political activities kept him close to the centre of society and often in the public gaze. At the outbreak of the First World War, though he had been critical of the warmongering attitudes that had marked the years from 1910 to 1914, Graham, at the age of 62, volunteered for service and was charged with two missions to South America, one in 1914-15 to Uruguay to buy horses for the Army, and the second to Colombia in 1916-17 to obtain beef supplies. The first mission enabled him to recapture some of the excitement of his early years on horseback in South America, although it made him desperately sad as a horse-lover to think of the dreadful fate awaiting the animals he bought. The second mission turned out to be unsuccessful, owing to a lack of shipping.

After the war, Graham continued to travel, now more for relaxation and for the sake of his health. He had a new close companion and friend, a wealthy widow, Mrs Elizabeth ('Toppie') Dummett, whose artistic salon in London he frequented and who travelled with him on most of his journeys. Back in Scotland, Graham continued to spend summers at Ardoch, and was well known round the Glasgow and Scottish literary scene, as well as being involved in Scottish political controversy. Among his literary friends were the poet Hugh MacDiarmid (C.M.Grieve) and the novelist and journalist, Neil Munro. Graham made a point of attending the dedication of a memorial to Munro in the summer of 1935. Graham was then eighty-three years old. A few months later, Graham set out on what he probably knew would be his last journey, back to Argentina, the scene of his first youthful adventures. In Buenos Aires, he contracted bronchitis and then pneumonia, and after a few days he died. His funeral in Buenos Aires was a large public occasion attended by the Argentine President, with two horses belonging to Graham's friend,

Aimé Tschiffely, the horseman-adventurer, accompanying the coffin as symbols of Don Roberto's attachment to the gaucho culture that had been such an influence on his life and philosophy.

Robert Bontine Cunninghame Graham is buried near his wife Gabriela in the family burial place at the Augustinian Priory on the little island of Inchmahome in the Lake of Menteith. A memorial to him is now placed near the former family mansion of Gartmore.

The Writings

It may not be too much of an exaggeration to say that the greatest blessing bestowed upon Robert Bontine Cunninghame Graham in his boyhood years was an incomplete formal education. Two years at prep school, two years at Harrow and one 'finishing' year in Brussels gave him little of the classical education deemed essential for the well-born Victorian gentleman. Instead he reached the age of eighteen with considerable fluency in Spanish and French, and an undoubted acquired love of reading gained from the books in the libraries of his family's Scottish houses and his mother's house in London. His extensive (if difficult to decipher) letters home to his mother from abroad make this latter fact clear. The proficiency in Spanish and French gave him immediate entry into two major literatures of the modern world in addition to English, a more bankable asset for the modern writer-to-be than any familiarity with the classical writings of Greece and Rome.

It is conventional to ascribe the beginnings of Graham's writing career to the period after he left Parliament and was settled back in Gartmore, in the last decade of the century. However, the habit of writing had undoubtedly been acquired by him over many years preceding, when he was writing long letters home about his experiences in the Americas, and, later on, writing speeches and articles as part of his work as a strongly involved and committed Radical Liberal Member of Parliament.

Nevertheless, we can only begin to speak of Graham as a true writer when in the years after 1890 he began to publish both fiction and non-fiction on a regular basis. Probably beginning with an essay, "The Horses of the Pampas", contributed to the monthly magazine, *Time*, in 1890, Graham went on to write extensively for the *Saturday Review* and other periodicals. There were essays, sketches and short stories, and, later, books of travel and history. Graham's confidence in himself as a writer can be seen to grow during this period, especially when he acquired the literary and critical friendship of the publisher, Edward Garnett.

What makes Graham very different in his writing from any other late Victorian upper-class traveller and man of action is his conscious awareness and absorption of the realistic spirit and literary techniques of contemporary European writers. His main subjects initially are his beloved South America and Spain, as filtered through his personal experiences as a younger man, and aspects of life in Britain, perhaps especially Scotland. Yet he describes these with, in the main, a detached unsentimental insight gained from his reading of the short stories and sketches of Guy de Maupassant and Ivan Turgenev. Equally, after reading *La Pampa*, a set of vignettes of gaucho life written in French by Alfred Ébélot, on the recommendation of his close friend, W.H. Hudson, he came to see how his memories of life among the gauchos could be structured into short tales blending close detailed observation and brief narrative. Yet it would not be true to think of Graham as always being a totally controlled and dispassionate writer. There is both fire and anger in those of his pieces that set out to confront rampant and racist imperialism, social injustice and cruelty directed against helpless human or animal targets.

There is perhaps a tentative quality about Graham's first two books. *Notes on the District of Menteith* (1895) is a highly personal short guidebook to the part of Scotland he knew at first hand surrounding the ancestral home. It almost seems to be a practice for the real thing, before going out into the territory of the big book. Similarly, *Father Archangel of Scotland, and Other Essays* (1896) is an initial attempt at the short story collection, in which Graham shares the contents with his wife, Gabriela.

Graham's first true full-length book conceived as a single narrative is his account of personal experiences in Morocco, *Mogreb-El-Acksa* (1898). The book, whose title translates as 'Morocco the Most Holy', deals in the main with Graham's time there in the later months of 1897. Paradoxically, for a man who travelled so extensively throughout his long life, it is one of the only two real travel books that Graham ever wrote. The other is *Cartagena and the Banks of the Sinú* (1920), which arose out of Graham's mission to Colombia in 1916-17. It is clear that he came to see his experiences in the wider world primarily as a fertile and energising source for fiction.

Between 1899 and 1936, Graham published thirteen collections of sketches and short stories. Generally, his approach for these collections was to bring together stories and short pieces of a rather heterogeneous nature, with settings ranging from his favourite locales of South America and Spain, and increasingly North Africa, to Scotland, London, Paris and more distant parts of the globe. Some of the stories are crafted narratives; others may be little more than detailed descriptions of life and manners with a minimum of narrative, or even personal essays on a range of diverse topics. Although his tone is mostly detached and often ironic, the persona of the writer is never far away and at times Graham's partialities emerge clearly through the text.

The first two collections, *The Ipané* (1899) and *Thirteen Stories* (1900), give the impression of being the most diverse, partly because of the throwaway nature of their titles. 'Ipané' is merely the name of an old river boat that appears in the title story of the first collection. The book has a random quality about it with no sense of a central thread behind the choices.

Thirteen Stories, as a title, suggests an equal randomness. Indeed the main story in the collection is in fact a novella, "Cruz Alta", which takes up fully a third of the length of the book on its own, the other stories being very diverse in their settings and themes. However, the collections that follow in the years before and during the First World War have titles that seem to show a more directed thinking by Graham about their central thrust or themes. *Success* (1902) and *Progress, and Other Sketches* (1905) imply an inspirational quality. *His People* follows in 1906, and *Faith* (1909), *Hope* (1910) and *Charity* (1912) seem to be linked as a group within Graham's mind. *A Hatchment* (1913) and *Brought Forward* (1916) bring to an end the first cycle of Graham's fictional output. Thereafter, there is a gap of eleven years before the final late collections, *Redeemed, and Other Sketches* (1927), *Writ in Sand* (1932) and *Mirages* (1936), the titles of which seem to suggest a disengagement from the serious business of life. And yet perhaps too much weight can be attached to the titles of these works. In all of them, the stories are equally varied and exotic in their sources, and Graham never lets himself be pinned down by a reader's or critic's desire to pigeonhole him as a fiction writer on a particular subject or theme.

It is in his historical writing that Graham does reveal himself as having a specific interest and purpose. Beginning in 1901, he published a sequence of works, mostly biographical, dealing with aspects of South American history from the time of the sixteenth-century Conquistadors right down to his own lifetime. For the writing of these books, he undertook extensive research into the original source documents, a labour in which his knowledge of Spanish proved to be invaluable. The largest group of historical biographies deals with prominent figures in the conquest of

South America by the Spaniards. *Hernando de Soto* (1903), *Bernal Diaz del Castillo* (1915), *The Conquest of New Granada* (1922), *The Conquest of the River Plate* (1924), and *Pedro de Valdivia* (1926) show his interest in most areas of Latin America, not merely his own beloved Argentina. Indeed, his travel book, *Cartagena and the Banks of the Sinú* (1920), includes a sketch of the history of Colombia from the Conquest onwards. In that same year Graham also published his biography of the Brazilian religious revolutionary leader of the 1890s, Antonio Conselheiro, under the title, *A Brazilian Mystic*. Two biographies of later figures in South American history are *Jose Antonio Paez* (1929), dealing with one of the heroes of the liberation of Venezuela from Spain in the 1820s, and *Portrait of a Dictator: Francisco Solano Lopez* (1933), about the leader of Paraguay through the disastrous Triple Alliance War of the 1860s. How popular these books about a continent and culture little-known in Britain could ever be is questionable. In writing them, Graham was undoubtedly trying to counteract the contemporary craze for writings about the British Empire, an institution about which he held distinctly unfashionable views. Probably the most enduring of his historical works has turned out to be *A Vanished Arcadia; Being Some Account of the Jesuits in Paraguay, 1607 to 1767* (1901), for reasons more to do with its later cinematic connections than any historical appeal. A historical biography of more personal significance to Graham was *Doughty Deeds* (1925), an account of the life of Graham's own direct eighteenth-century ancestor and namesake, Robert Graham of Gartmore.

Graham's wife, Gabriela, had literary aspirations of her own and published a number of works, frequently infused by the deep religious feeling that developed as she grew older. Her main work was a two-volume biography of Saint Teresa, to which she devoted years of travel and research. Graham clearly played a major role in encouraging her in her writing, and helped in its publication. He had collaborated with her in *Father Archangel of Scotland, and Other Essays* (1896). After her death in 1906, he arranged for the posthumous publication of a new edition of *Santa Teresa* (1907), her poems in 1908, and a new collection of her shorter writings, *The Christ of Toro and Other Stories* (1908).

This survey has touched on all the books that Graham published in his lifetime. Selections have been made by some of his many admirers from his considerable output of short stories and sketches, usually focusing on specific subject areas of his work, such as South America, Scotland or his passion for horses. One unfortunate effect of this may have been to stereotype Graham as a particular kind of writer, an exotic breed who sits uncomfortably in a literary climate dominated by the Modernists of the earlier twentieth century. The extravagant larger-than-life image that has built up about him has perhaps skewed our perceptions of his writing, which is more European in its sensibility than British Edwardian or Georgian. Paradoxically, despite his class origins and cosmopolitan experience, Graham can also often seem to be closer in tone and outlook to twentieth-century Scottish writers like George Douglas Brown, Hugh MacDiarmid or Lewis Grassic Gibbon, writers whose work he almost certainly knew well. There is a great deal of scholarly work waiting to be done on Graham as a Scottish writer, not least the unquantifiable task of bringing into print the large body of his articles, journalism and letters that have never been properly investigated. The full canon of his work has still to be established. Until that is done, it is not possible to make any true assessment of the literary significance of Robert Bontine Cunninghame Graham.

Alan MacGillivray

Note to Volume 3

Volume Three of the Collected Stories and Sketches contains three collections published between 1906 and 1910, years in which Graham, although no longer in Parliament, was very active in Labour and Radical politics. *His People* appeared in 1906, the year in which Graham's wife, Gabriela, died. He spent a lot of time over the next two or three years arranging the posthumous publication, or republication, of Gabriela's writings. Continuing his own writing, *Faith* and *Hope* were published in 1909 and 1910 respectively, suggesting a notional trilogy completed with *Charity* (1912) (a collection which will appear in Volume Four). This suggestion is not in fact borne out in terms of the contents of the collections. They each continue Graham's practice of bringing together stories of widely differing subjects located in his familiar Hispanic, North African and British (mainly Scottish) areas of experience and inspiration.

Alan MacGillivray
John C. McIntyre

His People

R. B. Cunninghame Graham

To
Edward Garnett

Some of the following sketches have appeared in "The Saturday Review", "The Speaker", "Dana", and "Guth na Bliadhna", to whose Editors the author makes his thanks and acknowledgments.

Introduction

The collection, *His People*, appeared in the middle of a very fertile period in Graham's writing career. In the four previous years, he had published two of his South American histories, *A Vanished Arcadia* and *Hernando de Soto*, as well as two volumes of short stories and sketches, *Success* and *Progress*. It is probably significant the new collection, *His People*, was dedicated to the man who was to a considerable extent responsible for Graham's obvious confidence as a writer, Edward Garnett, the publisher who acted as the reader for various firms including Duckworth, the firm which published this book.

Graham's Preface to this collection is presented as a kind of self-justification, an 'apologia' in the traditional sense, for venturing to present another gathering of stories and sketches. The Apologia suffers considerably from being very rhetorically over-written, as if Graham is too consciously straining for literary effect. However, three points emerge from it. Firstly, these stories emerge directly from Graham's own experience and observation of the world. Secondly, Graham is very conscious that such writing is ephemeral and subject to the vagaries of time. Like writing on the sand, it will be washed away by the tide leaving behind only a blank space. This is a theme touched upon regularly by Graham as he grew older, and indeed his second-last collection was entitled *Writ in Sand* (1932). Thirdly, despite this awareness of the transience of his writing, it is the product of an irresistible compulsion. So Graham has come to a realisation that now it is writing that governs his life. All in his life that has gone before, and is yet to come, serves the purposes of a professional writer. Perhaps it is fortunate that Graham has gained this sense of purpose, for it was in this year of 1906 that he lost his wife Gabriela and had to shape his future without a permanent partner.

"His People", the title story of the collection, is very relevant to the theme of time and the ways in which it creates a gulf between present and past, between us as we are now and us as we were, changing the place that we remember into a place of strangers. Juan Icazar, a successful man of business in Mexico, makes a sentimental journey back to the place of

his childhood, the Spanish city of Toledo.   During the voyage across
the Atlantic to Santander in the North of Spain and the subsequent
rail journey to Toledo, he thinks affectionately of the old acquaintances
he will renew and the familiar places he will re-experience. It is rather
disturbing to him when he begins to find the sights and sounds of his
native Spain strangely unfamiliar and discordant with his memories. He
is seeing and hearing as if with strangers' senses. However, he consoles
himself with the thought that he will find on his arrival home that Toledo
itself will be as of old. Of course, this is not the case. He finds that,
although the place itself accords with his childhood memories, everyone
he used to know is now dead and he is a stranger in his own city. It is
only when he goes out after dinner at his hotel and enters a theatre where
a play is already in progress that he has a vision that changes his mood.
Sitting alone in the stalls at the interval, Icazar realises that it is only in
the world of imagination, as realised in art and drama, that he can find
the familiar and feel at home. The characters of the play, the scenery
representing Toledo, speak more directly to him than the real Spain from
which he has been for ever alienated by time and distance.

   This expression of the power of art and drama is an occasional feature
of Graham's story technique. In this collection, it surfaces again in the
sketch, "La Zagala", where he holds in balance as of equal interest an
account of a play he attended in a theatre in the city of Burgos and a
description of its Spanish audience. The shifts and turns of the plot of
a comparatively new tragic-comedy by the Quintero Brothers, hugely
popular dramatists of the day, are well contrasted with the down-to-earth
reality of the bourgeoisie and ordinary people of modern Burgos, who are
nevertheless deeply affected by the tragic denouement of the play.

   For a man who on the surface was very much a man's man, an
adventurer in a world dominated by powerful and aggressive men of
action and politics, an exponent of supposedly manly pursuits like
fencing and horse-riding, Graham showed himself in his writing to be
very sensitive to the situation and feelings of women. Not surprising
when one considers that three women were central to his maturing
years: his maternal grandmother, Doña Catalina; his mother, Mrs Anne
Bontine; and his wife Gabriela. In several stories in *His People*, Graham
explores and meditates on the situation of women, very different in their
lives and characters, and made individually distinctive and interesting
through Graham's perceptive scrutiny. "A Botanist" presents Graham's

speculations about the life and character of the original owner of a book on botany that he had bought from a second-hand bookstall. Matilda Hutton, in Graham's sentimental imagination, is shaped into a retiring spinster of a previous generation whose passion for flowers and plants is conveyed through her copious annotations of the book. Graham even permits himself to speculate about her appearance, the circumstances of her simple life and her quiet, even lonely, death. Perhaps Graham goes too far beyond the scope of the available evidence, but he has certainly created a sympathetic and engaging character. In the story, "Signalled", Graham is on surer ground from his personal experience and observation. In a crowded French seaside casino, men and women of many nationalities are united in their gambling greed. Among the crowd, fashionably dressed prostitutes are on the look-out for clients and submit to the lustful, embarrassed or knowing gazes of the passing bourgeoisie. One girl, in particular, quiet and respectable-looking, sits on her own, aware of the hints of recognition from former clients. Suddenly she is joined by an innocent English girl who has felt drawn to her and is totally unaware of what she is and how she relates to all the men who seem to know her. In a few minutes of sympathetic communion, the two girls sit outside in the beautiful summer night, saying very little, the French girl overwhelmed by the innocence of the other and the gulf that separates them, unable to speak of her own life and its misery, until the English girl is called away. Like ships they have merely signalled to each other in passing.

In "A Wire-Walker", Graham reveals his distaste for the way in which supposed men of the world talk about women in their all-male gatherings, prosperous men smoking and drinking and depreciating women as beings of lesser account, unworthy and untrustworthy. As an advocate for women, Graham creates a figure very like himself who tells the story of a woman whom he had met, a circus performer, Victorina, whose life was a metaphorical balancing act between her dangerous occupation and her long-lasting relationship with a totally unreliable man. She and the man, René, adopt a child, but René betrays her with her own maid, who bears him another child. Victorina raises both children as if her own, and yet eventually the man deserts her, taking the adopted child with him. Victorina struggles on, faithfully looking after the maid and René's child, until her eventual death in a fall from the high wire. In an ironic ending, the "Graham" narrator finishes his story, intended to redeem the image of women, only to realise that his clubroom audience have nearly all fallen asleep.

Graham's storytelling methods are sometimes deliberately indirect. From time to time one can find oneself reading a story and imagining that it is going in one clear direction, only to find that suddenly it has taken a turn and is heading off towards an unexpected destination. This happens in two of Graham's stories about women, "Tha Til Mi Tuliadh" (Cha Till Mi Tuilleadh – "I shall never return"; Graham's use of Gaelic is often erratic) and "Miss Christian Jean", where the women themselves, two sisters living all their lives in a small Menteith cottage and a formidable spinster lady, Miss Christian Jean, with her own house and servants, are only gradually introduced, through the medium of other characters and indeed the whole district of Scotland that they inhabit. Part of Graham's subject is indeed the district of Menteith and the damp decaying house of Gartmore where he had come to live on the death of his father, trying to make the estate viable as the family seat. However, by the time of the publication of *His People* in 1906, Gartmore had already been sold and the evocation of the mansion and its rooms, with the policies surrounding it, that feature prominently in these two stories, and in the melancholy sentimental sketch, "Fate", which precedes them, was now part of Graham's memories rather than his current life.

Sometimes, a place is Graham's sole subject in a sketch. The location can be either local and Scottish or exotic, remembered from his frequent excursions abroad. "Tobar Na Reil" (Tobar na Reull – Well of the Star) describes a spot known to Graham in Menteith. In "The Grey Kirk", he goes further afield to the Douglas family burial spot, St Bride's Chapel in Douglas, Lanarkshire. By contrast, Gualeguaychu in the Entre Ríos province of Argentina is described vividly as Graham remembered it from his youth, a sleepy undeveloped, almost frontier, town; no doubt, he admits, it has much changed. And "La Camargue" captures the other-worldly atmosphere of a region seemingly alien to the rest of France, almost in Graham's eyes like a detached piece of South America that has strayed across the ocean. It too is subject to inevitable change. Graham's mood is determinedly elegiac, regretting the passing of a world he once knew.

To these subjects already considered, art, women and places with their relationships to time and mortality, must be added Graham's fascination with significant men and their contributions to life and society. The long story, "Le Chef", creates the character of a Frenchman, Louis Cossart, a real person whom Graham knew over many years. Cossart emerges from a gallery of vividly-drawn characters haunting Buenos Aires in the 1870s, a man met and re-met in the following years as he graduates to being a restaurateur and chef, prospering and expanding his business in different cities from Buenos Aires to London, by way of Madrid and Edinburgh, seeing himself ultimately as a true culinary artist. As a contrast to this man of his own time and social circle, Graham focuses in another sketch on the life and achievement of a little-known historian of the sixteenth-century Conquest of South America, the Flemish soldier of fortune, Hulderico Schmidel, who wrote in German the first history of Buenos Aires and Paraguay, and their Spanish conquerors. The sketch can be seen as a little companion piece to Graham's more ambitious biographies of the Conquistadors.

Graham's interest in the lives of significant players in the contemporary scene, who nevertheless must be seen as failures, can be seen in the treatment he gives to two men who were certainly well known to him personally. Elsewhere he wrote that failure was more interesting than success. Failure in politics was of particular interest to him, since his own political career could be said to have been a disappointment to him in terms of the Socialist principles he had come to espouse. Two examples of such failure were considered by him in three stories from *His People*. "On the Spur" and "The Emir" deal, from the point of view of his British readers, with an exotic personality. The Minister of War to the Sultan of Morocco during the First Moroccan Crisis of 1903-04 was the Kaid, or Emir, Sid Mehedi-el-Menebhi. At a time when the Great European Powers were disputing over which nation should control the hitherto independent Kingdom of Morocco (a diplomatic struggle finally won jointly by France and Spain), Menebhi travelled between the European capitals representing the Sultan. He fell into disfavour and had to return home. "On the Spur" deals with his return at full speed from the port of landing across the desert to see the Sultan at Marrakesh and forestall the appointment of a major rival, a race which he just manages to win. "The Emir" deals with events a little later, when, now in disgrace, Menebhi builds a magnificent new palace for himself at Tangier where he lives in a dignified retirement. Graham, who came to visit Tangier more and more in his later years, clearly knew and admired Menebhi personally at the time of these events, and wrote these stories as a tribute to his spirit and in respect for the Muslim ethos. Similarly Graham wrote personally and mostly in admiration about the Irish Nationalist leader in Parliament, Charles Stewart Parnell, whose political career was severely damaged by an adulterous affair. Graham's pen portrait of Parnell is one of the best pieces in the collection, assessing Parnell's great personal and political abilities and his contribution to the Irish Home Rule cause, without ignoring his faults. Graham's observation of the Irish Nationalists in Westminster was undoubtedly of great significance to his development as a leader of the Scottish Nationalist movement.

This collection of short stories reveals much about Graham's progressive social attitudes and his developing literary skills. We have seen how he is perceptive and sympathetic in his attitudes towards women, eschewing the easy sexism of his male companions. Unmentioned so far has been his awareness of and lack of sympathy with racist attitudes, even in his own countrymen. The short story, "Dagos", uses the cheap gibing term for persons of Hispanic origin to expose the shallowness of a loud-mouthed Scottish sea-captain's response to an anecdote that is told in another male social gathering. (That being said, Graham himself cannot be totally excused of the racist charge, given that in "Signalled" he compares a Japanese in Western clothes to a monkey escaped from the woods.) Above all, in *His People* we must be struck by the sureness of style that Graham has developed, with clear demonstrations of his mastery of vivid description, character presentation, colloquial dialogue, and tones of irony and elegiac melancholy. In this collection, Graham has definitely become a master of the writing trade.

A.MacG.

Contents

Apologia

It is (I think) a general belief, that every writer draws his matter straight from the fountains of his brain, just as a spider weaves his web from his own belly, as naturalists aver. This may be so, especially with folk of much invention and no imaginative power. The makers of Utopias and the like, forecasters of society under socialism, and those who write long novels about the theologic doubts which now and then attack a clergyman, and those who treat the lives of celebrated men made small by lack of comprehension, as objects are belittled seen through the large end of a telescope, no doubt enjoy the gift. Peace and good luck to them, and large editions soon sold out, with profits, and prospective knighthoods, and the respect of all right-thinking men. It may be that which I refer to as invention they style imagination, and if that is so, I am still content to wish them luck, and to repeat that I, in common, as I think, with most of those who write on what they see, or have seen, setting it out before the public through the medium of the vision of their brain, and from their point of view, are born entirely lacking in both qualities.

Still I believe that, be it bad or good, all that a writer does is to dress up what he has seen, or felt, or heard, and nothing real is evolved from his own brain, except the words he uses, and the way in which he uses them. Therefore it follows, that in writing he sets down (perhaps unwittingly) the story of his life, and as he does so, makes it worth reading only by chronicling all his impressions of the world quite honestly, as if he were alone upon a desert island (as in fact he is) and he were writing on the sand.

Upon this head at least, he need not trouble, for Time is like a strong north wind, which moves the sand upon the shore, and covers up all tracks which human feet have made upon it, however deeply they may seem to mark, no matter if the foot that made them were as perfect as the best Praxiteles designed or as a desert Arab maiden's, henna-dyed and light as a gazelle's.

One wave, of fashion or the like, one little change of language or of taste, and naught remains, and the blank sheet of sand lies out without a mark upon it, fresh and inviting for another kind of foot to dance upon, and dent it, if it can.

Therefore, oh writers of imagination or invention, or what you choose to call the thing that makes you write your monumental tomes, which fall out from the press, just as in olden times the hot cross buns fell from the oven upon Maundy Thursday night, do not, I pray, scorn men devoid of inspiration or afflatus, and who perforce must see and touch (like Thomas) before they can believe sufficiently, to take in hand the pen. Go on (after the manner of the pampered jades of Asia) and spin your gossamers, making the meshes of your web as fine as those which only dew reveals to mortal eye, stretched like a rigging through the grass, without apology.

In fact, there is no need for any, for it would seem that you (connected, as I think, directly with the cosmic spirit of the world) have in yourselves a faculty which acts like armour, keeping you safe from the attacks of the light cavalry of critics, shutting you up securely in a tower of strength, above the flight of all the arrows ever shot by man.

Why, if invention, or imagination (or what not) is, of itself, a thing apart, and the transmission of it into print causes no pain in parturition, as it were, how happy you must be. All that is wanted is a table and a chair, a ream of paper and a pen or two; these, with your bottle of fine blue-black ink, a modicum of power in the wrist, and perseverance to a limited degree, make you both rich and famous, and what has issued from your brain is never felt, for nature or some other mighty power replaces it, just as the sand upon a tidal river's bank comes back again with the tide's ebb and flow.

You are not torn and twisted, as with a thousand devils struggling to be free, nor can you feel the shame which burns the cheek of those who read in after years what they have written, as it were, against their will; for writing is so damnable a thing that no one (excepting always the Utopia weavers and the rest of those to whom I have referred) sitting down to write is ever certain what it is that he will do, for it may chance of mustard or some other kind of seed, after the fashion of the sower in the Word. A thing which sets one thinking on the curious kind of crops that farmers must have had to deal with in the Holy Land, when it was time to reap.

And it is true enough, men write against their will, constrained by some fell power, that they know perfectly they should resist, but cannot for their life; just as they say that sometimes women suffering violence have seized their violators round the neck and kissed them fiercely, as though not knowing what they did, or yielding to temptation, just as a writer does when he sees ink convenient to his hand.

With this apology, I venture forth again upon the highway, after the fashion of the far-famed goose of Cantimpalos, which, as the proverb says, came out upon the road to meet the wolf.

R. B. Cunninghame Graham
Ardoch, 7 August, 1906.

His People

His People

Full twenty years had passed since he had seen the once familiar streets.

Years had gone by — years of hard work, of heat, of long and dreary hours spent in the counting-house in Zacatécas, and in long journeys to Tampico, to Acapulco, and to Mexico. At last, his fortune made, and all the treasure of his youth wasted in making it, he had taken ship to Santandér. The unfamiliar sea, the people all so smartly dressed, the ladies finer by far than even were the daughters of the governor in Zacatécas, the strange refinements of the cabins, the ceremonious dinner, the band, the futile games in which the passengers engaged, the endless trivialities of European life, which Europeans have erected into fetishes, to which they bow, making them into gods minted in their own images — struck him as they might strike an Arab brought from his native plains, with feelings of contempt and envy bewilderingly mixed.

In the quiet nights within the Tropics, as he paced up and down beneath the awning upon deck, he thought how would Toledo look on his return. In the wild weather, as the ship neared Spain, he wondered whether he would find it changed. Whilst seated in the smoking-room playing at "tute," as he chewed a black cigar between his teeth, with his thoughts wandering from the game to the disgust of all his partners, he saw the ochre-red Castilian city, wind-swept, austere, and seated on the rocks above the yellow rolling Tagus, as he had seen it as a child.

He thought, "Will it look larger, smaller, be more ruinous; and will the trees upon the Alameda now have grown so much I shall not know them?" and then smiled at himself, knowing Toledo cannot suffer change. How many of his friends would be alive, he wondered, and he pictured to himself the look upon the faces of the men he once had known, and how they would be sure to say, "What, Juan Icázar? Yes, ah yes, the son of Pedro and Maria, may they both rest in peace. We thought you had been dead, man, years ago." Then, as if in a dream, he saw himself entering the shop of old Higinio Guarrázas, just at the corner of the Calle de las Armas, where as a child he had gazed with wonder at the boxes of sardines, the olives in their bottles, the bales of Iceland codfish, cases of macaroni, and all the wondrous products drawn from countries overseas, which filled the store and made it fairyland.

Of course, Higinio would be there, his bushy whiskers maybe a little greyer, and his thick hair turned white; but there, of course, smoking his cigarette, making his entries in his daybook, whilst the clerks ran about and served the customers; and he remembered that just opposite the shop there stood an archway built by the Moors, the infidels, the enemies both of our faith and God.

All that seemed real to him, for it was stamped upon his brain from childhood, just as the view was stamped that he remembered as he stood upon the terrace below the Puerta del Cambrón, and looked across the suburbs, known as Las Covachuelas and Antequeruela, with their tiled roofs forming long pent-houses of brown. Surely right underneath his feet he still would see El Alfar Blanco, where they made hard white pottery and even porcelain, and the two other potteries where as a child he played. These were all real, and their foundations deep as the foundations of the world; but the long years in Mexico, the drudgery, the struggle and the strife, the dull hot hours of listless waiting for the evening breeze, merely a bad dream. The long and dusty rides with his gun underneath his thigh, his striped serapé rolled behind the cantle of his saddle, and the stiff, heavily embroidered "poblano" hat upon his head — surely he looked a picture on his horse, but why, he wondered, did the Mexicans all smile and murmur "chapetón" as he passed by — had surely happened to another man. All was unreal, all except the *coup* upon the Stock Exchange, which, following on years of successful business, at length had made him free. But still the steamer always drew nearer day by day to Spain, and he, pacing the deck, thought on the future, for the past he put aside just as one does the oboe note of a mosquito, when one has squashed the piper on the wall. Sometimes his thoughts ran upon old Antonio Lopez, who, he knew, had left the mountains above Santandér, poor and unknown, just as he had himself gone from Toledo, and by degrees become enriched and founded the great transatlantic line, in one of whose best steamers he was coming home. How did old Lopez feel, he thought, when, after years of slaving in the Habana, he at length became possessor of a ship, and how, when in the plaza of his little native town, at last a senator, all had come forth to welcome him with bagpipes, flutes, oxen with wreaths of flowers on their heads, the bishop and the clergy of the diocese, and all bowed down before the golden calf, set up and incarnated in himself. Were not their lives and their careers alike, and might not he, too, be a senator? He saw himself just entering the house of Don Adolfo the apothecary, where, as he knew, at evening time, the doctor, old Guarrázas, some of the canons of the cathedral, the bookseller, and other worthies, used to congregate. Lifting his hat after a ceremonious "*Muy buenas tardes*," he would say, "By the by, did you know Pedro Icázar, who had his house in Covachuelas, eh?" Then cautiously, "And what of his son Juan, who went out to the Indies — is he alive, think you, or dead of those accursed fevers of the land?" For it is never good to do things with a rush. Then as a grave "Si, señor, Pedro Icázar; I should think so, and his son Juan also," went round the ring, touching his hat, he heard himself rejoin, "I am that Juan, much at your service, and at that of honest men."

How glorious it would be thus to revive old memories (he knew the last of his relations long was dead), and better still to say, "Gentlemen, I wish to offer you champagne"; then call for "Codorniu," worth ten francs the bottle, and watch it sparkle in the glasses, as all his old friends' faces kindled with delight.

The other passengers, mostly rich merchants from Habana, Tampico, Cartagena, and from Port Limón, all thought him odd, saying, "Icázar surely had heard bells, but he did not know where." Then they all gave him up, leaving him to his reveries, his silent pacing up and down the deck, and to the reconstruction in his mind of that Toledo which he had known so well — brown, wind-swept, melancholy, proud in her ruin; the widow of the Goths, the Romans, Jews, the Moors, and now neglected by her lord and mourning haughtily aloof, like a fair jewel lost on the floor of a deserted garret, its facets chipped and its whole setting tarnished by decay.

The icy winds of Europe chilled him to the bone, making him shiver in his unsubstantial clothes made for the Tropics, although he, half with uneasiness and half with pride, remembered in his boyhood he had gone bare-headed in the frosts which grip Toledo in a band of steel, pinching the people in their great barrack-looking houses, where they sat wrapped in cloaks about a pan of charcoal, waiting for the sun. Porpoises gambolled round the ship, making him think upon the buffalo which he had seen out in Chihuáhuá and New Mexico, and as they neared the coast, steamers passed by, exchanging signals, at which the returning "Indianos" looked approvingly, remarking that "The commerce . . . Si,

señor . . . was the great lever by means of which men moved the world
. . . that is, the commerce and the steam, for after all, where there is
commerce there is progress. . . . Si, señor . . . long live the commerce
and . . . and the steam." Then they, all having graduated in "the progress"
at New York, would order "whiskisoda" and drink to Spain, the steam,
the commerce, woman, black eyes, and bull-fighting, and as they drank,
unpacked their recollections of the Tropics, and of the ladies they had
known in Mazatlán, Salina Cruz (with anecdotes at this point about
the Zapotéca girls, mostly apocryphal), Cienfuegos, and the Habana,
yes, the Habana. Ah, what a place! . . . Its half-caste girls quite lost to
shame, but still agreeable, with underlinen starched so stiffly, it would, if
placed upon the ground, have stood up like a tub. Much as they lauded
the strange beverage, pressing it on him as a cure for melancholy, Icázar
did not like it, saying it did not make him happy, and cherishing the
recollection of a little wine which he remembered in his youth, that
came from Villa Cañas, or from Vargas, he did not quite remember
which, although he recollected that the women of the latter place used
to walk, carrying their shoes, the long two leagues into Toledo, as he
expressed it, at the donkey's feet.

At last the Asturian mountains, snow-capped and seeming to be
hung between the water and the sky, appeared far-off and cloudy; then
by degrees grew nearer, and, the mist lifting, showed the Cantabrian
coast, smiling and vine-clad to the shore, with the white villages nestling
about the hills; above them chestnut woods, then pines, then masses
of grey limestone, which by degrees melted away into the snow quite
imperceptibly.

Fishing-boats, with their sails tanned brown and pointed sharp as a
shark's fin when it just rises to the surface following a ship, were scattered
here and there; and soon the long and straggling town of Santandér, the
Sardineiro with its bathing-boxes, and the white villas smiling through
the trees, roused Juan Icázar to enthusiasm, making the blood course
through his veins and his eyes fill with tears.

Once landed on the mole, all was familiar, and yet strange to him.
To see white Christians bending under burdens, whilst others ordered
them about like negroes, shocked him, accustomed as he was to Mexico
and its strict colour line. The carabineers, with their green gloves and
well-remembered uniforms struck a note in his heart; but then again, his
native country seemed not to have progressed, and as the sleek mouse-
coloured oxen drew the creaking carts with solid wheels which turned

with the whole axle, at two miles an hour, his thoughts went back to Zacatécas, with its smart Yankee Milburn waggons drawn by a team of mules. But the harsh guttural cries of fish-hawkers and water-carriers sounded as sweet to him as did a nightingale, reviving memories of home, of childhood, and of the echoing notes which he remembered still, in his gaunt native town. Nothing seemed changed except himself. Men lounged about, wrapped in their cloaks and with a cigarette-stained hand appearing underneath their chins, holding the folds about their mouths. Ladies all robed in black came from the churches, followed by their maids, and as they passed along the streets the lounging men undressed them with their eyes, murmuring compliments in an undertone which brought the blood into their cheeks and caused their great black eyes to flame, though they appeared unconscious, but treasured secretly each word up in their hearts as a just homage to their charms. In Juan Icázar's ear, his native tongue spoken without the softness with which the racial or climatic influences of the New World endues both branches of the Spanish tongue, seemed harsh and unrefined, but he reflected that his ear was vitiated, and in the north men spoke abominably, but that in his own native town he would hear once again the right Toledan, with its clear utterance, full cadence, and the mysterious something which attaches to a speech when spoken in one's home. The railway-station seemed a little tumbledown, and the time wasted at the ticket-office needless, and it was strange to see so few advertisements, and those merely of steamship companies catering for emigrants, and now and then of bull-fights, with the cartoons adorned with pictures of some famous dancer, such as La Chirigota, with a man's hat upon her head, her hair brought low upon her forehead, almost covering her ears, and with a look deep-seated in her eyes of gipsy harlotry.

Still he reflected that all this was due to want of "illustration" and bad government, or perhaps he himself, in his long absence, had turned a foreigner, and saw things in a wrong perspective, and, sinking back into his seat, watched the train creep into Las Fraguas, diving into the bosom of the hills, waking the echoes with its whistling, and making cattle, feeding in the fields of clover and lucerne, stop and look lazily out of their beryl-coloured eyes, munching the while, with a green foam upon their lips.

The long delays at stations gave the returning pilgrim opportunity to hear the well- remembered cries of "Water," "Ground nuts," "Milk," and of the people who sold chocolate made by Matias Lopez of the Escorial, and note they had not varied since when, a youth in a bare third-class carriage, he had been jolted to the port.

Nothing was new except the gum trees, which, rattling in the wind, were planted round the stations, giving an air of an oasis of vulgarity, in the prevailing calm. Slowly the train wound like a snake out of the mountains on to the central plains which, brown and windswept, and guarded to the west by distant hills, spread out indefinitely.

At last he felt himself at home. Long strings of peasants, seated upon asses or on mules, were riding to the fields. Under their stiff black hats were tied checked handkerchiefs, the ends of which were knotted, forming a sort of turban, and their brown clothes and cloaks blended as well with the prevailing colour of the plain as does the colour of a rabbit or a hare with a bare stubble field. He saw the water-wheels, turned by a horse blindfolded with a clout, wearily pacing round, and marked the steam rise up from the hot soil, where each revolving pot poured its contents into the trough, from which it flowed upon the ground.

Little by little the land grew browner and more bare, and the white towns upon the hilltops looked more African.

Night caught the train between Arévalo and Ávila, right in the middle of the Castilian steppes, which, glacial in winter and in the heat a hell, fill all the middle of the land, windswept and shut from Europe by great mountain ranges, austere and melancholy as the brown folk they bear. Ávila, with its towers and castellated church, lay sleeping in the moonlight as it had slept for ages in the sun; and then the train, snorting and groaning, set its face up against the Guadarráma, passing through rock-strewn deserts and through pine woods, looking fantastic as the landscape of a dream through the white billowing smoke belched by the engine as it strove hard against the hill. The Escorial, the great grey epic which Felipe el Prudente thought out in his old age, gleamed on its hill like steel, and as the morning light tinged the far mountains of Toledo pink, Madrid, the royal village of the bear and árbutus, just showed against the sky. On every side the plain flowed round it like a great brown sea in which it stood an island, going down straight into the waves, without a suburb stretching out between the country and the town, to act as breakwater.

Short time the homing Toledáno stayed within its walls, but set his face towards his Mecca on the Tagus, counting the stations as they passed, and meditating on the flight of time, almost in agony between the joy of seeing once again his native town and terror that he should find all altered and himself forgotten by his friends.

The stations passed as slowly as had the years in Mexico, until the train arrived at Algodór, the junction where the branch from Aranjuéz joins the line from Madrid, and then indeed he felt he was near home, and, rising from his seat, paced up and down the carriage just as a sailor walks upon the deck.

Villages that he thought he had forgotten passed before his eyes.

Churches that he had dreamt of far away were there to welcome him.

All was unchanged; even the cattle feeding on the plain he recognized, knowing them for the fierce Veraguas breed, and feeling half inclined to shake his cloak at them as the train slowly jolted by.

Then, like a whitish cloud, upon a hill, Toledo burst upon his view. Clustering like bees about their queen, the houses nestled in the rocks beneath the great Alcázar, grim and four-square, topping the craggy height. Nothing had changed: the tall cathedral spire still rose into the air, and still the Tagus flowed beneath the walls in the deep rocky pass.

All was familiar, and he recognized it all without an effort, standing entranced, with a black burned-out cigarette between his lips, as the train steamed into the town.

Calling a cab, he told the driver, with the air of one who knew the place, to take him to the Hotel del Pino, and was answered with a stare: "The Hotel del Pino was shut up ten years ago," he said, with the astonished look of one who hears a man allude familiarly to long-forgotten things.

"Well, then, to the boarding-house of the Miss Figueroas, in the Calle de la Cruz."

"The Figueroas have been dead for years," the man replied. "The last, she whom the rest always referred to as La Niña, though she was sixty-five at least, is living still out in a town they call Navalmorál de Pusa, but miles away from here."

Icázar told the man to take his things up to the best hotel; then, hurt, after the way of those who, having waited long for friends, find that they miss the tryst, walked up the dusty road on foot, feeling that he had never left the place, and that the conduct of the Figueroas and the proprietor of the hotel was quite unpardonable. Decaying omnibuses drawn by mules, rattling and jingling on the stones, tore past and covered him with dust; and by the roadside women sat, with large red jars of water, covered with a board on which were set out glasses and lemons and a small pile of cakes sugared and stuck about with caraways, and looking like a quoit.

Instinctively he stopped upon the bridge, which is defended by the Puerta del Cambrón, and dropped a stone into the swirling river underneath, just as he used to do when sent on errands twenty years ago, to pass away the time. It seemed to take an age in its descent, and its dull splash awoke him from his dream, and as he gazed at the wide-spreading circles which it made in the yellow waters of the stream, a voice behind him fell upon his ear. He heard the well-remembered words "For God," and as he turned felt certain he would see one of the beggars he recalled out of the past; but though the man was dressed in red-brown rags but half concealed by an old tattered cloak, his face was unfamiliar, and he had almost murmured, "God assist you," but, altering his mind, gave a peseta as a sort of welcome to himself on his returning home. The blessings showered upon his head reminded him that he was in a land where, though most men give alms, none give profusely, and he walked on, feeling he was a stranger in the country of his birth, though he remembered every stone of the rough pavement of the bridge. Boys followed him, proffering their services to guide him through the town. Indignantly he shook them off, muttering he knew Toledo better far than they, but as he spoke he recognized his speech had altered in the long sojourn in America, and differed much from theirs. Breasting the steep and stony street, he stopped to breathe beneath the gate where, as tradition says, the skull of the alcalde who betrayed his trust, and outraged two poor women he found wandering in the fields, is still preserved behind the keystone of the arch. He looked at it as a man looks at an old friend, and to his joy saw that the sculptured stone still bore the figures of the women, with a new severed head between them, set up to mark that a good governor had done them justice, and placed the record of his act in stone to witness to all time.

Then as he passed into the little Alameda, just on the edge of the high cliff which overhangs the stream, he looked up at the trees and saw with pleasure they had grown taller and more bushy, patting their trunks, as if he thought that they could feel and answer his caress.

Then, leaning on the railings, with his arms folded and with his burnt-out cigarette between his lips, he gazed upon the well-remembered view. All was unchanged. Antequeruela underneath and Covachuelas struggling up the hill, seemed to look up and greet him with a smile. True that the houses had grown smaller as it seemed, and looked more weather-stained and more dilapidated. One that he turned to as by instinct met his eye, with the great vine on which had grown the sweetest grapes in all the world still shadowing the door. The yellow-ochre coloured walls, stained on the weather side with green, seemed not to have grown older, and the corral for chickens at the back, topped, just as he remembered, with a growth of marigolds, stood baking in the sun. The Alfar Blanco lay below his feet, the smoke just curling from the kiln, and with a line of brushwood-laden donkeys waiting at the gate, as they had waited twenty years ago, and just as patiently.

All was unchanged, and he, getting up from his seat, took out another cigarette, and, lighting it, resolved before he went to his hotel to visit some of his old friends and to surprise them by his knowledge of the town, before he told his name.

Just as a horse let loose upon the plains without a moment's hesitation strikes the trail for home, so did Icázar half mechanically take the short cut which leads up the steep, stony Calle del Alfilerito, passing the door of the old building, once a mosque, then synagogue, now turned into a church and duly consecrated, known as "El Cristo de la Luz." So much at home he felt that he would not have been astonished had he met boys, he knew were grandfathers or dead, come shouting out of school. The stony lane led out into the square, with its long rows of shops on a raised causeway under colonnades. The diligence for Vargas was just starting, crammed, as he recollected it of old, with peasant women, all carrying bundles, and with a priest crushed in between them, smoking and mopping at his face with a red handkerchief. The mules and the apocalyptic horses, harnessed with ropes, so thin it seemed they only stood by balance or by leaning up against each other, had not changed, and the unshaved and roguish-looking driver with his short jacket of black plush with silver buttons, as he sat on his seat, his foot just toying with the brake, and his hands grasping an enormous bunch of reins, appeared identical.

Boys selling papers two or three days old screamed like macaws upon a field of maize, and half the population seated on the seats enjoyed the sun, wrapped in their cloaks to shield them from the breeze which whistled from the hills. Icázar, smiling, recognized his native town at once, where on one side you burn under the torrents of the sun, and freeze upon the other, and, without knowing that he did so, turned up the collar of his overcoat to keep away the wind.

He struck into a little street which, as he knew, would take him to the Calle de las Tiendas, and as he walked, cut through the archways mounting the causeway to save the angles, after the fashion of the place.

He walked through well-remembered lanes, by Moorish arches, windows with wooden lattices and medieval ironwork, and passing houses whose heavy wooden soffits, carved by Mudéjares, were monuments of art, left to decay and crumble in the fierce sun of summer and the winter's frost. Used as he was to Mexico, and to its cleanliness, and to the air of wealth which marks its towns, he felt a shock at first at the neglect of all the buildings, which he remembered just in the same condition in his youth; but then, as he saw foreigners, with books beneath their arms, stop and admire, with that half-shamefaced look a man assumes when stopping to observe a building in a foreign town, began to feel an air as of an owner, and to half wish to step across and tell them all about the place, and what there was to see.

Without the least mistake he came out in the Calle de las Armas, crossing a dozen little streets, so steep you scarce could scale them, so narrow that a mule stopping to unload its bales of charcoal at a door entirely stopped the way. Guarrázas' shop was there, with the inscription "Ultramarinos," almost obliterated, but still visible. Holding his breath, he gazed at it, marking the bustle round the door of peasant women, whilst shopmen stood and talked to customers, just as in days gone by.

Entering the shop, he asked for Don Higinio, and a smart shopman answered, "Guarrázas, that was the man from whom the actual owner bought the business. . . . Yes, I remember now, he died some years ago out at his native place, near Talavera de la Reina; his widow, too, I hear is dead . . . and . . ." Icázar thanked him, and, hurrying from the shop, sat down upon a seat to meditate and smoke. And as he pondered upon this thing and on that, the elementary facts which lie forgotten, till a shock, such as he had received, forces them rushing to our minds, crowded upon him, and he thought, "Poor old Guarrázas, may God have pardoned him, he might have waited till I came, after so many years." Then as he sat, still smoking, over his head, with such a sudden shaking of the tower it seemed about to fall, the great cracked bell, which he remembered you could hear as far as Algodór, struck the half-hour, astonishing but still delighting him, as it had never failed to do when as a child he waited for its chime upon the way to school. He took it as a welcome, just as a man may clutch a superstition to his heart without believing it, and rising from his seat, half thought of dropping in on the apothecary, but a vague fear restrained him, and to put off the time, he strolled into the church to see if it was changed.

He gave some coppers to the beggars at the door, and as a mummified old woman drew aside the mat he passed into the church. Half furtively he dipped his hand into the holy water stoop and crossed himself, muttering it was a superstitious act, yet glad to yield to it, for a true Christian ought to testify, even though God for some wise purpose of His own has not vouchsafed him faith.

Through the dim aisles there came a sound of voices, which filtered through the piers just as the gurgling of a brook comes through the trees in some great forest, making the traveller turn to it, by instinct, without the wish to drink.

In the round chapel underneath the tower, the Mass of the Mozárabes was going on, with a scant congregation listening to it, the women sitting squatted on the ground, and one or two old men looking on listlessly and muffled to the eyes.

Icázar, standing at the door, turning his hat between his hands, after the way of an infrequent worshipper, recalled the ceremony, just as a man recalls the details of a dream seen through the mist of sleep.

The silver bells rang out to scare the fiends, who, hovering in mid-air, are on the watch to seize a soul when the chance offers, and if the priest should be remiss in offering up his prayers. All the strange ceremonies and curious rites so piously preserved in their captivity among the Moors by Gothic Christians in the south, were faithfully rehearsed. As the priest mumbled at his Mass, and as Icázar listened to him and the strange music which accompanied his prayers, the story of the strife in the old times between the northern and the southern rituals came crowding to his mind. Dimly he recollected he had heard his mother say that the thing came to trial in the great plaza of the town, when, after prayer and a due search for amulets was made, both missals were committed to the flames to test their holiness. The expectant crowd stood round, each prophesying victory for his own Mass book, and certain of success.

At the first touch of the consuming fire the Gregorian Psalter leaped out on the stones, and lay upon the street. All its adherents shouted victory, but still the fire burned on, and at the bottom of the pile, covered with ashes, but by God's grace and by the virtue of the Oriental patience, which perhaps it had acquired in its long sojourn with the Moors, there lay the book of the Mozárabes unharmed and sanctified by the fierce trial it had undergone, of its authority.

When the priest reached his "*Ita missa est,*" and the scant congregation had quietly dispersed, Icázar left the church, following the street known as the passage of the Wooden Man, to the apothecary's, refusing as a slight the proffered help of several street boys, who, when they spy a stranger in the dark lanes which in Toledo bore through the town like worm-holes in a cheese, all cluster round like flies.

Hardly observing where he walked, but going straight as does a pigeon through the sky, he came upon the shop. A jar of leeches hung beside the door, and on the shelves were the same pots of Talavera ware painted in blue with a great Austrian double-headed eagle, lettered in Latin "Cardamomum" or "Savina," which as a child had made him wonder how any single man could know as much as he felt sure that Don Adolfo knew and keep it in his head.

The selfsame smell of senna met him at the door, mixed with valerian and with dead flies, which made the ointments that his friend prepared send out a stinking savour, and which of old had sickened yet attracted him, as he passed by the house.

A row of chairs stood, as they used to stand, ranged up against the wall, some seated with rough cowskin, shiny with use and with a few white hairs still clinging to the hide, and some with tapestry.

Coming up to the door half warily, after the fashion of a man who has received a check and has his mind made up that it is possible fate still has blows in store to deal him unawares, Icázar asked, "Is Don Adolfo disengaged?" scanning the pimply-faced assistant, who was sitting on a stool, with some disquietude. "Don Atanasio, I suppose you mean," the man replied. "He has just lain down to take his siesta, but in an hour or two you can come back again, and I am sure that he will undertake your case if you are indisposed."

"Where, then, is Don Adolfo?" Icázar said, but diffidently, foreseeing that he must be dead, and that another of the links with the Toledo which once had been his home had parted, and that he had returned to be a stranger in the town where he had passed his youth.

"Exactly where is difficult to tell," rejoined the assistant in a strong Seville accent, and with an air as of a humourist *[sic]*, after the fashion of his kind. "For years before his death the worthy man never communicated, heard Mass, confessed, or in the least complied with any of the duties of the Church, so that, as Father Perez thinks — he comes at times to our 'tertulia' in the shop — poor Don Adolfo may lie howling. But — we men of science ridicule such things, putting our faith in Darwin and the great Draper, he who wrote 'Conflict with Science and Religion,' as I am sure you know."

Thanking the humourist *[sic]*, Icázar hurried from the shop and plunged into the streets. All day he roamed about, seeking his friends and finding none of them, knocking at houses where in times past the doors appeared to open of themselves before his knocking ceased. No one remembered him but one old lady, whom as a child he faintly recollected, and she had turned half-imbecile with age, taking him for his father, asking affectionately after his mother and hoping she was well. At nightfall he returned to his hotel, and, dining miserably alone, his joy at coming home turned to despair with disappointment and with loneliness, he half determined to go back to Mexico by the first ship that sailed.

His dinner over, with a cigar, which tasted bitter in his mouth, between his teeth, he roamed about the town half-aimlessly, passed by the theatre, and after going in found the first act half over; and as he gazed about, watching the people in the boxes and the stalls, he fell into a dream.

All his past life and all his present being seemed somehow welded; the world was empty, and he alone in it, wandering about and looking for a friend. Coffins and tombstones strewed the streets, which all seemed cemeteries, and he alone went sadly up and down reading the epitaphs.

He heard the singers vaguely, and all the actors had their faces veiled, whilst a thick mist covered the people in the boxes and the pit, and hid them from his sight. All seemed his enemies or, at the least, unsympathetic to him, and nothing he could do helped him to clear away the vapour from his brain, which kept him separate from every one he saw, in an unfriendly world.

Then, without knowing how it came about, a change came over him, and, looking at the stage, he saw the curtain had been lowered and that the audience was going out to smoke, leaving him sitting in the middle of the stalls, alone and solitary.

He sat half dozing in his seat, tired with his rambles up and down the town, and as he sat, scanning the curtain, lying back against the seat, he felt the sense of loneliness had gone and that the world still held some people whom he knew, without a barrier of intervening mist to keep them separate.

For instance, the tall gallant in the cloak, with his fair curls upon his shoulders, his pointed beard, trunk hose, and shoes with round rosettes which looked too big for them, was an old friend whom he had known from childhood upwards, and understood him well. His sword, with a long wrinkle in the sheath, which, had it been smoothed out, must certainly have made it more than a fathom from the pommel to the chape, he recognized with joy.

He thought the look upon the gallant's face, which wreathed his cheeks into a mortary kind of smile, as when the stucco gapes upon a wall, was one of welcome, and as he answered it himself it seemed to fade away into the paint, as if the smiler was contented, feeling the tension of the muscles might relax now he had found his friend.

The lady in the draggled satin gown, which once had been rose-pink, but now had faded to a sort of yellow-ochre, seemed to be bowing to him, keeping her eyes the while right in the middle of the tall gallant's back, and smiling roguishly.

The fluffy dogs, of no discovered breed, seeming a cross between a badly-bred King Charles and a fox terrier, which stood between the gallant and the dame, uncertain which to go to, being repelled on one side by the terrible long sword and on the other by the whip which sprang directly from the flesh of the fair lady's white-gloved hand and dangled in the air, he knew familiarly. What power prevented him from stretching out his hand to run it gently down their neatly frescoed backs, he knew not, feeling so certain that he owed them a caress for their fidelity.

Well did he know the palfrey of a light lemon colour, which a young page in a round cap and feather, bright scarlet trunks and orange hose, was holding by the reins. He heard it neighing, although no sound came from its widely opened mouth, and he felt tempted to exclaim, "Fair youth, take me the courser to his stall, water and feed him; for, look you, he has waited in the sun since I was little taller than yourself, and must a-weary be."

He knew a play was going on upon a stage set in the open air, on which four men wrapped in their cloaks, with swords like torches brandished in their hands, fought to defend or carry off a damsel, who, with her hair dishevelled, lay like a bag of rags upon the ground, whilst her distressed and aged father wrung his venerable hands and gazed upon the clouds.

The gallant and the lady and the page he knew were looking at the play, although their eyes were otherwise employed, and fixed on vacancy. The band, which, squatted on the ground, discoursing music of the spheres — through the unsympathetic medium of a long Arab-looking flageolet played by a pallid youth, with wind-swollen cheeks and eyes that started from his head, and a round drum on which a negro lad was beating furiously — ravished his ears with a strange melody which none but he could hear.

A town which simulated a Toledo drawn from phantasy, with an enormous range of snow-clad mountains towering up above its walls, surmounted by deep orange-coloured clouds, he half divined, half recollected rather than actually saw, was in the background, and underneath its walls sat a gay company at cards, whilst, with a touch of realism, quite in Velazquez' manner, two or three beggars stood behind them as they played, and criticized the game.

Then, as the curtain rose, and his old friends were rolled above his view, he slowly rubbed his eyes, and opening them again looked out upon the world and found it empty. Then muttering, "All dead; of all the people I had hoped to see, these are the only friends to welcome me," he walked into the street. Following the Calle de la Plata half mechanically, he walked down to the river, and, standing on the bridge, leaned on the parapet and gazed into the stream.

A chilly wind blew feathery clouds across the moon. Algól was rising and the Three Maries, with their gleaming lamps cut through the blackness of the night as diamonds cut glass, joining the earth and sky together with a long beam of light. The battlemented walls outlined against the sky seemed drawn in charcoal, and as the traveller stood leaning on the bridge the Tagus thirstily lapped up against the piers, whilst on its surface came a murmuring as of choked voices striving to be heard, which seemed to greet him, as if the Romans, Arabs, and the Goths pitied his loneliness, and were stretching out their hands.

His People

A Botanist

The book cost but a shilling on a barrow in a side street of a provincial town. The subject of it, botany, that gentle science, so fit for bruised and disappointed minds.

In it, the quondam owner had inscribed her name, Matilda Hutton, adding "her booke," perhaps to show her erudition, or perhaps in play. Apparently she lived in Bath, the refuge for old maids and generals who never handled troops but from the windows of a club, for on a little yellowing ticket it was set forth that Pickering & Son sold books, both new and second hand, at Bridge Street, opposite the Wells.

A gentle soul, Matilda, one feels sure, and one that probably had been, so to speak, stillborn from her birth, as far as passion is concerned; or maybe, she had had her brief unhappy passage in her youth, and been deceived, and then shut up her soul, pouring her love out on a cat or Blenheim spaniel, and falling back on botany, the all-heal of old maids. I take it that she was a most undoubted, right old maid, by virtue of her careful handwriting, her notes and her corrections of the press, written so delicately, that they seem half clandestine, and an apology for her continuance in life. Besides, between the pages of the book, which is itself a trifling and compendious affair, with blurry woodcuts of the plants (the Flora of our Isles), wild flowers were laid in press. Perhaps she called the book (companion of her rambles, her scientific vade-mecum and her joy) "my *hortus siccus*"; for all the hay, which once was leaves and petals, all instinct with life, but now as miserable and as out of joint with what they were, as are the birds, distorted by a stuffer in a glass case in some museum, not ghosts but tortured souls, and smelling of some disinfectant, has a small docket with its Latin name. Thus meadow-sweet, which still exhales a ghostly scent of its sweet self, and is labelled "the *Spiræa ulmaria*," as it should be, no doubt, in catalogues of plants; Speedwell, which becomes *Veronica officinalis*; and Love-lies-bleeding (as perhaps hers did up to her dying day) under the style of *A. caudatus*; are so transmogrified that if they met in some old garden in a country farm, they would not know each other, unless some kindly creature, such as the writer was herself, had introduced and put them at their ease. Not that such gardens nowadays are to be found, for all the plants with their old English names have lost their modesty, and smack of some emporium in a town, and lengthy catalogue.

I take it that the Latin was Matilda's joy, but that she loved the flowers for themselves. This, the floss silk which still confines them, and the thin leaves of tissue paper, to save the pages of the precious book and keep the flowers fresh as long as possible, most amply testify. Besides, the scientific names apart, the flowers she dried are all such as she must have loved and gathered in her walks, in the green leafy lanes.

Campion and eyebright, agrimony, with winter-green, St. John's wort, spearmint and tormentil, with holygrass and herb of grace (called, as she says, by some, countryman's treacle), prunella, gentian, moneywort, and viper's bugloss, of which she says, "I found this plant at Kenilworth, it grows just in the wall above the tiltyard," all witness to her taste.

Just fifty years ago she took her walks about the woodlands and the lanes, her book in hand and dressed after the fashion of the times, in a grey linsey-woolsey skirt, kept up from trailing on the ground by an elaborate system of silk cords. Her hair dressed low and covering her ears, and at the back neatly disposed beneath her hat in a loose net of black chenille, with her short gloves of brown or puce-colour laced up the back by a white tasselled string, gave her a look, even when all such garments were in vogue, of being out of fashion and ill-dressed, but not ridiculous.

Her book in hand, and an umbrella, which I feel sure was bulgy and had lost the india-rubber band which should have kept it elegantly furled, and with that air of diffidence that in those days was indispensable to all unmarried women not much blessed with money or good looks, she took her walks abroad. I feel her lonely in her life, living in lodgings, or in a family of serious disagreeable folk who, with the best intentions upon earth, rendered her wretched now and then, and sent her out for refuge, searching for flowers she never could have found. Herb-paris very likely was her dream, or Park Leaves, which she sought diligently, as knights sought the Grail, both in and out of season, hearing no doubt of them from herbalists, or reading in the press, they had been found at Taunton, or near Maryport, or Pevensey, or in the district of Menteith, perhaps in Lundy Island, or in some place quite inaccessible to one of modest means.

I like to fancy her straying on the roads with a tin box for specimens hung by a green silk cord across her shoulders, her book in hand, her bulgy sunshade tucked beneath her arm, and with her porcelain coloured eyes, shaded by spectacles of neutral tint, which she had varied year by year from her youth upwards (as the young Parthians changed their bows according to their strength), wide open, but not seeing very much or too acutely, and with an air of having lacked advancement from the first day she entered upon life. But still, a happy soul, as commonly are those born without guile; wearing her happiness, the chiefest boon that nature gives to man, quite unassumingly, feeling instinctively that to flaunt a quality so rare, would be unkind to ordinary men and smack of cruelty. She must have been contented, although at times the curious injustices and ills that an all-seeing Providence permits, may have astounded her, and set her pondering on the lot of those less blessed than she, who had no book of botany to solace and amuse, but passed their time in sickness or in toil; and as she mused on this thing or on that, the tears would well into her eyes so that she readily mistook gentian for gromwell, muddled up golden-rod and agrimony, and wrote down entries in her book which only that explains. But yet these moments of inquietude and doubt must have been fugitive, for as a botanist she saw that He who made the flowers in their degrees, inspiring, as it seemed, Linnæus and the rest of those his botanists to classify and set them in their books, must have loved all He made, and at the last no doubt, right would prevail, and so she praised His name. Then, calling to her Blenheim spaniel, for I am sure she had one, she would go into the woods, mildly excited and as eager for the day as is a fisherman when, in the morning, seated in his punt, he throws in ground bait, regulates his float, and settles down to fish. The dog with its large paws and flapping ears, stump tail and back as mottled as a calf's, loved but despised her, after the fashion of its race; coming back to her call just when it liked, and asking for applause. Those were red-letter days, and she has marked them in the margins of her book, setting forth briefly (but without method) everything she did. "Found a small cistus (yellow) on the chalk . . . hemp agrimony (cannabinaceæ) grows by a marsh near Ibblesworth, a charming graceful plant; wonderful order, the compositæ . . . sunset too beautiful for words," rounding her observations off with a quatrain from Herbert or from Quarles.

So did these simple joys (I think) sustain her in her life, as they do many subcutaneous pantheists who, unknown to themselves, unite their souls to nature in the fields as naturally as dragon-flies, which as they flit about above the grass with the sun falling on their gauzy wings seem happiness itself. No doubt these halcyon days were far apart, and the dull life of one in narrow circumstances and with few friends, for one so tender as the writer of the notes in the thin faint Italian hand could not have had a widespread circle, does not bring joy except of a subdued, almost clandestine, kind. Still, very likely in the quiet town, the few who knew her loved, though they half-despised, her, thinking her botany a weakness, when it was really the strength that gave her spirit to face life. It is not probable that even in that science, which the old maid forlorn, in every age, has made her own, she attained a great proficiency.

Linnæus, though as she says his scheme was "artificial," seems to have been a favourite, for opposite the *Ulex Europæus*, she observes, "This is the plant which in full bloom, in all its glory on a common, impelled the great Linnæus to shed tears. . . . I, too, have wept on seeing it in flower."

At times she stumbles on the harder words, and sets down "monohypogyneæ" when it is evident that "monoperigyneæ" was really in her mind; but trifles such as that do not impair enthusiasm, either in botany or in any other cause.

Her life was simple, of necessity, although I cannot fancy it as being otherwise had she had millions, still without doubt it would have pleased her to have money in her purse when an impostor followed her and begged. Sometimes, when down a street, a herd of oxen trotted to their doom, she must have shuddered, thinking that things were out of joint, and longed for money to redeem them from their fate, and to provide a field in which, happy and peaceful, they could ruminate their lives. Lost dogs and homeless cats, larks in a cage and rabbits in a trap, sore wrung the heart that knew itself without a place in the economy of man, making her lift her voice in faltering parable, knowing it was not womanly to teach. Near fifty, I should think, her health grew weaker and her walks more circumscribed, and by degrees she sank into that feebleness which sometimes wears away the lonely and neglected, as a flower wastes away from lack of tenderness and care, and withers at the root.

What was her ending? That is to me unknown, although I judge it peaceful, and of the sort we call, unkindly, a release. Her little property, if she had any, served but to pay her lonely funeral. Her much-loved book perhaps was sold with a job lot of tracts and homilies.

I fear that no one placed a bunch of myosotis on her grave, which possibly lies desolate without a headstone, a mere green mound covered with daisies, and with the grass all eaten up by moss.

So I take leave of her, having no idea in what green churchyard, with its dark lush grass, its time-defying yew, its lich-gate, cock-topped steeple, and tall clump of rook-filled elms, she lies. Still I am certain she sleeps well, forgotten by her friends and leaving for her only mourner but the spaniel, whose dumb grief most likely was unmarked and comforted by none; her treasured book, the one memorial of her life. It may be, though, that in the lanes round Bath, the flowers miss something, for surely none can gather them so tenderly as she who loved them all, and never sinned against them or their lives, except by giving them their Latin names when she embalmed them in the *hortus siccus* of her heart.

His People

Signalled

The Casino rooms were crowded. French, English, Poles, Russians, and an occasional Japanese, looking just like a monkey who had escaped from freedom in the woods and voluntarily had put the chains of trousers and of coats about his limbs, all jostled in the throng. Above them hung the concentrated scent of all the perspirations of their different races, mingled with every essence that the perfumer's art affords to mitigate the odours which humanity distils. All were well dressed, and eighteen centuries of culture and of care had culminated in making every one alike. Thus all spoke French, of course with varying accents; but as they all read the same books, had the same thoughts, and wore the selfsame clothes, the accident of accent did not separate them, and they formed one immense, well-scented family as to exteriors, though with their hands all secretly raised against each other, and their tongues wagging ceaselessly in calumny, just as a bulrush wags by the edge of some old mill-race, half filled up with mud.

All round the tables men and women stood, pushing and elbowing, and with their eyes fixed on the money on the cloth, adoringly, as it had been the Holy Grail and they all vowed to search for and to grasp it, at the peril of their souls.

Men who at home were magistrates and pillars of a church, or members of some county council, gazed at the *demi-mondaines* as they went to and fro brushing against the players to attract attention, with their eyes aflame or with a swinish puckering of their lips which spoke of lust unsatisfied, not from religious principles, but from the fear of spies and interfering friends.

They eyed the women just as a starving dog looks at a butcher's shop, sideways and lurkingly, for fear a blow may fall upon him, out of some quarter unforeseen. Smartly dressed women looked at their sisters of the *demi-monde* half with dislike half with approval, as if they somehow understood that they, although they were transgressors of trades-union rules, were helping them in their life's strife with man; whilst others with the colour rising in their cheeks pressed up against them as they passed, just as cats press against a chair, meeting their eyes with a bold comprehending stare. Remote from all the rest in a cane rocking-chair there sat a girl, thin, dark, and dressed quite quietly, so quietly that at first sight you might have taken her for a young married woman who had got separated from her friends and had sat down to rest.

Her high-heeled shoes just tapped upon the ground as the chair rocked, and as it balanced to and fro revealed her stockings half way up the calf, so fine and worked so open, that it appeared the hair upon the flesh might pass between the stitching, just as a little fish escapes through the fine meshes of a net.

Men passed before her, in the half-sneaking and half-swaggering way that men assume before a woman whom they have held between their arms a night or two ago, and whom they dare not recognize in public, although they want the world to see that they are well acquainted, and in its censure half applaud the fact. Their hands involuntarily just touched their hats, and as they looked an inch or two above her head murmured a greeting, and then straightening their legs they fell into a strut, as of a bull-fighter who has been nearly caught by the bull's horns, and wants the crowd to think he is not frightened as he edges to the limits of the ring. She gave her salutation by a half rising of her eyebrows, and a faint smile, half of amusement and half contempt, just flickered on her lips, as some one with his wife or daughter on his arm suddenly flushed or paled and looked with interest at the chandelier as he passed opposite her chair. Callow and fledgling youths boldly saluted her, colouring as they did so to their hair, whilst grave and decorated men just raised their eyes, and fat provincials wildly plunged and bolted at the sight of her, just like young horses faced suddenly in a deep lane by the fierce rattle of a motor-car.

Still nothing in her dress or manner was unlike that of a hundred other women in the rooms, as she sat quietly at the receipt of custom, watching her various acquaintances as they passed by give by their guilty looks the lie both to the faith and the morality they held, and which, no doubt, she held herself as sacred, and as fixed as are the poles, although she saw them outraged in her person twenty times a week, just as in Spain, 'tis said, that a society founded to protect the lower animals, finding itself in difficulties, arranged a bull-fight to increase its funds and clear away its debts.

But as she sat indifferent, waiting what fate should send her, to her amazement, another girl, but little younger than herself, sat down beside her, and with "*Il fait tray sho nais-cepars*," fell into conversation with her as easily as if they had been friends.

The girl, who knew the world, glanced at her quickly, half thinking that the stranger came from some island in the Ægean Sea, but saw at once her island lay to the north, and that she had addressed her in pure innocence of heart.

Though she had often seen fair English girls, dressed in short skirts, boisterous in manner, fresh-coloured and half manlike in their ways, striding along as if their knees would burst their petticoats, this was the first time she had met or spoken to one, and the experience somehow brought the blood into her cheeks.

"Yes, it is hot," she said, and stole a glance half of amazement, half approbation, at the fresh English girl, who seated by her side seemed quite unconscious of the difference in their lives and talked so naturally and in such curious French. She marked her sunburned hands, gloveless and strong as those of a young man, and, made observant by the manner of her life, saw she was pretty at a glance, although her clothes were ugly and her fair hair all gathered in a knot. As she thought upon this thing and on that, and on the shielded life of the fair English girl, so little younger than herself, and on her own, a flush rose on her face as she perceived that she was shy before the other's innocence and want of knowledge of the world. At first the conversation languished, till the stranger, who had sat down with so much lack of ceremony beside her, looking her over with wide-open eyes, said, "I liked the look of you, as I was straying up and down, looking out for my mother, who had got lost whilst I was watching the roulette. You looked so pretty, and you are well dressed, you know you are, and so does every one, all the men look at you, when they pass by, just as a schoolboy at a cake in a shop-window. How foolish they all are."

Used to all kinds of compliments point-blank, none that she ever had received, in all her life, had put her to such difficulty, and once again she stole a look at her fair complimenter's face to reassure herself that she was really as innocent as she appeared to be. "Well dressed," she murmured, "well, any woman likes to be well dressed." To such a commonplace of femininity no answer was required beyond a simple affirmation, and a look of admiration at the clothes.

"Why, what a lot of men you know!" the English girl exclaimed, as counts and viscounts whom she knew by name walked by, as they sat talking, staring a little at the strange companionship of the two girls, all making a half recognition as they passed. "Why is it, none of them take off their hats — I thought that Frenchmen always were polite?"

Then as she got no answer, but a tapping of her companion's heels upon the floor, and a faint blush as of annoyance at her words, fearing she had offended her acquaintance, whom she already had begun to admire on account of her nice clothes, and evident knowledge of the world, she said, just as a schoolboy might have said, "It's awful hot in here. Would you mind going out into the air, and we can sit and talk?" The other, like a person in a dream, got up and followed her, and the two girls walked through the crowd, the English girl quite unconcerned, pushing her way, after the fashion of a forward player in a football team, smiling and only anxious to get out into the air. The other, red and uncomfortable, but hypnotized by the frank manners and good faith of her she followed, hardly knew where she was until she found herself seated in a cane chair upon the terrace, and heard her guide say, "Well, this is better than the stuffy room."

From the Casino came the hum of voices, and points of light seemed to break through the windows, and a faint smell of perspiration and stale scent defiled the atmosphere as it came floating up to where they sat. A breeze sprang up and cleared away the fleecy clouds before the moon, whose rays, half deadened by the glare of the electric lamps upon the terrace, seemed to be concentrated shyly on the magnolia trees which formed the background of the artificial scene, falling on their metallic-looking leaves, which it subdued and turned to plates of silver in its light. Moths hung about the great electric lamps, like men about a courtesan, and seemed to swim in the long beam of light which issued from the globes. Sometimes they flew against the glass with a dull furry noise, and then fell stunned and lay upon the paths, with their wings fluttering, until some high-heeled shoe, just peeping out from underneath a cataract of lace, crushed them to pulp upon the stones, or carried off their bodies sticking to the sole.

Silence fell on the girls as, walking to the balustrade, they stood and looked over the wide white road, across the lawn set with its bunches of white pampas-grass and of euonymus, upon the sea, which stretched out cool and clean and undefiled even by all the tawdriness of the Casino and its lights. Up from the shore there came a long-drawn sigh as if the waves had brought to land the last expiring breath of some lost sailor as they swirled upon the beach. The light air stirred the curls upon the foreheads of the girls, and the mysterious companionship of youth drew them together without words making them feel a bond of sympathy.

Tears stood in the dark eyes of the French girl, she did not quite know why, and something seemed to force her to bestow her confidence upon the girl who stood beside her, although she felt it would be useless, as she could never understand.

As she stood hesitating, the other, seeing her tears, caught at her hands and said, "I say, whatever is the matter? I am so sorry. Tell us about it, it will do you good. Is it about any of those bounders who grinned at you, and did not raise their hats?"

The other looked at her, and, struggling to keep back her tears, said, "No, no, not about any man, I hate them all . . . that is, I am not sure . . . I think one is not quite so horrible as all the rest — but then I have no right to talk to you, so innocent, about such things." She felt the hand of her companion tighten on her own, and all her sorrows running from her heart; her prostituted youth, the recollection of her home, perhaps the thought of the one man less horrible than were the others, forced her to speak and lay her head upon the shoulder of the mysterious friend, who had come as it were out of the depths to comfort her.

As she was struggling to choke down her tears and speak, and as the English girl stood wondering, but sympathetic and expectant, clasping her hand in hers, a strong high voice broke through the stillness of the night.

"Ethel, my dear," it said, "where have you got to? We have been looking for you for the last hour, and father is so cross." The girls just pressed each other's hands, and separated, as ships which have but signalled may be parted by a mist, without the time to make out either their numbers or the ports from which they hail.

His People

La Zagala

I went once into the Cathedral of Burgos and paid to have the curtain drawn from before the figure of a most striking and realistic crucifix. Beside me stood a countryman dressed in his sheepskin coat, and with a blanket striped in brown and white over his shoulder; in his hand a staff. I saw him cross himself and fall upon his knees, whilst from his face ran drops of sweat. He gazed with the fixed eyes of faith, and as the curtain was whisked hurriedly across the crucifix, drawn by a bored, yet merry-looking acolyte, he rose again and murmured "It is finished." Perhaps, with the interior vision, he had seen the crucifixion, and had felt and suffered with his Lord. Again, it may have been he had felt nothing, and been but hypnotized by gazing on the Christ. Into these mysteries of the human soul the thinking man looks with reluctance, if he is wise, for it may be that looking, he may chance upon reflections in his own, which may surprise him, in despite of faith. But I, more lucky than my shepherd, or perhaps less lucky, for again the matter is one of the perspective of the mind, can say that at a theatre last night, here in this windswept mud-brown village, capital that was of all the Spains, when the piece was over not only did I say regretfully "It is finished," but I wanted it straight to begin again. And yet perhaps it would not have appealed to every one, because it had no moral precept to inculcate in the last act, after in the first three, the actors like unlicensed bridegrooms all had run their course. Religion seems to have left as an inheritance to its half-sister chill morality, that in the last act of our lives all should be strictly done within the limits of its law. And thus it seems that we have merely, as is usual, changed one collar for another, but have remained essentially the selfsame dogs. But in the theatre of which I write, laws were made merely to be broken, and serve as counsels of perfection, and quietly and bitterly, just as in life itself, the story was unrolled.

In the bare theatre, devoid of accessories, and decorated but by the ingenious installation of electric light, decked out in toilets which apparently were made on purpose for trans-Pyrenean use, and with their coal-black hair set thick with specious-looking diamonds, sat hard-eyed ladies, with their full busts bulging beyond the fronts of boxes. All were full armed with fans, as if each one had come to judge the world. But if the ladies in the boxes with their attendant men appeared as if they were but part and portion of a play in which they took the part of ladies and of gentlemen, the sovereign people in the gallery took the reproach away.

Well are they called in Spain the brazen folk (*gente del bronce*) and "los Morenos," for all were dark and many of them, through want of washing and with the glare of sun and burning of the fierce Castilian wind, shone bright as brass itself. Short and square-built, with eyes that twinkled merrily, something between the twinkling of the eyes of jockeys and of monkeys, their faces shaved but once a week and for the most part set in a stubble of black wire, their flat white hats from Cordoba or blue Basque caps formed as it were an aureole of rascalism.

Naturally, knowing nothing on any subject under heaven, they were critical of all. Actors and actresses, the piece, the theatre, the ladies in the stalls, the Government, all had their turn, and upon each and all they gave their absurd opinions, formed with much native quickness but without intelligence, just as a woman glancing at a horse sees at the first sight that it is a jade, but has no power to give her reasons words, or as a monkey looking at a nut sees at the first glance that it is rotten at the heart.

In rows they sat as thick as gulls upon a rock, their cloaks thrown back, their thin brown fingers coloured orange at the tips from the eternal cigarette, the only fire of Vesta never extinguished in the Spains. Their women in the mass were handsome, strong and even harder-eyed than were their sisters in the stalls. Their hair piled up in masses, or parted in the middle, half concealed their eyes, and the white powder daubed upon their cheeks dusted their brows, encroaching on their heads, so that the face and hair melted together in a coat of white. At first sight one divined the realistic view, both of the stalls and gallery, and it was faithfully set forth upon the stage.

The hard white light, brown land and windswept hills, the meandering rivers dry in the summer and in the winter torrents, the mixture of the Arab with the Goth, the Roman, and the Carthaginian cross, with garnishing of gipsy and of Jew, have all contributed to the material point of view.

The authors of the play, descendants by the right divine of genius from the great unknown writer who evolved the curious masterpiece of choice Castilian known as "La Celestina," had set forth as in a spectroscope the very pith and marrow of the life of Spain. Homelike, and biblical, and seasoned with the salt of Betica, it formed a southern complement to the plays of Ibsen, in its simplicity and truth. In a huge sparsely furnished house, somewhere near Seville, lived an hidalgo, who must have been descended from the Ingenious Gentleman, he of the running greyhound, the bold ferret, and the horse who had more corners than had a real from the mint of Potosí. Tall, grey, and upright, all his delight was in his horse and land, and all the world to him was full of people eager to do good, if they but got the chance. Withal no fool in things that appertain to daily life. In speech and dress precise; sober in diet and for morality a bar of steel. His wife having died whilst on a journey, for some strange notion of saving pain to his two daughters, he had concealed her death.

With various excuses and a wealth of lying letters only to be excused to conscience by the idea of doing good, he kept the fraud alive. At last his eldest daughter married, and the younger went on a visit to her, leaving their father, lonely, with his servants and his horse. Still he wrote on, and always held out hopes of his dead wife's return. Into the Andalusian Eden glided all unawares the female snake, creeping about the heart of the hidalgo after the fashion of its prototype of old.

She was a country girl, and her entry with her father, a stupid and yet humorous Andalusian clown, appeared quite natural, as she came to take a servant's place, left vacant by a death.

The solitary gentleman had a mania that all his servants in the evening should come into the drawing-room and learn to read and write. This led to intimacy, and by degrees to love. But still the simple gentleman would not confess it even to himself. Then came upon the scene a rough Asturian miller, one Polanco, whom in his loneliness the modern Quixote had invited to his house. He and his dog Veneno soon overran the place, the latter sleeping on the hidalgo's bed, the former talking and laughing with the maids. One day he pinched the Zagala (the new maid), and then her master found out what had been passing in his heart. He instantly boxed Polanco's ears, and turned him and his dog Veneno out of doors.

He went, protesting that his expulsion left a bad savour in his mouth. Next came the hesitations of a man of feeling and of sense, described with humour and with pathos, and at last a secret marriage, and a brief interval of transient happiness. Then one by one his servants leave him, some from jealousy of their old comrade, and others, as the old nurse who brought his children up, out of respect for the remembrance of his wife. As the old nurse went out, carrying her bundle, Spanish fashion, in a towel, the soul of the Zagala for the first time wakened into life. Till then she had accepted, in the Eastern way, life, love, and everything as fate. But then she suddenly became alive, and screamed impressively, "Go call her back." Then doubts assailed her, and she thought that she had been a traitor; but her old father came to visit her, and her pride in her smart clothes and jewellery stilled, for the moment, all her qualms. Her father is astonished, smells her pocket-handkerchief, touches her flounces timidly, and is delighted when she tells him "she is all lace inside." Then in the whimsical, half-stupid manner of his kind, says, "I feel half ashamed to be your father," which she takes as he had meant it, for a compliment.

But in the village where the drama passes, news of the marriage soon had filtered out. None would believe it, and Polanco, with his dog, determines to deliver up himself a victim on the altar of his friendship, and to learn the truth. He comes, is well received, and when he learns the truth is thunderstruck. In vain the poor hidalgo tries to make Polanco understand that he has tried to act, if foolishly, still like a Christian and a gentleman. By the inexorable logic of a commercial world, Polanco shows him that he has brought ruin upon himself and misery upon the daughters whom he loves, and probably upon the girl whom he has taken to his heart.

Indignantly he asks Polanco, "Would you not have acted in the same manner as I did?" and gets the answer, "I — I should have acted in a very different way."

Just as they are about to quarrel, comes a letter from his daughter saying she and her husband have returned from Italy, and will be with him in an hour. It seems they think the mother is at home. Then for the first time all the significance of his action rises before his eyes. How can he meet his daughters, and present them instead of the long longed-for mother, a young servant girl. The Zagala overhears him, and is mad with terror, and threatens then and there to run away. The daughters come, and then taking the elder one aside, he tells her of his pious fraud and after tears obtains her pardon; but he knows that there can be no pardon for the next action that he must confess. Days pass, and by degrees the daughters slowly begin to feel all is not right. Then they ask for the nurse who brought them up, and hear she is at home living alone in a small cottage in a village near at hand. The eldest goes and sees her, learns the truth, and comes back heart-broken. Still though, she doubts, until by accident she sees her father kiss his wife. At last her love prevails, and she forgives her father, and agrees to take the younger sister off and keep the truth from her. They go, and the poor father is left desolate.

He naturally turns to his wife for comfort, misses her; grows uneasy; searches the house, the terrace; rushes out to the garden calling upon her name. You hear him in the orange grove, and from the eyes of all the "brazen people" in the gallery real tears drop. They make their way through paint upon the faces of ladies in the boxes and the stalls. The theatre suffers and weeps, as if each man and woman lived the agony upon the stage. Lastly the poor hidalgo rushes back again, and in a moment, takes it in, and stands turned to a pillar of salt grief. Then cloaks are flung across the mouth, women tie highly coloured shawls under their chins, ladies throw furs about their powdered shoulders, and the audience, holding their handkerchiefs before their mouths, for it is good to take precautions in the subtile [sic] air, stream out into the night.

His People

Le Chef

Just at the corner of the streets called Twenty-fifth of May and Calle de Cangallo stood Claraz's hotel. In those days, long before the city of La Plata rose and fell, before La Union Civica was known, and whilst the echoes of the Paraguayan war were still resounding in the River Plate, it was a busy spot. The life of Buenos Ayres ran before the door. Only three squares away the two great Plazas, with their palaces and barracks, basked in the sun, or shivered in the wind, according as the Pampéro whistled, or the hot north wind blew. The Stock Exchange was near; the mole within a stone's throw, and up the deep-cut Calle de Cangallo, which looked more like a dry canal than a great thoroughfare, stood several of the principal hotels. The house was built all round a courtyard, with a great archway over which were rooms upon an upper floor where Claraz kept his saddlery, his books, and natural history collections, and in which he generally lived, to be away from noise. The rest of the establishment was but one story high, though being built upon a bank, it looked right out across the River Plate, in Buenos Ayres nearly thirty miles in breadth, so that the houses in La Colonia, on the other side, are only visible upon the clearest days. Claraz himself, a tall and black-haired Swiss, of all the men I ever saw, was the least fitted for the business of keeping an hotel. Well educated and with scientific tastes, his guests were almost all either commercial travellers or sheep and cattle farmers, who strode into the place, with a Basque porter carrying their saddles, took off their pistols, hung them on their beds, and called for drink incontinently, stamping about the brick courtyard in their long riding-boots and spurs. As all the rooms looked out into the yard, the fashion was to leave the doors wide open and to converse whilst lying on your bed, with any one you knew. In some respects the place was like a school, with the initial difference that you were pretty sure to learn some things worth knowing, after a day or two. Claraz himself, being a naturalist, knew all the animals and a percentage of the myriad shrubs and trees of the republic, and others in their several degrees were able to impart much knowledge of a varied kind and differing quality.

Kincaid from Patagonia had much Indian lore, and knew the chiefs of all the southern tribes. Though he lived out upon the fringe of Indian territory, and far removed from towns, his neighbours gauchos, and his life to herd his sheep and cattle all the day and sit down either alone or with his herdsmen in a hut at night to smoke and read a "Glasgow Herald" ten weeks old, which told him in eight columns all the ecclesiastic news of the Free Church and the Establishment, he yet remained a Scotchman, so Scotch that had you met him in a railway-carriage you would have thought him a new-comer fresh from Kirkcaldy or from Perth. Benitez Wilson, half Argentine, half Englishman, kept a *pulpería* in the south camp, and having been to England to be educated, had returned home again, more Argentine than ever, after the fashion of the Texan youth sent by his father to tour round Europe, who being asked on his return what mode of life he proposed to embrace, replied, "Guess, Poppa, that I'll have a horse-ranch out in Nueces County or down by Goliad." Thin, slight, and dark, with long brown hands, and feet eternally imprisoned in tight patent-leather boots, he did not look the man to keep a frontier drinking-shop; but was reported, when a fight arose, to be a master of the art of throwing empty bottles, which he delivered like a Benjamite, and seldom missed his mark. What was worth knowing about racing on the flat (three squares or fifty) bare-backed and owners up, he knew, and no one from the Tres Arroyos to Tandil was cunninger *[sic]* in the innumerable false starts which are the science of a gaucho race. His life had made him taciturn, but when he chose, he could discourse of many things with the strange double view of the mixed-blooded man, which makes him never quite at home with either race, and an eternal stranger in the land. The other guests were mostly bagmen, usually Frenchmen from Marseilles or Bordeaux, black-bearded, voluble and unilingual, for why should any one whom God has blessed by making him a Frenchman struggle with other tongues? "You do not speak the language of the place," Benitez Wilson had remarked to Monsieur Lagadigadon. "Certainly not," he answered. "*Je parle Français, et ça me suffit, voyez-vous.*" But notwithstanding their linguistic limitations, they were a jovial set, carrying destruction, as it seemed, amongst the female sex of every land, and passing hours relating all their conquests, although the listeners might well have been aware, by personal experience, that all the tales were false. They and a knot of Englishmen, mostly offshoots of county families, and known in Buenos Ayres as the "Gentle Shepherds," made the most noise of all the visitors, and passed their time in general in the billiard-room, playing the cannon game, with lumps of chalk held in the bridge hand, with balls like turnips, and with cues like table legs.

The fashionable streets in which were situated the best shops cut the Cangallo at right angles, and even in those days had tramways running down them preceded by a boy on horseback who blew upon a horn, so that the curious little inn, even then, was an anachronism, though Buenos Ayres still in some respects was primitive. Horses were commoner than dogs; they stood at every house, with their feet hobbled during the time their owners talked or drank, and now and then, when they got bored, they would hop off, raising their shackled feet like rocking-horses, and congregate in knots, where with their reins tied to the saddles drawing their heads into their chests, they stood and fabulated. Before the Stock Exchange dozens, or sometimes hundreds, stood, and stockbrokers felt their way cautiously amongst them with propitiatory words, hissing and chirruping, and sometimes coming to a standstill, so to speak, storm stayed, amongst a sea of tails and hoofs, too difficult to pass. The presidential escort, dressed as exaggerated lancers, used to ride down the streets behind the carriage of the president, just as a troop of Indians rides behind a chief, all with their toes scarce touching their small native stirrups, their bodies swaying easily above the hips, talking and laughing, and some smoking cigarettes. The upper classes dressed in black broadcloth, and all wore black felt hats which made them look like Maltese ship-chandlers or touts in the Levant. They held themselves the first of humankind, calling the English "gringos," the Italians "carcamaños," Spaniards "gallegos," a term which they resented, as in Spain the word *gallego* is used to designate a man of all work, and the Brazilians, monkeys (macacos), whilst referring to themselves as the Porteños (men of the port), though at that time there was no harbour in the place. Women, except the higher classes who had travelled and seen that Mecca of the *rastaquouère*, "Paris de Francia," dressed in a loose black skirt with petticoats much starched and laced, wore low-cut shoes and white silk stockings, and minced upon the stones. Over their heads they wore the *manta*, a thick black cashmere shawl which, crossing on the chest, covered deficiencies and served them for protection and disguise. They seldom ventured far from home, except to mass, or to walk three or four together in a row about the squares, when in the evening military bands discoursed the strains of Offenbach or clashed out patriotic music written in general by Italian music-masters.

The house of Juan Garáy, one of the *conquistadores*, still stood, a long low brick or mud adobé edifice, close to the corner of the square, and usually the architecture was half-Moorish, flat-roofed and flanked by towers called *miradorés*, all dazzlingly white. A few tall French-built buildings studded the town, breaking the line of long flat roofs, and looking vulgar and unsuitable both to the people and the place. One of these just at the corner of the largest square was let in furnished suites and called "La Casa Amueblada," and occupied in general either by French or by Hungarian women, who sat in dressing-gowns, with their hair most elaborately dressed, at all the balconies. Painted but unashamed they sat at the receipt of custom, which seldom seemed to lack, although their tariff was in general a gold ounce, a coin which in those days was plentiful. In almost every side street, red lamps and doors ajar held by a chain, denoted where a lower class of ladies lived, and not content with this, the bars and cigarette shops all held their houris, and that although the women of the place were keen competitors. So much so, that in a town in Entre Rios a Frenchman having called upon the ruler of the place with a request to start a tolerated house, was answered with an oath: "Yes, start it and be damned, but you are certain to be ruined, for here the women all are amateurs." General society scarcely existed in the modern sense, but followed antique Spanish or semi-Moorish rules, the men at parties congregating into knots, smoking and talking scandal, and the girls seated upon chairs against the wall, whispering in undertones whilst managing their fans. Sometimes a man approached them, and selecting one, led her with compliments point-blank about her "beauteous eyes," her "grace" or what not, to the dance, which was a slow and swinging Spanish waltz danced with much balancing of hips, the arms held out like pump-handles, and during which the woman's head rested upon her partner's shoulder with her eyes closed, as she had been asleep, and smiling rapturously. The ceremony over, she was led slowly to the refreshment-room and ate an ice or drank some lemonade, standing the while a fire of compliments, which as she knew them all by heart and they were fixed as is a liturgy, must have been wearisome, although their age did not seem able to impair their efficacy and personal effect. In the less fashionable circles, they danced the *pericón* and *el cielito*, quaint, old-world dances with much waving of their handkerchiefs, and breaking now and then into some verses which the unlucky man was held to improvise, though generally he broke down utterly and the song ended in a laugh. The older people sat and drank maté, smoking cigarettes of black tobacco made in Brazil, which they lit frequently from a hot coal kept on a chafing-dish, or from a slow match hanging to a chain. On one side all was new, that is in what concerned commercial life, and steamboats and hotels were certainly more comfortable than those of England in the days of which I write. Upon the social side, with the exception of some rich men who had been educated either in Paris or in Bordeaux, or who had travelled, customs survived from Spain, and not from modern Spain, but from the Spain of the pre-revolutionary age. As there was little mixed society, except that of the nymphs of every land that Europe sent as civilizers, we as a general rule remained at Claraz's at night, and either talked or played at billiards, drinking the while maté or caña punch, or a decoction which we called "*la boisson Cavantous*," compounded of such simples as white curaçao, gum, gin and bitters, and a little lemon-juice.

Most of the company is dead, the last-named liquid, helped by whisky, having proved too much for them, in spite of struggles almost heroic in their foolishness. Some have been killed by Indians, drowned at sea, knocked on the head in rows, or died in drinking-shops. Long John Arbuthnott, known to us all as "Jar," from the initials of his name, and by the reason of a flowing beard which, mingling with his hair, caused him to look like Jove, sailed in a schooner to the Falkland Islands, and the last seen of him was his tall figure wrapped in a pampa poncho, waving good-bye as she cleared in a gale of wind from Maldonado and dropped into the mist.

Lucien Simmonet, a young Parisian journalist, who gained his living in a mysterious way by writing paragraphs from Paris in a back street in Buenos Ayres, became head secretary to His Majesty Aureille the First, King of Arauco, and his last letter to me, dated from Union Bay in Patagonia, just as his chief and he were starting for their Mecca in the West, has formed his epitaph, for from the wilds of Araucaria, if he returned, that is to me unknown. Dunsmere was lost in those vague regions known as "down about the Straits"; all that remains of him is a blue poncho barred with red, which lay for years upon his father's sofa in his smoking-room, and a whip made of coronilla wood mounted with silver, which when I used to take it up from where it lay, would bring him back to me, and make the tears stand in his father's eyes, who knew intuitively where and with whom my thoughts were straying, whilst I held it in my hand. Others have turned respectable. Simon Uruchi has an *estancia* in the district of Tuyù, is wealthy, a senator I think, and now and then his name appears in "La Tribuna" as having spoken on free-trade, protection, or the inherent right of every man to cheat, or something of the kind. All the Italians have gone home, having made "leetel money," and settled down to smoke Virginia cigars, grow their own wine, and talk of the old days amongst the "Barbari." My partner is a country squire in Devonshire who hunts and sits upon the bench, is a staunch Protestant and true, keeping his sitting in the chancel manfully and standing up for Church and King, though he believes in neither of them, as far as I can see. John Bland, the "Rengo," has an Indian wife, ten children, and a rancho near Cala in Entre Rios, wears native clothes (the poncho and the chiripá), has almost lost his English, and, a friend tells me, is happy as a dragon-fly, watching his flocks increase and his own life slip peacefully away. One hung on till last year, and then departed, not the least inclined to go, for life was pleasant to him, his groove just fitted, and in his way he had achieved renown. At Claraz's we called him Treadway, though his name was Cossart; but certain difficulties he had when in the little frontier town called El Bragado, where, as he said, "I used to sing *basso cantante* in the church choir, and serve the Mass, *vous voyez ça d'ici, mon cher*," induced him for a time to change his name, although he still remained a stoutish Frenchman, broad-shouldered, and with a profile just below the waist beginning even then to show, though he fought with it manfully and possibly with stays. His dead white face set in a jet-black beard, looked like a pearl in black enamel, and his large beaky nose — "*J'ai un grand diable de nez comme tous les gens intelligents*," he used to say — gave a fierce look which his intensely black and simple eyes quite truthfully belied. He was perhaps a little truculent, and stood a good deal on his dignity at open doors and crossings, and when he walked the streets and had the wall at his right hand, for nothing in the world would he have given up his right. No, not if his chief hero, Napoleon III, whom he admired but yet called Badinguet, had risen from the dead.

Few people even in Buenos Ayres at that day, when life was cheap and every man went armed, cared to contest the matter with him, for he was strong as a West Highland bull, or, as he said, *un lapin*, and moreover his troubles in Bragado had given him a name which it was his chief care to keep alive. Though born in London he was French to the backbone, his family having come from Carpentras; but yet spoke English perfectly, with just a little foreign accent grafted on cockney, which did not in his mouth sound vulgar, but as it were a complement to his appearance, which certainly was French. Thus no one but a Frenchman of his type could, when a woman passed, look at her with a conquering air and say, "Not bad, that little girl, eh? Strange how she smiled at me — but then they all do; one gets no peace because of them — ah, *sacrées femmes!*" He could not have believed himself, but for their self-respect, men of his type and nationality were forced in those days to assume that attitude, as Englishmen of the same time and kind thought it incumbent on them when a horse passed by them on the road, to put their heads a little on one side and mutter critically, "He seems to me to go a trifle short on the off fore, or perhaps on the near hind." Just at that moment he was working as a diver, which his proportions did not seem to fit him for, but which, as he said, "after my trouble in the camp, a simple matter of an almost necessary homicide, is prudent, and the most fitting occupation for a man who wants to pass unseen." A statement which in itself was logical enough, had he but gone about the streets, lived, slept, and had his being in his diver's dress. But as, his duties over, he dressed himself in the black suit with low-necked shirt and black felt floppy hat, which was the uniform of every one, the reason was not plain. But, be that as it may, he dined at Claraz's, sleeping in what he called *"mon taudis"* in a by-street, and was ready at all times to talk and tell his strange adventures in the provinces, or to play billiards, at which game he easily gave fifty in a hundred to almost any one in town. This talent, joined with great generosity and natural kindness, a somewhat "pawky" humour, and the most perfect feelings of a natural gentleman, made him a favourite with all. Though not weighed down with money, he always had the "Vie Parisienne" sent to him from France, esteeming that thereby he kept himself in touch with what he called "Le Bitume" and "La Haute Bicherie," not that he had nostalgia of the city of the light, thinking that the life in Buenos Ayres was the pleasantest the world afforded, as many of us thought; but from a sense of duty, as it were, just as the Englishman pored on the "Licensed Victuallers' Gazette," reading accounts of prize-fights in the halcyon days of Sayers and the Benicia Boy, and other worthies, long departed to that limbo which presumably they share with jockeys, touts, and sporting noblemen. The "Gentle Shepherds" used to borrow the French papers, and pore on them, especially when they found anything indecent, and then among themselves aver with oaths the French were "an immoral crowd," returning to the pure columns of "Bell's Life" with Saxon innocence. Such differences of ideals, no doubt, are in the very life-blood of a race; and points of honour, which the "Gentle Shepherds" held in high esteem, were to the Frenchman quite incomprehensible, and each looked on the other with contempt tempered by whisky or by absinthe, according to their kind. Both of them looked down on the Argentines, calling them "niggers" or *des barbares*, whilst they returned in kind, heaping the English up together with the Germans under the name of *gringos*, calling the French *gabachos*, and looking with contempt on both of them, as men who could not ride. Still they jogged on together, misunderstanding one another mutually, as they were joined in holy matrimony.

I left the country thinking never to return, being seen off by many of the society at the quaint little inn, into the whaleboat which in those days took one out to the steamers which lay eight, ten, or twelve miles off, often hull down, in the thick yellow water of the River Plate. After two years, lacking advancement and with the nostalgia of the open plains, the horses and the wild free life, I sailed again, landed in Buenos Ayres, and found the place had altered in that time almost as much as European cities alter in an age. No longer whaleboats took one from the ship, nor did a cart drawn by three horses with a Basque riding the near-side animal, or a bullock-wagon with a man seated on the yoke, carry one to the shore where the water shoaling made it unsafe for boats. Steam-launches pitching on the choppy waves like buckjumpers, in half an hour or so, performed the passage which in the whaleboats often took more than two, and on arriving near the beach, I found a smart tin pier replaced the wooden wharf which had survived apparently from when the conquerors first landed at the city of Good Airs. But once inside the town, although fell progress had already laid its hands on many of the older buildings, sweeping away the house of the old conqueror Garáy as if, according to a friend of mine, it had been nothing but a disagreeable mother-in-law, the old life held its sway.

Still at the corners of the streets the hobbled horses stood. Hard hats, except amongst officials, and the like, had made scant progress. Few people carried walking-sticks, but in their hands held plaited raw-hide whips, with silver tops, flat lashes, and a thong to hang them to the wrist. Still women went to church all dressed in black. Basque milk-boys rode their ponies, seated between their cans, dressed half like sailors, half like gauchos, wearing the chiripá and the broad belt fastened with silver coins, with a black jacket and thick boots, a sort of cross between the kind a pilot and a cattle-rider wear. Beggars no longer rode, but with increase of wealth and of modernity, had multiplied a little, as if to prove that no one has devised a scheme to make the rich man rich, and not involve as its corollary the increasing poverty of our poor brethren in the Lord. Arrived at Claraz's a *changador* carrying my things up from the custom-house, all was unchanged. The owner still sat quietly in his upper room and classified his plants, whilst guests arrived and either at their own sweet will selected rooms, or were inducted into them by an old housekeeper from Biscay who spoke but little Spanish, and that all topsy-turvy, who could not read or write or far less cipher, standing for all that manfully between her master and his guests, and bustling about. The bagmen still disputed as of yore about their conquests, the "Gentle Shepherds" drank and idled through the day, cursing the country, but still loath to leave it, knowing that in a British colony they must work or starve, contingencies they did not care to contemplate, all being gentlemen. In such a place it did not take more than ten minutes to shake down and learn the local news, hear of the revolution up in Entre Rios, the Indian *malón* upon the frontiers, the death of So-and-so, the feats of some one's horse, and to absorb a cocktail, which done, the world appeared to fall again into its last year's rut. "And Cossart? Oh, yes, he has left off his diving," Claraz said, "and keeps a restaurant, makes a good living, and has a mistress called Emilienne." Dinner-time brought him to the inn, and it transpired that, being bred a cook, at the first chance he had returned to his profession, and now appeared rather bejewelled, but yet quite the gentleman, to play his game at billiards and incidentally welcome me effusively, and tell me of his altered circumstances and of Emilienne, whom he described with so much detail that I appeared to know her perfectly, both dressed and undressed, her ways, thoughts, habits, with *une tache vermeille* which she had upon her shoulder, her business aptitude, and other details which recited openly put the most hard drinking of the "Gentle Shepherds" to the blush, as their conventions and those of the possessor of *cette bonne brave fille* differed as much as do the stars, both in their glory and their magnitude. The restaurant turned out to be a stuffy, much beflied and dusty little place in which one dined extremely well and cheaply, and heard ten languages spoken all at once and loudly, and where *le chef*, wearing the habit of his craft, went round to every table and talked familiarly to all his guests, hoping their food was to their liking, and Emilienne, dressed in grey beige, her hair *en bandeaux*, presided at a desk, so quiet and businesslike that it appeared she just had left a convent to come and take the post. The guests departed; the *chef*, leading me to the desk, presented me to the fair priestess of *céans*, who bowed *très dignement*, accepted *mes hommages*, and comported herself generally in such a way as to quite justify the choice my friend had made. To the outward eye, the lady seemed one of those sensible commercial French women, who in a situation which an English girl would fill after the fashion of Moll Flagon, or half ashamed, knew how to conquer virtue by her seemly conduct, although she had it not, that is if after all mere virtue can be put beside good humour and real kindliness of heart.

Our talk ran on my friend's advancement, his future prospects, on politics, religion, the next president, the drought, the locusts, Indians, and other subjects which a year spent in Europe slackens the grasp of, and in all of them Emilienne gave her opinions when asked for them, in such wise manner and so foolishly, that at last the *chef* said to her with the kindly air with which a man speaks to a child, "*Ma belle*, go and see what the *marmitons* are at," and she, patting her bandeaux and smoothing out her skirt, tripped dutifully away. We sat and smoked Brazilian cigarettes, drank lemonade, and watched the fireflies flitting in the trees in the back garden, what time the chef unfolded all his plans. "You see," he said, "that diving business led to nothing"; then, for more emphasis, repeated it in French, "*menait à rien, pas même ça,*" and as he spoke he bit his thumb-nail and waved his hand before his face in token of disgust. "*J'avais mes quarante ans*, yes, forty years, so I said, Cossart, *mon ami*, after all, you are a cook, a cook professed, and it is in *les marmites* that your future will be found.

I thought of marrying, but then at forty years without a sou, not twenty paper dollars in the bank — a dot — you laugh, at forty years with my black beard becoming grey. I thought of shaving it, but . . . bah! So I went to a lady that I knew, what they call Trotaconventillos, eh, and asked her to get me somebody, not too pretty, not too young, neither too thin nor fat, a good arithmetician and *rangée*, and she, the Lord knows where, procured Emilienne . . . *il faut une femme, mon cher*, that poses you, especially in *ce sale métier* that I follow now." Laughing internally I told him that his lines had fallen not quite in a hard place, and he, loosening the buttons of his waistcoat, rejoined, "Yes, I have ambition, *quand on est chef* it always is like that. My hand, you see, what with the diving and the years I spent out at Bragado minding sheep, had got a little rusty, so I said, *Mon gars*, you take this little restaurant, get to your tools, and then when you have saved a bit, go home and settle down, after a month or two of course in La Ville Lumière; for before I die what I ambition is to be the *chef* at a swell London club, so that at last I shall be known for what I am, and make a name, eh — ." Every ambition being equal, and but measurable by the effort it entails, I cordially agreed, bade him farewell, and in the morning took the steamboat up the Paraná, landed at Diamante, found my tropilla waiting, and galloped to my house.

Two years brought me again to Buenos Ayres on my return to Europe, where I found my friend, still prosperous, his little café changed for a larger one, Emilienne gone, "*partie la mâtine, avec un riche Brésilien,*" and duly was seen off on board my ship by Cossart, from whom I parted not thinking I should meet him, for his ambition to be *chef* in a good London club seemed to be quite forgotten in his prosperity. Two or three, or perhaps five years had passed, when, lunching at a club in Edinburgh, and having got a mutton-chop, half raw, half burned, I sent (the first and last time in my life) to see the manager. The waiter said that Monsieur Trastour was away, but Monsieur something or another would come and speak to me. He came, and looking up I beheld Cossart, unchanged except that he had shaved his beard, and looked a little like an actor, with his blue stubbly chin. Speaking in Spanish, I asked him to meet me at a café in an hour or two, finished my lunch, and then sat down to smoke and ponder on the strange meeting after so many years. The *chef* appeared true to the tryst, embraced me, patting my shoulder with his great hairy hands, and hugging me. "You see," he said, "this is an *étape* on the way to London, but *ogni strada men' a Roma* — no, no whisky, it is an article of faith I know here in this North — but I will tell you how I came here — yes, a cigar," and he chose a long black oily one, not lighting it, but keeping it stuck in the corner of his mouth. "You see, *mon cher*, I think it was the sedentary life that got upon my nerves. Then, too, that matter of Emilienne — *les femmes, mon ami, ça vous abîme un homme.*" He paused, and looking at him I perceived that he was growing stouter, and no doubt in general *les femmes* did not appeal so much to him as in the days gone by, although a little later in the street he criticized them freely, as an old troop-horse out at grass is said in story-books to prick his ears at the sound of military music, even when yeomanry pass by. "Travel," he then continued, "is the best cure for all affections of the heart — you smile — well, well, that poor Emilienne was not perhaps so fatal to my peace, but vanity, and we all have it — *n'en doutez pas*. You see, I did not like the chaff about that damned Brazilian and his dollars, although, no doubt, had I been in his place, I should have done the same. Better by far to run about the world, even with such an ignoble *macaque*, than keep the books of a mere *guinguette* such as mine was, eh? Philosophy is in our Gallic blood, not of course the dull Germanic trash about first causes — woman is man's first cause — but, well — one resigns oneself to the inevitable — so I attached myself as cook and secretary to a diplomatist. Half the whole world I travelled with him for two years, going from Buenos Ayres up to Corumbá — you know, in Matto Grosso. Ah, yes, I recollect, you told me when you first went there after the Paraguayan war, the alcalde came down to the steamer riding on an ox. Well, not much changed, that Corumbá, when I was there. Nothing to cook, of course, but *charqui dulce* and some *mandioca*, and as there was no business, nothing to write. The people still washing out gold-dust, you recollect?" I nodded, and he seemed to remember his cigar was still unlighted and struck a match upon his thigh, though there were matchboxes upon the table, remarking as he did so, "*usage de la guerre.*"

"*Mon cher*, a desolating country, hot as the nether hell and damp — his excellency's boots were mildewed every day, and I, though cook and secretary, cleaned them, out of *désoeuvrement*, for they were London boots, and seemed a link with home. Mosquitoes like a thick cloud after rain, and every cursed crawling thing you ever saw, the people, negroes almost to a man, and yet, I liked the place — so did his excellency — it grew upon us both. Nothing on earth to do after the call *de rigueur* on the governor. We lounged about all day in our pyjamas, swung in our hammocks, listening to our lives. I cooked the breakfast, having a negro girl for *marmiton*, dished it myself, and waited on his excellency, who talked to me quite freely, for *entre nous* we were the only Christians in the place. Then he sat down to smoke, and I stood by and talked to him, telling him of all kinds of things and others, to pass the time away. Then came the siesta, and we got upon our horses and rode them down to bathe, going into the river on their backs for fear of the electric eels, the rayas, and some little devils of the deep they call a pejeréy. Then out into the forest, a veritable decoration of the opera, with climbing plants like ropes on every tree, monkeys and parrots and butterflies a foot across the wings. Then back to dinner and a stroll about the town, right through the grass-grown plaza, with the adobé palm-thatched houses whitewashed and gleaming in the night — *bon Dieu*, I grow poetical. But still I liked the place, and sometimes, walking down the street I hear the niggers scratching their guitars or playing the marimba, and wish that I were back again. It's stupid, isn't it? But it's stronger than myself — *mais on est philosophe*. With my diplomatist I went from Buenos Ayres to Madrid, where I got tired of him, gave him his *congé*, so to speak, and left him in the hands of the worst cook I ever met, a Greek, without an atom either of culinary knowledge or of dignity. I found myself in London, and in a month or two this billet has turned up, but I shall not stay long in this cold place amongst these people, whose chief pleasure is to talk about the quarrels of their Kirks. Not that I look down on religion; it is a useful scourge enough, and keeps them honest for the fear of hell, and comforts women and all those who never read Voltaire or Rousseau, but for the rest, God's not a bad man, as we would say, out in the River Plate."

So saying the philosopher lit his cigar again, shook hands with me, and went to look after *les marmitons*, who, as he said, were ever on the watch to spoil his plans and break his heart by letting saucepans overboil, entrées grow cold and tough, and bringing down discredit on his head. I watched him swagger down the street, looking at all the girls he passed, shouldering the men, and humming softly "Popol," a song in vogue in those days, with its absurd refrain of "*je me nomme Popol,*" and setting forth the adventures of its hero when "*au fond de l'Amérique, pays du Panama, il faisait de la botanique quand p'tite Française passa.*"

Six or eight months had passed when, passing that fine specimen of modern architecture, St. Peter's, Eaton Square, on horseback, riding to the Park, a voice called after me in somewhat Gallic Spanish, and turning in the saddle I saw my friend emerging from the church. A wondrous change had come upon him, for he was "*cinglé,*" as he would have called it, in a frock-coat, with a gardenia in his buttonhole. His hat shone shiny as a life-guardsman's helmet, and was cocked at such an angle on his head, it seemed capillary attraction only could keep it in its place. His boots were like the top layer of a pot of jelly, and in his hand he had a silver-mounted cane, the crutch of which was ivory, shaped like a woman's leg. In his left hand he held new gloves of a bright *sang de boeuf*, and on his cheek the barber's powder clung, like sugar on a cake. As a smart wedding was in process I was prepared for anything, to hear he was a millionaire, was married, or had made money on the Stock Exchange. "I come," he said, "from witnessing a marriage ceremony. One of my employers or my clients, all is one, has lost his liberty to-day." As I was still profane to what he meant, he said, "I have at last achieved the summit of my hopes, and there is no one rather than yourself whom I would make the sharer of my joy." Then straddling out his legs, he critically scanned my horse and tried to run his hand down its foreleg, almost receiving a slight kick whilst doing so. "Not a bad horse, *mon cher*, a little sickle-hocked I think — what, eh, from South America? — then not a word, we have been there ourselves." As I gazed speechless at him, knowing he knew as little about horses as I knew of his mystery, he drew out a cigar from an enormous silver-mounted case, lit it, and puffing out the smoke, scanning the while the ladies as they left the church, finding no doubt some of them "sickle-hocked" enough, he said, "At last I am the *chef* of a swell London club, and feel I am the right man for the place, for I have now the time to think my menus out; my *marmitons* are good, and," tapping on his head, "something here tells me that I shall succeed and make a name at last." Sending my horse home, I got into a cab and took him to a restaurant, to hear about his luck. As we walked through the grill-room, at the end of which the cooks, dressed all in white, presided at the fire, he whispered *pas de personalités*. We sat down at a table, and I think I ate a mutton-chop, red and enormous, and flanked by mushrooms and tomatoes, the moral cookery which England loves, and out of which have grown the brains and sinews of the Imperial race, so dear to editors. He watched me, as one might watch a cannibal with horror and amazement, and being without appetite, as often happens, I can well believe, to those of his profession, drank lager beer and crumbled up some bread.

He spoke about his plans and his ambitions, and how one day he should retire, and though he should keep on "my little digging" here in town, should buy some land at Carpentras to plant his cabbages as Diocletian did, because he said the air is good there, and that they grew a little wine, delicious, and as he spoke he blew a kiss at it, puffing his cheeks out like a cannon-ball. What more he might have said the Lord God knows, and himself only, for a portrait-painter came into the place, and, sitting down, began to talk to us. I introduced him as an artist, and the *chef*, bowing, said, "I am an artist, too," then lowering his voice, he added, "*culinaire*."

A Wire Walker

The talk had run on women in the club smoking-room of a small foreign port. In it were gathered all the heterogeneous waifs and strays, which, floating on the gulf stream of their lives, had for the moment swirled into the quiet eddy of the sleepy little town. Spaniards and Greeks and Englishmen all said their word; the solitary Frenchman who, by virtue of his race, was held a doctor in the matter, had set forth his crude philosophy born on the boulevard, culled from the simples of the "café concert," and duly sublimated in the crucible of prejudice with which men judge those without whom they cannot pass their lives, and which they who are judged repay with interest.

A Consul, thin, lean, and capriform in face, had given his opinion that wedlock was the thing — that is, of course, after a man has reached the time of life when — that is, in fact — as you may say he has become — and here he blew a cloud of smoke through his wide nostrils, looking at the ceiling, on which a crowd of chubby Cupids (or angels) sprawled, their bellies downwards — he has become fit for monogamy by force. His hearers languidly assented to so obvious a truth, and he took up his tale.

"You see," he said, "the family, and property, and personal dignity, and the desire of all men to live cleanly," and here a voice broke in, "When he cannot do otherwise," at which he gravely nodded, recognizing, as it were, a brother in the Lord, with a grave smile, and wetting with his tongue the corner of his lips — "all these things, I say, impel a man to matrimony. But, for all that, the innate antipathy of sex to sex remains unchangeable."

He paused, and those who sat around, knowing he was a master in the science which he treated of, took up their glasses with a brave "Jess so," "*Très bien*," or "*Vaya*," according to their race. No one had any single word of good to say, though all seemed to have looked into the subject carefully, without allowing prejudice of race or creed to stay them in their task.

Hoarse voices bawling vegetables or fish, with the last syllables so prolonged that the words melted into one another, and formed a cry as of a bird, broke the still air, and flies upon the sugar-basins hummed their pæans to the heat. Men shifted in their chairs, leaving damp patches when they moved, and drops of perspiration hung on their foreheads, whilst they sat waiting for the breeze which springs at evening from the overheated sea.

"*Ah, sacrées femmes,*" the Frenchman murmured, balancing his cane rocking-chair and knocking off the ash from a husk cigarette, "torment of all our lives, our only real pleasure, and yet cats all of them, yes, cats, who in the very moment of possession will strike their claws into the flesh of him who holds them in his arms, if but a thought occurs to them that they have thrown away a chance. No hearts, no heads, digestions like an ostrich, cold calculating, void of imagination, dead to the arts, and yet delightful, businesslike, sensual as monkeys, pious, by — *par bétise*, eh? — and, tell me now, who here can say a word in their defence?"

Just as he spoke a newspaper on a cane table stirred, and every one, looking out seaward, exclaimed at once, "The breeze!" and on the water of the bay a kind of shiver ran, a greenish tint shone on the waves, and on the distant hills the pink light deepened to a reddy-brown, the palm trees in the square seemed to erect their leaves, and in the smoking-room men gathered at the window wiping their foreheads, drinking in the wind.

The weary look which summer in the tropics brings to Europeans cleared away, and left their faces jovial or commonplace, honest, or mean or calculating, burned dark by sun and alcohol, but natural, without the corpse-like pallor which the long-heated hours had set upon their skins.

Ice chinked in glasses, and in the leaves of the hibiscus hedge about the club the fireflies darted, and the green frogs croaked musically, whilst all mankind, refreshed, laid in a stock of energy for next day's conflict with their enemy, the sun.

The Consul, having said his say, called for an *advocatus feminæ*, amongst the smiles of his compeers.

One who had sat and smoked, taking no part in the debate, knocked the ashes of his pipe upon the table, and, looking round, remarked: "I knew a wire-walker whose history, I think, might interest some of you, and perhaps go a little way towards altering some of your opinions about the enemy."

Voices broke in on him, saying the tale was of no value if he had been the lover of the girl, for, as a fat man sagely said, speaking in broken

English: "In that case you would have either hate her all your life, or else, so that you had no quarrel with her, which is impossible, or nearly so, be influence on her behalf."

The smoker, with a smile, rejoined: "Nothing of that sort. My interest was half-platonic and half-literary, with just a dash of Socialistic bias and contempt of the society in which she, I, and all of us exist."

Eyebrows were raised, and some formed an unspoken "crank" upon their lips, as he took up his tale.

"I met her at a charitable lady's house, who, though a poetess herself, or perhaps on that account, had interested herself in Victorina's fate. I forgot to tell you Victorina was her name. She looked to me exactly like a sailor, dressed as a woman — short, fair, and broad, flat-breasted as a man, her flaxen hair cut like a boy's, her hands thick, square, and muscular, duckfooted like a ballet-dancer, and dressed in reach-me-downs."

"Yes," said the fat man, "hardness of feature is a great help to virtue. Go on, old man, no one had thought of scarecrows, and it appears to me the lady's clothes put her clean out of court at the first pop, as you may say, speaking profanely in the Yankee style."

He leered and nursed his stomach after the fashion of the obese, blew out his breath in a half-whistle, wiped his perspiring head, and settled in his chair.

"That's where you're wrong; you bet your bottom dollar," answered the story-teller, "for there was something in the sturdy little girl not unattractive, a sort of look of one well crucified by life, which, well, I don't know how, seemed to convey — that is — I liked her — that's the short of it. Wire-walking at the time was not so common as it has since become, and nets, although, of course, one knows that they are chiefly for the public, not for the acrobat, were quite unknown, so that the danger, though not much greater, seemed so, and if the walker fell he had the chance of hitting some one who sat smoking in the stalls. This made the thing alarming, that is, of course, to the general public, who now insist on nets, saving thereby their conscience and their bones.

"She used to walk across a music-hall on a wire stretched from the flies to the top gallery, a man she called 'my poppa' hauling her up with a rope round her leg, letting her down again with a half coil right round the body, which by long use had left a mark, just like a serpent, in the flesh.

(No, I did not examine it myself, and if you interrupt I shall dry up.) The performance was a good one of its kind, dangerous, of course, for people go to music-halls just as they go to bull-fights, or to see gladiators if they could get a licence from the County Council — hoping that some one may be killed.

"Strangely enough, once on the wire she became graceful, and the square figure in pink tights — she used to think that black were far more decent, and lament that taste forced her to pink — swayed easily and lightly in the air. As I looked at her on the wire I always used to be reminded of a flying-fish, which as it darts upon the waves is magical, but if it lands on board is but a clammy, leaden-coloured fish, gasping its life out on the deck."

In the black darkness of the tropic night, lighted but by the fireflies and the stars, for in the clubroom lights had been put out not to attract the insects, a voice remarked, "Even a sparrow shall not fall, etc., but that says nothing about fish."

"Who flo' dat brick?" the narrator of the tale exclaimed, as said the negro, rubbing his head, when some one hit him with a stone. "But life even to wire-walkers is not all walking in the air in pink silk tights, stared at by venerable lechers, examined curiously by ladies through their opera-glasses, and when the walk is over and the neck yet unbroken, cheered by the crowd who, disappointed of the half-expected accident, applaud vociferously, partly from custom and partly for the joy of noise innate in all mankind.

"She did not know exactly who she was, where she was born, or anything about her birth. One day in Austria somewhere she remembered that a woman whom she thought was her mother, had taken her to see a man who travelled with a show. They had talked long over some beer, and then the woman went away, leaving her with a man whom after that she called her 'Poppa,' and who had trained her to the wire. With him there was a woman, an Italian, who was cruel to her, beating her when she fell, and starving her. This she did not resent, although another child who lived with them was better treated, for she said ' "Poppa" was making me a star.'

"Time passed, and she travelled round the world with 'Poppa' and the tent, performing now and then till she grew strong and skilful on the wire. 'Poppa,' it seems, was not attracted to her as a woman, and kept her safe from men, because he wished her to live cleanly, to become a star, for stars must suffer if they wish to shine, even in circuses.

"After having travelled half the world, and been in every town of Europe and America, but seeing nothing of them but their music-halls and the mean lodgings where she slept, it seems she tired of 'Poppa' and of the cruelty of the Italian woman, who was his mistress or his wife, as she believed.

"She left him and set up for herself, and having made some money, met her fate in a French engineer who hung about the wings. René had just the little culture that she lacked, although by that time she had learned to speak most of the tongues of Europe, half like a parrot, half like a child, with all the verbs in the infinitive. René, she said, was 'rather *fainéant* because the world was hard to him, and so I thought, as it was hard to me, there would be two of us.' In person he was slight, short, dark, and sallow, his fingers stained with cigarettes, his pointed boots worn almost without heels, curved like canoes, and his large necktie of black *crêpe de chine*, tied in a bow, betrayed the man of genius who disdains hard work as too mechanical. He told her that he had waited all his life for a good woman, and that his heart was pure and undefiled, for, as he said, the body sins, we all know, but the soul is stainless, and all that matters is intention, and he was certain that his own were pure.

"That sort of man, if he be weak in body, always proves irresistible to women such as Victorina, who have been starved of love.

"She loved him as a strong-bodied, simple-minded woman loves a man weaker in physique than herself, as a dog loves his master, and as abjectly. He gave up instantly all attempt to work, and used to lounge about the circus, holding a rope occasionally or pulling at the corner of the net spread underneath his wife with much solicitude, as well he might, seeing his fortune dangling in the air.

"They rambled through the world, she happy in her work and love; and he, getting a little weary of her as time went on, made love to other women, for, as he said, 'man is an animal just as polygamous as another, and it is wise to follow Nature's law.'

"He drank a little now and then, and in his cups beat his wife ineffectually, for the disparity between their strength was great. She, who could easily have strangled him or killed him with a kick, never resented it, thinking apparently that beating was a necessary part of married life, sanctioned by custom and sanctified by use.

"Finding themselves at Ipswich, and with the longing for a child, for which most likely she had married René, still unsatisfied, she bought one from a tramp, giving its mother three pound ten for it, and treating it as if it were her own. René and she alike adored it, and it became the bone of their contention, each struggling for its love and striving to supplant the other by all the arts with which a child's affection can be won.

"They fought about it almost as fiercely as theologians fight about some dogma which neither understands. Both seemed to have forgotten that it was not their own, and spoke of it as 'ours.' 'My girl shall be a nun,' the pseudo-father said, not that he was religious, but having read Lamartine in his youth, was sentimental in a half-educated way, holding a nunnery to be poetical and a fit place for one who, as he called her, was a child of misery. The woman, far more practical, after the fashion of her sex, wanted to bring her up to commerce, seeing her, no doubt, in her mind's eye, dressed in grey beige and seated at a desk setting down figures in a ledger, and in time well married to some shopkeeper, who should never know her mother's name. Both were agreed, although the child was only three years old, that she must never know her mother's calling or smell the scent of sawdust and of gas mixed with the smell of horses and of gunpowder which float in circuses."

As he talked on the moon had risen, and his hearers, half asleep, sipping at their drink and holding in their mouths cigars and cigarettes, mostly burnt out, cursed the mosquitoes, whilst from the sea the white, wet mist crept over everything, shrouding the mangrove swamps in silver cobwebbing and hanging on the palm-leaves till it fell dripping on the stones.

The drowsy negro waiters looked in and hoped the time had come to close, then grinned mechanically, and slipped out at the door to doze upon the floor of the verandah whilst the narrator again took up his tale.

"You fellows do not make what I call an invigorating audience," he said, "but I must finish, for you know a tale untold is like a love that never is enjoyed — both make your heart ache and, besides, are bad for the digestion — Oh, Jango, some gin and ginger —Where was I? —Yes, I remember.

"The funny thing about the whole affair was that poor Victorina, who had passed all her life in music-halls, never suspected René, who on his part took but small trouble to conceal what he referred to as his little frailties; so that his goings on with her own maid who dressed her for the wire, when she perceived, she took as a thing natural, although annoying, just as she would have borne the toothache or sea-sickness, or any other ill of life which falls like rain upon the just and the unjust, with perhaps a partiality for those less fit to bear it and to suffer its effects.

" 'Men have far more temptations than ourselves' was her remark; 'no wonder that they yield to them,' and although to her, reared in some vague and kindly superstition, half Greek, half Roman, she no doubt thought marriage a sacrament to be observed by women, but to men a counsel of perfection and to the full as unattainable as is the moon.

"No doubt she suffered, but suffering was the lot which she had taken up at birth, as she had taken blows, starvation, and an occasional fall from off the wire.

"So when they started out again upon their rounds she took the girl with her and cared for her as she had been a sister; and when her child was born never reproached her, as she said, 'The child is René's, and after all it has no blame; the blame is his, and he will leave the girl now he is tired of her.'

"But René, having tired of both of them, slipped off, taking her savings with him, and to make all complete he carried off the adopted daughter, leaving a letter saying 'he thought it was his duty to the child to save her from a life in music-halls.'

"Still Victorina struggled on, growing a little more disillusionized *[sic]* than before, and with her husband's mistress and her child upon her hands.

"She took to hearing Mass, not, as she said, 'in a religious way, though it is good, but chiefly it is quieting, and as I do not understand a word he says, it sounds impressive, and the incense makes me sleep.'

"Not a bad reason for a religious faith, which, had the ceremony been in the vulgar tongue, would have seemed common, for what we understand, though it be beautiful, we never value, thinking that mystery is a veil to beauty when in reality it is a shroud.

"But to return to Victorina, if you are not asleep. She never seemed afraid, and yet was certain always that she would die in harness, so to speak — that is in tights and in a circus —'for that is how we all die late or soon,' she told me, 'in our trade.'

"So I was not surprised one day to get a letter from her 'Poppa,' posted in New York, and read the cutting of a newspaper in the familiar style the great Republic has invented for itself.

" 'Woman falls from her wire in Coney Island, misses the net, body bounds off upon an awning — horrible panic in the theatre — society women faint — victim never moves, carried out dead. But for that tragedy it was a red-letter day for Coney Island — not only human but animal performers excelled. Elephants, horses, and a bear showed the effects of long rehearsal and of careful work.' "

The narrator stopped, and looking round the room saw that his audience mostly were asleep, only the Consul sat upright and smoked mechanically. Laying his cigarette upon an ash-tray he thanked the story-teller, and remarking, "Poor little devil, she had come into the category of women by her suffering," strolled out into the night.

The mist had lifted from the mangroves, and the moon shone down upon the sea, turning it into a vast silver shield, whilst on the beach the sobbing of the waves raised Nature's threnody.

Hulderico Schmidel

Of all historians (after the Greeks), perhaps the directest and most simple-minded were those who chronicled the exploits of the discoverers of America. It may be that as some of them, like Xenophon, treated of what they had seen and done themselves, it seemed invidious to them to do more than set down what they saw. In their bald narratives, in which one sees the pen was not the instrument they had most used, sometimes there are little bits of self-revealment worth preservation by a curious man. In all their writings, treating as they did of what the world had never seen, and what they took good care for the most part the world should never see again, are many curious facts. One of the most original and most forgotten writers is Hulderico Schmidel, the first historian of Buenos Ayres and of Paraguay; but then how many historians, worthy of a better fate, sleep disregarded under the dust of libraries, on a secure top shelf. Like Bernal Diaz in Mexico, Hulderico was both an historian and a soldier; faith they both had, befitting "Christianos Rancios" in those days, but not the faith removing common sense and mountains.

Had any one appeared with a story of Santiago on his well-known milk-white charger rallying the Spanish arms, Hulderico would have answered as Bernal Diaz did on a similar occasion in Mexico: "It may be so, but to me, sinner that I was, was vouchsafed nothing but the sight of Francisco Morla on his old grey horse." Probably both of them would have allowed the apparition of a saint in a battle or otherwise, as a thing possible, but their credulity went no farther than it was obligatory to go. In the narratives of both, inches and feet, hundreds and thousands, get jumbled up together now and then, as they do in even more important scriptures than those which they have left. Both of them relate stories of wondrous animals and strange adventures, and of enchanted cities, but neither speaks of having seen them; both were good soldiers and criticised their generals freely. But here the likeness stops; for Hulderico had not the touch with the pen, no matter how he used the sword, of the historian of Montezuma and the good horse "Motilla."

Hulderico Schmidel was a Fleming or a German, and that is all we know of his nationality, except that he sailed from Antwerp, and on his return retired to Strasburg. His work originally was written in German, but a Spanish translation exists, from which I take these notes. He seems to have constituted himself historian of the expedition, on the principle of the Spanish proverb, "*A falta de buenos, mi marido alcalde.*"

Many of his Spanish names are twisted in the most marvellous fashion, and when he uses names of places and things in Guarani they become (to me at least) inextricable. Sometimes the translator seems to have been puzzled with a phrase, and leaves it in German, spelling it phonetically like Spanish. Hulderico seems to have been an honest, simple-minded man, whose greatest care was to keep his arms, especially his arquebuse, in order, for he mentions with pride that his accoutrements were always bright, and that "*Mi arcabuz siempre relucia como las estrellas.*"

In 1511 Juan Diaz de Solis, seeking for a passage to the Moluccas, had entered the estuary of the River Plate, and given it the name, then, landing on the island of Martin Garcia, had been killed by the Chanà or the Charrua Indians. Some fourteen years before the expedition of Mendoza, Sebastian Cabot had sailed some distance up the Paraná, and built the fort of Espiritu Santo on the Caracañá, close to where now stands the city of Rosario de Santa Fé. The leader of the expedition was one Don Pedro de Mendoza, a gentleman of the town of Guadix, in the province of Almeria. Don Pedro had been secretary to the Emperor Charles V, and a courtier, and was the last man in the world to command an expedition of the kind. He undertook to pay the expenses of the expedition and to found a city, on the condition he was made *adelantado* (governor) and had certain privileges accorded to him. With him went two thousand five hundred Spaniards and one hundred and fifty Flemings and Germans, amongst whom was Hulderico Schmidel. Also in the fleet were seventy-two horses and mares, from which have sprung the countless herds of horses in the River Plate. Schmidel sailed from Antwerp in 1834 *[sic = 1534]*. In fourteen days he arrived in Cadiz and joined Don Pedro de Mendoza's fleet, which was just about to sail. From Cadiz the fleet sailed to the Canaries, thence to the Cape Verds, and thence "to a certain island" called Rio de Janeiro.

In this "island" the first ill-luck happened to the expedition. "There our general, being ill and very weak, named as his lieutenant one Juan de Osorio; but shortly after, suspecting his faith, commanded four of his friends to kill him, which they did, sewing him up [*cosiendole á puñaladas*] with dagger thrusts." Hulderico, who though a good soldier was free with his comments on his officers, remarks, "This did not please us all, as Osorio was brave and prudent, and beloved of all the soldiers." To be loved of the soldiers was the highest praise that Hulderico had to give to any one; and, as his history shows, to receive their love an officer had not to look too closely at what his soldiers did.

From Rio de Janeiro the fleet sailed to the River Plate, and "entering the estuary we came on a town of almost three thousand Indians, called Querandis. There we built a town, and called it Buenos Ayres on account of the wholesome airs which there prevail." A curious little town it must have been (to judge by the woodcut in the first edition of the work), built of wood and mud, and with little turrets at every angle, a sort of transatlantic Nuremberg, at least as imagined by the designer of the print.

"These Indians [the Querandis] brought fish and meat to the town for fourteen days, and because they missed a day, the general sent out an armed force, commanded by his brother, composed of three hundred foot and thirty horse; amongst the latter I went myself." From the very first the blessings of civilization seem to have been made apparent to the wretched Indians. One wonders, had an armed expedition of Indians landed in Spain or England, if the inhabitants would have brought them provisions, without payment, for fourteen days.

"We found the Indians encamped to the number of four thousand, and having attacked them, they killed the brother of the general, Don Diego de Mendoza, and twenty soldiers. Their arms are tridents pointed with flints, arrows and bows, and three balls of stone tied together with a string; with these they caught and brought the horses to the ground."

This is, I think, the first mention of the *bolas*, a weapon which has played so great a part in the life of the River Plate, and with which the gauchos caught the soldiers in the ill-fated expedition to Buenos Ayres under General Whitelocke. Provisions seem now to have begun to fail, for "our general commanded to give out to each one three ounces of flour a day, and each third day a fish, and he who wanted any more to get it for himself." In spite of the ration of fish and bread, hunger increased so that many of the soldiers died. The Indians, too, besieged the new-built city, and almost burnt it by shooting arrows with burning straw tied to them.

The general, after having dispatched Juan de Ayolas on an expedition up the Paraná, and after leaving a garrison in Buenos Ayres " provisioned for a year at reason [*á razon de*] of a pound of bread a day, and if they wanted more to look for it," embarked for Spain, and, after having spent more than four thousand ducats and seen the expedition reduced to five hundred and sixty men, died on the voyage.

Hulderico says little or nothing about the country, nor does he tell us what the Pampas appeared like, solitary, without the horses and the cattle, peopled only by the wandering Indians, the deer, and ostriches. Nor does he, like the author of the almost contemporary poem of the "Argentina," embellish his recital with the story of the ill-fated love of the Indian chief Siripo for the wife of the Spanish captain Hurtado, nor yet with the story of Maldonado and the lion, which in the "Argentina" is depicted so movingly that a modern naturalist from Buenos Ayres almost believes it.

Juan de Ayolas ascended the Paraguay and founded the city of Assumption. There Hulderico meets the "Carios," who eat the root *padades* which tastes like apples, and who have fish, pigs, ostriches, and Indian sheep as big as mules (perhaps the tapir), goats, chickens, and rabbits. These Indians are short and fat, and harder workers than the rest. Their city is called Lamperé (Lambaré) and is well fortified. "Now these Carios would not keep quiet [*no quisieran aquietarse*], for they had not experienced our swords or arquebuses; so we drew near and fired an artillery upon them, and they, seeing the wounds and holes in all their bodies, fled, leaving about three hundred dead."

So far so good; the most usual and expeditious way to make an Indian keep quiet has always been with swords and arquebuses. Nothing so readily convinces him of European superiority. "We then attacked the town, and the Indians, fearing for their wives and children, asked for pardon, offering to do our bidding. Admitted to peace, they regaled [*regalaron*] our captain, Ayolas, with seven Indian girls, the oldest of eighteen years. To the soldiers they gave two girls apiece, with food and other things, and in this manner we made friends, and founded the city of Assumption, in the year of God one thousand five hundred and thirty-nine."

The method of making friends seems to have been of the roughest, but not more so than in Matabeleland to-day, though our arquebuses are an improvement on those of Hulderico's time.

"The Cario Indians make a wine of algarroba," called by the Germans, Joannebrot or Bockorulein; "their city is on the river which flows into the Parabol" — Hulderico always calls the Paraguay the Parabol — "and is called Fuechkamyn."

The unfortunate translator, in a foot-note, says: "It is not easy to find out this place or to make plain the error of its name"; and, indeed, there is a most strange air of Thuringia about the spelling, which must have been most puzzling to a Spaniard. After having made friends with the Carios, his captain sent Hulderico to Santa Catalina, in Brazil, and on their return they were wrecked in the River Plate, and all lost "except myself and five others, who swam to shore holding to the mast. We reached shore naked and without food, and had to walk eighty leagues to the town of San Gabriel, by which the grace and care of God was abundantly made manifest." The grace is, of course, a matter for theologians, but the care is not so manifest to ordinary mortals as it seems to have been to the writer of the narrative.

"Things being thus," begins the next chapter after the narration of the shipwreck, "Alvar Nuñez Cabeza de Vaca arrived from Spain with four hundred men and thirty horses." He landed in Santa Catalina and marched overland to Assumption, in Paraguay, a distance of nearly two thousand miles, with the loss of only a single soldier.

Of all the conquerors of the Indies, Alvar Nuñez was perhaps the most remarkable. Born of a great family, he had distinguished himself in Mexico, and already undergone ten years' captivity in Florida. Alone of all the conquerors he treated the Indians with strict justice, so that, as Hulderico says, "did but an Indian wench squeal, the soldier had to suffer for it."

Ayolas, the lieutenant appointed by Don Pedro de Mendoza, being dead, the soldiers had elected Dominguez Martinez de Irala to succeed him. Irala was a Biscayan, a man of low origin but of considerable character; he eventually became Governor of Paraguay, and had already commenced the series of intrigues by which he succeeded in disgracing Alvar Nuñez, and in sending him a prisoner to Spain. For the present the pleasant days of pillage and Indian wenches' squealing disregarded were over for Hulderico, for "our new general treated the soldiers harshly, and forced us to pay for all we took." Was ever such injustice heard of? Men had not left their countries to pay for things as if they were in a mere shop in Antwerp or in Rotterdam.

Alvar Nuñez started shortly on an expedition to reach Peru by land. This was the dream of all the explorers of the River Plate as soon as they discovered there were no precious metals in that country, and in such an attempt Ayolas, the lieutenant appointed by Mendoza, died. After sailing up the river "we came to the country of the Lasacusis, who go naked and painted in blue patterns (especially the women), and with such art that even in Germany I doubt that any of our best limners could exceed the fineness of their designs. They wear a crystal through their lower lips, and are not handsome." Here I can add my testimony to Hulderico's, for a Chaco Indian with a hole in his lower lip and a piece of crystal in it, saliva exuding through the hole, is not a pleasant sight. "After asking for peace [this seems apocryphal], we fell on them and killed many of the men, and captured many of the women, who were of great value to us."

In what their value consisted Hulderico does not reveal; but a terrible disillusion was soon to come upon him, "for the cacique came to the General Alvar Nuñez, and promised to obey the king if the women were returned. The general consented to this, considering that the Indians were subjects of the king." So that "the women of value" were lost to the soldiers, "at which they murmured." This is one of the many instances, both in Hulderico's narrative and Alvar Nuñez' own memoirs, in which he seems to have incurred great odium by protecting the Indians.

In the battle, "so numerous were the infidels that many of our men were massacred." But "the multitude of dogs is the undoing of the hare," observes the writer. So Hulderico went on doing his duty and slaying Indians, keeping always his arquebuse "in order and fit for service," and noting down with some little prolixity all that he thought worth noticing, even to the dimensions of a crocodile. The study of natural history always presented a fine field for the early discoverers of America. Certainly it had difficulties unknown to-day, notably in the fact that in those days there were more animals to study. Thus we learn that the "carbuncle is a little animal which has a mirror in its forehead which shines like fire." Also that the only safe way to kill a crocodile is to hold a looking-glass before your face, for if its eyes meet yours you certainly turn mad. "This, though, cannot be true, for I have killed above three thousand of them, and never had a looking-glass in my possession during all my pilgrimages in the Indies." There is a butterfly, also, which turns first to a worm and then into a rat, and which destroys the crops; it feeds on human flesh, and is discriminating, too, as to the kind of man it feeds on, for "*Mas le sabe carne de un Pagano que no de Español o Castellano.*"[1]

[1] *"La Argentina"* (canto iii), contemporary poem descriptive of conquest of River Plate, by Barco de la Centenera.

This was fortunate, as the number of the Spaniards was relatively small. It should be observed, though, that Hulderico never says he saw these wonders, but only relates them as having been told by others. Many of his observations on the Indian tribes leave little to be desired for terseness, though they are not exactly descriptive, as when he says, "the Sebenes, these Indians have moustaches." One is glad to hear this, though I believe it to have been a mistake. "The Ackeres have larger stomachs than other Indians, and are swift of foot." Largeness of stomach is not invariably accompanied by fleetness of foot, but the power of observation involved does great credit to the narrator.

So he chronicles his adventures, sometimes "marching for days in water to the knees," sometimes "marching for days without a drop of water, so that even the most avaricious amongst us came to think of water as of more account than gold." At last, "having marched and sailed more than three hundred leagues, according to the calculations of those who understood the stars," the expedition came to the Lake of the Xarayes, and saw "*la casa del gran Moxo.*" This palace was "built of stones four square, with many flanking towers, and as fair in its proportions as any castle of Spain or Flanders." This is the only instance where Hulderico's enthusiasm seems to have got the better of his judgment, for no such building of stone with towers was ever found east of the Andes. Here the expedition turned, on account of the illness of the general. The description he gives of the intrigues of Irala and final banishment of Alvar Nuñez is very much biased, as befits a soldier writing of a general who was particular about "Indian wenches," trifles into which no self-respecting conqueror should have looked too closely.

Hulderico returned to Assumption, and tells us no more of himself, of Alvar Nuñez, the "carbuncle," "the Indians with moustaches," or anything of note till at last "one day I was on guard over the well, for there was scarcity of water and the people had to drink by turns, when a letter was brought to me saying my brother was dead, and that my family prayed for my return; the letter had come in fourteen months from Cadiz." He does not seem to have considered the time excessive, but without words "I dressed myself in my best clothes, and putting on a fine red mantle I went to the general, and laying my services before him, asked for permission to return." This was granted with many flattering phrases and a letter for the king. The general said that "I had been a faithful soldier, not anxious to slay, but always performing orders and keeping my arms and armour in good condition." "Not anxious to slay, but always performing orders," seems to reveal that "orders" had been often peremptory.

In six months, and after dangers not a few, he reached a point in Brazil, "*llamado San Gabriel asi de Cristianos como Ingleses.*" [1] Here he took ship to Lisbon, and arrived "with all my luggage and many parrots" after a voyage of five months. In Cadiz "I engaged a passage in the 'Henrique Lebertzen' for Antwerp." The parrots and the luggage went in another ship, and a great tempest having arisen, the ship went down, so that "I arrived in Antwerp as poor as when I left." "Still ["still" seems ambiguous], after twenty years it pleased Providence that I should arrive at the port from which I sailed, but what miseries and hungers, perils and journeyings I passed in my sojourn in the Indies is only known to God himself, to whom all praise, etc. Amen." So far Hulderico, but in a note he informs us he retired to "Estrasburgo." Perhaps when there he sometimes doubted whether Providence had really been so kind in bringing him back home. Perhaps he wandered up and down the streets seeking for sun and finding none. Perchance (like others who have known the Indies) the recollection of the adventurous life came back at times, and turned the *Leberwurst* and *Sauerkraut* to Dead Sea fruit. Perhaps he heard the parrots scream through the woods of Paraguay and saw the Paraná, its thousand islands almost awash, thicketed with seibos and lapachos with their yellow and purple flowers, smelt the sweet espinillo blossom in his nostrils, and hated Estrasburgo when he thought upon the past. Seated in a trim Dutch garden with cut box hedges and clean brick walks, dozing in some arbour over his pipe of right Varinas, perhaps he wished he had remained in Paraguay to fall by an Indian arrow like a *conquistador*, and that some other soldier had received the order to write commentaries.

[1] The Englishman is still a doubtful Christian to the Latin races, and they, I suppose, are pagans to the Englishman.

Gualeguaychú

The steamer glided from the yellow waters of the River Plate into a narrow channel over-arched with trees, which almost swept her deck. A thick white mist rose from the stream, which shrouded both the banks and rose half up the masts and funnel, leaving the tops of trees hanging like islands in the air. Upon their highest branches cormorants and vultures sat asleep, which at the passing of the boat awoke and screamed, then dropped into the mist.

The channel narrowed, or appeared to do so, in the gloom which brooded on the river and its banks, although the moon shone brightly and the Southern Cross was hung above our heads, the black Magellan clouds looking like mouths of funnels in the sky, deep and mysterious. Capella was just rising, and the stars, though not so bright as in the northern hemisphere, seemed far more luminous and gleamed more yellow and more phosphorescent, than do their sisters of the North. Carpinchos, startled from their sleep, plunged with a splash into the stream and swam for refuge to the reedy banks, their backs awash, and their flat heads stretched out upon the water, looking like giant prediluvian rats.

Moths, large as humming-birds, hung round the binnacle, making the helmsman curse, although his compass was a sinecure, as from the bow, the pilot, sounding with a cane, guided the vessel up the stream. From both the banks and from the islands with their feathery canes, the shrill mosquitoes' oboe piped its unpleasing tune. Nothing was heard but now and then the pilot's nasal cry as the stream shoaled, or the faint distant neigh of some wild stallion gathering up his mares. All was so still and ghostly that the snorting of the steam seemed like an outrage upon Nature, which wept great tears of dew upon the deck, to see herself defiled.

Hours, which seemed long as days, went past, and still the steamer struggling with the current pressed into the night. At times she ran her nose against the bank, and from the trees the mist, congealed upon the leaves, poured down like rain upon the awnings and the shrouds. At times she grounded on a sandbank, backed, and was helped by all the crew, pushing her off with poles, then, shivering, swung into the stream, strove for a minute with the hurrying water, and once more glided through the mist.

Great wreaths of *camaloté* floated past her her sides, and now and then she swerved to let a tree come swirling lazily along. At last the mist grew lighter, and the moon, sinking below the trees, showed that the morning was at hand. The stars waxed paler and the air more chilly, and men, sleeping upon the deck beneath the awning, their heads upon their saddles, with their long silver-handled knives close to their hands, stirred and drew close their ponchos in their sleep. Others sat up and lighted cigarettes, smoked silently and then lay down again, the white dew glistening on their blankets and their hair.

As the dawn brightened, and Capella fell behind the trees, the whistle sounded, echoing through the woods. The vessel edged into the bank, as if by instinct, and her sides rubbed against a pier made of rough planks and almost level with the stream. Some sleepy soldiers, smoking cigarettes, came through the mist like spectres and a man dressed in uniform stepped from the pier on to the deck, went down below, and in a little while came up again, wiping his lips, and with an air of having done his duty to the State.

The passengers, each with his hand-bag, or his saddle, as the case might be, stumbled ashore, and took their way through a rough path cut in the woods, which, after half a mile, came out upon a plain, and a short league away beheld the town, flat-roofed and white, silent and shining in the rising sun.

A diligence, which should have met the steamer, drawn by six horses driven, and one in front on which a ragged boy, half gaucho, half town loafer, rode, whirled in a cloud of dust towards them, and they, scaling it as it were a fortress, were jolted to the town.

Stuck like a chessboard on a table, on the plain, and with the streets all intersecting one another into squares, the houses all flat-topped and painted white, and with the towers called *miradorés* looking like minarets, and the church dome resembling a mosque, it had a sort of Oriental look. The sandy unpaved streets, in which lean yellow dogs prowled after offal all the day, and howled at night in chorus at the moon, smacked also of the East. There the resemblance ended, and the line of posts, to almost every one of which a horse was tied, and the great stores, in front of which stood horses hobbled, for no one went on foot above two squares, was purely Argentine. Horses pervaded all the place, in every open space they fed attached to ropes, in all the yards they stood up to the fetlocks in black mud, or in hot dust, according to the season of the year, and ate alfalfa, or were led down to water by their owners, with the long picket rope known as a *mañador* curled like a lasso in the hand. Men dressed in loose black cashmere trousers, with high patent-leather boots, the tops all worked in patterns with red or yellow thread, their ponchos fluttering in the wind, rode past on silver-mounted saddles and with bits furnished with cups of silver on each side the mouth, and with an eagle wrought in silver moving with every step below the horse's mouth. Their horses, with manes hogged to the middle of the neck, leaving upon the withers a long lock six inches wide to mount by, snorted and passaged at the strange sights of town, tried to whip round and spring across the street like goats, if a dog stirred, or a door fastened with a bang. Sometimes if they had eaten corn, a feat which often took them days to learn and which they only learned on being tied up without food, they trotted slowly at the *paso castellano*, their long tails squared off at the fetlock joints, swinging as if in rhythm to the short jogging trot. Their riders with their hats kept on by strings of silk with tassels underneath the chin, their bridle hand held high, and on the right their flat hide whips just dangling on their horse's quarters to keep him to the bit, assumed the far-off look of an ineffable content which horsemen, mounted on a horse that does them credit, put on quite naturally in every quarter of the world.

Wild and barefooted boys, on bare-backed ponies, careered about the outskirts of the town, and the one beggar of the place, an old Canarian, rode a thin horse and when he saw a charitable face, took off his hat and mumbled, "For the love of God," receiving what was given, as his due, for alms are not a favour to the receiver, but to the giver, who thereby lays up for himself treasures beyond the skies, where beggars are not, and where horses, if they exist, are winged like Pegasus. It was a gaucho town that lived upon the "camp," as people styled the adjoining country in the pidgin-English of the place. A town in which all men went armed, their knives and pistols sticking out below their coats, and where, if you were so inclined, on any pretext you might fight with any one, no questions asked, and if you killed your man, get on your horse and ride into the "camp," secure of never being caught, so that you did not venture into town, or run by accident into the hands of the police.

During the hot hours of the day all slept, leaving the streets deserted and the stores wide open, so that a man could walk into them and knocking with his whip upon the counter or the door, find no one, till at last some sleepy shopman would appear and say that business was suspended, and retreat, cursing, to his bed. The sun declining put new life into the town, and in the various stores men sat and talked and criticised the horses and the women as they passed. Still later on, the evening brought the ladies of the place into the plaza, all dressed in Paris fashions of a year ago, to saunter up and down in groups beneath the orange trees, in which the fire-flies flitted, making the heavy leaves seem all alive with light. As they passed by, a fire of compliments was turned on them, which they pretended not to hear, and yet were piqued if no one paid them, for as the saying was, even a compliment from a black man is better than indifference from a prince.

In the still air the tinkle of guitars sounded like Cupid's sheep-bells, and at the iron-grated windows on the streets men stood, flattening themselves against the bars, to talk to women, whom the judicious custom of the place only allowed to see their lovers with a stout iron railing set betwixt the two.

Between a male and female saint a wall of bricks and lime, the proverb says, but a stout iron bar aids virtue plaguily.

Although the streets were all deserted after ten, through the wide-open windows and the doors of patios you saw the richer people of the place, seated at tables playing cards or dancing, and at the window-bars the loafers stood, as at a theatre, but now and then giving forth their opinions of an ankle or a foot, not disrespectfully but with the freedom of the Spanish race, which holds all men, as men, are equal, and that the want of money does not debar a man from being human, or its possession raise him to a god.

The lower classes congregated in the *pulperías*, and there drank gin and maté, danced the "*cielito*, the *gáto*" and the *pericon*, and not infrequently got drunk and fought with their long silver-handled knives. They played at monté, each producing his own pack, marked at the back (so that he knew each card as it was dealt), and striving to impose it on the rest. They, knowing well the trick, preferred a neutral pack, which, although marked, was yet unknown to any of the players, and having made a bank, they gambled desperately, so that a man, having begun well dressed, with silver-mounted arms and belt well stocked with dollars, not seldom left the place stripped to his trousers and his shirt.

The foreigners assembled at one of the hotels, either at Ellerman's or at the Fonda del Vapor, kept by a Basque, Don Pedro, where they drank and sang, roaring the choruses of comic songs, after the fashion of boys at public schools or sailors in a port.

Don Pedro owned a long and flat-roofed house, built round a courtyard in which there was a well. Above the doorway hung a model of a steamboat made in wood, from which the *fonda* took its name. Broad in the beam, and painted blue and red, the funnel like a mast, and with enormous paddle-boxes, on one of which the captain, dressed in a general's uniform, girt with a sword, appeared to bellow through a speaking-trumpet to the stars, the model might have served for a museum in some inland capital, where none had seen the sea. But yet it was Don Pedro's pride, and pointing to it, he would say, "Steam, . . . si, señor, the steam is the great power which I have heard Prometheus stole from heaven; it means our life, for life is progress, and there can be no progress without steam." Not that, for all his aphorism, Don Pedro differed from his fellow-countrymen, who slow and steady, and as obstinate as a male mule, are able, it is said, to drive a nail into the door by beating on it with their heads, and then when driven home, to draw it with their teeth.

The rooms all looked upon the patio, and it was well, after an evening of caña punch and song, to shut the door and put the candle out of sight, for the chief form of wit was shooting at the lights, and as you sat and read, a pistol shot was pretty sure to knock the plaster from the wall, close enough to your head to make things dangerous, as the man firing generally was drunk. The rooms were bare, but for a wooden folding-bed known as a *catré*, a chair, a table, and a washing-stand. Don Pedro's pride was centred in his dining-room, which was adorned with various French prints of hunting scenes, all highly coloured, in which the hunters in high-collared coats and bushy whiskers, girt about with knives, rode centaur-like. One was entitled "Fox-hunting to the Wild Boar," and showed a monstrous beast as bulky as a hippopotamus careering on the grass. The hunters to the boar rode after him, all clad in green, with high and shining boots, from their left sides there dangled cutlasses, and round their bodies horns like ophicleides. "Fox-hunting to the Deer" showed a strange animal much like an antelope, loping across the fields with a great company of beagles following at his heels, all lolling out their tongues. Last scene of all set forth the kill, which was enacted in a pigsty, wherein the deer had fled, and where a huntsman manfully butchered her with a cutlass; the pack of beagles sitting on their hams, look like peccaries when they have run a man into a tree, and watch expectantly.

To the hotel there gravitated the more respectable of the young English cattle-farmers, a fair proportion of French bagmen, and some substantial Basques who, as Don Pedro was a countryman, gave him patronage. One or two wool-buyers from Buenos Ayres, and an Italian engineer or two, who loafed about, waiting for contracts to build a bridge or make a railway to the moon, and several experts in what were known as fruits of the country (*frutos del pais*) consisting of, in general, hides, with hoofs and horns, and salted beef to send to Cuba and to Brazil, to feed the slaves on the plantations, made the contingent commerce furnished to the house.

Science contributed two German lepidopterists, who in their rooms pursued their mystery in a strong smell of camphor, and at meals ate solidly, their knives and forks clinking upon their teeth like foils in a sharp bout. Captain McCandlish, too, was there, a worthy mariner, who, having lost his ship for drunkenness, passed all his life regretting the old days, when in the 'fifties he had had a brig in the South Seas. Much did he dwell upon the islands and the life: "Conceity folk, yon Kanakys, ye ken. The weemen too, sort of free living . . . juist vera leetle prejudice aboot them. I mind one o' them doon in Eromango . . . dod no, long before the missionaries cam', spoilin' the place. I cana' bear a Kanaky, in breeks, ye ken . . . seems to corrupt them . . . fine buirdly [sic] bodies, but European clothes mak's them upsettin'.

"Weel, this gurl, ye see; lads ... I dinna care to mind aboot her, whiles I juist think I never should have left the islands. . . . Awfu' easy life; taro, ye ken, is handy planted, handier far than tatties . . . a bonny climate too, and then the weemen. Man, I think I was a fool to leave the islands, and to fetch up in this mud turtle, round-bottomed sort o' a smouchin' toon, where everything is dear, and no a body kens the dogvane from the kingston valve. Hech, sirs, I think I was a fool."

Then he would snort in his red pocket-handkerchief, light up his pipe (he "couldna' stan' thae cigareets"), call for more whisky, and stagger down the street, lurching a little in his gait, as if he was at sea.

Within a square of the hotel was set the police-station and in a lane hard by some huts in which some half-caste "Chinas," with several

Mulatas, and two or three Hungarian and German girls, become too faded for the capital, sat painted at their doors. Vice was so unattractive, set as it was in a mud hovel, thatched with straw, that many, whom the love of virtue bound but lightly, yet were virtuous from disgust. Whether the moral gain was great, only the moralist can say, and he was an infrequent visitor in those days, either at Ellerman's or at the Fonda del Vapór. In fact morality was looked at in the larger or the Latin way, with the result that on the whole life was far cleaner than in Anglo-Saxon lands, where nature being what it is, the same things happen but are rendered meaner by concealment; the homage, as they say, vice pays to virtue, but which makes virtue, as it were, compound a felony and smirches both of them.

Racing and cock-fights were the national sports, the former for short distances, two or three furlongs, with innumerable false starts, all of set purpose and with the object of tiring out the weaker horse before the race began. Barefooted and with silk handkerchiefs tied round their heads, a custom which they evidently took from the Indians, who tied a woollen string called *vicha* round their brows, and with their flat-thonged whips hung on their wrists, the riders made pretence to give their horses all their head, leaning well forward on their necks and shouting wildly, but all the time they held them well in hand. As all the starts were flying and by mutual consent, if one man saw his horse was but an inch behind the other's, or if he noticed that his adversary's horse (for all the races were confined to two) was getting out of hand, he stopped and, getting off, walked slowly back again up to the flag. This naturally upset the temper of a violent horse, who at the next attempt would rear and plunge, and break out sweating, and perhaps run half the course before he could be stopped. When at the last they got away, each shouted "*Vamos*" and then they plied their whips, the horses close to one another, for if a man could bore the other rider off the course he won the race.

But at this game all gauchos were adepts, as well as that of trying to kick the opposing horse's chest, to put their feet below the other rider's heel and hurl him to the ground, all which was reckoned fair, and part of racing, just as at cards they had a code of signs which were allowable, but in both cases, tricks and signs were all conventional, and nothing might be done, except what wont and immemorial use had rendered sanctified.

To a low building built in a circle and looking like a little bull-ring the sportsmen of the town repaired on Sundays, nearly all carrying cocks beneath their arms, or balanced on the pommels of their saddles as they rode. To show that nationality was no bar to sport, the committee had drawn up rules and invitations in several tongues; the one in English ran: "Sunday and other holly days there are large cock-fight. The native and the foreign cock is both accepted, and are accepted all kind of cock whatever his prevention." To make all clear, at the bottom of the page was written "The direction," which the composers of the document imagined had the same meaning in an English as in a Latin tongue. English or French or Spanish, or no matter what the tongue, all men were equal in the arena of the cocks. The love of blood and money, the two strongest passions, write what they please of love, levelled down most of them to a mere mass of animals, with bloodshot eyes, mouths open and their lips drawn back upon their teeth, sweating with interest, and following every wound the birds inflicted with their sharp steel spurs, all pity laid aside, and for the time savage as tigers, ready to quarrel with their brother if the red cock struck out the other's eye and he had criticized the stroke.

The remnant, those who cared not for the blood, and in whom the skill and fortitude of the trained cocks neither excited nor evoked compassion, called the odds with regularity, marking each turn in every combat, and when at last the victor dashed his spur down through the brains, and then himself fell dead beside his foe, just crowing out his victory as he fell, stretched out their hands to take the dollars that their bird had gained them with his life, with a low chuckle of content.

But when in England or in South America did life, either of man or beast, stand any chance when there was money to be made? The only difference is, that here we try to hide from others and ourselves the motives of our deeds, and there they stuff the dollars dripping red with blood into their pockets and light their cigarettes.

The town, such as it was, when first the little stern-wheel steamer groped through the mist, her decks swept by the dripping boughs of ñandubay and espinillo, no longer now exists.

No doubt the house in which they tortured Garibaldi, hanging him by the thumbs and flogging him across the face with raw-hide whips, has long made way, perhaps for a new church, perhaps for some smart bar-room, in the Yankee style.

No longer in the shady lanes Paz and Dolores sit waiting for their customers, playing guitars, and with their pictures of a saint above their beds. Ladies from Paris and from Buda-Pesth, not so religious, but as superstitious to the full, no doubt adorn the town, driving their trade, and keeping their accounts by double entry, with the view of honourable retirement in their riper years when paint has failed and drink imparts no lustre to the eyes. The loafers cannot any longer stare in through the *rejas* on the ladies at a ball and criticise their clothes. Increasing wealth no doubt has set a bar betwixt the classes, making the poor man feel his poverty, and the rich know that isolation is the best weapon in the fight that he must wage. Who would allow a horse to stray about, now that no doubt his price is trebled, or to stand hobbled in a street, when all drive motors, and he would be in danger of his life? A vast and tin-roofed "terminus," in which the engines scream and whistle all the night, is the chief labarum of progress, and all who see it, with the smoke from its workshops hung across the sky, bow and adore it and are satisfied. Few still remain, who can recall the days, when taking horse a man could ride to Corrientes, without an obstacle to stop him on his way, but flooded rivers, if it should chance to rain, or want of water if there was a drought.

Those were the days when on a journey man took no thought for food, for riding to a house, if by some chance there was no meat in the *galpon*, they said, "You have a *lazo* — eh? The cattle are but half a league away — out on the rise, beyond the round Ombu. Well, go and kill a cow, take all the meat you want, but leave the hide; the owner does not like his brand to turn up in a parcel of strange stuff . . . and so. . . with God."

La Camargue

Swept by the winds of Africa which meet the winds of the Swiss mountains and the north; winds and more winds which never cease; scorched by the sun in summer and in the winter scourged by cold, it looks upon the sea.

Salt marsh and waste of aromatic herbs, great heathy plains towards the east, and to the west alluvial steppes without a stone, but broken here and there by patches of grey olive woods and vineyards, a line of sandhills runs along the beach which opens to a little bay where the three Marys landed from the East. It still remains a shadow of the past — a melancholy region of decaying towns with medieval walls, in which the sparse inhabitants look out of place, as beggars herding in some vast Italian palace which has seen better days.

It seems as if a portion of the Pampa between Bahia Blanca and the Romero Grandé had got adrift and floated out to sea, and then got stranded on the fertile plains of France. A land of vast horizons, mirages, quick change of temperature, of violent tempests, mosquitoes, ague, fever, of flights of red flamingoes, fierce black cattle, and the white horses which tradition says the Arabs left there after the rout at Tours. In hardly any other part of Europe does the old world, the world before the Middle Ages, still maintain itself as strongly as in this island in the marshy delta of the Rhône.

When Caesar knew it and long afterwards when Musa and his Saracens passed by upon their march to Tours, it could not have been very different from what it is today. The railway crosses it, but railways in a plain have not the strength to force themselves upon the landscape as amongst hills, and only make a track such as a snail leaves on a window-pane.

The island does not seem intended to be lived in but by the horses and the kine, and should be kept, just as Segovia and Toledo should be kept, as a memento of the past to show men what the world was like before they spoiled it with their manufactories. The scattered hamlets grouped around their churches look primitive and at the same time unsubstantial as if they had been built by the lacustrine dwellers of a bygone age, or like an Indian camp of wickeyups.

Round most of them the marshes stretch, and from them rises up a hum of shrill mosquitoes' pipes, as if they challenged man to live there at his peril and presaged fever and unquiet sleep to the invaders of their realm. And in effect inhabitants are few. Your plainsman seldom is gregarious, and on this heathy sea of scrubby aromatic plants the infrequent herdsman with his lance looks like a Guaycurú or Arab, and as remote from modern European life as either of them, sitting immovable in his high-peaked Montpellier saddle and looking out across the plains.

'Tis said that long before the Romans, Greeks, and Saracens, the inhabitants adored the sun. Perhaps of all the peoples of their continent, they were alone in this, their almost reasonable faith. No doubt to wile them from their bright belief, to the sad Galilean mystery, the Marys, she of Mágdala, Maria Jacobé, and Mary Salomé with Trophimus and Saturninus, Cleon and Lazarus, Sidonius, Joseph of Arimathea, and the rest of the strange errant saintly company which landed on the dunes just where the old Byzantine church is built, sought out their shores.

Mary of Mágdala who, one would have thought, had long ago wiped off her sins upon the Saviour's feet, retired into the desert; one of those earthly purgatories which all saints had ever at command to serve them as a step to heaven, and having sought the Holy Cave, she passed her life in prayer. The other Marys, one the mother of St. James the Great, the other of the lesser James, with Sarah, an old servant who had been a slave, lived and died where they landed, on the spot where afterwards their church was built, and which still bears their name.

Joseph of Arimathea, who, though a Christian, yet was a rich man, passed on to England, and was lost among the mists. The rest remaining in the land preached and evangelized, and for a testimony of their success they left their features stamped upon a rock so that all men might see them and venerate their deeds. They wrote their names in stone, but Mary Magdalene, more pious and poetical than they, preserved her name in tears, which, falling from her eyes, were, by the grace divine, turned to a river, which issuing from the cave, where she wept daily at her prayers, carries her sins out to the sea, where they are lost amongst the waves.

Their memory will endure whilst the stone still retains their images, and whilst the creed they preached is venerated, but hers can never die as long as water runs and grass grows green and the mistrál raises her córonach.

But in despite of saints and of their shrines, of pilgrimages, of holy caves, legends and miracles so well attested that to believe them would imply a faith in human testimony that contact with humanity rubs off, the ancient faith still lives.

Neither in Naples nor in Seville is life more joyous, nor does the fear of the dread mysteries which the virgins and the saints crossed over sea to inculcate, weigh less upon the mind. In all three places a reasonable and satisfying superstition fills men's souls, but does not influence their lives, more than the faith in Jupiter and Mars, Diana, Venus, and the rest of high Olympus influenced the ancients, that is, those ancients who, like the people of La Camargue, thought the first duty of a government was to give bread and bulls.

In the old towns which ring the river island all about, each with its aqueduct and temple, the Roman type remains, and any woman in the streets with her black hair, full bust, and low broad eyebrows could step into an amphitheatre, and gloat upon a gladiator's agony, turning her thumb down if he fought badly, or was not a personable man, with as much relish as she now enjoys the dying struggles of a horse, or, as in England, ladies watch a pheasant writhing its life out by a green covert side.

But the intense and ancient life runs stronger in the country than the towns. The guardians of the cattle form a race apart, unique in Europe, for the brown herdsmen of the plains between Lebrija and the hills of Ronda, although they pass their lives on horseback, are in the main men of the village or the town, whereas the Camarguais are as true countrymen as are the Arabs or the Mexicans. In this forgotten nook of Europe, hedged about by the tall reeds which fringe the Rhône, and the white sands which border on the sea, if it is true that Saracens once passed, it is quite certain that they left some of their customs deeply rooted in the land.

Whence comes the high Montpellier saddle, with its cantle rising well above the waist, and its iron stirrups covered in to save the toes? Where in all Europe but in Southern Spain, where men are partly Moors by blood and by inheritance, is to be seen the bit with the high port, and the long reins, joined at the middle and finishing in a flat whip, and where the hand held high, to turn the horse upon his neck, and not to heave him round by pulling at his mouth? The active horses and the tall, silent, swarthy men, might all be African, although veracious history, so careful of her generalities, so careless of her facts, does not inform us that the Saracens had time to intromit, as Scottish law-books phrase it, with the women of the land.

To give the infidel his due — and if we give it to the devil, why not extend it to the infidel? — he usually did not take long to intromit with all the women that he came across, but in this instance time was wanting, so it seems strange he should have left his horse-lore; but the fact remains. These customs are not relics of the Middle Ages, for the old knights rode differently and the bits they used were such as were required to pull up Flemish demi-elephants and not to turn a pony lightly as a seagull whirls upon the wing, after the fashion that the men in the Rhône delta use.

To see them bring a "point" of cattle up to the rude corral in which they shut the bulls before a bull-fight, takes one back to Mexico or the South Pampa, Nebraska or to Queensland, and makes one wonder why it is these centaurs do not emigrate with their wives, families, and stock to Venezuela and settle up some "llano" hitherto unpeopled, founding a race apart and uncommercialized as the Moors from Granada might have done, when the Red Towers were won.

Just swaying in the saddle, with the bridle hand held high, the hat blown back, and kept in place by a black ribbon underneath the chin, and in the right hand the long lance, tipped with the crescent and called a "trident" in La Camargue, the herdsmen dash about the sandhills (there is no sane man on a horse's back), their ponies' shoeless feet cutting the ground just as a skate cuts ice, shouting the while, out of the joy of life, and the proximity of death. The bulls, just as in Spain, led by an ox or two that wear bells, come snorting up to the corral, then stop and wheel, and plunge away into the maze of sandhills by the sea. The guardians float after them, their ponies' manes and tails streaming like foam from off a wave into the air, just as a swallow rushes at a gnat. The people shout, and in a cloud of dust the bulls are brought up with a rush, causing the men and boys to fly for safety up the posts of the corral, on to the wheels of carts, or up the gratings of the windows of the houses, to which they cling like flies.

The wooden bars are let down with a clang, the animals driven into an inner pen, and the whole village breaks out in a shout of "*Lagadigadon,*" as if each man by his own strength and skill had done the feat, instead of having stood and gossiped till the bulls rushed past.

The riders slowly dismount, unloose their girths, light cigarettes, and taking out their knives scrape off the sweat from just behind the girths where the hard spurring leaves a bloody foam. The horses stretch themselves and yawn, and then stand panting, looking at one another out of the corner of their eyes.

The corralling over, in the Byzantine church of the three holy Marys the bell "chaps" out, and the whole population headed by the mayor goes in to mass, the horsemen, after the fashion of their kind, sitting down in the sand, to talk of horses and of cattle, and illustrating what they say with diagrams drawn with the points of knives.

Mass over, and the whole village having dined, seated at wooden tables before the cafés in the main street, the bull-ring fills, the local firemen's band braying out the strains of songs from the music-halls in the sailors' quarter of Marseilles.

Three or four chosen guests mount a rude "shoggly" platform, only just beyond the reach of the bull's horns, and the mayor tells the chief fireman to blow a fanfare on the horn, announcing that he will give, drawn from the funds of the municipality, five francs to any one who can pull off a tricolour rosette pinned to the forehead of the bull.

In a moment all the huge corral fills up with ragamuffins and fishers from the shore, the nameless loafers who in every town throughout the world work hard at keeping up the houses by leaning up against the walls, and one or two assistants from the little shops, who give themselves what they think is the air of Spanish bull-fighters. As no one has a cloak, and for all means of keeping off the bull his jacket or a sack, the task is not so easy as it might be thought. Not that the loafers care to risk their skins, with the exception of the one or two who, having drunk sufficiently, get rolled about like barrels by the bull. After some twenty minutes, and when the bull stands panting in the middle of the ring, and all the loafers having fled for refuge are seated safely on the bars of the corral, the cornet sounds again, and the mayor beckoning for silence as did St. Paul at Athens, rises and says that the sum now is doubled, and the sport begins again.

The mayor's munificence by this time had attracted to the ring a plumber, who putting down a basket with his tools, walks into the ring. The people seem to know him, and mutter that he is a "*lapin*, who has no cold about his eyes," a thing quite evident, for, taking off his coat, he makes some "passes" quite in the style of Cúchares, and as the bull charges and passes him, snatches the cockade from its horn, and walks up quietly to the mayor, amongst the people's cheers. He gets the largess, and another bull is let into the ring, the first being taken out by the tame oxen, who decoy him to the gate.

After a sailor from Marseilles has got more largess, two herdsmen, armed with "tridents," come into the ring, and when the bull runs at them, catch him on their poles, and hold him for an instant, bellowing. Loud cheers salute the feat, which wants a good eye and a steady hand, and then the populace, just as they do in Spain, invades the ring, and has a pleasant twenty minutes with the bull.

Lastly, the mayor, placing himself before the firemen's band, adorned with his three-coloured sash, and in a hat coeval with the Third Empire, marches majestically across the ring, and the day's sport is done.

Then evening falls upon the little town, and in the vast and solitary marshes the herdsmen with their long "tridents" in their hands, held high like spears, convey the bulls back to their pasturage, their ponies snorting and passaging as the stiff breeze blows up the spindrift from the sea. Night shuts the scene, and the dull roar of surf upon the beach fills the immensity of marsh and sandhills, whilst from the pastures where the cattle feed come bellowings and the strange sounds which rise at night from lands uncultivated, where man has not been able to subdue and fetter Nature, forcing her with his plough and spade to give him crops, enslaving her just as he is enslaved himself by progress, with its ten thousand unnecessary wants, become necessities.

All that is left of the old disappearing life is doomed — the small black cattle will give place to shorthorns, the semi-wild white ponies to that well-bred stock, as little interesting as is the man who breeds it, and the black smoke of factories desolates the sky.

A melancholy and mosquito-haunted land it is, where beavers still are said to lurk, although unseen by all except tradition's piercing eye, which has immortalized them, and will not wot of their decease. A land once seen, which haunts you always, with its white horses and its fierce black bulls, its sun, mistrál, its fevers, ague, and the mist which floats above the marshes where the cattle harbour, seeking protection from the flies.

Charlemagne and Roland, Saracens and Goths, the Greeks, the Romans, Cæsar and the Phoenicians saw it and passed by, upon their way to history. Perhaps they thought it not worth occupation, and left it desolate, to the flamingo and the ibis to possess and populate. They saw and left it; but for its chiefest honour it still holds the bones now purified by tears, of the adulteress whom Jesus loved, and its chief saint is Mary Magdalene.

On the Spur

Princes had smiled upon him. All London had admired the tall lithe figure dressed in white. Uncomprehended and uncomprehending, he had talked with ministers and statesmen, and had sat silent with restless eyes at theatres and at reviews, glancing with tacit approbation at the battalions of strong sun-burned men, and at the ranks of bare white shoulders in the boxes and the stalls. What he had thought, when he returned to the great stucco house in Bayswater, thronged all the day with Jews and *rastaquouéres* and at night silent, and with some of the mystery of the East, redeeming even the commonness of mid-Victorian architecture, no man can tell.

No doubt, the two veiled women, who like bundles had accompanied him, asked questions as to the wonders of the mighty Londrès, which roared all day and night outside, but which they, bound in their haiks and the convention of their husbands' *[sic = husband's]* faith, had never seen but through their veils when peeping from a window, or through the blinds when driving in the town. But in the intervals of visiting our public institutions or our cotton mills, and as he listened to the promises of statesmen assuring him of England's interest in the welfare of Morocco, and of protection for himself, the tall young Arab Chief Menebhi no doubt thought anxiously of what was going on at Court in far Marâkesh, where, as he knew, his rivals were at work. At last, word came that all was over, and that England which had lionized him for a whole month had got another idol, and with the cross of some Victorian order was waiting civilly to send him on to Germany, where the same flatteries and promises were ready at Berlin.

There without doubt he saw the pomp and state of German militarism, watched educated men turned to machines skirmish and countermarch, whilst all the time rumours arrived from home that his liege lord the Sultan was being warped against him by his foes. Days followed days, and still the weary round of ceremonies, which held him half impatient half attracted, succeeded one another, whilst telegrams and letters from his friends urged his return if he set store upon his life.

When, from the quay at Bremerhaven he stepped aboard the steamer, with his two wives well veiled, his suite and all the useless things, as snuff-boxes from which sprang singing birds, electric toys, repeating watches, and all the costly trash which Orientals buy in Europe, his heart must have rejoiced.

Our pomp and state and noise, our crowds and all the rushing to and fro of modern life, delights an Oriental for a time. He sees our trains and steamers, our telegraphs and telephones, and marvels at them, but in a little while they pall upon him, and his mind, not to be deceived with symptoms, goes at once to causes and sometimes actually, at others with a sort of instinct, he asks himself, are these men happier than we for all their miracles?

He knows a watch is useful, and prefers a gun that kills a mile away to one that carries but a hundred yards, and is quite ready to accept all our inventions, even to railways and to telegraphs, for they seem natural things and admirable in that they save exertion, but on the understood condition that he shall take and use them, but not change the essence of his life. So would a cave-dweller, and almost every savage, eagerly clutch a sword and throw away his club, if it were offered to him, but each would know, as does the Oriental, that for himself his way of life is best.

During the voyage the ex-ambassador must have paced anxiously enough about the deck, or, squatted on a cushion, looked out on the horizon as earnestly as did the sailor in the "Pinta's" shrouds, when the New World was known to be at hand. No doubt occasionally he asked the officers why, if the ship could steam her sixteen knots, she could not manage sixty, for with a miracle so great as was the art of navigation, surely all things were possible, and but a matter of more coal.

When the low coast line with the lonely sea without a sail appeared, and the brown walls of Mazagan, with its mosque towers, and its half-dozen palm trees came in sight, and as the boats came dancing through the surf, the tall white figure paced about the deck. To land, to meet some faithful friends, to greet the governor, all with an air of being still in favour, and as a man who, having stood before the kings of Europe, was anxious for an audience with his lord, must have been as the rack to him, but still he bore it quietly, speaking to all, with the attention due to each particular and individual man. Then as he ambled on his mule through the unpaved and dusty streets, a messenger from his own tribe walking beside his knee, as if to welcome him, gave him the news of his disgrace. He learned the Sultan, young and inexperienced, and left to flatterers, all of whom were eager to supplant the minister, too far away to speak a word in his defence, had turned away his face.

Horses, the tribesmen said, were ready, and on the road a strong detachment was in waiting to ride with him to Court and to protect him on the way. He made no sign, but rode impassively out to a saint's tomb, just beyond the walls, ostensibly to pray. Sending his secretary, a thin brown doctor of the law from Mecca, to get his wives and property ashore, he prayed with all the bowings and prostrations which his faith required, and which as in like cases in most creeds, have by degrees become more vital than the prayer.

His tribesmen waited silently until the long formalities which pass between an Arab and his God had been completed, and then when he had shuffled on his shoes and stood erect, poured out their news in the succession of quick snapping gutturals which makes a stranger think that they are on the point of murder, when but engaged in a quiet talk about the price of cows or barley at the sok [sic=souk].

Whilst absent in Berlin and London, it appeared that, bit by bit, the confidence of the young Sultan had been undermined. Menebhi, so it seemed, had been accused of having borne himself more as a Sultan than an envoy; of having worn the hood of his burnous drawn forward covering his head when he had stood before the Christian kings, as if he were their equal, and the like. Such accusations, if they be vague enough, always impress an Oriental's mind, and in this case the poison had sunk in, and El Menebhi was advised that on his arrival at Marákesh he would be straight disgraced. Disgrace with Orientals usually carries loss of property, and not infrequently, of life. Some urged immediate flight to Europe, others that refuge should be taken with some consul in Tángier; some that he should remain encamped and send a messenger to argue out the case.

He, getting off his mule, called for green tea, drank the three semi-sacramental cups in silence, holding the silver ring which keeps the amber ball in place inside the cup, with his lean index finger, and then calling the head men of the deputation, said: —

"I start at once for Court; bring me a horse, one that can do the distance within thirty hours, and send a man on a swift-pacing mule to warn the tribe. Three hundred men of powder are to meet me at El Saghariz."

As he ceased speaking, the setting sun just falling on the yellow walls of Mazagan turned them to orange, then to rose-pink, and lastly to a violet tinge, which made the whitewashed houses look unnatural and ghastly, as the sea-breeze sprang up and caused the leaves of palm trees to rattle on their trunks.

The call to prayers rang out, prolonged and quavering, and the grave storks upon the battlemented walls appeared to listen to it, turning their heads and chattering their beaks. At corners of the streets and in the open spaces in the negro village just outside the walls, dotted with castor-oil plants and with cactuses, those of the faithful who felt themselves impelled, engaged in prayer, rising and falling like automata.

Men led their horses down to water, letting them jump about and wallow in the sand like buffaloes, and at the wells the women filled their water-jars, whilst the sea-breeze just rustled from the west.

As the last call rang out, repeated from the different towers and taken up in the straw hut which, in the negro village, serves as a mosque, and given back reverberating from the hot walls in one continuous peal as if the callers were determined to take Allah's ear by storm; wake him, if sleeping; or call him back, if on a journey; Menebhi mounted, settled his haik, raising himself erect in the short Arab stirrups, and leaning back against the cantle of his high red saddle, touched his horse sideways with the spur, and struck into the road. His friends and tribesmen, after a hurried blessing, swung themselves some upon their horses, others on their mules, and then the shadowy white figures melted into the night, their horses' footsteps muffled in the sand, making the line of horsemen look like their own ghosts. They pushed along, their bridles jingling, and their horses swerving now and then as a wild boar broke from the bushes with a grunt, through the thick scrub which for a league or two circles about the town. Then striking into a grey stony tract in which grows now and then a caroub tree, and now and then some patches of white broom, they reached a well just as the false dawn reddened the sky, and as the freshness of the night turned chilly, making them draw their haiks and their burnouses tighter and tie their handkerchiefs around their necks to stop their hoods from falling back in the cold air.

Hard by a saint's tomb near the well where grow palmettoes, dwarfs of their species, twisted and gnarled, fantastic-looking in the half light when moon is down and sun not risen, and stars above shine coldly through the night, they lighted down. Taking a carpet from a mule, they squatted silently upon it, whilst a black slave made tea, their horses standing with their girths loosened, and the blood dripping down from their flanks, where in the rapid march the edges of the stirrups and the spurs had bitten through the skin. They yawned, their eyes disappearing almost in their heads, rested a leg, and laying back one ear pricked the other forward, listening to every noise, neighing occasionally, and now and then rising and striking at each other with their feet. The mules dozed quietly, their huge red saddles making them look like hobby-horses in a pantomime. Drinking his tea, which he did noisily as a duck eats a weed beneath the water of a pond, a sign of breeding amongst Arabs and the Moors, Menebhi sat, his shoes kicked off, pale and fatigued, for during the past months he had not ridden, but yet resolute.

"How are the beasts," he said, "Si Hamed? I want to reach the tomb of Sidi ibn Nor at daybreak, for if we do, and meet the tribesmen with fresh beasts, we can arrive in Marrakesha at the evening call."

Si Hamed rose, a lean brown Arab, tall and taciturn. Shuffling along in horseman's boots and long straight spurs, such as those worn by knights of old, he scanned the animals. Some he pulled by the tails to see if they resisted; for if they stand as firm as trees, it is a sign that they are strong. Others he patted, dragging down their eyelids to see if they were red; for when a horse upon the road begins to flag, his eyelid and the flesh about the eye grows paler, as the heart weakening in its action pumps less blood into the veins. He took the mules' long ears and tweaked them, watching most carefully if it took long for them to go back to their pose; and these formalities gone through without a word, he silently came back, seated himself upon the carpet's edge, and in a guttural voice ejaculated "Good." The false dawn waning gave place to dark and heavy clouds, obscuring all the heavens, and rendering the roads almost impossible to travel but at a walk, stumbling in the deep ruts left by the feet of countless travellers for generations past. Then by degrees the first grey light of day appeared, the dark black clouds rolled past, and on the trees and shrubs great drops of moisture hung, wetting the long blue Arab cloaks as they brushed swiftly through the bushes on their way. The stars were setting, and the road lay white before them as they struck into the plain, which, like a sea, stretches from just outside the bushy country of the coast, right to the foot of the low hills, which lie between it and the stony steppe, on which Marákesh, girt with its palm trees, stands as in a sea.

As the first rays of sun fell on the company they felt the exultation which buoys up a man who has been riding all the night, and finds himself untired, his horse still fresh, and all the terrors of the darkness blotted out. They shifted in their saddles, rising erect, then settling themselves again pushed on in groups of threes and fours, talking and looking out across the plain.

In half an hour the round white saints' tombs of the Sok Thelatta ibn Nor appeared like mushrooms, and every eye was strained to see whether the tribesmen had arrived. As they rode on, a cloud of dust just rising to the west showed their arrival, and soon the sun shone on the slender single-barrelled guns that Arabs use, holding them upright in their hands, after the way their ancestors held spears.

Out of the dust the tribesmen charged, firing their guns and whirling round like seagulls on the wing. Then pulling up, their horses snorting and passaging, they passed at once from wild excitement to the grave silent attitude which Arabs all affect, just as day changes into night within the tropics, without the twilight intervening to give semitones.

Quickly Menebhi and his band changed horses, and in haste swallowed some food, and then he gave directions to his friends. "Follow us," he said, "about a rifle-shot behind, and send at once back to the tribe for reinforcements; tell them to hold the bridge across the Tensift at Marákesh when I have crossed it, and have gone into the town."

Once more they took their way across the plain, now heated almost to a furnace by the sun. With faces covered up by veils and handkerchiefs, they looked like maskers in a play, and as they went the lizards darted through the heated stones, snakes basked, and now and then mysterious pools appeared, which, as the horsemen neared them, took themselves farther off and reappeared, mocking them in their thirst, they seemed so real, just as our life seems real until death comes in and cheats us, ere we can slake our thirst upon the road.

Hours passed, and still the horses jogged, trying to keep up with the mules' swift swimming walk, the heat increased and every stone reflected it, so that it struck both from above and from below and seemed to burn into the bones. The horses sweated and then dried again, the particles of salt glistening upon their skins, and still they pushed along, a cloud of dust blown by the following wind, enveloping and hiding them from sight. At last about the noonday call to prayers, the trees and gardens of the saints' tombs at the oasis of the saint Rahál appeared on the horizon, as it seemed. But the deceiving mirage this time was a friend, for in an hour they reached them, and dismounting, breathed their horses, halting for half an hour beneath some orange trees.

In front the plain stretched on to Zagheríz, which they reached, now fatigued, at three o'clock. Leaving the weaker animals, they set their heads towards the hills of El Gibila, knowing that if they reached them with an hour or two of light, that there were hopes of getting into town before the gates were closed. Changing his horse for a swift-pacing mule, Menebhi led the way, dashing along the stony path, spurring and pulling at his bit, after the Arab style when they ride mules, which answer better to the bit than even to the spur. Right at the summit of the pass, Marákesh burst on them, the Kutubieh like a lighthouse of Islám, springing sheer from the plain like a tall palm tree of brown stone. They raised a shout, knowing that they were well ahead of news, and, without looking at the palm wood or the swift green-grey river running on the stones, dashed down the road to join the level plain. They passed the little saint's house on the hill, and as the sun was sinking, leaving but one short hour of light, reached the long bridge which spans the Tensift and then called a halt. The men arrived in groups, their horses panting and gasping, and Menebhi said:—

"Hold me the bridge until more men come from the tribe. Let ten men follow me, and in ten minutes ten more men, and in an interval another lot of ten. When I go in beneath the gate, let a man ride three or four hundred paces back and call a halt, and so on with all the other bands of ten. Be ready, keeping your horses bitted, and if at dawn you do not see me coming through the gate attack the town and seize some notables to serve as hostages."

Settling his clothes and haik, he rode into the palm woods which seethe about Marákesh like a flood. He rode through palms and still more palms, whose trunks, touched by the setting sun, glowed red, and then entering the zone of gardens, paced along between high aloe hedges or brown tápia walls. Crossing the wide maidán, which serves as horse-market, he entered by the lofty horseshoe gate, the guards not seeing in the dusty, road-stained horseman, muffled to the eyes as is the fashion in the land, the powerful minister and his familiar friends. Passing the gate, their horses slipping on the stones, they rode through crowded streets, and open spaces, where the jugglers and the story-tellers gather crowds, right to the palace walls. Dismounting, with a sign he gave his horse to one of his attendants and saying to the captain of the guard, "The Sultan sent for me and I am here," walked to the courtyard where he knew his master would be found.

As he passed through the various yards and ante-rooms, from the high Kutubieh tower the call to prayer rang out, booming and echoing, and taken up from every minaret. He shivered, knowing his danger, and recognising that the conflict was at hand.

Crossing the last of all the courtyards he came to where the guards keep watch, just where the Sultan sits. The soldiers knew him and respectfully made way, no news of his disgrace having reached them, and as he gave the Peace, his rival dressed in white, and with his face shining with joy, as does the face of him who has found favour with his lord, stood in the gateway. Just for an instant, in the pale dust-stained man, he did not know his foe. But as he would have spoken and have barred the way, the other, throwing back his hood, looked him between the eyes, and said, "Our Lord expects me," and as he spoke he passed into the court. The soldiers closed the gate, and the once joyous and successful rival sank, a white heap of rags, upon a bench.

All night he sat, waiting his fate, and as the morning sun just kissed the mosque towers, flushing them rose-pink, the gateway opened and El-Menebhi, pale with fatigue and dust, but with his eyes alight with victory after the night's debate with his liege lord, appeared before him, as he sat upon the ground. He rose, saluted and stood silent, and the successful rider, throwing his haik across his shoulder, and beckoning for his horse, looked at him stonily and muttered, "Dog!"

An Emir

Only two years ago it was a waste of sand, which from the edge of a high cliff looked out across the straits at Spain, that submerged fraction of the Eastern world. On it dogs, yellow and as thin as jackals, played. When it was dark they howled, making night hideous or melodious, according as the listener's ears were tuned to the roar of cities or to the silence of the East. Ragweed and mignonette, and now and then a bur and now and then a gentian struggled from the sand, their stalks grown woody with the drought. Dead dogs and cats strewed it abundantly, with offal of all kinds, and on the scanty grass an ass or two fed without appetite, resigned to fate.

At times some Arabs from the interior camped upon it, their bell-shaped tents sewn with squat bottles of blue cloth springing like mushrooms from the sand, their mules and horses standing listless in the sun, stamping at flies or neighing shrilly when they were fed at night. Their owners wandered on the cliff looking across toward "El-Andalus," pondering, perchance, upon the black, the incomprehensible, the element on which Allah has given scant dominion to his faithful, and of which Musa, he who conquered Spain and died in far Damascus, poor and a prisoner, said, "It is a thing the mind of none can compass, vast and ungovernable; fools ride it to their ruin in their hollow ships. . . . Such is the sea, no man hath bridled it."

Perhaps the campers wondered why the people of the faith, those who alone can properly pronounce the letter *dod*, did not again attempt the conquest of the land which once they ruled, or perhaps their thoughts but ran upon the price of eggs in Tángier, or in the sok *[sic=souk]* of Jabaltár.

Jews and more Jews, the women handsome, but graceless as must be all condemned for centuries to persecution, and the men more Spanish than the Spaniards in their faces, but much more European in their minds, lived in long rows of pink or sky-blue houses, upon every side. The little plain called the Marshán, on which in Carolean times battles were fought against the Moors, under the chief the English called Lord Gáylan, spread out between the cliffs above the sea and those which run down to the River of the Jews. Just at the end a Moorish cemetery, a field of stones, cut into little paths on every side, in which the feet of all the passers-by for centuries had left deep ruts, seemed to connect the living and the dead, in the familiar way of Africa, where no God's acre, railed and cut off from all the world, forms both a barrier against the quick, and yet a link with those who sleep beneath the grass.

The waste of sand, the cemetery, the howling dogs, and all the features of the life of Tángier, which have endured since first Ibn-Batúta left its walls to set forth on his travels, seemed likely to go on for ever, as changeless as the tide-rip which foams and billows in the middle of the Straits.

Then on a day a gang of builders suddenly appeared, Arabs with sacking tied about their loins, talking and shouting, and falling over one another in their zeal to do as little as was possible. A Spanish foreman, solemn and olive-coloured (a Moor in trousers and a cap), speaking a jargon between Andalúz and Arabic, and half incomprehensible to all his workmen, walked about, looking intensely grave, and now and then cursing his men for dogs of infidels.

A Jew, thin, lithe and eager, acted the part of clerk of works, and in a month or two walls and more walls of courtyards, the scheme of every Moorish house, rose as by magic from the sand. The noise and the confusion of the men would have shamed Babel easily, and yet the work went on, went on by force of human strength and sweat, men raising stone by pulleys, in which palmetto ropes creaked noisily, whilst donkeys waited patiently with lime.

So did they build the Pyramids, the temples at Palenqué, and thus did the Alhambra rise out of the rocks which crown the gorge above the courses of the Darro and Geníl. Grave, bearded, white-clad men, holding each other's hands, as children do in lands where custom sets a gulf unbridgable betwixt the actions of the old and young, came and sat down on heaps of stones and criticized. They gave their reasons solemnly, and with much calling upon God, raising their hands with a slow motion from the wrist, and turning up their palms towards their auditors, who listened to them silently with now and then a pious phrase, which whistled through the larynx as the wind whistles through the trees. Some held the employment of the Christian would bring bad luck, whilst others gave as their opinion that the infidel was given might by God over the steam and electricity, and it was right to profit by his lore, as Allah, for wise reasons of his own, allowed him greatly to enjoy the earth, reserving to himself the power, the world's play done, to cast him into Tophet, where he should wither for a thousand years.

Men swarmed like ants about the walls, chattering like parrots in a field of maize, and mules and donkeys carrying bricks and lime went to and fro, men urging them with blows and shouting curses on their mothers, all which they took unmoved and uncomplaining, their round black eyes looking amazed and philosophically upon their fellow-slaves who ran beside them yelling in their ears.

Word came from Suez or Port Said that soon the owner of the place might be expected, and that all work be finished by a certain day, on which he with his women and his suite would be in Tángier, and would take possession of the house. Painters and decorators, working with a will, soon gave the interior a habitable air, glazing the windows with parti-coloured glass, and painting dados of great stripes of blue picked out with orange, and finishing pink window-frames with green, a scheme of colour which to a Western eye seems crude, but which in Africa the light tones down and softens as in a garden flowers are blended by the sun into a harmony.

Then, all desisted from their work, and the great house stood silent in the sun, as some huge palace in the realms of the "Arabian Nights" called up by genii, springs in a night, and perhaps vanishes away as speedily, into the sand from which it rose. Though built so hastily, it yet looked solid, the long white walls without a window, giving it an air as of a fortress, which the great gate did not belie though plated with sheet tin.

The master landed at the port, his baggage packed in carpets and in great wooden cases, filling a lighter to the water's edge, and he himself, dressed all in fleecy white, was welcomed by his friends. He got upon his mule, settled his clothes, and followed by a friend from Mecca, rode slowly through the town. Women and eunuchs followed, and the whole train emerging from the walls, clattered and slithered up the slippery street paved with rough cobble stones, and stood before the house. Cushions were brought and, sitting down, the owner's part was done, for he sat drinking tea and opening letters, handing them to his secretary to read and comment on, as if he had already lived a lifetime in the house new risen from the sand. His household silently fell into its accustomed round. A throng of wild retainers lounged about the door, which opened on a narrow street, giving no inkling of the splendour of the place.

Horses and mules were hobbled in the grounds, and tents were pitched in corners, in which mysterious men dozed on their saddles, or sat drinking tea, and at which messengers arrived bearing exaggerated news about the doings of the French upon the frontier, the fights between the tribes, and of the struggles of the various European Powers for the predominance at Fez.

The owner having been a minister of state, one of those men who in the East are sure to sow the seeds of jealousy in sovereigns' minds by standing out too high above the crowd, and who had fallen into disgrace, losing most of his property, and running in danger of his life, looked on his palace as a sort of exile, not that he, as an Arab, probably was more attached to one place than another, but as a banishment from power, which so appeals to all men of his race, that Diocletian, the one philosopher in practice, who has sat upon a throne, to them would be a madman, and his retirement, the wisest action history has set down of any ruler in the world, incomprehensible. Their subtle, quick and yet material minds rise to few flights of fancy. That which exists, for them is absolute, and Allah sent his sun, his rain, his power or poverty for men to bear, enjoy or profit by, but not to criticize.

So in his garden, which had been made as quickly as the house, and which his taste had set with beds of Indian corn and vegetables, after the fashion of his race, that holds all gardens should be used for profit, and flowers as incidental, and not necessities as in the West, he passed the portion of an Oriental's life that Westerns ever see. Dressed all in spotless white, eager and lithe, and never still an instant when upon his feet, he roamed about much as a tiger roams about its cage. At times he sat, quiet and impassible, as is a joss upon its shrine, in one of those small narrow rooms the Moors construct in which to see their friends who cannot pass into the house. Beside him sat his secretary, a young black-bearded Arab doctor of the law, who had passed years in Mecca and at Cairo, and yet had learned no word of any tongue but Arabic. Quick and intelligent, almost vivacious in his speech, his manners courteous, and his smile as ready to break out as sun in April, and to illumine all his face with seeming kindliness, some thought he was a fanatic at heart, others that in the holy city of the Haj, seeing the mystery too near, he had become indifferent, even a sceptic, as happens now and then to ardent Christians who have lived long in Rome, and become too familiar with their faith. But, if his thoughts were difficult to fathom, as no doubt the thoughts of

Europeans, ever a mystery to Easterns, were to him, they were as clear as crystal beside those of the accomplished ex-minister, now fallen from his high estate, to whom the house belonged.

Jews, Moors and Europeans and an occasional out-at-elbows Turk, all thronged his doors, most of them anxious for assistance of some kind. To some he gave hard cash, to others promises, but always courteously, so that none said of him as says the adage, "The man has neither charity nor a kind word to give."

But, on the other hand, the richer Europeans, in want of lions (which had long ago retired into the Atlas Mountains beyond Fez), had hailed with acclamation his advent in their midst.

No party was complete without him, and as the dancers whirled about, with arms and shoulders bare, he sat and possibly discreetly wondered at the show.

Silent and bored, but smiling, he sat at parties, timid but haughty, for no one better than an Arab knows all the gradations of society, or is so quick to take offence at courtesies omitted, or any social sin committed by his host. Women, young, beautiful and half-undressed, stood by his side, their petticoats just mingling with his flowing robes, and he who from his youth had never looked a woman in the face, except she was his sister or his wife, stood unconcerned, although his blood, no doubt, ran boiling through his veins. Still he smiled on, a smile so enigmatical that even diplomats who put him down as a hot-headed Arab chief, must surely now and then have wondered what he thought.

The hospitalities that he received from German, English, and from French alike, he paid back amply in his new palace, in which the plaster and the paint were hardly dry, and where the flowers in the garden seemed to have been planted all in bloom, and yet which, by the virtue of the climate and the custom of the land which makes it natural to let a house decay for want of necessary care, then build another by the side of it, neither seemed old nor yet conspicuously new.

Playing at tennis with young ladies in his court, which, painted green to mitigate the glare, looked out upon the sea, he still looked dignified. Walking about the open yards, which serve in Arab houses as reception-rooms, after a dinner party, and no doubt conscious that a dozen curious eyes of carefully veiled women watched from upper windows, envying or perhaps despising the greater opportunities their European sisters had, he looked as must have looked the Emirs of Granada, when they entertained a batch of Christian knights and ladies, in the last bulwark of Islám, in Spain.

So, in the house which he had built, as it were by chance, and in the garden looking on the sea, he passed his days, for the most part, after the fashion of his fathers, half of his life shut from the world behind a curtain, from which at times came voices in dispute and sometimes songs, harsh and high pitched, but haunting as is a cricket's pæan to the sun, heard in a noonday halt beneath the trees. Sometimes he rode abroad, erect and swaying on his horse, his long white draperies afloat, with his eyes fixed upon the distance, after the manner of his ancestors who, as they rode across the sands, looked out for enemies. His, though concealed, are just as imminent, and he awaits them still, uncomprehended and incomprehensible, courteous and cruel, rash and yet diplomatic, lounging the hours away upon the cliff, from which he sees the land where his race flourished, and from which, constrained by circumstance or fate, it sank again into the sands.

Fate

In a long corridor of an old Georgian house, lit by a skylight and by a window over the hall door, there hung a piece of needlework in a dark rosewood frame. In silk, some lady of the family had worked a landscape setting forth the district and the house in which the picture hung. It stood four square and looked out on the east, across the moss which once had been a sea. On either side of the great strath ran lines of hills, one rough and heather-clad, as when just at their feet the Romans were rolled back, the other smooth and green, and sloping off towards the south. The moss itself was brown and on its face the shadows came and went, chasing each other as the hours pursue eternity, leaving no trace where they had passed.

Trees stood about the house and in the pictured needlework; in one case stiff and formal, looking like ineffectual monuments of grief in cemeteries, and in the other whispering in the wind, labouring and groaning in the storm, and in the sunshine all alive with bees.

The careful needlewoman had displayed each stone and window in the house; colouring those black which had been closed during the operation of the window tax; and had dwelt lovingly on walls and pediments. The range of hills under her magnifying steel had changed to mountains, and a small lake had come into existence supplied with water from the fountains of her brain. Right carefully she had devised the cedars, with the beech avenue, the sycamores, the weeping yew, and the stiff terrace upon which the house was set, whilst every post in all the fences was portrayed both with elaborate stitching and with circumstance.

Just as much inkling of perspective was employed as to make all unnatural, and yet on looking at it, you felt it had been done with tenderness, and the contriver must have put her soul into the task.

Such artless works sometimes more nearly touch the heart than the most airy flights of genius, when the place represented has been dear to the beholder and the artist; for places, unlike men, can never vary, and time itself breeds no satiety of love.

The faint, fresh smell of fir trees in the wet, that scent of dampness rising from the moss and the perfume of bracken, sweet and sharp, must have been present always to the worker as she sat sewing at her window-seat, whilst gazing at the rain.

Time does not mellow needlework as it does pictures, yet still it gives it interest, and as the colours fade and ends of silk grow rough, it seems a soul is born in them which speaks to us out of its nothingness, bringing us somehow nearer to the dead.

So it hung on, getting a little yellower, more flyblown, and with the varnish scaling from the rosewood frame and the gold falling off in particles from the interior rim, as winter damp and summer sun succeeded year by year in the long corridor of the old Georgian house. Birds sat upon it now and then, and bats occasionally hid themselves between it and the wall, and darted out again as fearlessly as if the lonely passage had been an alley in a wood. Nothing appeared less likely than that a tragedy should be unrolled with it as background, or as the world, in which after the fashion of the greater world outside its frame, birth, life, and death should pass all unperceived.

Life was serene as usual in the corridor, whilst the dust gathered on the picture-frames and clung upon the looking-glasses as frost clings on a cabbage leaf in the late autumn after a cold night. The house itself, buried in woods, woods and more woods, stood lonely, and in the avenues guttered and channelled by the winter rains, the grass grew rank. The terraces were pitted here and there with holes made by the rabbits in their play, who left a little heap of sand outside them, to which occasionally clung brown silky fur.

The roedeer, venturing from the copses, strayed in the summer nights and belled close to the windows; and the soft flying owls wafted from tree to tree like kites, or hooted litanies from the tall larches, whilst from the woods and mosses rose the faint noises which at night wake recollections of the time when men and animals perchance all spoke one tongue.

The charm of desolation had descended on the place, and the rare lights and few inhabitants seemed to be lost in nature, which invaded them, swallowing them in her amplitude as the stray vegetation swallows up a church deserted by the Jesuits out on the Chaco or in Paraguay. Gnomons had fallen from sundials, and the stone slabs of terrace steps yawned open: from some of them sprang ferns, whilst on the coping of the walls the moss grew tenderly. The ponds were half grown up with flags and bulrushes. Great banks of sand and mud stretched into them, brought by the burns in winter, and on them feathers stuck, looking like snowflakes and fluttering in the wind. All was so quiet that the mast falling from the beech sounded like raindrops pattering upon ice or on a window-pane.

Nothing disturbed the quiet of the place, which slowly seemed to fall to ruins and become more beautiful each day. Then, on a summer morning when the swallows darted through the trees, hawking at flies, and on the grass the squirrels ventured timidly to play, springing upon the overhanging boughs at the first sudden noise, a bubble seemed to swell below the glass and force it outwards at the corner of the frame. It grew mysterious and white, next turned a rusty brown, then was forgotten as the days slipped past, each one so like the other that the flight of time was imperceptible, darkness succeeding light as stealthily as the owls floated through the wood, lighting like thistle-down on the elastic branches of the trees.

Weeks passed and still the mystery was unsolved, only beneath the envelope a fluttering motion now and then was seen, as if a spirit prisoned in its cell stirred faintly, struggling to free itself from matter and to escape into the sky. But no one marked it much, for tragedies may be enacted at one's elbow, and none the wiser; for indeed, most tragedies seem comic to the looker-on, who does not comprehend the motive, and takes the sufferer for a mere ill-bred person, who might have lived and died, just like the rest of us, had he had common sense.

So the bees hung about the lime trees, making their music in the flowers, the cedars' branches swayed like windmills' sails, and in the thickest of the woods the capercailzie crowed, flapping their wings with a strange hollow sound which echoed through the trees, like negro tomtoms by night up some mosquito-haunted river on the Coast, or like the mournful drum which Bernal Diaz heard during the siege of the great temple of Tenochtitlán.

Then, on a morning in late June, when the soft air just curled the rising mist from off the moss into tall pillars such as rise in a simoom, one who had looked by chance at the old needlework in passing, saw that the tragedy had taken place.

The temple's veil was rent, and fallen asunder, and underneath the glass a brown and fluffy moth had come into the world, been born, had stirred, just fluttered and had died, seeing the air it could not fly in, feeling the life within it, which fate that laughs at all things, moths and men alike, said it should never taste.

To wish it peace, it who had not known trouble, were in vain, and for repose, its wings had never fluttered in the air. Care, sorrow, love, hate, pain, revenge, and still less avarice, or ambition by which the fool and not the noble falls, it should know none of, and probably would not have felt in its brief joyous life.

But to be cabined in a cage of glass, to suffer the *peine forte et dure* of death by pressing, for no committed crime, poor, fluttering fairy round the lamp of life, 'twas hard. How brief your pleasures and how innocent, merely to play about the corridors of the old melancholy house to prove your wings, and then to soar into some fir tree on the lawn, equipped at once with all the lore inherited from those your ancestors in Eden, who flitted through the cypresses of that fair garden on the Tigris, and then after a day or two, at most a month, to love, to rove at night amongst the trees, to fall at the first frost or heavy shower, and lie amongst the needles of the pines without a single crime upon your conscience, tender as your wings, this would have been your fate.

Alas, poor fellow, would-be flutterer in the realms of a hard world, perhaps the fate presiding at your birth who with her unkind shears cut off your destiny, was kind. Who knows? You might have come to ruin or mishap, e'en you who surely had no unkind thought in your minute and microscopic brain.

Circling about at night, thinking no evil, after the fashion of your clan, a candle light which to your complex eyes might have appeared a sun, vast, round, and vivifying, might have attracted you and left you writhing agonized and maimed, a prey to children who in their rage for self-improvement, or from the cruelty which we who have no wings bear in our blood as the true sign of the great curse our common Maker set upon us at the Fall, might have transfixed you with a pin.

Perils we know not of and which have never entered our dull brains, so ill attuned to all the mysteries of your world, may have awaited you. Some pestilence which no physician of our kind has diagnosed might have attacked and struck you blind, crippling your flight or rendering you unsightly to the companions of your merry little world. This might have been, or the fell spider with his web of fated filaments entangled your soft wings and drawn you struggling to his den, cut off your life and fed upon your flesh, for these are dangers even we who know so little of your lives can comprehend. From these your fate has freed you, making you equal to great Cæsar, Hannibal, to Alexander, both to the greatest and the least of all mankind, by the mere fact that you have lived.

Rail not at fate, poor iridescent moth, although the hues upon your wings were meant to shine at twilight as you flickered through the trees with just as fair a lustre as the most gorgeous butterfly who hovers in the sun on the Tijuca's slopes can ever boast. Do not repine, although no snowflake would have floated from the sky more delicately than the unfollowable pulsations of your wings would have conveyed you through the twilight air in your brief honeymoon with life. You will not know the joy of liberty, tender and innocent in its conception, as moths alone conceive it, of all created things. Let no cursed man of science with his dog Latin and apocalyptic Greek dispel my ignorance, telling me that the family of moths is as rapacious as the vulture or the crow. I'll not believe it, but will mourn thy fate, condemned to see for a brief moment all the beauties of the light, never to flit at evening in the dark recesses of the trees. Poor pilgrim to a world unworthy of your innocence, who lived and died so quickly, surely you solved at once the mysteries which we live for a lifetime and still never grasp. My fellow-sufferer by fate, you, who left instantly the world in which we tarry longer instants, with as scant comprehension of our lives perhaps as you, do not forget us prisoned in our glass; but in the limbo where you flutter now, think that a fellow-moth remembers you, just as you lived and died, with your soft body, iridescent wings, and sharp antennæ.

Ha Til Mi Tuliadh

All was unchanged, and Nature cared not, being occupied with sun and moon and stars, the tides, the mists, the dew, rain, snow, the fall and reproduction of the leaf, and the great mysteries, the cause of which evades and always has evaded man. She smiled, as she does sometimes at a funeral, sending a glimpse of sun upon a coffin-plate, so that the cold-nipped mourners read the age of the deceased whilst they stand peering down into the grave, as in a blaze of light.

All was unchanged.

The two tall lime trees towered above the rough field-gate contrived of poles running through horseshoes wedged into their trunks.

The leaves just swept the roof, and in the evening air they seemed to sigh for the departed, who for so many years had watched them green in April bursting into life, and glorious in autumn as they fell carpeting the road, and piled upon the level doorstep with its concentric pattern drawn in chalk; the rush-thatched byre, upon whose roof grew fumitory and corydalis, looked just as it had looked for forty years, and the low door flanked by great tufts of golden-rod and of angelica, and painted blue, was shut for ever on its late owners and on me. Through it, from earliest childhood, as I passed, I led my ponies, tying them in the dark beside the cow to the tall uprights which in Highland cowsheds serve for stalls.

Two sisters, almost the last survivors of an ancient race, had lived for years in the old cottage by the reedy lake. Descendants of the retainer of a feudal chief, their ancestors had been hereditary ferrymen, for, in the days of old, caste, now confined to India and the East, was spread throughout the world.

In what rough coracle or boat their remote ancestors had ferried over to the island, men dressed in skins, no one can say, for from the dawn of history in Menteith marauding clansmen, coming with a creagh from the laigh, had been rowed over to the castle in the isle by some one of their race.

In the deep bay, rush-locked and clear, they or their father had constructed a rude pier of stones and wattles, to which a boat was tied, the paint all sun-cracked, and with an inch or two of water in the well.

So in the days gone by, in houses occupied by gentlemen whose pedigrees were longer than their purse, an antiquated carriage, used as a roosting-place by hens, slowly decayed in some gaunt coach-house, given up to damp.

Carriage and boat were evidence of better times, a link with days of glory long departed, drawing a smile or tear, according to the point from which the man who saw them looked upon the world.

So in the cottage the two sisters lived; relics of days when men were civil in their speech, had time and did not spare it in its use. They never travelled far, but, for all that, they knew the world in which they lived themselves in all its niceties. Constrained by poverty to work, the sisters yet appeared two ladies in distress, not fallen in fortunes, though their Potosí was but the little croft and garden with "its hantle of sour plumtrees," but, so to speak, having suffered wrong from Nature, which had not placed them free from all necessities at birth. Not that they lacked advancement either, for in their heart of hearts they held themselves the equals of the highest in the land; a tacit claim which all admitted, but their equals, in the old-fashioned district where they lived. Raw-boned and rather hard of feature, the eldest had the soft Highland voice and manner, which somehow seems not to belong to modern life, and places the possessor of them in a world outside the present age. The younger, gentle and delicate, had never married, must have been pretty in her youth, and lived her life subordinated to her sister, admiring her, and in her turn being admired and cherished by her in a half-tender and half-peremptory way.

Their father was an ancient Celt who formed a link with olden times, being compounded of quite different essences and stronger simples than men of latter days. Born as he was, just where the Highlands and the Lowlands touch, he had amalgamated much of the characteristics of the two. His manners were all Highland, his knowledge of the world partly his own and partly that of the Low Country, as we style the realm of bogs and marshy fields that swells and billows like a sea up to the lumpy range of tawny hills that cuts them from the north, and, till the days of railways, formed a bar as strong and as insuperable as is a navigable river, or indeed the sea. Short, and in later years bent almost double, but to the last alert upon his legs, time and the rain, which when it ceases for a fortnight is the theme of prayers in church, had turned him a light fern colour, and his clothes, and hair — originally grey (for no one living could remember when his head was brown) — had weathered to a lichen-looking green, and his blue twinkling eyes, not bleared with age, could, as he said himself, "discern a gentleman almost a mile away." Gentry and gentlemen, by which he understood those of old family, for money could not make, nor the want of it mar, in his opinion, were the chief objects of his creed.

"The Queen can mak' a duke, she canna' mak' Lochiel," he would observe with pride, not that the limitation of the royal power rejoiced him, for he held, as do Mohammedans, that he who reigned did so by right divine, but it seemed to him evident, or else the prayer for those "set over us and under Him" had been of no account.

Withal he was himself a gentleman, if natural good-breeding makes one, conjoined with courtesy in speech. Upon a visit, when he had showed [sic] you round his croft, with what an air he used to offer you fruit in a cabbage leaf, saying, "Will ye tak' berries, laird," or "leddy," as the case might be, thus exercising hospitality in its best sense, by giving what he had without false shame or with excuses for his poverty. One ate them, listening all the time to local lore, distorted through the vision of his years, and rendered picturesque partly by want of education and partly by the way he touched his subject, embroidering and adorning it with sidelights of his own, just as an artist draws from what he sees in his own brain, and neither copies nor extenuates his theme.

Seated upon the gunwale of his boat, and talking volubly in the soft Highland accent, which makes you think that you knew Gaelic once upon a time, the landscape all unchanged, the scrubby oak copse straggling up the hill, the bracken yellowing in the autumn breeze, and leaves of sycamores, mottled and black, like trout in moorland burns, all falling softly round about, whilst the white mist crept up and hung the castle and the chapel in the air, making the great stag-headed chestnuts in the Isle of Rest look like gigantic antlers thrown against the sky, the things and men of which he spoke became alive again and the long, broken link with the old world was welded into shape. You heard unmoved, and as a thing quite natural, and which it seemed had happened to yourself, how he had walked to Eglinton to see the tournament, taking three days to do it, in the rain; had slept beneath the trees, had seen it all, especially the Emperor of the French, "Napoleon Third, ye ken," the Queen of Beauty carried through the mud, and then tramped back again.

Who, in these days of education and of common sense, made manifest and plain by copy-book, would do the like, out of pure love of sport, lightness of heart, or the sheer devilment of youth?

All the old legends of the Borderland he knew; with much about Rob Roy, who as he used to say was "better in a tuilzie than a fight, for all his skill o' fence, and they long arms o' his, ye mind, he could untie the garters frae his hose without a stoop or hogging up his back." He talked about the man just as he were alive, so naturally and without effort, having heard all he told you from his grandfather, that it would not have startled you on looking round to see Red Robert in the flesh come trotting down the hill, his target at his back, and his long Spanish "culbeir" in his hand, humming a waulking song or whistling a strathspéy.

All the old legends of the district and his lore of times gone by he left his daughters, which, working in their minds and coming to the surface in their speech, stranded them lonely in the world, without a fellow, just as a glacier-carried boulder in a glen must feel deserted in the tall heather where it lies, far from the hills and stones.

The younger sister first departed, going on before to tell their father that the world was changed, and that no place was left for them or theirs, and that the osprey built no more in the old chestnuts which the monks had planted round the grey priory in the isle, and that the trees themselves were growing balder and more sere. The elder lingered on alone, brisk but alert, driving her cow down to the mossy "park," and stepping east to church when it was fine, not following the road, but going through the fields (though it took longer by them), perhaps from the hereditary Highland habit of avoiding stones in days when every man made his own brogues at home. In summer time she took into her house artists and fishermen, and those whom the fine weather drives into the country for a time, and who lounge through their time smoking and bored, but conscious it is right to do as others do, and therefore satisfied. They thought her odd, and she esteemed them common, but "awfa' clever folk, ye ken, ane o' them painted me a bit picture o' ma sister from a fotygraph, ane o' they dagyriotypes, ye mind them, done on glass, which I have by me since it was ta'en back aboot sixty-three, the time o' yon review at Paisla', the verra image o' her, laird, I'm tellin' ye." The effort of the limner's art (to which even a "dagyriotype" on glass was preferable) hung in her little parlour, resplendent with megilp, shining with poppy oil, and setting forth the patient with a grin upon her face, and with the clothes in fashion forty years ago, themselves not beautiful, rendered ridiculous by newness, just as a play of the same time appears to us absurd, not that our own are better, but because folly is a changing quantity and different in degree.

Our friendship, fast but intermittent, lasted many years, and the byre door through which my ponies used to pass became too small to lead my horse through, and so we generally talked outside the house, not that we said much, for she was growing deaf, and I knew all her stories years ago, but it pleased both of us, and when I mounted and rode off she used to stand, holding her hand above her eyes, after the fashion of a sailor on a pier, looking out seaward, even when not a sail is on the sea.

Her death was in the olden style, after the fashion she had lived; so to speak, not premeditated, but natural, just as a tree dies at the top, decaying downwards, till it is gone almost before those who have known it all their lives are well aware of its decease. The neighbours told me, for I was absent in that region which folks in Menteith call "up aboot England," that she was "travellin'" from church, felt ill upon arriving at her house, took to her bed, and "sleepit bonnily awa'" upon the following day. A man, that is a man who feels the ancient Highland spirit in his blood, would like to die with his boots on, but for a woman this was the nearest thing to sudden death, and quite became the last of an old violent race of men.

In the old churchyard by the lake, amongst the Grahams and the Macgregors, some of whom have swords upon their headstones, for all their trade-mark and memorial of their lives, she sleeps. With pride of race and Scottish thoughtfulness she left sufficient to erect a stone, in which is cut her name, her sister's, that of her father, and those of many of her clan. It stands in the wet grass, close to the wall of the kirkyard, a sort of landmark in the history of Menteith, showing a page turned down; a page on which but few could read, even before the book was shut for the last time. To bid her sleep in peace is but a work of supererogation, after full eighty years of life. Those who remain tossing and turning upon life's uneasy pillow stand more in need of such a wish.

So I "stepped west," and, coming to the Highland cottage by the lake, found the door shut, the hearthstone cold, the garden eaten up with weeds, the flauchtered feals upon the cowhouse roof fallen from the poles, and the old boat, hauled up upon the beach, paintless and blistering in the sun. No cow fed in the little rushy park, even the withies which had once confined the gate were burst and swinging in the wind. The door was shut, shut against me, and shut upon the last of my old friends; so, sitting down upon the step, on which no longer was a pattern laid in chalk, I smoked and meditated, seeing a long procession pass upon the road, all riding ponies which grew larger towards the end, until a man upon a horse brought up the rear. They stopped before the house, which seemed to have turned newer, and in which a fire of peats burned brightly on the hearth. Then, from the door . . . but . . . I will return no more (*Ha til mi tuliadh*); he who waits at the ferry long enough will get across some time.

Miss Christian Jean

Two pictures hang upon my study wall, faded and woolly, but well stippled up, the outlines of the hills just indicated with a fine reed pen, showing the water, coloured saffron, deepening to pink in the deep shadows of the lake. Although one picture is a sunset and the other done as it would seem at sunrise, they show a country which even yet is undefiled by any human step.

So accurately is the dark brown tree set in position on the border of the fleecy lake, one feels an artist, superior to mere nature, has been about the task. The castle on the mountain top, in one of the two masterpieces, is at the bottom of the hill in its compeer, and in the two a clear blue sky throws a deep shadow over the unruffled water, on which float boats with tall white sails, progressing without wind.

Still, with their frames, which are but fricassees of gingerbread well gilt, to me they say a something all the art of all the masters leaves unsaid.

A masterpiece speaks of imagination in its maker; but those pale blue-grey hills and salmon-coloured pinkish lakes, castles which never could have been inhabited, boats sailing in a calm, and trees that seem to rustle without breeze, set me reflecting upon things gone by, and upon places of which I once was part, places which still ungratefully live on, whilst that of me which lived in them is dead.

A long low Georgian room, in which the pictures hung, with its high mantelpiece, its smell of damp and Indian curiosities, and window looking out on the sunk garden underneath the terraces, the sides of which were honeycombed by rabbits, rises in my view, making me wonder in what substance of the body or the mind they have been stamped.

How few such rooms remain, and how few houses such as that, to which the dark and dampish chamber, with its three outside walls, and deep-cut mouldings on the windows and the doors, was library. We called it "book-room," in the Scottish way, although the books were few and mostly had belonged to a dead uncle who had bought them all in India, and on their yellowing leaves were stains of insects from the East, and now and then a grass or flower from Hyderabad or Kolapur (as pencilled notes upon the margin said), transported children to a land so gorgeous that the like of it was never seen on earth. These books were all well chosen, and such as men read fifty years ago — Macaulay's Essays, with the Penny Cyclopædia, Hume, Smollett, Captain Cook, The Life of Dost Mohammed, Elphinstone's Cabul Mission, with Burckhardt's Travels, enthralling Mungo Park, and others of the kind that at hill stations in the rains, or in the plains during the summer, must have passed many an hour of boredom and of heat away for their dead purchaser. The rest were books of heraldry and matters of the kind, together with a set of Lever and of Dickens, with plates by Cruikshank or by Hablot Brown. One in particular set forth a man upon a horse, with a red fluttering cloak streaming out in the wind, galloping in the midst of buffaloes with a long knife between his teeth. But books and furniture and Indian curiosities, with the high Adams chimney-piece and portraits of the favourite hounds and horses of three generations, were, as it were, keyed up to the two water-colours, one of which hung up above a cabinet sunk far into the wall and glazed, the other over a low double door, deep as an embrasure.

All through the house the smell of damp, of kingwood furniture, and roses dried in bowls, blended and formed a scent which I shall smell as long as life endures. This may, of course, have been mere fancy; but often in old houses some picture or some piece of furniture appears to give the keynote to the rest. But it seemed evident to me that, in some strange mysterious way, the pictures, outstanding in their badness, had stamped themselves upon the house more than the Reynoldses and Raeburns on the walls, though they were pictures of my ancestors, and the two water-colours represented no known landscape upon earth. They entered into my ideas so strongly (though they were unobtrusive in themselves) that, looking from the window-seat in the deep bay of the sunk window in the dining-room, across the terraces, over the sea of laurels, beyond the rushy "parks," and out upon the moss and the low lumpy hills that ran down to the distant lake, almost divided into two by a peninsula set with dark pine trees and with planes, the landscape seemed unfinished and lacking interest without the castles and the chrome-laden skies of the twin masterpieces.

It may be, too, that the unnatural landscape caused me to form unnatural views of life, finding things interesting and people worthy of remark whom others found quite commonplace, merely upon their own account, and not from the surroundings of their lives. So every one connected with the house of the two works of art became mixed up somehow with them in a mysterious way, as well as things inanimate and trees, the vegetation and the white mist which half the year hung over moss and woods, shrouding the hills and everything in its unearthly folds, making them strange and half unreal, as is a landscape in a dream.

Perhaps the fact that the house stood just at the point where Lowlands end and the great jumble of the Highland hills begins, and that the people were compounded of both simples, Saxon and Celtic mixed in equal parts, gave them and all the place an interest such as clings to borderlands the whole world over, for even forty years ago one talked of "up above the pass" as of a land distinct from where we lived. Down from those regions wandered men speaking a strange tongue, shaggy, and smelling of a mixture of raw wool and peat smoke, whose dogs obeyed them in a way in which no dog of any man quite civilized, broken to railways and refreshment-rooms, obeys his master's call. The bond of union may have been that both slept out in the wet dew, huddling together in the morning round the fire for warmth, or something else, the half-possession of some sense that we have lost, by means of which, all unknown to themselves, the drover and his dog communicated. Communion, very likely, is the word, the old communion of all living things, the lost connection between man and all the other animals, which modern life destroys.

But, be that as it may, the men and dogs seemed natives, and we who lived amongst the mosses and the hills seemed strangers, by lack of something or by excess of something else, according to your view.

The herds of ponies that the men drove before them on the road fell naturally into the scheme of nature; sorrels and yellow chestnuts, creams and duns, they blended with the scrubby woods and made no blot upon the shaggy hills. Instinctively they took the long-forgotten fords, crossing below the bridges, and standing knee-deep in the stream, the water dripping from their ropy tails and burdock-knotted manes. The herds of kyloes too have gone, which looked like animals of some race older than our own. The men who drove them, with their rough clothes of coarse grey wool, their hazel crooks, and plaids about their shoulders, whether the wind blew keenly or midges teased in August, all have disappeared. Their little camps upon the selvedge of the roads are all forgotten, although I know them still, by the bright grass that grows upon the ashes of the fires. Or have they gone, and are the hills brown, lumpy, heather-clad, and jewelled after rain by myriad streams, merely illusions; and is it really that I myself have gone, and they live on, deep down in the recesses of some fairy hill of which I am not free?

Men, too, like my friend Wallace of Gartchorrachan, have disappeared, and I am not quite sure if we should bless the Lord on that account. All through Menteith, and right "across the hill" as far as Callander and Doune, he was well known, and always styled Laird Wallace, for though our custom is to call men by the title of their lands, thus making them *adscripti glebæ* to the very soul, the word Gartchorrachan stuck in our throats, although we readily twist and distort the Gaelic place-names in our talk just as the Spaniards mutilate the Arab words, smoothing their corners and their angles out in the strong current of their speech.

Dressed in grey tweed with bits of buckskin let into the shoulders of his coat, for no one ever saw him leave his house without a gun, he was about the age that farmers in the north seem to be born at — that is, for years he had been grey, but yet was vigorous, wore spectacles, and his thick curly hair was matted like the wool upon a ram, whilst from his ears and nostrils grew thick tufts of bristles, just as a growth of twigs springs from the trunk of an old oak tree, where it has got a wound.

His house was like himself, old, grey, and rambling, and smelt of gun oil, beeswax, and of camphor, for he was versed in entomology, and always had a case of specimens, at which he laboured with a glass stuck in his eye, reminding me of Cyclops or of Polyphemus, or of an ogre in a story-book. Botany and conchology and generally those sciences which when pursued without a method soon became trifling and a pastime, were his joys, and he had cabinets in which the specimens reposed under a heavy coat of dust, but duly ticketed each with its Latin name.

He spoke good English as a general rule, and when unmoved, as was the custom with the people of his class and upbringing, but often used broad Scotch, which he employed after the fashion of a shield against the world, half in a joking way and half against the sin of self-revealment which we shun as the plague, passing our lives like pebbles in a brook, which rub against each other for an age, and yet remain apart.

In early life he had contracted what he called a "local liassong," the fruit of which had been a daughter whom he had educated, and who lived with him, half as his daughter, half as housekeeper. Her father loved her critically, and when she not infrequently swept china on the floor as she passed through the drawing-room (just as a tapir walks about a wood, breaking down all the saplings in its path), he would screw up one eye, and looking at her say, "That's what you get from breeding from a cart-mare, the filly's sure to throw back to the dam."

Withal he was a gentleman, having been in the army and travelled in his youth, but had not got much more by his experience than the raw youth of whom his father said, "Aye, Willie's been to Rome and back again, and a' he's learnt is but to cast his sark aince every day." But still he was a kindly man, the prey of any one who had a specious story, the providence of all lame horses and of dogs quite useless for any kind of sport, all which he bought at prices far above the value of the most favoured members of their race.

His inner nature always seemed to be just struggling forth almost against his will, mastering his rough exterior, just as in pibrochs, after the skirling of the pipes has died away, a tender melody breaks out, fitful and plaintive, speaking of islands lost in misty seas, of things forgotten and misunderstood, of the faint, swishing noise of heather in the rain moved by the breeze at night, and which through minor modulations and fantastic trills ends in a wild lament for some Fingalian hero, like the wind sighing through the pines.

Nothing was more congenial to his humour than to unpack his recollections of the past, seated before the fire, an oily black cigar which he chewed almost like a quid between his teeth, and with a glass of whisky by his side.

After expatiating upon the excellencies of his lame, jibbing chestnut mare, that he had bought at Falkirk Tryst from a quite honest dealer, but which had gone mysteriously so lame that even whisky for his groom had no effect in curing her, he usually used to lament upon the changes which the course of time had brought about. All was a grief to him, as it is really to all of us, if we all knew it, that some particular landmark of his life had disappeared. No one spoke Gaelic nowadays, although he never in his life had known a word of it. The use of "weepers" and crape hat-bands by the country-folk on Sunday was quite discontinued, and no one took their collie dogs to church. Coffins were now no longer carried shoulder-high across the hills from lonely upland straths, as he remembered to have seen them in his youth. Did not some funeral party in his childhood, taking a short cut on a frozen loch, fall through and perish to a man? — a circumstance he naturally deplored, but still regretted, as men of older generations may have regretted highwaymen, as they sat safely by their fire. Although he never fished, he was quite certain no one now alive could busk a fly as well as a departed worthy of his youth, one Dan-a-Haltie, or make a withy basket or those osier loops which formerly were stuck between the "divots" in a dry stone dike, projecting outwards like a torpedo netting, to stop sheep jumping from a field. Words such as *flauchtered feal* and *laroch* were hardly understood; shepherds read newspapers as they lay out upon the hill, the Shorter Catechism had been miserably abridged, and the old fir-tree by the Shannochill was blasted at the top.

All these complaints he uttered philosophically, not in a plaintive way, but as a man who, at his birth, had entered as it were into a covenant with life just as it was, which he for his part had faithfully observed, but was deceived by fate.

Then when he had relieved his mind he used to laugh and, puffing out the smoke of his thick black cigar, which hung about the tufts which sprung out of his nostrils, just as the mist hangs dank above a bog, he would remark, "I'm haverin'," as if he was afraid of having to explain himself to something in his mind. On these occasions, I used to let him sit a little, and usually he would begin again, after a look to see if I had noticed the gag he suddenly had put upon himself, and then start off again. "Ye mind my aunt, Miss Christian Jean?" I did, eating her sweetmeats in my youth, and trembling at her frown.

"Ye never heard me tell how it was I kisted her," he said, and then again fell into contemplation, and once again began. "My aunt, Miss Christian Jean, was a survival of the fittest — aye, ye know I am in some things quite opposed to Darwin, the survival of the potter's wheel in the Fijis and several other things . . . aye, haverin' again . . . or the most unfitted to survive.

"She was a gentlewoman, . . . yes, yes, the very word is now half ludicrous, ye need not smile, . . . lady is a poor substitute. Tall, dark, and masculine, and with a down upon her upper lip that many a cornet of dragoons, for there were cornets in those days, might well have envied, she was a sort of providence, jealous and swift in chastisement, but yet a providence to all the younger members of her race who came across her path.

"I see her now, her and her maid, old Katherine Sinclair, a tall, gaunt Highland woman, who might easily have walked straight from the pages of Rob Roy, and her old butler, Robert Cameron, grey and red-faced, and dressed eternally in a black suit, all stained with snuff, a pawky sort of chiel, religious and still with the spirit of revolt against all dogmatism which modern life and cheap and stereotyped instruction has quite stamped out to-day. My aunt kept order in her house, that is as far as others were concerned. Each day she read her chapter, in what she styled the Book, not taking over heed how she selected it, so that the chapter once was duly read. It happened sometimes that when she came into the room where, as my cousin Andrew used to say — ye mind that he was drowned in one of those Green's ships, fell from aloft whilst they were reefing topsails in a dark night somewhere about the Cape.

"I've heard him say he could come down the weather-leach of a topsail, just like a monkey, by the bolt ropes. . . . Where was I, eh? Aye, I mind, he used to say that my aunt's prayers reminded him of service in a ship, with all hands mustered; so as I said, my aunt would sometimes open up the book and come upon a chapter full of names, and how some one begat another body and sometimes upon things perfectly awesome for a maiden lady to read aloud, for 'twas all one to her.

"Then the old butler would put his hand up to his mouth and whisper, 'Mem, Miss Christian, Mem, ye're wandered,' and she would close the book, or start again upon another chapter and maybe twice as long.

"My aunt and her two satellites kept such good order, that a visitor from England, seeing her neat and white-capped maids file in and take their seats facing the menservants, expressed her pleasure at the well ordered, comely worship, and received the answer, 'Yes, my dear, ye see at family prayers we have the separation of the sexes, but I understand when they meet afterwards at the stair foot, the kissing beats the cracking of a whip.'

"Poor Aunt Christian, I used to shiver at her nod, and well remember when a youth how she would flyte me when I pinched the maids, and say, 'Laddie, I canna' have you making the girls squeal like Highland ponies; it is not decent, and decency comes next after morality, sometimes, I think, before it, for it can be attained, whereas the other is a counsel of perfection set up on high, but well out of our reach.'

"A pretty moraliser was my poor aunt, almost a heathen in her theory, guided by what she said were natural laws, and yet a Puritan in practice, whereas I always was a theoretic Puritan, but shaped my life exclusively by natural laws, as they appear to me.

"Let ministers just haver as they will, one line of conduct is not possible for nephews and for aunts. Take David, now, the man after the Lord's own heart, and ask yourself what would have happened if his aunt . . . aye, aye, I'm wandered from my tale . . . I ken I'm wandering.

"Well, well, it seemed as if my aunt might have gone on for ever, getting a little dryer and her face more peakit, as the years went by and her old friends dropped off and left her all alone. That's what it is, ye see; it's got to come, although it seems impossible whilst we sit talking here and drinking — that is, I drinking and you listening to me talk. One wintry day I was just sitting wiping the cee-spring of a gun, and looking out upon the avenue, when, through the wreaths, I saw a boy on a bit yellow pony-beast come trotting through the snow.

"It was before the days of telegrams, and I jaloused that there was something special, or no one would have sent the laddie out on such a day, with the snow drifted half a yard upon the ground, the trees all white with cranruch like the sugar on a cake, and the frost keen enough to split a pudding stone and grind it into sand.

"I sent the laddie to the kitchen fire, and ripped the envelope, whilst the bit pony rooted round for grass and walked upon the reins. The letter told me that my aunt had had a fit, was signed by 'Robert Cameron, butler,' and was all daubed with snuff, and in a postscript I was asked to hurry, for the time was short, and to come straight across the hill as the low road was blocked by the snow drifting and nobody could pass. I harnessed up my mare — not the bit blooded chestnut I drive now" — this was the way in which he spoke of the lame cripple which had conveyed him to my house — "but a stout sort of Highland mouse-coloured beastie that I had, rather short backit, a little hammer-headed, and with the hair upon the fetlocks like a Clydesdale. . . .Maun, I think ye dinna' often see such sort of beasts the now." I mentally thanked God for it, and he again launched out into his tale.

"An awful drive, I'm tellin' ye! I hadna' got above Auchyle — ye mind, at the old bridge just where yon English tourist coupit his creels, and gaed to heaven, maybe last summer — when I saw I had a job. The snow balled in the mare's feet as big as cabbages, and made her stotter in her gait, just like a drunken curler ettlin' to walk upon a rink. I had to take her by the head till we got on the flat ground, up about Rusky. Man, it was arctic, and the little loch lay like a sheet of glass that had been breathed upon, with the dead bulrushes and reeds all sticking through the ice! The island in the loch seemed but a blob of white, and the old tower (I dinna' richtly mind if, at one time, it belonged to some of your own folk) loomed up like Stirling Castle or like Doune in the keen frosty air. The little firwood on the east side of the old change-house — that one they called Wright, or some such name, once keepit — was full of roe, all sheltering like cows, so cold and starved they scarcely steered when I passed by and gave a shout to warm my lungs and hearten up the mare; and a cock capercailzie, moping and miserable, sat on a fir tree like a barn-door fowl. I ploutered on just to where there used to be a gate across the road, where ye see Uamh Var and the great shoulder of Ben Ledi stretching up out by the pass of Leny and the old chapel of St. Bryde. It was fair awesome; I did not rightly know the landscape with the familiar features blotted out. I very nearly got myself wandered just in the straight above the Gart, for all the dikes were sunk beneath the snow, and the hedge-tops peeped up like box in an old cabbage-garden. At last I reached the avenue, the mare fair taigled, and the ice hanging from her fetlocks and her mane and wagging to and fro. The evergreens were, so to speak, a-wash, and looked like beds of parsley or of greens, and underneath the trees the squirrels' footsteps in the snow seemed those of some strange birds, where they had melted and then frozen on the ground. Across the sky a crow or two flew slowly, flapping their wings as if the joint oil had been frozen in their bones and cawing sullenly.

"On the high steps which led up to the door the butler met me, and as he took my coat, said, 'Laird, ye are welcome; your poor dear auntie's going. Hech, sirs, 'twill be an awfu' nicht for the poor leddy to be fleein' naked through the air towards the judgment-seat. Will ye tak speerits or a dish o' tea after your coldsome drive, or will I tak' ye straight in to your aunt? I'm feared she willna' know you. But His will be done, though I could wish He micht hae held His hand a little longer; but we must not repine. I've just been readin' out to her from the old Book, ye ken, passin' the time awa' and waitin' for the end.'

"All day my aunt lay dozing, half-conscious and half-stupefied, and all the day the butler, sitting by the bed, read psalms and chapters, to which she sometimes seemed to pay attention, and at others lay so still we thought that she was dead. Now and again he stopped his reading, and peering at his mistress with his spectacles pushed up, wiped off the tears that trickled down his face with his red handkerchief, and, as if doubting he were reading to the living or the dead, said, 'Nod yer heid,

Miss Christian,' which she did feebly, and he, satisfied she understood, mumbled on piously in a thick undertone.

"Just about morning she passed away quite quietly, the maids and butler standing round the bed, they crying silently, and he snorting in his red pocket-handkerchief, with the tears running down his face. The gaunt old Highland waiting-woman raised a high wail which echoed through the cold and silent house, causing the dogs to bark and the old parrot scream, and the butler stottered from the room, muttering that he would go and see if tea was ready, closing the door behind him with his foot, as if he feared the figure on the bed would scold him, as she had often done during her life, if it slammed to and made a noise.

"All the week through it snowed, and my aunt's house was dismal, smelling of cheese and honey, yellow soap, of jam, of grease burnt in the fire, and with the dogs and cats uncared for rambling about and sleeping on the chairs. The cold was penetrating, and I wandered up and down the stairs quite aimlessly, feeling like Alexander Selkirk in the melancholy house, which seemed an island cut off from the world by a white sea of snow. None of Aunt Christian's friends or relatives could come, as all the roads were blocked; even her coffin was not sent till a few hours before the funeral, the cart that brought it stalling in the snow, and the black-coated undertaker's men carrying it shoulder-high through the thick wreaths upon the avenue.

"The servants would not have a stranger touch the corpse, and the old butler and myself kisted my aunt, lifting her body from the bed between the two of us. A week had passed and she looked black and shrunken, and as I lifted her, the chill from the cold flesh struck me with horror, and welled into the bones. I could not kiss her as she lay like a mummy in the kist, for the shrunk face with the white clothes about the chin was not the same Aunt Christian's, whom I had loved and before whom I trembled for so many years, but changed somehow and horrible to see.

"The butler did, looking at me, as I thought, half reproachfully as I stood silently, not once crying but half stupefied, and then as she lay shrunken and brown on the white satin lining of the kist, we stood and looked at one another, just as we had been partners in a crime, till they began to hammer down the lid. A drearsome sound it makes. One feels the nails are sticking in the flesh, and every time ye hear it, it just affects ye more than the last time, the same as an earthquake, as I mind I heard a traveller say one day in Edinburgh. What the old butler did, I do not mind; but I just dandered out into the garden, and washed my hands in snow, not that I felt a skunner at my poor Aunt Christian's flesh, but somehow I had to do it, for ye ken 'twas the first time."

Laird Wallace stopped just as a horse props suddenly when he is fresh and changes feet, then breaking into Scotch, said: "I have talked enough. That's how I kisted my Aunt Christian Jean, puir leddy, a sair job it was, and dreich. . . . Thank ye, nae soddy, I'll tak' a drop of Lagavoulin." Then lighting a cigar, he said, "Ring for my dog-cart, please," and when it came he clambered to the seat, and pointing to his spavined mare, said, "Man, a gran' beast, clean thorough-bred, fit to run for her life" (and this to me who knew her); then, bidding me good-night, drew his whip smartly on her scraggy flank, and vanished through the trees.

His People

Tobar na Reil

Right at the summit of the pass it lies, nothing above it but the sky. On every side the billowing heath-clad hills engirdle it about. Flat stones encircle it, and on its surface water spiders walk. Red persicaria, with wax-like stalks and ragged leaves, grows by its edge. Below it stretches out a vast brown moss, honeycombed here and there with black peat hags, and a dark lake spreads out, ringed on one side with moss, and on the other set like a jewel in a pine wood, with a white stretch of intervening sand. On it are islands with great sycamores and chestnuts, stag-headed but still vigorous, and round their shores the bulrushes keep watch like sentinels. Mists rise from moss and lake and creep about the corries of the hills, blending the woods and rocks into a steamy chaos, vast and unfathomable, through which a little burn unseen, but musical, runs tinkling through the stones. So at the little *bealach* the well lies open to the sky, too high for the lake mists to touch it, as it looks up at the stars.

They say that on a certain day in mid-summer, a star when at its zenith shines into the well. Which the star is, if Rigel or Algól or Aldebáran with his russet fire, is clean forgotten, for nowadays tradition has scant place in men's imagining. He who looks on the water at the fateful hour, and sees the star reflected in the well, acquires again the ancient universal tongue, by which in ages past men and the animals held speech. For him the language of the birds becomes intelligible. The trees that groan or whisper in the breeze divulge their lore, and disclose all that they have seen in their long peaceful lives. Fish in the rivers and the lakes have no more dread of him, and, rising to the surface of the linns, tell him the marvels of the deep, whilst snakes and lizards, with newts, the moles and bats, impart their troubles or their joys, making their little secrets plain, by the strange virtues of the mystic star transmitted through the well.

There is no record of any one who, having drunk, obtained the power and straightway got into communication with all animals and things. No doubt if at the appointed hour the fountain had turned all to gold, a town would have arisen on the pass, and Baal's priesthood or an aristocracy would have reserved the right to drink and gaze upon the well, and temples of Algól or Aldebáran would have sprung up as if by magic from the hill. But man, who lives an outcast from all living things, cut off by pride and want of sympathy from beasts and birds, and careless of his own connection with the world except so far as it may bring him the twin curses, wealth and power, which have combined to make him vile, cared not for such a gift. So trees and animals and beasts, with stones and streams, watched vainly every recurring year throughout the centuries for some adventurer who should break through the bonds which held the self-crowned monarch of the world in silence, condemned for ever to live dumb but to his own kind's speech, whilst on all sides secrets he never dreamed of were waiting to be heard. So as a Highlander went past, driving his cattle from the low country in Menteith, or in the summer evenings a group of men wrapped in their plaids, with curly hazel shepherd's sticks, and carrying long single-barrelled Spanish guns, trotted along the steep and winding path, their deerskin shoes making no sound upon the stones, the rabbits sitting at their holes watched them expectantly. The birds upon the branches turned their round heads and looked towards the well. The trees and plants and heather on the hill seemed to sigh softly in the summer air, as if inviting them to halt until the mystic star should rise, then drink and break the spell.

But they, absorbed in the affairs of life, which lead men onward prisoners to the grave, discoursed of hogs and pownie-beasts, of trysts and markets, and of the price of hirsells and of queys. At times they stopped and drank, but never lingered, scooping the water in their palms or in their *cuachan* of birch-wood hooped with silver, drawing their hands across their mouths, and sometimes murmuring, "Aye, och aye, they say that when a body drinks here, when the stars are up, he learns a vast o' things, that's why they ca' it *Tobar na Reil*, but I mind lying here aince o' a summer's nicht, sleeping ye ken, after some awqua that I had doon by at old McKureton's, and never learned a thing."

And whilst they talked, the trees and stars, half-sleeping in the cold moon's light, listened but drowsily, and all they heard was Angus answer Finlay, "Och aye, McKureton just keeps the finest awqua that I ever drank no more, Finlay McLachlan," and his compeer and fellow-driver, looking up whilst kneeling by the spring, would answer sapiently, "And neither did I too." And so the well slept on, having for its one tragedy the fight between the Grahams of Menteith, and Stuarts on a raid from Appin, whose leader's head, struck by a sword-cut from his body at a blow, rolled down the pass, calling out imprecations even after death.

With the exception of this brief tragedy, history the well has none. Its very name means nothing to the men who now inhabit, where once its namers dwelt. The legend lives as a tradition, to be laughed or wondered at, according to the attitude of mind of him who hears it, for education has new superstitions of its own, which have expelled those of the older race. Who that to-day, when all flee from responsibility as from the plague, would incur the burden of the sorrow of the trees, the winds, the beasts? for man aspires not to equality but to command, by which, when he possesses it, he straightly becomes an outcast from his kind.

Yet, had it been but for the pleasure of another sorrow to his life, 'tis strange that no one quenched his thirst, for joy is transient, whilst sorrow lives for ever, and to prove sorrows yet unknown might have stirred some one with imagination, had there been any such a traveller on the road which winds by Glenny to the valley of the Teith. And yet the district set with *Sith-bhrughan* and with traditions of a fairy causeway in the lake, a borderland of races in the past, a frontier where the Lowland hob and Highland pixie met on neutral ground, to dance upon the green, seemed to invite experiment, and call for its Columbus to explore a newer world than that he saw in Guanaháni from his caravel.

A gentle world in which no hatred reigns; where envy and all malice are unknown, where each one tells his secret to his friend unwittingly, because the speech they use is universal and without volition, and not as ours, confined to persons and articulate. The speech that lives in the clear water of the well, at the conjuncture of the star, has no vocabulary, no rules, no difficulties, but he who has it, speaks as does the wind, and saying nothing in particular, is understood of all. Thus it can never lie, or lead astray, and so is valueless to us, as valueless as gold upon a desert island, with no one to enslave.

No one has claimed it since the first framers of the legend paddled their coracles upon the lake; no one will claim it, or ever think but for an instant of the treasure waiting to be grasped. Red-deer and roe and kyloes on the hills are all born free of it, and swallows from the south need no interpreter, but straightway tell their travels to the birds who but a week ago have left the pole, or to the weasels and the wrens who never wandered more than a mile or two from where they saw the light; they find themselves as much at home amongst the scrubby copse, as they were, only a month ago, in cane brakes and in palms.

But if the birds and beasts, the trees and grasses and the stones, mourn the estrangement and the want of faith of man, so does mankind feel vaguely its own loneliness amongst created things with which it cannot have communication, and before which it always must be dumb. What tender idylls moss and lichens could unfold, if only some one of the passers-by throughout the centuries had learned their speech, and taught his children, taking them, as the most sacred duty in his power, upon the star's appearance in its round, to drink and learn, and thus transmit their knowledge to their children, making them all hereditary dragomen by right divine, betwixt their race and the creation of the beasts.

Drink and admire, the motto says, upon the well in far Marrákesh set among its palms. Above the fountain, built by some pious pilgrim, who perhaps had felt the desert's thirst and reared this monument to the one God — He who alone brings comfort in the sands — the horseshoe arch is blue with pottery. Intricate patterns marked in lustrous tiles cross and recross each other, and arabesques repeat some pious saw or play upon God's name. Over the humble fountain on the pass unknown to fame, the skies are canopy, and the stars set in them, celestial glow-worms of the firmament, which mark the hours the passers-by neglect. No pious pilgrim there has hedged about the spring with masonry; no sculptured stone relates its virtues, for it serves but as a drinking-place for roe, who as they drink admire and give their thanks instinctively, wiser by far than man. No one remembers the lone well among the heath or cares for it, but to smile scornfully at the old simple legend of the past. In all the district where it lies, few know its bearings, and for the name, refer to it "as a sort o' Gaelic fash aboot a star; I mind my feyther kent the meaning o' it," dismissing it at once as "juist a haver, auncient but fair redeeklous, an auld wife's clishmaclaver," beneath the notice of an "eddicated man."

So it sleeps quietly upon the pass just where the road descends to Vennachar and rises from Menteith. Winds sweep the bents and rustle in the ling, setting the cotton-grass a-quivering, bowing the heads of the bog asphodel, and carrying with them the sharp perfume of the gale, sweeter and homelier than the spice of Araby.

In the dark mirror of the lake below, the priory and the castle hang head downwards, and on the bulrushed shore the wavelets break amongst the stones. The earl's old pleasance, now neglected, is a park for cows, its few surviving sycamores have withered at the top, and soon will follow those who planted them into the misty region of the past.

The well, the star, the scrubby oak copse on the hill, the old Fingalian road, distinct in moonlight, or in the morning after frost, for time itself appears unable to efface the taint man's footsteps leave upon the ground, remain and call to the chance passer-by to stop and drink at the conjunction of the star. They call in vain, and nature in the breeze still raises its lament, uncomprehended by the ears of man, who, in his self-forged fetters, fails to understand.

His People

The Grey Kirk

In a grey valley between hills, shut out from all the world by mist and moors, there lies a village with a little church.

The ruined castle in the reedy loch, by which stand herons fishing in the rank growth of flags, of bulrush and hemp-agrimony which fringes it, is scarcely greyer than the hills. The outcrop of the stone is grey, the louring clouds, the slated roofs, the shingly river's bed and the clear water of the stream. The very trout that dart between the stones, or hang suspended where the current joins the linn, look grey as eels.

Green markings on the moors show where once paths the border prickers followed on their wiry nags led towards the south, the land of fatted beeves and well-stored larders, clearly designed by Providence or fate to be the jackman's prey, but long disused, forgotten and grassed over, though with the ineffaceable imprint of immemorial use still clear.

Dark, geometrical plantations of black fir and spruce deface the hills, which nature evidently made to bear a coat of scrubby oak and birch. Wire fences gird them round, the posts well tarred against the weather, and the barbed wire so taut that the fierce winds might use them as Æolian harps, could they but lend themselves to song.

A district which the wildness of the past has so impressed, that the main line of railway steals through its corries and across its moors as it were under protest, and where the curlew mocks the engine's whistle with his wilder cry.

The village clusters round the kirk, as bees crowd round their queen, the older houses thatched. Their coping-stones carved with a rope, remain to show how, in the older world, their rustic architects secured their roofs against the blast.

No doubt the hamlet grew between the castle and the church. The jackman of the chief, the sacristan and kindly tenants of the church, ready and near at hand to put on splent and spur, and able to take lance or sprig of hyssop in their hand at the first tinkle of the bell or rout of horn.

The castle in the loch has dwindled to a pile of stones, from which spring alders, birches and sycamores, whose keys hang yellow in the wind, unlocking nothing but the sadness of the heart, which marks their growth, from the decay of the abandoned keep.

A modern mansion set with its shrubberies and paltry planted woods, where once the Caledonian forest sheltered the wild white cattle in its glades, seems out of place in the surrounding grey. Its lodge, with trim-cut laurels and with aucubas and iron gate, run in a foundry from a mould, is trivial, comfortable and modern; and the low sullen hills appear to scorn it in their fight with time, for they remain unchanged from the bold time of rugging and of rieving *[sic=reiving]*, when spearsmen, not a pensioned butler, kept the gate.

The crumbling and decayed stone wall, secluding jealously the boggy meadows of the park, shuts off the modern mansion with its electric light, its motor-cars, its liveried servants and its air of castellated meanness, from the old houses huddling in the wynd. They look towards the chapel with its high-pitched roof, its squat round tower with crenellated top and its sharp windows pointed like a lance. It seems to gaze at them, as if it felt they were the only links that time has left it with its old own world. The eye avoids the modern buildings in the town, the parish church, four square and hideous, with windows like a house, and from the hills falls on the chapel and is satisfied. Only in some old missal, with the illustrations by some monk adscribed to his small round of daily cares, can you behold its equal, as it stands desolate and grey.

The chapel of a race of warriors, men dark and grey as is the stone of which its walls are built, once a lone outpost of the great mother fort in Rome, it lingers after them, sheltering their tombs and speaking of their fame. Instinctively one feels that once its doors stood open, just as it were a mosque or church in lands where faith continues the whole week, and men pray as they eat or sleep, just when they feel inclined, and naturally as birds.

In the green churchyard, whose grassy hillocks wave it like a sea, the long grey tombstones of the undistinguished dead appear like boats that make towards some haven, laying their courses by the beacon of the tower.

The church itself floats like a ship turned bottom upwards on the grassy sea. Its voyage is ended, and the men who once clattered in armour in its aisles and through its nave now sleep below its flags. A maiméd ritual and a sterner creed prevail, and those who worship in the church have shown their faith by laying down encaustic tiles over the spur-marked stones on which their forebears jingled in their mail. A fair communion table of hewn stone, smug and well-finished and with the wounds upon the bleeding heart all stanched (as one would think), stands where the altar stood, cold and uninteresting, a symbol of the age. *Non ragioniam*; on every side, lie those who, in their time, carried their wars across the border, and on the bridge at Rome charged on the people who pressed round them, just as they would have charged in Edinburgh, had any other clan presumed to take the croon of the old causeway of the High Street, and brought upon themselves an excommunication from the Pope.

Stretched under canopies of stone they lie, looking so grim and so impenitent, that one is sure they must be satisfied with their presentments, if, looking down on their old haunts, they see their images. Many are absent who would have filled a niche right worthily, Tineman and the Black Knight of Jedburgh and others of the house, who, in their time, shook Scotland to the core. But in the middle of the aisle, in leaden caskets hooped with iron and padlocked, lie two hearts. One, that of Archibald who belled the cat. The other heart has travelled much, and in its life beat higher with all generous thoughts than any of its race.

He who possessed it (or was possessed by it), liked ever better, as he said, to hear the laverocks' singing than the cheeping of the mouse. His hands were able, all his adventurous life, to keep his cheeks from scars, as he averred in Seville to the Spanish knight, who wondered at their absence from his face. Carrying a heart to Palestine, he fell, not in the Holy Land, but on the frontiers of Granada, that last outpost of the Eastern world. The heart he carried lies at Melrose, and his own, sealed fast in lead, soldered perhaps in some wild camp lost in the Ajaráfé of Sevilla, is the chief ornament of the grey chapel of his race.

Set like a ship, the chapel lies in the long waves of sullen hill and moor that roll away towards the south.

In its long voyage through the sea of time, crews of wild warriors have clung to it, as their one refuge from the spear of life. Each in their turn have fallen away, leaving it lonely, but still weather-tight and taut; a monument of faith, as some may think, or of good masonry and well-slaked lime, as the profane may say, still sailing on the billowy moors which stretch towards Muirkírk; so little altered that any one of those who in the past have prayed within its walls, if he returned to a changed world, would cling to it as the one thing he knew.

So it drifts on upon its voyage through time, bearing its freight of warriors to their port.

His People

Dagos

Cadiz was stifling, and all the world sat waiting for the breeze. In the dark streets, which cut like drains right through the town, not a breath stirred to break the heat. The cries of water-sellers, with their guttural "Aguaa," long prolonged and Arab sounding, broke the still air, just as a corncrake's cry falls on the ear as a relief, when in the wheat-fields of the south the sun pours down as he would bake the earth, and seems to set the air in motion by its sound. The gardens in the plazas drooped, and the long bells of the daturas closed up as if they slept the siesta during the hot hours.

The city lay, a very cup of burnished silver, in the fierce glare, and in the waters of the bay the pink and blue and yellow houses were reflected, looking as if a coral reef had turned into a town. The waves just crept about the great black shoal known as "Las Puercas," lazily swashing on the cruel stones which have so often pierced the sides of ships, in winter, when the Levanté blows.

Men slept in rows on the lee side of boats. The horses in the cabs hung their tired heads, and where a man threw water at a café door upon the street, a steam ascended, as if the stones were heated underneath.

Only upon the alameda, that of Apodaca, where the sea-breeze first strikes, the palm trees braved the sun, seeming to draw new life from out its rays; and at their tops there ran a murmur, as when a little air just plays upon the outside leach of a lateen, making it crinkle up before it fills the belly of the sail and strains upon the sheet.

But in the cafés of the Calle Ancha the people, sitting drinking their *horchata* and *agráz*, talked just as loud and just as earnestly as if their conversation ran on some great principle, or as if something was at stake. Upon the shady side, the ladies, their faces white with powder, which made their great black eyes look larger and more lustrous, walked up and down, swaying a little on their hips, just as a thoroughbred walks in the paddock before saddling, receiving as they went a shower of compliments and *quodlibets*, which would have made a woman unaccustomed to such fire fairly turn tail and run, but which just made the colour heighten a little underneath the powder on their cheeks, increased the flame of their black eyes, and made the swaying of their walk a little more pronounced as they held on their course, as the feluccas in the bay stood up to a beam wind.

Just at the corner of the Calle Columela at a small café where sailors congregate, a fan shop on one side and on the other a *refino*, a group of men sat talking lazily.

At last, one rising, said, "I hear it coming," and as he spoke, up the deep street there came a sighing, and the breeze, bearing a little flight of bats before it, which passed like swallows just above the heads of all the idlers with a shrill twittering, came rushing through the funnel made by the houses, after the fashion of a bore, when it ascends a river on a low, shoaly coast.

It came, bending the palm trees with its sweep, making their leaves all rustle on the trunks, and spreading a red haze over the low and arid hills above San Lucar, and by Rota, and making ships at anchor at the Trocadero balance a little as the white lacy net of foam ran seething past their bows.

Within the town it worked a wondrous change, for when the dust it brought at first had cleared away, the horses in the cabs pricked up their ears and looked as if ten years had been rolled off their lives; the loafers on the quays got up and shook themselves, throwing their tattered jackets, which had served for pillows on the stones, across their shoulders, and, after having looked out seaward with a long stare at the horizon to see if any vessel was in sight, straggled in groups towards the plaza to pass the evening on the seats.

Fans worked less lazily, and in the cafés men, after lighting cigarettes, mopped their wet brows and settled down to talk, which in the little fairy city, with its long piles of dazzling salt ringing it round like outworks to landward, and its blue sea which, dashing up against the walls, showers spray upon the blood and orange banner on the low ramparts of the fort, is the chief object of their lives.

The sailors in the little café, captains of ships of every nation upon earth, all felt the spell of the invigorating breeze, and by degrees their talk after a few attempts at topics which to most landsmen have a certain vogue, as horses, women, theatres, and politics, soon by degrees drifted back naturally to the one subject of real interest, the sea, the element by which all lived, and which whilst all abusing so had wound itself about their lives as to exclude aught else as absolutely as if they had been born in it, like porpoises or whales. Mostly the men were northerners, blue-eyed and freckled Swedes, Danes, or Norwegians, whose rough serge clothes and heavy boots contrasted strangely with the stray Spaniards and Italians who in their pointed-toed, white canvas shoes and spotless linen scarcely looked sailors beside their brethren from the North, whose huge red hands beat on the table when they emphasized their points, like a door banging in the wind.

Two things, however, formed a link between them, the sea, and that they all spoke English, more or less broken, as a common *lingua franca* in which they all could meet.

Captain Karl Harold, who had sailed for five-and-thirty years out of his little native port in Norway, bringing down deals to Malaga, to Almeria, and to the other ports in what he called "the Middle Sea," sat smoking a great meerschaum pipe, on which a boar-hunt was depicted carved in high relief. His great red throat was cut across by the thin narrow linen band of his grey flannel shirt, till it looked like one portion of an hour-glass, and you divined that underneath it must be thinner and probably quite white. A small straw hat was set upon the back of his enormous head, and on his forehead stood great beads of perspiration, which he mopped up continually with a red pocket-handkerchief quite large enough to hoist upon a raft supposing he had suddenly been wrecked.

Quiet and unassuming, he sat drinking beer which disappeared down his capacious throat just as a fishing-boat may be sucked in and disappear from sight when caught at certain junctures of the tides in Coirebhreacain whirlpool or in the Moskoe-Strom. His speech was slow, and as he talked of countries he had seen, of port dues, of the villainies of certain governments which kept no lights on dangerous places of their coasts, his curly golden fleece, flecked here and there with grey, shaken by his emotion, set one a-thinking of what a sheep would look like if it could be endued with understanding and wake up to a sense of all the wrongs it and its kind endured at the fell hands of man.

"Gadiss," he said, "is fine little town; not too much cultivated the people in it; no man have heard of Ibsen; . . . de beer is goot too, but not very strong. I bore myself soon in Gadiss, and never can get any repairs done to my ship. I have mine main-yard littel sprung now, and have to go round to Gartagena to get it fixed. The theatre too is elementary, and have no psychologic in it. . . . . Their dancing is goot, the Romans knew that. 'Impropa Gadiss,' they say, but I think perhaps Liverpool or

Gardiff is more wicked as Gadiss, for the peoples is not so elementary as here. . . . Uf, ah, it is still hot! Can none of you tell us some story, eh? You, McMillan, or Fernandey, eh? Don Joesay, Why you not tell us littel something, eh?"

Before Fernandez had time to speak, Captain McMillan cut in with: "Ay, Fernandey, something aboot yon time you had the blackbird-catching schooner, when ye ran niggers up to North Queensland from the New Hebrides. Man, a gran' business that slaving — I mean the importation of indentured labour. I've heard it was a fair saxty per cent job. . . . Saxty per cent! — worth a little risking in these days o' low freights and big insurance money. I mind I had a wee bit flutter, way back in the sixties, wi' a bit cargo, ane o' the last was run. I landed them in a wee port — na, na, I'll no tell ye the name o' it — doon aboot Rio Grande do Sul, the Brazeels, ye ken. A queer felly yon king up at Loandy; we ca'ed him Brass Belly, and a Christian too, except of course when there was business on. Weel, they just had a friar up in the bit port, before I got my stuff on board . . . thae "Portygees," ye ken . . . and had them a' baptized . . . just throwing holy water on them in a horn, and mumbling a wheen Latin, and makin' crosses in the air — fair superstition, I ca'ed it; and I'm telling ye, when aince I got to sea I had out the old Book, and just undid his job . . . had them a' resprinkled, and pit up a bit prayer ower them in the Free Kirk o' Scotland style. There was no reunion o' the free churches in thae days . . . nane o' your U.F's set them up. A wheen o' they newly admitted Christians died on the passage, but the lave o' them I got safe enough to Rio Grande do Sul, and, man, a gran' price I got for them. Nae one ever jaloused they were all sort of members of the Free Kirk, or God knows what would ha' happened. They Brazeelians are a superstitious lot. . . . Tell us yer yarn, Captain Fernandey; oot wi' it, Don Joesay."

He paused, and opened a bottle of soda-water, letting the cork fly with a bang and most of the contents spurt out, and then pouring himself about a claret glass of whisky, tempered it slightly with what soda still remained, and drained it to the dregs, but slowly and with as little effort as if it had been milk.

Boys selling lottery tickets dangled them underneath the noses of the customers, beseeching them to buy and win the biggest prize; beggars came in and stood behind the tables resisting all the objurgations of the assembled northern skippers and disappearing instantly when they heard

Captain Fernandez say "May God assist you" in a quiet tone of voice. Silent and rather dapper-looking, he sat sipping lemonade, smoking innumerable cigarettes, and now and then assenting gravely with a "*Bueno!* Yes, that iss so," or merely by a slight clicking of his tongue against the palate and a faint upward motion of the head.

Short, slight, and burned so dark you might have thought that he had Indian blood; one thin and nervous hand, on which a heavy diamond ring shone like electric light, held his eternal cigarette; the other now and then stole almost unconsciously behind his back and rested for an instant, as if to reassure himself that it was there, upon a little hump formed by the handle of his pistol underneath his coat.

As all his fellows looked at him he slightly flicked the ash off from his cigarette against the edge of the white marble table around which they sat, and blowing out an interminable cloud of smoke from both his nostrils, said: "Why, you fellows want to hear a tale; it is still time to see the third piece at the theatre, or we can go and hear the Mochuelito sing 'Las Chiclaneras.' How he bewails himself, the little gipsy rogue; not his like in all the Spains to hang upon a note." No one adventuring anything except a grunt from Captain Harold that "De folk music of the zooth, with de irregular intervals it have, say nothing to me." Fernandez slowly began to speak, half automatically: "My friends, I think of something happen to me long ago; plenty of the psychology in it, Captain Karl, enough to satisfy your Ibsen, he who have so much grace." The passing jibe left Captain Harold quite unmoved save for a puffing out of his great cheeks and a slight blowing sound as when a whale has finished spouting and lies upon the water as if it contemplated whether it should begin again or sink into the depths. "It was way back — my God! I think it was thirty-five, perhaps forty year passed. I was third mate in a Peruvian barquentine trading from Paita, up the coast to San Francisco, Guaymas, San Blas, and Mazatlán, Salina-Cruz, Tehuantepec, and Acapulco, and all those littel ports in Mexico.

"The barquentine was built in Paita. Beautiful she was; they never build no such vessels now these days."

"Stow the description," cut in McMillan; "I never had a guid conceit o' thae bit Paity barquentines. . . . Yon way of staying forward the topgallant mast and lashing every sail down to a spar, looks fair theatrical. . . ."

"All is in the taste, my McMillan. You talk about your Scotch girls and say nothing like number one West Highland lassie; she have straight back, short leg, and head like sunset, I think she look like German dachshund. . . . All is in the taste. . . . Where was I now? Ah, yes, the barquentine. She was called 'La Estrella de Paita.' She was clipper number one. . . . I see her now; she sit upon the water just as she had been blown there like a leaf off a tree.

"She was all right, it was the people that was in her that was bad. Most of them Indians — Cholos from the Bolivian ports and from Peru, one or two Correntinos from the Argentine Republic, half gauchos and half sailors, and with another part half devils, the cook a negro from about Panama or Savanilla, and two or three quite decent fishermen from Chiloé. You bet your ole sea-boot you have to keep your weather-eye well skin with all those infidels.

"The skipper was a Mexican, hail from Arispé. Cristo, what a man! He knew the coast blind-drunk and blindfold, and that was all he know.

"Ah, yes, Captain Karl Harold say, come heave round Rodney, and it is time, and it is true I am a little slow in making plain sail on my yarn.

"Well, let me see. . . . Yes, we were dodging up the coast of Lower California, inside what we call Sea of Cortés and you the Californian Gulf. We have well passed the islands at the mouth; islands of Revillagigedo they are call, and their names San Benito, La Nublada, and cetera. We lay a little in towards the coast between San Blas and Mazatlán to catch the lightest air; the 'Estrella' sail almost if a lady move a fan. . . . But I say no more of her, eh. You know that coast, eh, friends?"

"I know him well," said Captain Karl, "just like the coast where Peer Gynt's yacht was lost and he find Providence not economical. Wonderful man dat Ibsen, what you call bawky up in Aberdeen."

"Pawky, you mean," said the indignant Scot, and once again Fernandez launched into his tale.

"Baffling light winds force us across amongst the islands opposite Cabo Haro upon the other coast. What so many islands and none of them inhabited by man — La Trinidad, Espiritu Santo; what you call Holy Spirit, and Branciforte, Isla del Carmen — islands and still more islands, till you can have no rest. Just about midday we were running under easy sail under the lee of the large Isla del Carmen, hoping to get a slant of wind across to Guaymas to take us through the strait.

"What salt there is in Carmen Island, eh — green, white, and rose colour, almost as much as Cadiz — and, in my time, no one live on it, and only schooners from El Puerto de la Paz occasionally call. What you call jumping-off place, I think, though where you jump to except into

the sea? But I remember; I was young then, five-and-thirty years ago —
where have the years gone, tell me? . . . It was so interesting, for as you
sail along the coast you feel like Alvarado or Cortés, and always think
you come to something new, just as you think in life.

"What a fine day it was; and all that salt it looked like crystal in
the sun, in some places like a garden, and all the streams run through
a reddish sort of grounds. Scarcely a ripple on the sea, which have an
oily look; just enough wind to keep the sails just drawing. You recollect
that 'La Estrella' sail if you move a fan, eh; three or four fan make a stiff
gale for her. Well, well, island of Branciforte was on her weather bow,
three or four league away, and we just weathered Cabo de . . . I forget
his name, but it is just where the salt finishes and the thick forests all
begin, for island of Carmen is about twenty mile in length, and broad,
broad as from here to Rota, say about three league. When we pass by that
little cape all changed at once, and it was fairyland — island of Carmen
pretty, pretty when you pass that cape. Trees coming down right to the
water edge, and little cove of sand so white you want to go ashore and
bathe. All the crew came on deck to look at him, and the Correntinos,
they say, 'Ah, . . . like the country up the Paraná, by the Esquina,' and
they fall talking their Guarani, a heathen tongue it is. They say the devil
go twelve years to school to learn him, and come away a fool.

"The two Chilótes stand open-mouth, like children at the window
of a pastry-cook, and when the captain came on deck he looked across
the bay and say: 'Si, señor. Yes, a man could build a neat jacál there and
have good time with a nice Indian wife, one of those Zapoteca girls if
you could steal one from about Salina-Cruz, or if not a good Yaqui.' 'I
always like an Indian girl,' he say; 'they are cooking well, and have no
nonsense like white woman, and if you beat them, not go stick a knife in
you when you are drunk or sleep.' Not too much of a Christian was our
old man, but he know all the coast from Guaymas down to Paita as well
as if he was a shark. His mother I think she was a Pima or a Yaqui, and
you know no one can make good Christian out of an old Moor. Just as
we were standing by to go about, and the wind looked like fresh'ning a
little bit, he say, that is the captain say — (I think I tell you that his name
was Guadalupé Perez. — No! ah, I thought I did) — he say there is a
man upon the beach, running down to the shore. I jump upon the rail,
and see him waving his arms and making signals with a bough. 'Strange,'
say the skipper, 'a man on isle of Carmen, where there is no Indians, and
only schooners touch from Puerto de la Paz to load up salt, and now

and then hunt the wild goats that swarm about the place.' Well, the poor devil on the beach go on like semaphore, waving his arms about, and then he run down to the edge and go upon his knees. The old man curse a little about losing a fair wind, but give the order to back the fore topgallant sail and send away a boat.

"I went away with the two Correntinos in our dinghy to find out what was up. As we come close in the man ran to the boat up to the middle, and clamber in as if a tiger running after him, and lie down in the bottom gasping like a fish.

"I give him littel mescál. The 'Estrella' never carry rum, only mescál, because the skipper get it cheap up in Arispé, where they grow plenty aloes, what they call there maguéy. 'Ah,' say the man, and shake my hand as if he pull it off. He say in Spanish, for he was Chilian down from Talcahuano, 'That do me good. Mother of God! three months and never see a man; I think I going mad.'

"He was burnt almost black, and ragged I tell you, ragged like a saint down about Casablanca or at Mazagán; his hair like bird's nest, no shoes, and his feet all cracked with walking up and down hunting for shell-fish on the rocks. He look back always towards the island as if he thought the devil was behind the trees, and so I clap him on the shoulder and say, 'All right, ole man, cheer up your pecker, there is not nothing to be 'fraid of, and I shall take you to the ship.' At first he speak a little slow, but when he once get fairly under weigh *[sic?]* the words come out like water from a barrel when you have set it run. He tell our skipper he have sailed from Copiapó and bound to San Francisco, and that the vessel founder out at sea, and that he alone have reached the island floating upon some wreckage, about six months ago. He seem a little hazy about things and have a hang-dog look; but we say that the poor man is mad with solitude, and have him shaved and washed and give him suit of dungaree and send him down below. He speak with no one, and when he eat a little come up upon deck and fix his eyes upon the island as if he sorry after all to leave it, so that I tell him, 'Eh, you, do you want go ashore again?' and he laugh like a rabbit when you kill him, and lights a cigarette. I tell you I did not much take to the fellow, he have a pug-dog look.

"We ran along the coast a bit, maybe an hour or two, as the wind had veered a little round, and doubled another little cape, and once again stand by to go about and stretch across the gulf. Just as the ole man going to give the order, up go his glass again, and he call out, 'Jesus Maria! I think I see a smoke. Surely,' he say, 'devils are in the island,' and as he speak a column of black smoke rise up just by the wall of forest which stand behind the beach. Looked like as if some one had thrown green wood upon the fire to make the smoke more black. We edge her little nearer in, and once again a man come running down the sand and wave his arms about. Same old nonsense — send a boat ashore, and come back to the ship with one more ragged Chilian very like the last. When he come up the side and see the man we first took off he stare a little, and with a yell grab a belaying pin and spring at him just like a jaguar.

"One of the Correntinos threw a rope about his neck. They were, I think I told you, half sailor and half gaucho, and with another half of devil in their blood — that make them ready for any kind of thing.

"Well, the ole man he look at them and say 'Virgen de Guadalupé! Put her about; let me get off from isle of Carmen before some more poor shipwrecked Chilians come out of the woods and make my ship a lunatic asylum, for they are all stark mad.'

"We go about and lay our course for Guaymas, with a lively little wind, about a five-knot breeze, I think, and then the skipper have the two Chilians aft and question them about their devilment.

"It came out then that they were really the only two men saved out of their vessel which have founder in a fog. They reach the shore upon some wreckage, and pretty nearly starve.

"Two months and three pass by, they all the time hunting for shell-fish and snaring birds to eat. Then something happen and they fight, then separate, for island of Carmen get too little for them if they live close and speak. Each think the other come and kill him in the night, and they pass all their time, each with a stick under his hand to keep his friend away. Then we come on the scene, and the first man hope that we never find the other — leave him there to die."

He ceased, and the sea-breeze swept through the funnels of the streets in the now silent and deserted town as it would tear the cobble-stones out of their bedding, and the light scud raced overhead towards the east like feathers through the sky. The audience sat silent for a time, and then McMillan, taking up his parable, observed: "A curious case, Fernandey. Aye, oo, aye, I'm glad your fellows both were dawgos. I canna' think that a white man could ever have descended to such a meanness. . . . Now I ca' it just incredible in a full chop white man."

Fernandez, holding a glass of water in his hand, looked at him gravely and rejoined:

"You see this water. All my life I have loved water, . . . good air, good water and good bells, the proverb says, and yet, when I have been in an old sailing-ship out in the eastern seas, and when the water had run short been put upon two pints a day for drink and cooking, I have stand round the barrel, and though it smelled just like the drainings of a tanyard, counted the drops when it was poured into my pannikin as if they had been gold.

"Si, señor, . . . that is I mean, . . . how do you put it, eh? — it is not good to say fountain — out of your basin I shall never drink .... eh, no señor."

A Memory of Parnell

He always seemed to me a creature from another world, or a survival of some older type of man. Not that in ordinary respects he differed from the usual race of all mankind, having their passions, weaknesses, and all the rest developed to the full, together with an incapacity to get his stirrup-leathers the same length, on horseback, when he rode. His strangeness was, as is the strangeness of a faun or hamadryad, beings we all know did exist and have their being, so strongly has their personality been drawn for us and petrified in stone.

Occasionally we feel that characters in poems and in pictures are far more real than the sham human beings who go about in millions, pretending to be men.

The subject of my recollection, and how sad it is to rack the half-sealed chambers of the mind for the impressions of dead friends left on it, as the sun leaves pictures, so some think, indelible on every stone, was one of those whose death strikes us as an injustice and in some way a mistake.

Crossing St. James's Street I well remember seeing on a bill, "Death of the Irish Leader," and thinking that it was some error of the press.

Your politician dies, and it appears quite natural. Last week he had his knighthood; a month ago became the last of all the peers, received the garter at the last royal birthday, and now resumes the sleep which was but three parts broken during the whole course of his life. One pauses, recollects his small peculiarities, his tricks of speech and manner, and then forgets him, half-pitying, half with contempt, thinking an ill-graced actor has passed through the wings, into the freedom of the street, and left behind him nothing but the remembrance of his faults, when once the electro-plated glamour of the daily press has been rubbed off, leaving the tin all bare.

But when a man, such as was Parnell, passes, all the infirmities of life fall off, and only his originality and greatness stay. Then it becomes a marvel that the multitude of rats has been the undoing of the lion.

One tries to cipher out in what his influence lay, then gives it up, and is content to say, "I knew him, may he rest well at last."

In the dull, drab and common world of English life where everything is done upon the lowest level that the intellect of man can compass, in which our Gladdies and our Dizzies, with Pam and Bright and Buckshot Forster and the rest, appear like vestrymen unglorified, a figure such as his seemed almost insolent.

It is too soon perhaps to try to mark his place in history, but since Old Noll (hero in England, and in Ireland devil), perhaps no stronger character has played its part upon the boards of the great theatre at Westminster. He had not eloquence as it is generally appraised, although at times the intensity of hate he bore us and our twaddling institutions, gave him a glacial fire, which scorched even the dull wet-blankets of the House, where all is commonplace.

He was not deeply read, not even in the history of the land for which he fought. He was not humorous, nor had he wit, but now and then inflections came into his voice, which stirred one more than all the spurred-up caperings of orators, as when he finished up a phrase with "This is going on to-day in Ireland," in which he put such force and venom that the word Ireland seemed to die upon his lips in froth.

I cannot think of him as popular even at home upon his own estate, nor yet at school, still less with his own followers, especially with those of them who sold their Lord, and quite omitted to make sure the thirty pieces should be paid; and when they lost them did not have the grace to hang themselves.

Not popular, in the hail-fellow-well-met and loudly cheered conception of the word, but yet with an attraction for all women whom he came across, who were drawn to him by his careless treatment of them, and by the wish that nature has implanted in their sex, to be the rulers of all men who stand above their kind.

Straying about the House of Commons after the fashion of a new boy at a school, I chanced to sit down quite unthinkingly upon a bench. An Irish legislator edged up and whispered, "You're sitting in his seat."

To this I answered something about the seats being free unless they had a name attached to them, and I fear bade my interlocutor fare to Gehenna by the shortest route. A gentle voice behind me almost whispered in my ear, "Quite right, the seats are free."

This laid the first stone to the building of a desultory friendship which lasted till his death.

Occasionally we dined together, not talking very much, as we had nothing very much in common, except a love of horses.

Of them Parnell knew little, and the little that I knew was almost absolutely from the colonial point of view, so that our theories did not conflict, as often happens between friends. On politics we never talked, as upon almost every point we disagreed, he leading a great party, I being a mere unit of an amorphous crowd of Nonconformists, Temperance Reformers, Deceased Wife's Sisters Monomaniacs, and Single Taxers, with all the faddists and the dried fruit of outworn Liberal politics which at that time the tide of Liberalism had left like jelly-fish and seaweed, stranded and dying on the beach.

And what a beach it was, strewn with the dead remains of Leagues and Federations and Societies, mostly composed of Treasurer and Secretary, long-haired and stammering speakers, all with their theories of prompt regeneration for the body politic, and a collecting box to shove beneath the public's nose.

We raved, we ranted, and we called on Englishmen to rise, to embrace the movement and ourselves, and comprehend that social and political emancipation was at hand and that we were the men.

Amongst this herd of addle-brained and sometimes generous, sometimes self-interested reformers (but in all instances belated), which the late lowering of the franchise had let loose upon the world, and most of whom had not sufficient wit to run a coffee-stall, the figure of Parnell stood out, like the Old Man of Hoy stands out against the sea. The little waves of the above referred to muddletonians, who with their iteration damnable and advocacy of reforms long dead, surged round him, almost unnoticed and unnoticeable.

The larger scum of Liberal and Conservative, each again occupied with questions which had long been superannuated, left him unmoved.

The party leaders feared and hated him, for he despised them, and his outlook upon politics seemed but to point out all their lack of strength and incapacity.

Gladstone, who though in talk for fifty years, never contrived to say a single thing either original or worth remembering, was overbalanced by him, and Salisbury looked on him as Turk looks at a native Christian who rebels, whilst Morley, from the dreary, arid heights of Mount Philosophus, admired and wondered but supported loyally, although perhaps feeling a little hurt at having to play the second violin to one who knew no Greek. Balfour, by virtue of his æstheticism, was repelled, and did not hesitate to shoot out mildly philosophic lips. Churchill admired, and perhaps intrigued with him whom without doubt he thought a rebel, but in politics and love all that succeeds is fair. Chamberlain very likely dreamed of some municipal Home Rule, with Parnell as a county councillor glorified, a parliament for gas and sewage, existing by his will in Dublin, and all the Irish Nationalists, apparelled in frieze coats and battered hats stuck with dudheens, shillelaghs in their hands, dancing round and singing "Long live Birmingham!"

No one else counted, and in this motley crew of dreamers and of dullards, with here and there an able man upon the make, to give consistency, the Irish Leader jostled for a place.

Whatever were his faults, and I suppose that being human, he had many of them, one thing is clear to me, that above all he hated England and her ways. With what a seething coldness, as of ice upon the edges of a crater, he would say "your country" or "your Queen." Even the House of Commons, stupid as it was, would shiver, and red-faced Tory Squires, and Nonconformists reared on seed-cake and lemonade, rise in their seats, shaking their mottled or their plebeian fists at his calm smiling face.

It did us good to hear him stammer through a speech, misquoting all his notes, halting and trying back, and pouring all the vitriol of his contempt upon us as we sat.

It seemed as if some sort of incoherent Daniel had come to judgment and was about to pass his sentence on us all.

The British Parliament for generations had listened to the tirades of all kinds of Irishmen, but they had all been of another sort and different magnitude.

In them, the Saxon was a tyrant and a brute, a sort of Juggernaut, feared and yet envied, who had laid waste the land. But now he figured as an ass, and as ridiculous, whilst all the Irishry, taking their cue from their chief's speeches, publicly thanked their gods that they were Irish, and professed to think that the word English, applied with reference to themselves, was more than infidel, and quite as bad as Protestant, or thief. Thus did the Chief make it impossible for British ministers to take up the "poor Patrick" attitude, which in the past had always been a trump.

No one, I think, was ever hated by the House as was Parnell, and he returned its hate a hundredfold, taking delight in gibing at it, and making it absurd.

Nothing offended him so much as when some hypocritical "Noncon," whom he and Gladstone had kicked round into Home Rule, would talk about the "union of our hearts," and prophesy that soon all difference of race would be obliterated. Then as he ground his teeth, and his pale cheek grew white with rage, he sometimes muttered "Damn them," with so much unction and such fervency, that one felt sure his prayer, if not immediately vouchsafed, would yet be taken *ad avizandum* as the lawyers say, and perhaps be of avail. But whether it was answered, or fell harmless on the unwholesome air of parliament, it had the effect somehow of setting one a-thinking of how great a fraud the British Empire was, and rousing one out of the feeling of sublime contentment with ourselves, with which we of the Celto-Saxon race are prone to look at all things here below, knowing that we enjoy a place apart and specially reserved for us in mansions in the skies with all repairs performed for us, by the Creator of the World.

When we debated with much circumstance, and with citation of innumerable unnecessary figures (the ever-present refuge of a dullard in a speech), some weighty matter of a railroad in the Midland Counties, it was a sight to see the Irish Leader lounge into the House, stroking his beard and pulling his moustache with long white fingers, on which dull sparkled his historic sapphire ring. He would remark half confidentially to his lieutenant, "Biggar, I think that this debate ought not to finish before twelve o'clock." To which his Sancho Panza would reply, "It's quite impossible; I've let the boys away." Then, absently, as if he had never seen the man, or at that instant suddenly became aware that he persisted still in living, Parnell would say, "Tell Gallagher to speak." "Gallagher, sir, the only thing he knows is butter." "Well, let him speak on butter."

And in an instant Gallagher would rise, quite unprepared, and speaking, maybe, for the first time in that august assembly which, as a general rule, strikes us of the predominant partnership stark dumb and curdles all our brains.

With figures and with facts, which all looked feasible, the string-pulled member-marionette would thunder forth on the injustice done to Irish industries in general, and that to Irish butter in particular, by the abominable Bill before the House. After an hour, with perspiration running down his face, he would begin to talk upon the Irish question as a whole, be pulled up by the Speaker, engage in wrangles with the Tories, and speak and speak, with illustrations of his theme, with so much vigour and such aptness, that you began to think a hideous wrong was going to be done. Just about midnight Parnell might saunter in and either say "I think I will not speak," or "Biggar, tell that fool to stop; I wish to say a word." Then word would somehow be conveyed to the rapt orator, who would subside, perhaps in the very middle of a phrase, and Parnell, rising, would proceed, apparently quite coldly, but with shut fists, and a light foam about the corners of his mouth, to distil vitriol, drop by drop, into the very souls of Englishmen, till Gladstone, putting on his hat, would leave the House, and comfortable Liberals, who had been cultivating a Cork or Limerick brogue, by means of which to show goodwill to Ireland, would shiver in their broadcloth coats, and curse the day that made him their ally.

No one, I think, since Oliver the Great and Good (I write for the mere Englishry), has made the House of Commons tremble to its cowardly depths, as did Parnell, and never Irishman before or since his time, if we except Hugh Roe O'Neill, has ever treated, upon equal terms, with the old English foe.

Undoubtedly, he both despised and hated Gladstone, who on his part showed plainly that he was in the presence of a stronger man, and though after his death he damned him with faint praise, could not have been much disappointed when, after his nine days' waiting, the Nonconformist cat jumped as it did, and shut Home Rule off for a hundred years.

Not that I think that Gladstone did not believe in Ireland's wrongs, but that he did not wish to see an Irish parliament led by a man far stronger than himself.

During the days of *sturm und drang* when he was fighting for his soul, I saw him now and then as one sees figures in a dream.

Once seated in an old-fashioned eating-house off the Strand, he wandered in, and seeing me, sat down and talked during the dinner which he could not eat. We spoke of horses, of which, as I have said, he knew but little, and I not overmuch, and then sauntered down to the House, to find it counted out.

Then came his death and funeral, with as it seemed, no one ashamed in Ireland, and almost everybody secretly pleased in London, as if they felt an enemy of England was gone, as in fact was the case, for he who lets a Briton see he does not reverence him and his country, commits the crime against the British Holy Ghost, a spirit plethoric and heavy, generous but overbearing, and as well stuffed with pride as is an airship or a fire-balloon with gas.

Let him sleep well, a Protestant amongst the serried graves of those who lie looking towards Rome, whilst they await the Trumpet's call. A Saxon leader of a Celtic race, a man who, though no orator, yet held enthralled a parliament that lives on talk. Well may his spirit hover hesitatingly between the towers of Westminster, where he enforced respect, and the grey columns upon College Green, the unfaithful Mecca, which he never lived to reach.

Faith

R. B. Cunninghame Graham

To
Signorina Antonietta Segré

Introduction

Between 1909 and 1912, within the space of just over three years, Robert Cunninghame Graham published three collections of short stories and sketches. The brief time that elapsed between each one suggests that this was a very fertile period for Graham's writing. The titles that he gave to these collections suggest, furthermore, that they were seen by him as having some degree of inter-connection. They were, in order of publication, entitled *Faith*, *Hope* and *Charity*.

Faith, published in 1909, contains eighteen stories with the same eclectic mix of subjects and locations as we have come to expect from Graham on the evidence of his earlier collections. The volume is dedicated to an Italian lady, Signorina Antonietta Segré. This lady does not appear in a list of Graham's correspondents held by the National Library of Scotland, but from possible internal evidence of two stories in *Faith*, "Transfigured" and "Brutta Passeggiata", set in Italy near the city of Rome, it is possible that Graham came to know her on a visit to Rome and dedicated the book to her as a mark of respect. The Segrés, an Italian Jewish family, were and still are of some significance in Italian life, being especially connected with industry. Members of the family suffered during the Holocaust years.

In his Preface to *Faith*, Graham stresses what a sorrowful thing it is to be a writer. Much of the sorrow comes from the realisation by the writer that, however successful the writing may be, however pleasant the subject, "there still wells up the bitter-sweetness in the mind that passages, scenes, and events are past and cannot be recalled." Later in the preface, Graham repeats that "to record, even to record emotions, is to store up a fund of sadness, and that is why all writing is a sort of ice-house of the mind . . . almost all of the stories, sketches, or what you choose to call them, in this book are sad. None of them . . . end in a blaze of sunset, actual or moral; virtue in none of them is in the least atom better rewarded than it is actually rewarded in the world." For Graham, the merit of the stories is that they are as truthful as he can make them. To the reader, this may seem to add up to a bleak collection. However,

Graham is overstating the latent pessimism. Many of the stories are lightened by the colour and vividness of Graham's observation and the vigour of his writing.

The two later collections, *Hope* and *Charity*, each begin with a story with the same title as the whole book. *Faith*, however, differs in that there is no story entitled "Faith". Yet the first story, "Sor Candida and the Bird", could perhaps have had that title, in that religious faith is the significant theme. Sor (or Sister) Candida is a nun in a convent in the city of Avila, the place in Spain closely associated with St Teresa. St Teresa was the object of Gabriela Cunninghame Graham's special interest and research, leading to a well-received biography (1894, reprinted 1907). Sor Candida rescues a bird from dying of thirst in the intense summer heat and, contrary to convent rules, keeps it in a makeshift cage in her cell. It becomes a great favourite with the other nuns and is tolerated even by the Prioress, who obtains a special dispensation from the provincial, or convent supervisor, to allow it to be kept. However, in the outflowing of faith and piety attending the celebration of the day of St Teresa, the bird is forgotten and dies imprisoned in its cage. Sor Candida is left oppressed by a sense of her sin in permitting the bird to come between her and Christ in her thoughts. Her faith has been tested and she has failed. A more detached observer might, however, think that her true sin was in depriving the bird of its liberty in the first place. Graham's ironic observation of the situation, presenting the different characters in a sympathetic light yet without sentimentality, enables the readers to feel for Sor Candida in her distress and still remain ambiguous in their judgements.

"Sor Candida and the Bird" is one of only four stories in *Faith* that are set in Spain. "El Pastor de Las Navas" is a historical piece, recounting how, during the Reconquista (Reconquest) of Spain from the Moors, the Christian armies of King Alfonso inflicted a crushing defeat on the Berber invaders from North Africa at Las Navas de Tolosa, having been led by a shepherd by a secret path to catch their enemies unawares. It is a vivid piece of writing by Graham detailing the build-up of the opposing armies, the victory of the Spaniards, and the escape of the Moorish Emir after the battle. Unfortunately, Graham has confused two different Moorish invaders from different centuries. King Alfonso VI of Leon and Castile fought a battle against the Berber Almoravid invaders under the supremely able Moorish leader, Yussuf-ibn-Tachfin, in 1086, but it was the Battle of Sagrajas and Alfonso was defeated. This Alfonso is the king who is associated in the romances with the famous Spanish champion, Rodrigo Díaz de Vivar (El Cid). The battle of Las Navas de Tolosa was fought much later in the long struggle of reconquest between Alfonso VIII and the Almohad armies of Caliph Mohammed al-Nasir in 1212, and Alfonso won a great victory supposedly with the help of the knowledgeable shepherd. In memory of his almost divine intervention, the shepherd is immortalised in a stone-carved figure above the high altar of Toledo Cathedral. Graham's mistaken identification of the Moorish leaders does not, however, detract from the vigour and interest of the story.

The other two stories with a Spanish setting belong to Graham's own personal experience. "Los Peares, Un Minuto!" is an intensely observed and strongly felt account of a brief stop ("One minute!") by a train at the little station of Los Peares in Galicia in northern Spain. There it is expected, not by a mere handful of intending travellers, but by a crowd of hopeful emigrants with their wordly belongings. Virtually the whole population of the hamlet of Val de Cabras is leaving to seek a new life in Argentina. Graham describes the group and individual partings and meditates on the traditional hard but idyllic life that is being left for a future life in the New World where the people will be irrevocably changed. In this story Graham has captured a tiny episode in the great nineteenth-century economic movement of population from all over Europe to the beckoning open spaces of the Americas. The last Spanish story in *Faith* is "A Saint". In this story, Graham is writing about a man he actually knew in person. The "Saint" of the title is the Anarchist politician-hero, Fermin Salvochea y Alvarez (1842-1907), who lived and worked in Cadiz in Andalucia, widely respected and loved in his lifetime and coming to be known after his death as "the Saint of Anarchy". Graham's story follows the main pattern of his life without becoming specific about places and times, simplifying and to a degree idealising his subject. The extent to which Salvochea was actively involved in the Anarchist movement as a public figure, even becoming Mayor of Cadiz, is downplayed in favour of presenting a simple private personality, who lives and dies in poverty and obscurity. This is probably because Graham is letting his artistic creative instincts take over the direction of his writing at the expense of literal truth. He is concerned with presenting a "saint" rather than a real complex-natured political activist. It is fiction, not literal fact.

It is interesting to compare Graham's approach to the anarchist "saint" with how he treats another committed political worker in the story, "The Idealist". Graham was himself a man of strong Socialist principles and might be expected to give those who shared his opinions a sympathetic, even indulgent treatment. So it was in "The Saint". In "The Idealist", however, it is interestingly different. The sketch begins with a description of a Socialist public meeting in London with its varied audience and the typical fiery rhetoric about social injustice. The narrator (Graham?) expresses a kind of aristocratic disdain for the people who surround him, "workmen of the London type, sallow and slight and dressed in cheap slop clothes", out-of-place middle-class observers made up of awkward students and well-dressed ladies, bored reporters and committed Socialist comrades full of talk and nothing else. Graham's social alienation from the audience and the proceedings is clear from the condescending tone of his description and from the Cockney dialogue he patronisingly creates for the speakers. It is only when he moves from the meeting to follow a particular speaker, a dedicated activist and pamphleteer named Betterton, and outline his beliefs and the circumstances of his life that Graham shows himself to be sympathetically involved. Betterton is sincere and happy in his poverty and the limited sphere of his activities, futile though they appear to be. Graham clearly liked him, but he is not a saint in the Spanish anarchist mould, being "ridiculous...half-mad", so that Graham viewing his life does not find it "easy to be sure, if one should laugh or cry". Perhaps the story is examining the paradox that Graham saw in the Socialists with whom he often consorted. Collectively, their activities and methods invited ridicule for their awkwardness and futility, while individually there was much in them to admire. Certainly, for Graham, the cause was real, ever-present and deeply felt. The sketch that acts as a companion piece to "The Idealist", "In Christmas Week", is a strong essay of meditation on the injustice and inequality in society, which is particularly visible in London, in the depth of winter, in the week of Christmas that is supposed to celebrate love and charity to all mankind. Graham highlights vividly the suffering and cruelty and deprivation to be seen on the London streets, affecting both humans and animals. The atmosphere is cold and dark, both literally and metaphorically. The final image is of a soup-kitchen for down-and-outs, with one of the men sarcastically commenting to a chum, "Blime me, cheer up! it'll be better under Socialism," before spitting upon the stones. The words are more angry and dismissive than hopeful.

After the death of Gabriela in 1906, Graham more and more came to divide his time in Britain between London, where his mother lived until her death in 1925, and Scotland, in his final home at Ardoch on the north bank of the Clyde. Gartmore had been sold in 1900, and Graham felt its loss keenly, avoiding as much as possible coming within sight of it. Whenever Graham writes of it and the surrounding area thereafter, it is from his memory of past times that he draws his material, as probably in the two sketches with a Scottish setting, "Lochan Falloch" and "At the Ward Toll". In the two London pieces treated above, Graham's role was as observer and commentator on the social inequalities particularly evident in the metropolitan scene. "Lochan Falloch" (Hidden Loch), on the other hand, is an evocative piece of topographical and natural description, with a sense of history. The little secluded loch is carefully and beautifully described in its Menteith setting with its changing aspects according to the seasons. The loch is finally seen as existing merely in and for itself and the rest of the natural world. Mankind is forever excluded from any share in its being; it is truly hidden. Graham indulges a fanciful, even sentimental, strain in his writing for this sketch, which is at odds with most other stories in the collection. "At the Ward Toll" begins in a similar strain of natural description and is very specifically located. The narrator (undoubtedly Graham) is on horseback, riding home in the late evening through the Vale of Menteith near Buchlyvie. The road is taking him northward to Gartmore House two or three miles distant, towards the Ward Burn and the Kelty Water. The atmosphere of the misty landscape with its sights and sounds is carefully detailed, and images of past history swirl through the narrator's imagination. Reality breaks in when he is suddenly hailed in Spanish by a man on foot. This turns out to be a Spanish sailor from Vigo in Galicia, Ildefonso Lopez, who is walking from Leith to Glasgow. After the exchange of a few words and cigarettes, they part, and the narrator continues his ride to Gartmore, pondering on the meeting and imagining himself about to arrive by sea in Vigo, a port seemingly as well known to him as the district of Menteith. Graham and his wife, Gabriela, had in fact lived in Vigo for a time in the early 1880s after their return from Texas. So in a sense Graham is making two returns in the story, to Gartmore, the lost family home, and to Vigo, where he had shared a home with his young wife, now lost to him. The story, which at first sight was a slight descriptive piece with a random (perhaps invented) encounter in the mist at its heart, seems to reveal itself as an artistic construction from deeply-felt memories addressing Graham's personal desolation and loss.

Loss is central also to the two stories with South American settings, "Paja y Cielo" and "A Silhouette". "Paja y Cielo" (Grass and Sky) is a description of the Argentine Pampas in their natural state as Graham knew them in his youth, before the modern world discovered them through the advent of railways and fenced them into estancias and farms. The abundance of animal and bird life in the great ocean of grass under an endless sky, and, above all, the freedom enjoyed by all who lived there, even if it included casual cruelty and violent death, is lyrically evoked by Graham as if he is still vitally present in that paradise. Yet this idyll is framed at beginning and end by the awareness of its total loss, destroyed inevitably by the march of so-called civilisation. Yet Graham is not blind to the horrors that could find expression in such a fair setting. In the story, "A Silhouette", Graham returns to the pampas of the Argentine province of Entre Rios around the time of his first visit to South America in 1870. At that time, the province was racked by civil war following the murder of the local caudillo, or strong man, General Justo de Urquiza. The two opposing factions of Blancos and Colorados (Whites and Reds) were ravaging the countryside and murdering anyone thought to be associated with the other side. Graham recounts an incident of particular brutality inflicted on a small family of two brothers and their mother making a peaceable living from cattle-ranching until they are caught up in the conflict. One of the brothers is kidnapped and made to serve with a band of Reds until he escapes and returns home. However, he is pursued and caught within sight of the ranch and murdered for desertion and suspected White sympathies. Graham spares no feelings in his account of the murder, and catches a note of total desolation and loss in the final image of the story, the bereft brother and the victim's horse silhouetted against the dawn sun. The story itself is like a silhouette picture, the image of human cruelty in stark contrast with the brightness of the natural setting.

As we have seen, when Graham writes about South America, he is usually drawing his material from his travels there as a young man. His association with another of his favourite story settings similarly goes back to his young manhood. Graham first visited Morocco in 1875 in company with his friend George Mansel on board the trading ship, the "Wilberforce", under Captain Bilson, the subject of an earlier story,

"Bristol Fashion", in *The Ipané*. They sailed south from Gibraltar down the coast of Morocco and on round West Africa and the Canaries to the Congo and beyond, before returning to Gibraltar. They called in at ports in Morocco, above all the city that Graham was to revisit many times in his later life, Tangier. This was the beginning of a long relationship with Morocco and its people, involving respect and admiration, which was to produce many stories over the years of his literary career, as well as a committed involvement in the question of the political control of Morocco which divided the Great Powers of Europe in the early years of the twentieth century. In *Faith*, Graham has a group of four stories set in Morocco and examining different aspects of Berber Arab character and culture. "At the River" is a slightly surreal story of an encounter between the Sultan of Morocco and a European piano on a river-bank. "Bu Gidri" tells of the paternal faith and duty exhibited by an Arab guard at the British Consulate in Fez when he feels impelled to carry the body of his son back for burial to their home village near Tangier. "An Arab Funeral" is a colourful account of a traditional ceremony. "Mektub" ("Faith" in Arabic) tells of the life of a blind man, known as "El Rubio" (Blondie), and his misplaced faith in a German doctor who promises to restore his sight by an operation. The disappointment at its failure is mitigated by El Rubio's higher faith in God, enabling him to accept it philosophically and say, "Weep not. It was not written."

As was suggested at the outset, at some point Graham paid a visit to Italy, particularly Rome, which gave rise to two stories in this collection, "Transfigured" and "Brutta Passeggiata". As a boy, he did not endure the rigours of the full classical education inflicted on the public schoolboys of the Victorian age. However, "Transfigured" makes clear that he shared the feelings of admiration and awe common among the governing class of Imperial Britain in regard to Imperial Rome and its history. On the Appian Way he meditates on the glory that was Rome and the pathos of its remains. Where he differs from the common view is in seeing that all this was founded on and arose from the labour of peasants and small farmers. So the archetypal figure that appears before him, not just in imagination but in modern reality, is that of a common working man, a battered world-worn Italian labourer bearing the scars of a hard life upon his physical person. The man describes his experiences as a labourer at many different jobs all round the Eastern Mediterranean over the years until he became unfit and had to return to his home in the Campagna near Rome, only to continue working on the land. Graham sees him finally as a modern equivalent of the common Roman legionary, on whom the Empire had depended, and the last sight of him is as a symbol of something greater – a universal Socialist ideal transfigured by the setting sun, as if by the spirit of the classical world. The story with which "Transfigured" is paired shares the setting of the Appian Way just outside Rome. "Brutta Passeggiata" (meaning an "evil passage", or a "bad progress") begins with a similar description of the beautiful natural surroundings suffused with classical images and references to the mythology and life of pre-Imperial Rome. Unfortunately, through this idyllic setting passes a constant stream of modern traffic, including motor-cars and bicycles, raising clouds of dust. Towards evening, the traffic disappears and peace and tranquillity return. The final image is of a herd of oxen moving gently along the famous road. It suggests a happy close to the day. The mood that Graham has created is, however, undercut and destroyed when, through the words of a woman sitting by the road, it is revealed that these beautiful creatures are taking their last walk, since they are on their way to the slaughter-house. The sadness which Graham had promised in his Preface is at its most poignant here.

A sadness, if of a lesser intensity, lies behind the story, "Dutch Smith". Smith is an English corn-merchant, whose passion is for art of the Dutch School and visiting Haarlem in Holland each spring to paint in the Dutch style. Hence his nickname of "Dutch". He is a kindly, charitable but ineffectual man, with no knowledge of the world or experience of women and love. So, when he goes on a cruise to the Eastern Mediterranean and is led into a night on the town in Spain, he is totally out of his depth. Along with his cruise companions, he is led to a brothel where the other men fix themselves up with the women of the house. Smith is left chatting to the brothel madam and believes all that she tells him about her respectable past and her charitable feelings towards her "doves". Full of sympathy and kind impulses, he is eventually led upstairs. After this experience, his life continues as before, except that now he has to pay periodic visits to a spa to treat the sexually-transmitted disease that he has contracted and that will be with him for the rest of his life. Dutch Smith has become a victim through his own ignorance and innocence and his unfounded faith in what he was told. Graham touches delicately on sexual matters in a number of his stories, generally displaying sympathy for prostitutes and women mistreated by men. Here he deals tangentially with an aspect of Victorian and Edwardian life that he must have been familiar with, the blighting effects of innocently-contracted sexual disease upon people's lives and families. Dutch Smith is the only person affected in this story and is to be pitied. Had Graham wished, he could have written an infinitely sadder story on the same subject, in the manner of his model in the field of social realism, Guy de Maupassant.

The longest piece in *Faith* is an account of Graham's travels in the small Pyrenean state of Andorra. He writes with lively engagement and keen observation about a little-known part of Europe, following in the steps of the mid-nineteenth century travel writers, Richard Ford and George Borrow. Graham informs and entertains in equal measure, and although there is no pretence of fiction or artistic narrative, the essay fully deserves its place in the collection on literary grounds.

Faith is a collection that demonstrates a further development in the writing of Cunninghame Graham. It was largely written and collected in the years immediately following the death of his wife Gabriela and inescapably carries a significant charge of loss and deprivation. As Graham says in his Preface, saying to the reader, "In the balance of your brain, is it not better to write truthfully, when all is sad, than to write on sad things after the manner of your only jig-maker?", meaning that sadness and loss are the real environment in which he is writing rather than being a pose that he adopts as a literary artist purely for effect. *Faith* is one of the products of a dark period in Graham's life.

A.McG.

Contents

Preface

To the Illustrious Reader

Everything that a man writes brings sorrow to him of some kind or other. Especially is this the case as time goes on, and catches one a-thinking on the days when that which now is but a shadow, even though fairly stamped upon a page in moulded letters, was once a living thing. Let nobody deceive himself (as is the wont of many, here in this island home of ours) that books are spun out from the inner consciousness, after the fashion that the learned German evoked his elephant, or of him who made the fiddle out of his own head and still had wood sufficient left in it to make another violin.

Such processes are well enough for silk-worms, but men spin little silk from their own bowels, and still less from their brains.

All that they write, even the sonnets, those of Shakespeare and of Keats, has cost them labour and much biting of their pens. This is so, and artists of all kinds, whether in paint or letters, in marble, bronze, or in what medium they work, all know it thoroughly. Those who contest the point are the idealists, that is to say, the men who as they pass their days in business or the like, cherish devoutly the idea that art of any kind is of the nature of white magic, and comes into the world as easily as does a calumny or an unnecessary lie.

All that we write is but a bringing forth again of something we have seen or heard about. What makes it art is but the handling of it, and the imagination that is brought to bear upon the theme out of the writer's brain. It follows therefore that all writing, as I said before, brings sorrow in its train. Even when one looks back and reads the few rare passages that flowed off from the pen so easily, that on finishing them one was half tempted to exclaim, "Then I too am a writer!" and even when those passages were written about scenes one loved or of events pleasant to dwell upon, there still wells up the bitter-sweetness in the mind that passages, scenes, and events are past and cannot be recalled. It may be that a painter with his long stroke of the brush, so different to the niggling of the pen, is differently affected; but then his work is beautiful in itself, and must remain perforce a thing of beauty, even to himself. Painters, I fancy, are the pleasantest companions of all the race of men who follow any kind of art, either for bread, or as a man loves a capricious mistress, who on her part half scorns him, and of whom he has no need, but still adores, chiefly perhaps because no bond, either of law or of necessity, enforces him to love.

Whether it is or not as I have fancied with the painters, certain it is that writers store up sorrow for themselves, by setting down some of the myriad thoughts on paper, for all time (or unto such time as the unsaleable edition of their book is pulped), that course through every brain. Had he not chanced to write, the thoughts had been forgotten, and not remained to plague the thinker of them and to remind him that time flies.

What reason pushed the inventive Arab or Chaldean to invent a water-clock I never understood. Why could he possibly desire to know what time of day it was, and thus remind himself another hour had slidden past into the vacuum of time?

In the same way (at least, so it is said) that when the rainbow falls upon a tree no caterpillars hang to the leaves, time unrecorded does not cling about the soul.

To record, even to record emotions, is to store up a fund of sadness, and that is why all writing is a sort of icehouse of the mind, in which that which once was a warm and living action, a feeling, scene, experience, joy, or sorrow, is now preserved, as it were, frozen, stiff, deprived of actuality, and a mere chopping-block on which fools exercise their wits.

From this it would appear that none of us should write, except a poet here and there, or a compiler of a railway time-table, for they clearly are wanted in a well-constituted state; but, oh illustrious reader, for I assume you are illustrious, because you cannot write yourself, and hence are well endowed with the divine and sacred fire of criticism, you will find that almost all of the stories, sketches, or what you choose to call them, in this book are sad. None of them, that is if I remember rightly, end in a blaze of sunset, actual or moral; virtue in none of them is in the least atom better rewarded than it is actually rewarded in the world. In none of them is any moral drawn, or if it is, it is attempted to be drawn, it is set down as truthfully as possible, which naturally has the effect of making it seem false. Tell me though, oh illustrious reader, you who though, as I said before, cannot write yourself and yet are born a judge of wit, of pathos, style, of composition, and who can weigh imagination to the last scruple, in the balance of your brain, is it not better to write truthfully, when all is sad, than to write on sad things after the manner of your only jig-maker?

Cooped underneath the sky, like butterflies shut up by schoolboys under a finger-bowl, we can but flutter, or if we fly, rise only to the middle of the glass. What we can do, is to look out as far as possible through the imprisoning crystal and set down what we see. So, I have written all the sketches in the book, as clearly as my vision serves me to peep out. If they seem false to you, oh most illustrious, surely it is a little hard to blame a post if a blind man runs up against it and batters out his brains!

R. B. Cunninghame Graham.

Faith

Sor Candida and the Bird

The long grey buildings of the convent with their overhanging red-tiled roofs threw a refreshing shadow on the heated street. The sun-parched trees stood stiff and motionless as sentinels frozen at their posts. For months it had not rained in Avila. For miles on every side of the old town, the stone-strewn plains were heated like a kiln. The dark grey walls gave out the heat as you passed by and touched them with your hand. The distant mountains shivered in the heat. Upon the plains the last dead stalks of fennel loomed in the mirage of the heat like palm-trees in the sand. Lakes formed in front of men upon their mules, their faces shielded from the scorching sun by handkerchiefs, and with their stiff Castilian hats pulled down almost upon their shoulders to protect their necks, and then as the mules clattered on the stones, or brushed against the withered herbage with a crackling noise, took themselves further off, as fortune does in life, after one tantalising glance. Sheep and the cattle stood round the deep-dug wells, their heads bowed low, and their flanks heaving in the sun, waiting till evening for the coming of the men to draw the water in the long leathern bags. The yellow swirling rivers had dried up, leaving the mud as hard as kaolin, and here and there held thick, green water, with a dead horse or cow, bloated and swollen enormously, just floating on the top. All nature suffered with the heat, and birds approached the houses seeking help, just as they do in northern climates in the frost.

Is there at bottom some mysterious bond between all living things, which, but for our religion and conceit, should have made all the animals and us one clan? Who knows? Upon the strip of sand, which in old Spanish towns lies at the edges of the streets (just where the cobbles end), and makes a sort of neutral territory between them and the gutter, right opposite the convent door, a bird lay fluttering with its beak open, and its eyes almost closed. It lay half choking in the sun, its beady eyes becoming glazed, and its perhaps immortal little spirit just trembling to be free and join the universal soul; a minute or two more and it would have gone to swell the army of tired soldiers, camels, and horses who have died of thirst amongst the sands. It may be, as they say in Spain, God was not willing, or the slight fluttering of the feathers raised a little dust, for at that moment a side door opened, and with a cautious glance to see that no one was about, a nun stepped out, and taking up the bird, bore it into the shade. It lay almost expiring in her hand as she, with many little cries of pity, took a piece of rag and gently dropped some water in its mouth. As the drops followed one another, it slowly came back to the life it had so nearly left. Its head became less languid, and its eyes brighter, until at last it feebly pecked the hand that held it, making the nun smile, muttering it acted just like a Christian, as she released it, and let it hop about her cell. Then taking up a cane, she split it for a perch, and stuck it in the darkest corner of the cell, making some holes in the rough plastering. All had gone well so far, and on its perch the bird sat resting, and recovering its strength. Quickly she made a little cage out of split canes, not thinking for a moment that after giving life she thus would take away life's chiefest treasure — liberty; but all in tender heart. The cage contrived, and the revived and still half-drooping little bird duly inducted to its prison, she put a broken saucer and some bread-crumbs by its side, and sat down, proud and happy with her work.

Sor Candida was tall and dark, with large black eyes and a slight pencilling of hair upon her upper lip. Though she had left the world and all its vanities, losing her liberty, perhaps to save herself from want, just as she had herself deprived the bird of his for the same cause, her walk was springy, and she retained that easy swinging of the hips which is the race mark of the women of the Spains. Had she been in the world, no doubt, as she walked through the plaza or the street, "God bless your mother," "Long live grace," and other cries of admiration would have followed her, and even as it was, the priests who visited the convent, and talked occasionally in the dark "locutorio" through the grating to the nuns, would sometimes say to one another that "Sister Candida was the fine essence of true salt, a pearl that God Himself, no doubt, was pleased to wear." In the same way, a bull-fighter who has left the ring, if he pass near a bull, rarely refrains from "challenging," as those intelligent in such things say, by shouting loudly, and by stamping with his feet.

Her happiness was at its height, and she was praising God for having sent her just in time (another proof, if one were wanted, of His goodness towards all created things; well is it said that not a sparrow falls without His ken) to save the little life, and thinking to herself what name to give her prisoner, when a doubt arose. Her heart stopped beating for a moment, as she thought the convent rules allowed no property. Nothing but articles of individual use, a rosary, a book of hours, a hair shirt, or a scourge, was fitting for a nun professed, of the discalced and blessed order, which the great Saint of Avila herself had purified. Pets were not to be thought of, and she reflected that it seemed ages since she had known the bird, and he on his part twisted round his head, seeming to watch her movements in the cell.

All might have yet been well, had she but yielded to that unstable guide, mere reason, and opening the cell door, allowed the bird to fly. He would have launched himself into the air with a glad chirp, for by this time the heat had moderated as eventide drew near, and flown refreshed to greet his friends, and tell them in the trees, or in the corner where he had his little home beneath the overhanging roof of some high belfry, of the amazing charity of a great being, tall as is a tower.

Sor Candida, young, kindly, and deprived of love by the religious life, felt if she let her new companion go that she would feel as does a man cast on a desert island with but one fellow, if that fellow dies.

Surely God would not be enraged if she allowed the bird to stay! Had He not sent him to her, or her to him, just in the nick of time? He looked so pretty with his round beady eyes, which followed her about. Besides, she felt he was too weak to fly, so as the convent bell rang out for benediction, and the shadows lengthened, stretching across the cell till they bathed half of it in a cool darkness, she took a handkerchief, and having covered up the cage, hurried off to the choir.

Perhaps her thoughts strayed from the contemplation of the Saviour's passion, realistically set forth ("to a bad Christ, much blood"), and from the antiphones [*sic*], to her own cell, where in a corner the precious bird was sleeping, after his escape. The office over, all the nuns walked in the garden, pacing to and fro, glad to escape the heat the stones threw out at sunset, and to enjoy the air. Some sat and talked about the little gossip of the place, whilst others roamed about alone, turning incessantly when they reached the wall, just like wild animals shut in a cage in public gardens, to be gaped upon by fools. Others, who had the gift of prayer, sat alone enrapt, their lips just moving, and their beads slipping mechanically between their fingers as their souls strove to join themselves with God. Friends walked about in pairs, chattering and laughing almost as gaily as girls do in the world, and even pinching one another on the sly. And as they walked, the bell of the cathedral rang out, sounding as if, from the stiff arm of some recumbent warrior in the choir, a shield had fallen upon the stones, so martial was its clang.

The breeze just rustled in the trees, stirring their parched and thirsty leaves with a metallic sound. A coolness fell upon the land, and from the country came the lowing of the cows as they approached the well, where, since the sun had set, stood shepherds, their sheepskin jackets thrown upon the ground, as they strained on the rope which, passing through a wooden pulley, held a leathern bucket, just as in farthest Nabothéa, Esau gave water to his herds.

So still the air was that the warning of the clock in the great tower upon the walls, before it struck, was heard across the town, whilst from the thirsty ground a scent of freshness came, as if to tell mankind that, down below the surface, all vegetation was alive though sleeping through the heat.

Still all against the convent rules, the bird continued to sing on, and in the summer mornings, before the enemy, the sun, came out declaring war upon mankind, Sor Candida's most intimate and dearest friends used to assemble stealthily and fill her cell, to hear its melody. The delightful sense of doing something wrong — surely stolen music is as sweet as stolen waters — increased their pleasure, and they would sit enrapt, closing their eyes, to hear it lift its little canticle.

Holding each other's hands they sat, whilst one placed at the door looked through a chink, to give the alarm if the superior should come upon her rounds. All prospered, and the bird waxed fat, fed with nefarious rape and hemp-seed, introduced contraband into the convent by a sympathising lay sister who went into the world to buy provisions, and his sweet singing ravished the nuns into an ecstasy of innocent delight.

At times Sor Candida would say, "Sisters, it seems impossible, but that the Lord is pleased to hear the harmony the little one pours forth, all in His praise." And they, answering, would repeat gravely, "Yes, little sister, it must be so"; then they would push a piece of groundsel into the cage, for never had the garden of the convent been so free of weeds as since the advent of the little minstrel, saved so providentially to sing the praises of the Lord.

All went on well, day following day, and though no doubt the bird mourned for the reasonable converse of his kind, and wondered how the world wagged with his fellows, he still grew fat, as it is said did Silvio Pellico, although we have no record of his song.

But, one fine morning as they sat listening to the feathered psalmody, all lost in admiration, and with the ready tear of simple souls glistening in all their eyes, a knock was heard, and the cell door flung open showed the superior standing in their midst. Sternly she gazed, her broad white "tocas" looking like driven snow against the dark brown habit which she wore, of the same make and quality as that worn by the foundress of their order, she who, although she sits at the right hand, perhaps by virtue even more of her humanity than of her saintship, is yet a colonel of artillery, where the blood-red and orange banner floats against the sky. Her rosary hung by her side, the beads of coral and the little chains which held them, hammer wrought, with the "'Maria" made in Zaragoza, bearing the figure of the "Virgen del Pilar." A round medallion of the blessed foundress hung about her neck, and her bare feet, thrust into hempen sandals, were white and clean, the blue veins standing out upon the insteps, showing she followed the injunctions of her saint who said, "'My daughters, it is dreadful to be foul." Her shale-black hair, half hidden by the "tocas," was silvering at the temples, and her round, fat, good-tempered face was puckered to a frown.

"Daughters," she said, "what brings so many of you here into one cell, as if you were conspirators? You know our rules forbid one nun to go into another's cell without permission, and never with closed doors."

The nuns stood silent, cowering together like wild mares in a corrál. Then from the corner of the cell there came a muffled chirp, where the cage, hastily covered with a pocket-handkerchief, did not exclude the light. The prioress made a step forward, and, uncovering the cage, saw at a glance the motive of the nuns' silence, and the offender against all her rules, serenely seated on his perch. Setting her face as sternly as she could, she said:

"Which of you is it who has brought this bird into the cell? All of you know that anything, animate or inanimate, which causes a nun's heart to stray from its allegiance to her spiritual husband, Christ, not only violates the spirit, but the letter of our rule."

Still no one answered, till, at last, pushed by the rest, Sor Candida, drying her tears and with one hand upon the little cage, as if to save it from the wrath of heaven, stood forth, and with the eloquence which has absorbed the entire activity of her race, in latter days, took up her parable.

She laid herself upon the mercy, both of heaven and the prioress; told how, from her window, she had seen the bird lie choking in the sand, felt for its little agony, and had remembered that, when upon the cross, our Lord had suffered all but thirst, without complaint, and how something, she knew not what, had bade her venture, although she knew that by thus stepping out into the street she had fallen into sin.

Then as her voice gained strength, and as she saw the encouraging glances of her fellow-culprits, she explained how that ("and this the prioress knew well") one sin leads to another, and by degrees all she had done seemed to grow natural, and it at last appeared that she had known the little bird for years.

The prioress stood listening, letting her beads mechanically slip between her fingers, whilst her eyes now and then looked vacant, as if her thoughts were straying to the patio of some brown Castilian grange, where children played about, and where, just underneath the eaves, birds hung in cages, singing all the day.

The nuns all marked the look, and pressing closer to Sor Candida, encouraged her to speak. She told how, when the bird first sang, she thought the angels had come into the cell, and how she felt that all its singing was to God's glory, and then, the words half choking her in the sudden rush of explanation, she begged forgiveness, saying that if the prioress opened the cage and let the bird escape, she had better also open the convent door and thrust her out into the street. She stopped, and for a moment nothing was heard, but the nuns' stifled sobbing, until the prioress, with the frown almost vanished from her face, said:

"Daughter, you have acted wrongly, but we are human; let me see the little creature closer," and when they brought the cage, put out a plump white finger, and allowed the bird to peck at it, so naturally, it seemed as if instead of a grave nun of high position, she was a simple woman in the world.

Unwittingly she had exposed herself to the dread influence of sympathy, and as she stood a moment undecided, one of the sisters seized the hand which hung down by her side, and kissed it, whilst the others, crowding about her, all found voice to beg for the retention of the little bird, which seated on its perch seemed to survey them critically, an attitude which it is not impossible is frequent in animals towards men. The prioress, after a moment or two's silence, drew herself up and gave her dictum:

"Daughters, our good provincial comes tomorrow on a visit of inspection, and I will tell him what has occurred, and as he settles, so it shall be done." As she stopped speaking, the angelus called the nuns into the choir, and trooping out, they took their places in their stalls.

Next morning brought the provincial, who, in a shaky cab, drove to the door, looking incongruous, just as a nun looks out of place when travelling in a train. Had he but ambled to the door upon a mule, all would have been in keeping except the canvas sand-shoes which he wore in lieu of sandals, perhaps out of a half-felt spirit of homage to external progress, content to pass as a reformer to the outward eye, so that he kept the inward vision well obscured with the theology which he had learned in youth, or maybe for his corns.

Withal an able man, and active in the business of the order, untiring in all things pertaining to the welfare of the province over which he ruled. Well educated, but not intellectual, for "quod natura non dat, Salamanca non præstat," he yet had that dry humour, so common throughout Spain, together with a democratic freedom in address, unknown in northern countries, and which perhaps the Arabs left as a memorial of their sway.

When he had had his chocolate, and gone minutely into all the details of the convent with the prioress, and when the sweets, for which the nuns were famous, the hard quince cheese and sweet-potatoes swimming in syrup thick as honey, with the turrón from Alicante, and the white cakes with caraways incrusted on the paste, were set upon the table, seated in a high-backed chair, the seat, of leather deeply stamped, held to the framework by brass-headed, hand-made nails, he took up his parable:

"How go our daughters in the Lord? Nuns, as your blessed foundress said, are ill to rule, and I to whom it is appointed to govern and inspect, know that they sometimes prove as difficult to manage as a flock of sheep. I speak under due licence and with pardon, for we should not compare a Christian to a beast."

Then, drawing out his snuffbox, he tapped it in a contemplative way and took a pinch, brushing the residue from off his nostrils with a brown, hairy hand.

The prioress, who saw her opportunity, smiled and said:

"Surely your paternity does not imagine that I guide my flock after the fashion that a muleteer drives mules by shouting 'Arré' at them and by throwing stones?"

He laughed and said the answer was as full of grace as is an egg of meat, and after he had blown his nose with a not overclean red cotton handkerchief, the prioress placed before him the difficulty that had arisen, and asked advice whether the bird might be retained, and, if it were retained, was it not likely it would prove a stumbling-block, turning the minds of those who ought to think on spiritual things to the mere matters of the world?

Taking a piece of sweet-potato on the end of his broad-pointed knife, the provincial conveyed it dexterously into his mouth, and swallowing it with a sound as when a duck plunges his beak below the water of a pond to eat a weed, and having wiped his mouth upon the tablecloth, for a moment closed his eyes, and then began to give his dictum on the case.

"Most of the trouble that we have in life," he said, "is due to human nature, which we can modify and alter, just as we can convey the water from a spring in a lead pipe into a house, so that the pressure be great enough to make it rise."

"Ah," the prioress cut in, "it is then pressure that makes the water rise. I never understood it, or how it was the water came into a house simply by laying down a pipe. . . . Wonderful, indeed, are the Almighty's ways; but there are other things, and how a key turns in a lock, and why the water rises in a pump, I cannot understand . . . but life is full of mysteries that no one can explain."

"Mother," the visitor rejoined, "the mind of woman is not made for science; there are mysteries which it is best that only men should pry into; believe me, peaches lose their bloom by being rubbed, even with a silk handkerchief. Faith is your province, and the things that you have mentioned you had better take on trust, knowing that those, competent by their sex and education to deal with problems such as these, have solved them once for all. What says S. Chrysostom, 'Mens feminæ non est . . . ,' but why quote Latin? and besides, we stray far from, our text. I have been thinking as I spoke, on this thing and on that, and as I said, nature cannot be stifled, and it may be that it is not entirely without some great design that Providence has thus permitted this litle creature of His own creating to have come into your lives. I would not that the sisters set their affections too much on the bird; but it may serve perhaps to show them resignation to the conventual life, being as it were itself an inmate of a cell, within a cell. So, for the present it can remain, and I will ask our Vicar-General when I see him, if I have acted well."

The prioress thanked him, and said she would convey what he had said to Sister Candida and to the other nuns, and he, having taken leave, got back into his cab, and disappeared down the steep, stony street, the driver cracking his whip noisily as he sat with a rein in either hand, chewing the burnt-out stump of a cigar.

The rescued bird little by little grew in favour with the nuns, who all declared to hear him sing was next to listening to the celestial choirs. Even the prioress brought him some sugar now and then, and smiled good-naturedly upon Sor Candida when she launched out into his praise. Occasionally, so much he waxed in favour and in grace, his cage was taken into church, and as the organ pealed he twitteringly sang his little pæan to the Lord, making the nuns rejoice.

A year passed by, and once again the short, but fierce Castilian summer heated the rocks of Avila, making the lichens and the mosses, with which the winter rains had clothed them, here and there shrivel like leather, left out in the sun. Once more the parameras turned as brown as is the Sáhara, and round the wells once more the expectant cattle waited for evening with their heads hanging to the ground. The convent once again threw a cool shadow on the street, and on the distant mountains of the Gredos only faint lines of snow remained that looked like veins of quartz or marble, seen in the clear white light. The heat continued into autumn, till the great day when Avila turns out to honour her who, born a simple gentlewoman, died the most human of the saints.

The convent was astir, and all the nuns from early dawn were running up and down, decking the church with flowers. Even the prioress abated somewhat of her dignity, and as she mopped her face and drank repeatedly from the white porous bottle from Andújar, hung up in the draught to keep the water cool, said she had never seen the blessed foundress' day so stifling, and that she understood how much the Blessed Mother, born in cool Avila, had suffered in her journeys to the south. Services followed fast on one another, and high mass over, the nuns all crowded to the windows to see the image of the saint borne in procession through the streets. Aloft upon men's shoulders, and swaying to and fro as they with difficulty passed through the crowded streets, the saint appeared, her halo round her head, and in her hand one of her books, the other stretched in attitude of benediction to the crowd.

All the old palaces were crowded to the roofs. On all the balconies women with flowers in their coarse black hair leaned on each other's shoulders, and in the blazing sun, the men and boys, their sleek and close-cropped heads impervious to the heat, stood and admired, taking their cigarettes out of their mouths just as the saint drew level with them, and replacing them at once as she passed on, the bearers holding theirs unlit between their fingers stained with tobacco juice. From the adjoining country tall and sinewy men, clad in short jackets and in knee-breeches, stood holding their stiff felt hats, their heads bound round with handkerchiefs, which they wore turbanwise with the ends dangling underneath. Their wives and daughters, dressed in short bell-shaped skirts, puffed out with many-coloured flannel petticoats, had handkerchiefs crossed on their breasts, and their hair plaited into tails. As the procession passed they crossed themselves and fell upon their knees.

It took its way down tortuous cobbled streets, past mediæval houses with their coat of arms speaking of when the mystic city deserved its name of "Avila of the Knights," by little plazas in which acacias grew, by the cathedral door, half fortress and half church, whose battlemented walls contrast so strangely with its belfry and its bells, until it reached the gate, where it came out upon the road to San José, the first foundation of the saint. All day the cannon roared, and in the churches services succeeded services, and Avila, for once, woke up in its desire to honour her who has made it known to all the world.

Inside the convent, when at last the services were done, and as the nuns sat talking in the refectory after their evening meal, the door was opened, and Sor Candida appeared, pale and with staring eyes, and in response to their inquiries exclaimed the "sin against the Holy Ghost," and rushed back to her cell. The nuns sat horrified, and the prioress, taking some holy water and a taper as arms against the evil one, who, she averred, must suddenly have fallen upon Sor Candida, went, amongst exclamations from the sisterhood of horror and alarm, to see what had occurred.

She paused before the door and, looking in, saw kneeling on the floor Sor Candida, sobbing and calling down the curses of the Lord upon her head. Before her on a chair was set the little cage, where once the rescued bird had sat upon his perch, and had poured forth the melodies which, as the nuns averred, were praises to the Lord.

The cage was there, a lump of sugar and a piece of groundsel, dried brown with heat, were sticking in its bars. The earthen water-vessel was upset and dry, and in the bottom lay a little bundle of dishevelled feathers, out of which stuck a head with glassy eyes and beak wide open, showing that the poor occupant of the cane cell had died of thirst; but rescued, as it seemed, to taste once more the bitterness of death, by an inexorable fate.

Tears blurred the eyes of the good-natured prioress. Twice she essayed to speak, and then Sor Candida, rising from her knees, looked at her wildly and exclaimed, "This is the sin against the Holy Ghost I have committed.

"Whilst I prayed in the church and sat and watched our saint borne through her town in triumph, this little one of God lay choking in the heat.

"How could the saint forget? It would have cost her nothing to have put a thought into my mind.

"This punishment perhaps has come upon me as a warning that we nuns should not attach ourselves to any one but Christ."

She sank again upon her knees, and the poor prioress, having again essayed to speak without avail, stood playing nervously with the Maria of her rosary.

Faith

A Silhouette

The great brown plains of Entre Rios wore an unfamiliar air. Herds of tame mares had run half wild. They snorted and made off, a thousand yards away, their tangled manes and tails all knotted up with burs, streaming out in the wind. The cattle had become as fierce as buffaloes, and anyone who lost his horse had to make long detours, for to approach them was as dangerous as to come near a tiger or a lion. Only about the flat-roofed, whitewashed houses, set in their frames of peach groves, did a few animals remain domestic, and even those, at the approach of man, often made off and joined their fellows on the plains.

Sheep were close-herded, not by mere boys who climbed up to their saddles by placing a small, brown, prehensile toe upon their horse's knees, but by armed men.

The deer and ostriches ran if they saw a man a mile away, and disappeared down the brown grassy swells, just as a flying-fish shoots down the watery hills raised by the North-East Trades.

Men, "campeando" horses that had strayed, if they were forced to ascend a little hill, got off, and creeping on all fours, surveyed the country cautiously, and then, having made sure that all was quiet on the plain beyond, remained as short a time as possible standing against the sky. If at the crossing of a river, where the thick belts of hardwood trees obscured the view, two travellers came unexpectedly upon each other face to face, their hands at once sought pistol or "facón," and as they crossed at a sufficient distance to escape a sudden shot or lasso cast, cautiously passed the time of day, and not infrequently, seized with a panic, spurred their horses, and galloped for a mile or so before they drew their reins.

The sight, on the horizon, of a band of men made the few dwellers in the scattered mud-built ranchos flee to the woods, driving their horses, carrying their wives and children, at full speed, leaving their scanty household goods to the protection of their dogs.

For months the revolution had been going on, the rival bands roaming about and stealing horses, slaughtering the cattle, and now and then, if they could catch a man or two alone, cutting their throats just as they cut a sheep's, driving the knife in at the point with the edge outwards, and bending back the head.

The death of General Justo de Urquiza had broken up the province into two hostile camps, and Reds and Whites maddened and raved about the land, avoiding one another for the most part, but fighting furiously when circumstances brought them to striking distance and there was no escape. Prisoners had little chance, and those who fell alive into the enemies' hands were foolish not to have kept a cartridge, as now and then they were sewn up in hides fresh stripped from off an ox, then left to die, exposed to sun and rain, and eaten by the flies. Others were killed in various ingenious ways, and the best anyone could hope for was to be shot, or have his throat cut out of hand. No hypocritical pretence of treating fallen enemies as friends had ever crossed the minds of anybody, and war was carried on just as it might have been between wild beasts, quite naturally, and with the full amount of cruelty with which our nature has endowed us, free and unrestrained. Still, on the whole, things were no worse than they are in European wars, except that every man who fought, knew that he did so with a halter round his neck.

As all the rank and file on either side were pressed, occasionally fathers and sons or brothers found themselves opposed to one another, and, strange to say, the claims of party as a general rule proved stronger than the call of blood, and not infrequently it chanced that friends were called upon to kill each other, and did so, as it appeared, without a qualm of conscience, so strong is discipline, and so amenable mankind to every influence, whether of custom or of use.

It chanced upon a day, near Villaguay, two brothers owned a small estancia, known as "Las Arias," close to a strip of monté near a river in which carpinchos swam and tortoises abounded, and where green parakeets flew shrieking through the maize field, and built their hanging nests in the old espinillo trees, which here and there stood up amongst the corn. The thick green grass fed mares and cattle, and kept them fat and sleek, when on the outside "camps" animals starved from the lack of pasture, and trailed themselves laboriously for miles to drink at water-holes, upon the face of which carcases bloated in the sun, floated like bladders, and in whose mud, cows and thin mares got stuck like flies in treacle, and slowly starved, surrounded by a troop of vultures, who sat and waited patiently, just as the faithful followers of some great politician sit faithfully expecting the glad moment when his death shall free them and unchain their tongues, which have got stiff for want of exercise during their leader's life.

The brothers lived the ordinary life of men in those days, on the plains. From their youth upwards they had scanned the Pampa as sailors scan the sea, reading it like a book, and knowing almost instinctively, all the lore men learn when born to look at nature as an enemy, between whom and themselves a temporary truce exists, but which at any moment may be broken in the twinkling of an eye. Men were, of course, all hostile to them, and their philosophy, short, pithy, and extracted from the simples of their lives, bade them beware, and as they said themselves, "Never facilitate," that is, never to sit down on the left of anyone, for by so doing he had you at a disadvantage when high words ensued, and you essayed to draw your knife. So, at the passing of a river, if you could well avoid it, you did not ride into the water first, especially if you were wearing silver spurs or reins, or any of the massive trappings with which on feast days men adorned their horses, for it might chance that you received a knife-thrust in the back from a too much admiring friend, or perhaps merely because the sudden lust to kill, so frequent amongst dwellers on the plains, rose in the heart of the man following you, just as in islands far out at sea a roller suddenly sets in during a calm, and sweeps away boats anchored off the shore.

To these two brothers, with their quiet, but occasionally bloody, pastoral life, whose only care was to acquire some silver horse gear, to keep their cattle fat, and their "tropilla" sleek and tame, and in whose minds a vague but stimulating idea that they were free, with no one daring to constrain them in their lives, the fear of revolution hung like a black cloud, which somehow it had always seemed impossible should burst. Not that they cared about the matter in the abstract, knowing that when a Government went out a revolution followed, just as inevitably as blood pours out after you plunge a knife into a sheep. It seemed to them quite natural, for judging by themselves, they knew no one gave up a woman or a horse without a fight, and what so natural as that a man who had enjoyed the sweets of being "government" should struggle to retain his place at the knife's point, and to the utmost of his might?

So, as they lived their lives, religiously catching a horse at night, to stake out ready to stand all day and blink and hang his head, if not required for work, and sitting hours in the kitchen drinking their maté, and illustrating all their points by diagrams drawn with the point of a "facón" on the mud floor, upon them came one morning, as a Pampéro comes up on a summer's day, the news that General Fuláno had "pronounced." Soon came the usual rumours in a revolution, of men impressed to serve, of horses taken, of cattle killed, and now and then mysterious parties of armed men passed, almost, as it were, hull down on the horizon of the Pampean ocean, a gleam of sun falling occasionally on a lance head or rifle barrel, before they sank beneath the grassy waves which roll towards the south.

Much did the brothers and their mother deliberate on what was best to do to avoid the ruin which they foresaw would fall upon them. The mother, an old "china" woman, wrinkled and brown, was urgent that her two sons should get together all their best horses and "emigrate," that is, cross either into Santa Fé or Uruguay, and as she said, "Play armadillo." But they, used to the district, and knowing the recesses of the "montés" by the rivers as well as if they had been tigers or carpinchos, thought it was best to stay at home and wait.

They held their council, after the gaucho fashion, in the kitchen, sitting upon hard blocks of ñandubay or horses' heads, passing the maté round, and now and then holding it in their hands and listening, as a horse snorted, or a stallion, gathering up his mares, galloped past in the dark. Occasionally the tame "chajá" gave its shrill cry, causing the mother to look up and say that either it would rain, because, as all men knew, when the "chajá" cried, that it had to rain, even against God's will, or that there was a thief afoot after the horses staked out near the house.

They sat and talked, watching the negro "capataz" Gregorio come in and out, the fire-light falling on his silver-handled knife as he walked to and fro as noiselessly as if he were a ghost, in his white "potro" boots. His "santas tardes" broke the silence, and, sitting down, he took the maté from the attendant negro girl who stood by, with a small kettle ready on the fire to fill the gourd, and suck at the bombilla to see it was not choked before she handed it about. The others looked at him in silence till he had drunk his maté, for it would be bad manners to speak first to anyone who comes into a room. Unsheathing his long knife, after apology for drawing it before a lady, he laid it by his side, and, taking out a lump of black tobacco, dexterously cut enough, and tearing from a sheet of paper, about as large as a good sheet of foolscap, a piece of the right size, and holding it between his toes which stuck out from his "potro" boots, made toeless so as to catch the stirrup, he rubbed the cut tobacco fine and made a cigarette. Lighting it with a cinder held upon his knife, he blew a thin blue cloud from his thick nostrils, and began slowly.

"Si, si, señor, they say that parties of the Reds have been about the Gualeguáy, not twenty leagues away. Lopez Jordán is moving southward with a horde of Correntinos, infidels who all speak Guarani. From Villaguáy down to Calá, and right through Montiel, scarcely a horse is left, and all the beasts they kill, they roast with the hide on, so that there is a double loss, both of the meat and hide."

A "Si, señor," half whispered, was his answer, and through the door, glistening amongst the leaves of the peach "monté," the giant fireflies known as "tulipanes," flitted like humming-birds that had been rubbed with phosphorus, and from the plain stretching out white in the bright moonlight, the acrid scent of sheep floated upon the air, their bleating in the fold seeming like distant bells. Occasionally dogs barked, and now and then the shrill "chajá" repeated his wild note, and flapped his horny wings with a strange hollow sound.

Gregorio, suddenly starting to his feet, went out, and after listening anxiously, lay down, and, with his ear close to the ground, remained a little motionless, then getting up said, "Just at the pass, you know, where the tall seibo grows, I hear the noise of a large body of armed men."

"Why armed?" one of the maté drinkers said.

"Firstly, because no body so considerable as this is likely to be out at night except in arms, and secondly, because I hear steel scabbards ring, which probably are those worn by the officers, for the men wear them sticking through their girths."

In the twinkling of an eye the quiet kitchen was in confusion, and the two brothers hurriedly kissed their mother and, rushing out to where their horses fed attached to stake ropes, mounted in haste, barebacked, and quickly gathering up the horses feeding round their mare, whom they released as if by magic, one brother slipping off his horse as lightly as a leaf falls from a tree, to take the bell from off her neck, like shadows disappeared into the night, all the loose horses galloping in front.

A dropping shot or two and a wild galloping of unseen horses showed that the brothers had been seen by the advanced guard of the marauding party, but soon the unfamiliar noises died away, and left the plain silent and peaceful and as if nothing more was passing than the quiet setting of the stars.

Inside the kitchen the night wore on, with now and then a prayer, and with the maté going round from hand to hand, and now and then the negro capataz went out, lay down and listened, and coming back, sat gravely down, saying that he heard nothing, but that the Three Marias were getting low on the horizon, and it was time for sleep, seeing that even they, the blessed three, set in the heavens by God Himself to keep the holy Trinity before men's eyes, would soon retire to rest.

The mother of the boys, escorted by her negro maidservant, carrying a kettle in her hand so that her mistress might take a maté before she went to bed, went out, and passed into the grey light of the coming dawn; passing beneath the stunted China trees, skirting the well round which a pack of yellow dogs as lean as wolves were sleeping, who blinked at them and then dozed off again.

The women stopped before the entrance to the low white house, listened intently for a moment just as wild horses listen, even before they are alarmed, and then quietly closed the door, almost mechanically, as if they had been walking in their sleep.

The capataz, left all alone, smoked silently for a few minutes, then rising, he extinguished the "candil" which burned in an inverted mare's bell, stuck between the mouldings of a broken cattle brand driven into the earthen floor. Then, taking off his "chiripá," he placed his knife close to his hand, just underneath his saddle, and stretching himself out, his feet towards the fire, wrapped himself in his poncho, and fell asleep. Towards daylight he was roused by the dogs barking, and, looking out in the first light of the false dawn, saw a man riding a tired horse, hatless and wet, advancing to the house. Taking his long silver-handled facón in his left hand, concealed beneath the poncho which had covered him asleep, he cautiously advanced to the "palenque," and waited till the man came up. At twenty yards away he knew him, and called out, "Ah! patroncito, what has happened? Where are your brother and the horses?" But a glance at the exhausted rider showed him that something untoward had occurred. Sliding off, all in one motion, so quickly that his right foot almost seemed to touch the ground before the left, and yet so quietly that he scarce moved the dew upon the grass, the young man slipped the bridle from his horse, which stood a moment hanging its head, with flanks tucked up and the wet dew clinging upon its quarters; and then, shaking like a retriever dog, lay down and rolled, then shook itself again, and quietly began to feed.

Lifting the dried mare's hide, that hanging from two pegs, served as a door, they passed into the kitchen, and when the capataz had blown the ashes of the banked-up fire into a glow, and thrown a bundle of dried thistle stalks upon it, he heated water, and, handing the young man a maté, said, "Drink, patroncito, and tell me what it is. Where is your brother? Is he alive, or riding in the plains of Trapalanda, as the Indians say?"

Sucking the hot and bitter liquid to the dregs, Panchito then began: "No, ño Gregorio, my brother is not dead, and luckily only rides with a party of the Colorados who came upon us with our horses swimming the river, and waited for us to come out, just as a man sent forward in an ostrich hunt waits for the driven birds. My brother turned his horse to cross again, but as he did so, a party lined the bank we just had left, and took him prisoner at once. I let my hat drop in the stream to draw their fire, and threw myself beside my horse, and when we touched the shore, darted at once full speed into the woods. They fired, but missed me, and the trees prevented them from throwing 'bolas' at my horse. So here I am safe, tired and wet, with all our horses gone, and my poor brother Cruz obliged to serve amongst the Colorados as long as General Lopez keeps the field."

As they sat talking, little by little the sun rose through the mist, which hung on every blade of grass and fell in drops off the low eaves of the estancia buildings, and clung about the coats of animals. Vizcachas peeped out timidly from their holes, and tucotucos sounded their last note from underneath the ground, before retiring for the day. Sheep bleated in the fold, and cattle, sleeping on the highest ground that they could find, stretched out their heads, but did not rise to eat, knowing the wet, white dew upon the grass would be injurious to them, whilst from the monté by the riverside the noise of myriads of birds just waking, filled the air with sound.

"Let us go out and meet the sun as do the accursed Indians in the far south of Buenos Ayres, where I once was a soldier," Gregorio said.

Rising, they went out to the door, and as they stood and scanned the plain, a noise of galloping fell on their ears.

"What have we done," Panchito said, "to irritate the Lord that he allows another band of these accursed Reds to visit us? Providence surely cannot remember that our father was a White?"

Suddenly over a low hill a man appeared racing upon a barebacked horse, his knife between his teeth. After him swept a band of ragged soldiers, some getting out their "bolas" for a throw. Both onlookers recognised at once the rider and his horse.

"My brother Cruz." "Yes, on his blue roan horse," the capataz replied. Even as they spoke, the foremost soldier, with a long cast of the "bolas," caught the blue roan round the hind legs, and with a plunge or two he fell, and the pursuers gathered round their prey. Leaping upon their horses, the agonised onlookers scoured to the place, and just arrived to hear a sergeant say, "We must make an example; the young man has been once within our ranks; besides, his father was a cursed White . . . you negro there, dismount and cut his throat."

Pale and disordered with his fall, Cruz stood, disarmed and helpless, looking mechanically at the rising sun, knowing, he saw it, for the last time upon earth. Its light fell on his face, flushing his cheeks and bathing all the group of gauchos and their horses in its life-giving rays. Facing about, the sergeant cried, "Keep those men back till I have finished with this dog," and then signing the negro forward, who advanced, drawing his knife and scenting blood, just as a wolf lays bare its fangs before he pounces on a lamb, with a quick movement threw the prisoner on his face, wrenched back his head, and plunged his dagger in his throat. With a convulsive movement and a whistling sound, as when the air is suddenly let out of a pricked bladder, the blood gushed out, staining the grass, and feet of the impassive gauchos who stood round. The victim's eyes glazed slowly, then turned back horribly, exposing all the white, and a convulsive grin deformed his features, whilst the negro pressed his body with his foot, just as a butcher presses the body of a sheep, to cause the blood to flow. A few convulsive movements of the legs showed life was passing, and then the body lay extended on the grass, helpless and limp, and looking like a bundle of old clothes.

The sergeant spoke the funeral oration, as the negro wiped his knife, saying, "The young man might have made a soldier, for he was brave, and was no miser of his throat."

Then they all mounted, lightly as a flock of birds, and struck across the plain, their horses leaving a dark trail as they brushed through the dew-bespangled grass.

Panchito, slipping off, cast himself on his brother's body with a groan, mechanically throwing the reins over his horse's head, upon the ground to stop him moving off. The horse snorted a little at the fresh-spilt blood, and then stood like a statue, outlined and motionless against the sky, in the full glare of the new-risen sun.

A Saint

The days of saints are past. We never see them in these latter times. Our eyes are just as slow to mark them as were the eyes of those who slew and tortured them in days gone by, giving them thus the chance of immortality and of a place apart, in calendars.

I knew one though, that is, if stripes and prisons oft, the scorn of men, a life of poverty and a pure nature, with a soul afire at all injustice, constitute a saint. As many of the breed were born in most unlikely places and surroundings, so was the one I knew, for I feel certain that he was a saint in truth, in deed, and thought and life, although no church has canonised his name. The race has sprung before, in palaces, in hovels, farms, in armies, convents, and again in towns, in country districts, and perhaps in gaols. But Cadiz, "Improba Gades," the laughing, whitewashed, sea-bound, salt-ringed town, which rises from the waves and seems to float, just as a nautilus lies rocking in the trades, does not at first sight strike one as a cradle for a saint.

The little town of Hercules, built on its tongue of land jutting far out into the sea, and with the great black shoal, Las Puercas, standing sentinel just in the fairway of the port, with its long rows of dazzling houses chequered with bright green jalousies, its streets in which a crowd is never seen, in which the tramp of horses is not heard, sans trade, sans manufactures, peaceful, and seeming far removed from all the troubles of the world, does not seem fitting for the birth of one destined to struggle all his life.

Your perfect rebel, and there can be no saintliness without revolt in some shape or another against the myriad meannesses that dwarf mankind, makes his own struggle, if he but strives against himself. Easier far it would have been to have sunk into mere resignation (by that sin men have fallen deeper than even angels fell by pride), and to have found all fair, as did the Lord in Eden, till man appeared to break the spell. In the soft wind-swept, sea-lapped town, where stars come out like fireflies, pale, and sink back into the sky, and where day melts into the night as imperceptibly as if it were a tide, it is so easy to forget.

Dressed in his unsubstantial, southern children's clothes, made out of stuff like bed-ticking, he must have gone to school, to some poor starveling schoolmaster (the hunger of a schoolmaster is a stock jest in Spain), or some old snuffy priest. Still, in his youth he could not but have showed the promise of his life, just as musicians and great painters composed and painted as soon as they could speak, for saintliness is of the nature of an art.

Even in Cadiz, with its quiet ways, its streets so shady in the heat, so sunny in the cold, its grass-grown plazas and its air as of a woman, fair in youth and yet more beautiful in age, the ordinary injustices of life must have revolted him.

The overladen ass, girth-galled and patient, treading its weary Calvary which leads it to no heaven, except the rest from toil that death affords, must have stirred all his blood. Cats tortured and dogs stoned, no doubt set all his childish nerves a-tingling and his sympathies on edge, as they do those of many children, but with the difference in his case that the indignation lasted all his life, and did not settle down into that careless acquiescence that makes cowards of us all.

Whether he stood and whispered at the grated window, when he grew older, to some girl half seen, or, standing on the pavement, formed with his lips dumb words to some fair Gaditana on a balcony, I do not know, but I imagine that his only love was his old mother, and that, although throughout his life he never knew the name of fear, with women he was timid and did not know the worth of his timidity in women's eyes.

Fortune had given him a little manufactory of playing-cards, left by his father, which in a year or two of philanthropic management soon went to ruin, though I remember now and then, long years ago, to have remarked upon the ace of gold, in Cadiz packs, his name, and to have thought the cards were dingy and looked like blotting-paper. This hindrance to his life having been thus removed, the way was clear for him to run his course. Never again did he own property or any money, but what was necessary for the subsistence of his mother and himself, and that from day to day.

Thus being independent of the world, he naturally, after the fashion of his brother-saints, set out on his career to redress injustices, make things grown crooked, straight, and generally to court the martyrdom mankind is ever ready to inflict on all who do not put their necks beneath its yoke.

How he became an anarchist, that is to me unknown; but probably, after the fashion of his countrymen, more by experience of life, than by long poring upon books.

In such a little town as Cadiz, where everything is known, nothing but vice is possible to hide, and that but by the complicity of others, who shield their fellow-sinners for the need they have of them, his views were known to all, and he became a sort of bugbear to the population, who, in the vegetarian dreamer, saw a dangerous revolutionist, and yet received a pleasurable qualm as he passed by, feeling a pride their city had produced so terrible a man. As he walked through the streets, dressed in his threadbare suit of shoddy Barcelona tweed, a soft grey hat upon his head, with his weak eyes shielded by neutral-tinted spectacles, people stepped off the narrow pavement on to the cobble-stones and murmured, "There goes Antichrist." Strange rumours that he maintained a correspondence with the murderers of the Czar gained ground, and sounded terrible to those who had the vaguest of ideas what a Czar really was, and in what portion of the globe Russia was situated. The police began to dog his footsteps, and to endeavour to get proof against him of some mysterious crime. Was it not patent to mankind that one who lived on bread and milk, who never smoked, or went to bull-fights, and whom no soul in Cadiz had ever seen emerge from out the narrow lane that leads down from the Paseo de Apodaca to the house where dwells La Barquillera and her nymphs, must be a man who cherished dark designs? No Christian ever would have taken to his house lost dogs or kittens, or stopped light hearted boys from putting out cats' eyes, and pouring paraffin upon them and setting it ablaze. Such practices the Church itself does not condemn, at least by precept, for it knows well that animals are not endowed with souls, and he who seeks to mitigate the torture of their lives is a mere heretic and well deserves the stake.

So, by degrees, the hero of my tale became unpopular with all right-thinking men, and though he shared his pittance with the poor, the very men he helped distrusted him, for charity, although it suffereth long, is never popular.

A famine broke out in the south, with lack of rain for months, so that the earth dried up and cracked, and in the cracks millions of field rats bred, that, issuing from their holes, devoured the remnant of the crops the locusts and the drought had spared, and the sun turned to fire. Month after month it blazed upon the fields, drying the springs and rivers, and parching up the trees. Water was dearer far than wine, and in the little laughing town a hush fell on the streets, whilst in the country hunger stalked abroad and struck men to the ground. Then came the movement of "La Mano Negra," and the authorities, anxious to pay in full all that they owed to one who, in and out of season, always opposed all governments, arrested him and shipped him off incontinently to the Peñon de la Goméra, with shackles on his feet.

For years he sweltered in the sun, wearing the blue and white striped drill in which the Spanish Government dresses its convicts, on the coast. The little money that his mother sent him he laid out in tobacco for the other convicts, who, used to what they called "the vice," were mad for want of it, and by degrees his fellow-prisoners grew to know him as The Saint. The school he started, teaching the rudiments of education on an old slate, is not forgotten in the wretched little place, which stands up like a miniature Gibraltar, united to the shore by a mere tongue of land.

Somehow or other he escaped, and wandered up and down for months amongst the tribes upon the Riff. Though as a general rule the Moors give up all convicts, except those who, as the phrase goes, "throw away their hats" and join their faith, they seem to have been impressed with the inherent goodness of this prisoner in especial, and passed him on from one tribe to another until he reached Tangier. The Spaniards, in their human, careless way, did not repatriate him to complete his sentence, but let him live as best he could by writing, teaching, and the other little industries of the unlucky man of education compelled to toil for bread.

Something took place in Spain — perhaps the unnecessary birth of some unnecessary prince, the marriage of a princess, or the like event of national importance, and what is known as an "Indulto," that is, the letting out of prisoners (who should never have been sent to gaol) occurred, and once more he was free. His name was growing as a saint, that is, a man who had no vices and spent his life in doing good, but still was quite unfitted for the world he lived in, by his outrageous love of truth.

Then came a half rebellion, and though the saint of Cadiz was not in the town, some speeches he had made, served as a pretext to arrest him, and, once arrested, he was doomed to be condemned. Again he found himself in prison, though with the feeling of half Spain upon his side, after his speech in his defence.

Years dragged along, and though from time to time accounts leaked out of all that he endured, he might have rotted and been buried in a ditch had not a general pardon once more taken place. Broken in health and prematurely aged, he wandered back to Cadiz, just as a wounded animal returns to die where it was born, and as instinctively.

Those who had shunned him all his life now stopped him in the street, and warmly wrung his hands. Prosperous citizens saluted him, and he became an object of respect, just as a conqueror is worshipped, after the victory is won.

As the sun rose he walked down to the beach, bathed and then basked a little in the sun, and wandering back again, ate with good appetite his bread and milk; and, sitting down to work, translated English scientific works for the Madrid or Barcelona Press at miserable pay.

Death took him quietly, coming as a friend, and in his only clothes, a worn and battered shoddy suit of tweed, his mother seated by his side, dressed in the livery of black that Spanish widows wear, her worn merino shawl setting her walnut-coloured face in a dark frame, he lay upon his bed.

All Cadiz blocked the street, and through the little whitewashed, flat-roofed house a long procession filed. Ladies in mourning, and workmen in their ordinary clothes, passed through and gazed at him, and at his mother sitting silently.

Some kissed his hand, and others, patting his mother on the shoulder, essayed to comfort her, just as a horse nestles its nose against the shoulder of its fellow, when he sees it is in pain.

Outside the house the "Comrades" waited in the sun, smoking and talking and spitting in the dust, without the show of grief we in the north affect, but taking everything as natural which happens to a man.

Juan, Pedro, Gil, and Saturnino, taking off their hats, shouldered the bier, still smoking, and the procession took its way through the dark street of Columela, to the cemetery. Emerging on the alameda by the sea, it halted, and another band of "Comrades," brown, bullet-headed, and with their cigarettes either behind their ears or in their mouths, relieved the bearers, pushing their way through the thick crowd that swarmed on every side. Women in black, on every balcony, gazed silently, and as the body passed, signed themselves with the cross, making it first upon the breast, and then in miniature across the mouth. Again the bearers changed, and as they passed the cemetery gates, the civil guards, sitting like figures cut in walnut, on their high crested horses from Jeréz, saluted almost as if by instinct, their captain looking vacantly before him, so that discipline was saved.

Pushing its way through the dense mass of people, the bier arrived before the grave.

Around it stood a group of workmen, with here and there a person like a schoolmaster out of employment, dressed in black, faded clothes. When the grave had been filled, the sandy soil falling like hail on the cheap coffin lid, a man stood out, and plunged immediately into a maze of words about the virtues of the dead, the rich, the poor, the social revolution, and the glorious red flag. He ceased, amid some rather faltering applause, and a rough comrade took up his parable, his eloquence at times just touching folly, and his folly rising occasionally to eloquence. He finished, sweating and hoarse, muttering, "... he was a saint . . . Adios Firmin . . . long live the social revolution . . . long live anarchy."

The ground was beaten in upon the grave, on which the blows of mattock and of spade fell heavily, just as the blows of fortune had descended all his life, on the man resting underneath. The crowd dispersed, and in an hour, once more the town had taken on again its air of emptiness, and in the streets the women walked swinging and balancing upon their hips, just as a square-rigged vessel sways and balances, with a light, leading wind.

At the River

Along the bank of the brown, swirling, southern river fringed with tamarisks, the army straggled, in a confused, tumultuous mass. The sun was sinking slowly, although there remained an hour or two of light. Alone on a white horse, in the fine rain that hung like dew upon his fleecy haik, the Sultan sat, leaning back lazily against the cantle of his high red saddle, and looking at his army with an air half of amusement, mixed with boredom and yet with some remains of pride, as if he felt he was, out there in the brown sand, close to the rushing water, underneath the sky, and in the middle of the half-nomadic horde, more the Commander of the Faithful, than in his palaces at Fez or Mequinéz.

His umbrella-bearer on a chestnut horse with a white tail and mane, and seared with marks of firing against contingent equine maladies, sat with the umbrella folded, letting the raindrops trickle from the folds. The men who trot beside the Sultan on the march, sprawled about carelessly upon the sand. The infantry in dark blue jackets and pink or scarlet trousers to the knees, barefooted and with ragged fezes on their heads, were huddled like a flock of sheep, all in disorder, carrying their rifles with fixed bayonets, or in any way they chose; their officers, dressed in half-Turkish, half-European uniforms, looked just like monkeys on a barrel-organ, seated on their enormous Moorish saddles which need the haik or the burnoose to make them picturesque.

Behind the infantry came a confused and mixed-up mass of horsemen, drawn from the tamer Arab tribes. All wore their national dress of dusky white, and all sat on their wild-eyed horses, as only those who pass their lives on horseback sit, easy and unconstrained and swaying to the slightest movement, with the set features and the roving glance of men accustomed to look out upon a wide horizon, and to behold an enemy in everything that moves.

They held their guns upright like spears, or else beneath their thighs between the saddle and the girth, in the same manner that the Spaniards and the Mexicans have taken from them, together with the long and open reins, the bit with solid curb, and the light way of mounting in one motion, just as a bird starts on its flight without an effort that the eye can see, so different from the uncouth gymnastics of the civilised, when they climb on a horse.

No one dismounted, though the army had been halted almost for an hour during the time the Sultan was receiving a deputation from a tribe, which came, bringing an offering of sheep and oxen and a long train of covered dishes piled high with couscoussou. Some of the horsemen sprawled flat upon their horses' necks, and others sat, one leg across the pommel of the saddle, and now and then a man twitched his bit sharply, when a shrill scream proclaimed that someone had allowed his horse to approach too near his neighbour's, and a fight was imminent. Three or four mountain guns, on camels, constituted the artillery, and in the rear an heterogeneous mass of tribesmen, of women, negroes, and all the flotsam and the jetsam which in North Africa accompanies an army on the march, on foot, on horseback, perched on asses and on mules, waited impassively, just as they had arrived upon the river's bank, till orders came to cross. Upon the flank of the strange, wild battalions a little to the right the Sultan's baggage mules had halted, fine, fat beasts, bearing his tents, his treasures, and the necessary rubbish that in Morocco every Sultan always has carried on the road. A guard of tribesmen from the south attended them, thin, wiry men, whose tattered haiks were all dyed brown with sand. Some of them carried hooded hawks behind them on a pad, which swayed and balanced, as their owners' horses moved, just as a man sways with the motion of a ship. Each chief had his own train of baggage animals upon a smaller scale, which were mingled with the rest and huddled round his flag, just as the Sultan's personal attendants were grouped about the blood-red banner, which once the Salée rovers flaunted on the sea.

Some European officers, dressed in fine uniforms of scarlet cloth, over which hung a light and fleecy white selhám, their heads adorned with the round Turk's-head turban which only members of the Government may wear, were near the Sultan, and now and then he talked to them, about photography, the Röntgen rays, and all the wonders to be seen in Paris and in London, and the delights of Europe, which he, by the virtue of his holy station, could but behold in newspapers; but which appeared, by virtue of their unattainability, a thousand times superior to the delights he knew.

And as they sat and talked, the army gradually became mixed up with the camp followers, and the long straggling lines of pimp-faced, pink-clad infantry sat down upon the sand, sheltering themselves in groups of twos and threes, under a haik held up by rifle-barrels. A non-commissioned officer, dressed in dark blue, with brown bare legs, and with his European boots slung round his neck, stepped to the baggage mules, and drawing out a tray of sweets went from group to group calling out, "Ya Muley Edris," the cry with which the sweetmeat sellers hawk their wares in Fez.

Trade never has dishonoured in the East, at least amongst the Arabs, so a grave smile flitted across the Sultan's negroid features as he turned sideways on his fat white horse and watched the faithful buy from the huckstering sergeant, as he moved through the ranks.

The European officers were scandalised, but in response to their remonstrances about the lack of discipline, that discipline which makes machines of men, the easy-going Sultan answered that it was but a custom of the country, and they, knowing the man they had to deal with, sat straight upon their horses, looking as mortified as he who sees a miscreant enter a church and put his hat upon the altar, for custom is as great a tyrant in the West as in the East, and that which outrages it appears as blasphemy to every sort of men.

At last the guides who had been sent to explore the ford, and see if it were passable, returned, and said it would just serve, but that the stream ran deep. All was now hurry and confusion, and the mixed, heterogeneous mass of men and animals stood waiting for the word.

The sun began to slant amongst the rain-clouds, towards the white roofs and towers of Azimúr, about a league away, just shining like a fleecy cloud, where the plain shades into the sea, as a long train of camels, bearing enormous burdens, slowly came up and joined the army halted on the bank.

Gently they sailed along, like great Dutch galliots, their noiseless footsteps giving them an air of flight. From side to side they swayed, their packs looking like sails, and seeming to sustain them in the air. Beside them walked their drivers, men brown and lean, sun-dried and spare of frame as was the youth Mohammed, before Allah had marked him out to drive his Arabs on the path of victory, ordained by Him, when He created time. Lastly, there came a negro riding on an ass, instinct with the true dignity to which only a fool attains, his snow-white clothes seeming still whiter, against his blue-black skin, scurfy and rough as is the hide of some great water buffalo or hippopotamus. With the true Oriental unconcern for dignitaries the negro halted his caravan a hundred yards or so from where the Sultan sat upon his horse. The camels kneeled, sinking down as it were by sections, the packs standing out for a moment like huge hummocks, and then subsiding on the sand. The Sultan, always craving after something new, asking from life more than it has to give, and finding nothing interesting, because he always looked for something non-existent in the marvels that surrounded him on every side, signed to an officer and sent him off to ask what merchandise was carried in the packs. After the lengthy interval which, throughout North Africa, it would be wanting in respect for anyone charged with a message to abridge, the messenger returned. "Bianos," he said, were what the camels bore, and then explained they were a kind of Christian instrument, with an infinity of notes, which played strange music, which to the faithful sounded like the howling of a dog. The Sultan, after listening to the man, as if he had forgotten all about the camels and their packs, said with a shade of interest, "It is well, bring me a 'Biano,' I want to play that tune I learned from the French dentist who was in Fez a year or two ago, and put the bits of gold into the ladies' teeth, which made me laugh so when I looked at them." Then he sat back upon his horse, throwing the ends of his long silken reins across his shoulder, whilst on his face there came a look of interest, which the sight of his army waiting a sign from him to cross the river, had been impotent to raise. In vain his European officers, the only men of all the host who dared to raise a protest, argued against the loss of time; the Commander of the Faithful still replied to all their arguments, "Bring me the Biano, I want to play on it." In haste a French mechanic and an English groom were sent for, as being men able to deal with every kind of mechanism, whether of beast or man.

In a rough halting Arabic interspersed with oaths of their respective countries, they set a gang of Arabs to undo the cases, and the component parts of a grand piano, looking like bones of some gigantic fossil animal, were laid upon the sand. The knot of Europeans stood apart disgusted at the loss of time, the certain ruin of the piano, and the futility of the proceeding, which in their eyes was almost criminal, trained as they were to order, and to regard things that had cost much money, far above human life. The army, on the other hand, took it as natural, and interesting, for almost every man who waited by the river's bank would certainly have done the same, had he but had the might. Time was of no account to them, for even if the army crossed at night nothing more serious could happen than the drowning of a score or two of men, and loss of baggage animals, a thing ordained by Allah, and against which it would be impious to strive. Quickly the body of the instrument was set upright, the other pieces put into their places, and the great concert grand by Broadwood stood a little tilting to one side, but still fit to be played on by a monarch, in the light drifting rain. A thrill of expectation ran through everyone, though no one dared to approach the instrument, the first-fruit of our European culture, thrown out by progress as a defiance to the old world, in which music is made upon an earthern [sic] drum with ends of parchment, a rude reed pipe, or a long three-stringed guitar, with the neck stuck into a calabash.

Slowly the Sultan rode his horse up to the spot, dismounted, and, as the wet trickled down from his haik, stood like the Lord in Eden, and, looking at his handiwork, proclaimed that it was good. One difficulty more still lay between him and the accomplishment of his desire. The key was lost, and though the music waited for his touch, a lid of rosewood still veiled the keyboard, keeping the Sultan still apart from his enjoyment, waiting impatient as a bridegroom waits for the disrobing of the bride. Signing mimetically to a soldier who stood near, the man advanced, and driving his bayonet underneath the lid, it opened, carrying the brass plate on the lock with it, and clanging back upon the body of the piano with a loud jarring sound.

Gravely the lineal descendant of Mohammed stood by, as careless of the eyes fixed on him, of the approaching night, the rain, and everything, either in heaven or earth, as he had been alone, upon the plain.

After a moment of reflection, as if collecting all his energies, he ran his hand across the keys, and then slowly, and with one finger, and making several wrong notes, picked out the Spanish Royal March. Then, closing the lid down with a bang, walked to his horse, which had remained watching him gravely, and mounting in one motion, raised himself in his saddle for his attendants to arrange his haik, and signing with his hand, his European officers and his Kaids, his umbrella-bearer, and the men who run beside his stirrup, gathered about him, and without turning to the army, rode down into the stream. The water foamed about their horses, banking up on the stream side, until their saddles almost were awash, whilst the fierce current bore them struggling sideways, sitting immovably with their eyes fixed upon the further bank. There they emerged, and stood like statues in the sand, watching the army cross like a great shoal of porpoises, shouting and struggling in the stream, the smaller luggage animals swimming, whilst men guided them by the tails, or walked above them to break the current's force, holding their guns above their heads.

The camels followed gravely, their slender necks making them look like some vast water serpent, rising from the flood. Soon all had crossed, and on the sand, in the light, penetrating rain, the piano stood alone, looking ridiculous, but somehow menacing, as if the halting air that had been forced reluctantly from its insulted keys had been the death-note of the old, wild barbaric life which had surged past it, and now was swallowed up in mist.

Bu Gidri

The little holes which seamed his rugged Berber face had given him the title of the Father of Small-pox, which he — after the fashion of his countrymen, who take all, rain, wind, sun, good and bad fortune, wounds, prison, mutilation, even death itself, as being actual and direct manifestations of the Will Divine — had cheerfully accepted, and bore as uncomplainingly as he had borne the illness from which he took his name. Half Pagan, half Mohammedan, (after the fashion of the race from which most likely sprang St. Augustine), although he thought himself a firm believer, Bu Gidri was employed as soldier in the British consulate at Fez. Dressed in the Arab clothes which rarely suit a Berber, for the two races are as distinct as are the English and the French, he strove, though mean of stature and appearance, to look a swaggerer, and had grown the two long locks on either temple which are the outward visible sign of the official of the court. His pointed fez, and sword cocked up behind in the Arab style, gave him an air as of a monkey on a barrel-organ. Such was his outward mien, but those who knew him, knew that he was brave, staunch, obstinate as a mule, and one of those able to knock a nail into a plank by beating on it with his forehead, and then, if the necessity arose, to draw it with his teeth. Being a Berber, he had the catlike love of places, unknown to Arabs, who for the most part live and die, as it were on a journey, sleeping and dying on the road. Their very cemeteries are often unenclosed, and merely set about with pieces of rough stone, through which run short-cuts, death-traps to horsemen, who, trusting to the will of God, at night cross them at highest speed, knowing that those who sleep below the stones all were bold riders to a man.

Withal, Bu Gidri was an honest and a conscientious man, one that no gold could buy, thing unknown amongst the Arabs, with whom a key of gold opens all locks. Slow-witted, but tenacious of ideas when once they filtered through his skull into his brain, those who employed him knew him for a man to send upon a desperate errand should the necessity arise, certain that he would reach the place to which they sent him, or die upon the quest.

One portion of his life was shut from all mankind, although he was not so impenetrable as are the Arabs, with whom a frank exterior serves as a water-tight bulkhead between them and the world. At times, when asked about "his house" — the formula employed by Mussulmans when asking after one another's families — he would launch into details, and say that "she" was well, and then, pull himself up and stammer and drift off into praises of his little boy, who he averred, with the innocent fatuity of fathers, Mohammedan and Christian alike, was quite a paragon.

To the outward eye, the marvel was a dirty little boy in a torn yellow shirt, barefooted and black-eyed, and with a little close-shaved bullet-head, on which you could have struck a match had it not here and there been spotted with a white eruption, nauseous to behold. But, for his reticence about his family affairs he quite made up by his garrulity about a certain little pacing pony that he had bought in the Ait-Yusi country, and which he swore could go from Fez to Tangier in three days, and that, so smoothly that he could carry in his hand a glass of water and never spill a drop. This equine wonder was a cow-hocked and fiddle-headed beast, of a light cream colour with black points, and had an eye bloodshot and dangerous-looking, which did not in the least belie his temper, for to approach him was to expose oneself to be kicked or bitten, or to receive a blow from his fore feet, which if it carried home would have been fatal, for rising up, he used to launch his feet into the air, just as a boxer hits, and scream with fury, if he did not know his man. Once saddled and the Moorish bit jammed home between his yellow teeth, which operation usually entailed tying his feet together with a rope, or putting on a twitch, he then became as gentle as a sheep, after the way of many horses in the East.

Tied to a tree or post, nodding his head, with the flies clustered in bunches round his eyes, the high red Arab saddle towering like a howdah on his back, he looked fitted for nothing, but to draw water from a well. Yet when his master got upon his back (which feat he executed indifferently from either side, holding his gun, full five feet long, enclosed in a red case), and drove the edge of the sharp Arab stirrup into his belly, he pricked his long lop ears and a light shone in his red eye which gave a promise of interior graces not revealed by his exterior, impressing you, just as St. Paul when he had begun to launch into his theme must have impressed the men of Athens, who had despised the ugly little Jew. Still, with defects and all, he was the apple of Bu Gidri's eye, and though he seldom rode him, but for powder-play, when he would gallop him about as if possessed, wheeling and turning on the strong Arab bit just as a gull turns wheeling in the air, it yet was his delight to tend him and, above all, to talk about his powers. Most of his time the horse spent in a yard, exposed to rain and snow, up to his fetlocks in the mud in winter, and in the heat a prey to flies, and screaming savagely if any other horse came near him, as he laid back his ears.

His master during the daytime generally sat inside the doorway of the British Consulate, looking at nothing, now and then drinking a cup of sweet green tea flavoured with leaves of mint. His duties sometimes took him to the post office or to some other consulate, and now and then mounted upon his horse, his gun in hand, he rode behind the consul into the country to a picnic, his features fixed and impressionless, with his blue cloth "selham," which if he had but been an Arab would have been draped in graceful folds or flown behind him as he rode, swathing his body like a shroud.

Never in all his time of service, which had extended over years, had he been sick or sorry, or been away upon a holiday, so that one morning when he appeared, expressionless as usual, to ask permission to be absent for a week to go to Tangier, he got it willingly. Thanking the consul in the unceremonious way a man returns his thanks in countries like Morocco — where, if permission is not given at once, the man who asks, usually takes it on himself to grant it — he said, as if the thing had happened to another, "My son is dead; little Hamido whom you knew. I want to bury him amongst my people, after the fashion of my folk." Without a word about the will of Allah, which, had he been an Arab, he would have quoted gravely, partly to show his faith and partly to conceal his grief, he turned and left the room. What passed that afternoon in the mysterious interior of his house only himself could tell. Early next morning, just as the furtive streaks of red which split the sky into a sort of pattern had appeared, about an hour before the dawn, the sleepy gatewards in the dark passage under the massive archway of the Bab-el-Gizeh saw him strike into the road.

Mounted upon his pacing nag, his gun beneath his thigh, and balancing a little bundle wrapped in white rags upon the pommel of his saddle, he twitched his bridle, making the pony toss his head, and change his feet twice or thrice hurriedly before he fell into his pace.

The crenellated walls of Fez, flanked here and there by towers, on which stood storks asleep upon one leg, or flapping lazily as the dawn slowly crept across the sky, ran on the right, and on the left a vast flat plain, dotted with tents which sprang like mushrooms from the sandy soil, extended to a range of hills, now wreathed in mist through which the scattered houses just appeared, ghostly and white, and dripping with the dew. When he had passed beyond the walls he turned, and, looking back at Fez, saw it rise from the sandy hollows where it lies, transformed and glorious, dazzlingly white as is a water-lily, silent and ghostly in the early morning air, with every marking on the houses and the mosques so clear and well defined that it appeared that he could touch them with his hand. Rising a little in the saddle, he settled all his clothes, then pressed the stirrup in his pony's flank, who whisked his tail and struck into a pace between a trot and canter, swaying his rider to and fro, just like a camel, as he shuffled through the sand.

Muffled in his white halk, which swathed him like a mummy, silent and sorrowful, bearing his little dusky bundle balancing between his body and the pommel of his high red saddle, the pony's footsteps deadened in the sand, Bu Gidri passed so quietly through the now sunlit plain, that he appeared like death on his pale horse, prowling round stealthily to mark his prey. All day he paced along, jerking his pony's mouth occasionally after the Arab fashion, making the bridle ring against his teeth when the beast broke his pace or seemed to weary, and with his stirrup pressed into its side. He passed the great red hill, traversing first the sandy lanes, hedged on both sides with aloes, and then the wood of olives, till he stood on the ridge, from which Fez looks like a mere blotch of dazzling whiteness floating in the air. The noonday heat caught him close to a brick-arched well, beside which springs a palm tree, with its roots in water and its head in fire.

Lighting down carefully as must a man who wears voluminous clothes and keeps his slippers on by a perpetual contraction of the feet, he led his horse into the shade, balancing carefully the precious bundle on the saddle with his other hand. Laying it down upon a stone, he pulled his horse towards him sharply by the tail to see if it stood firm and had not felt the five hours' steady work upon the road, then loosening the girths, he put the hobbles on its feet and let it browse upon the scanty grass which grew about the well. Then sitting down he ate a piece of brown and gritty bread, moistening his thumb to gather up the crumbs, not on account of hunger, but from the sacred character bread has amongst the Moors, who hold it impious to waste a particle of the chief blessing God has given man.

Kief, smoked in a minute and curiously shaped pipe, the stem of which was a light cane about a foot in length, carved in concentric patterns, he fell into that state of half contemplation, half of dreaminess, which overtakes all those who have the habit, and then, rising to drink a little water, tightened his girths, bitted his pony, and swinging slowly into his high saddle, leaned back against the cantle, rubbed his stiff knees, and once again took up his march, refreshed by his brief halt.

Night overtook him at the Hájara Cherifa, on the Sebou, where he entered a zariba, and, after looking to his horse, sat talking of the price of barley, the doings of the tribes, always either in rebellion or ready to break out, till food was ready, and after eating heartily of the wheaten porridge, known as couscoussou, threw out more barley for his horse upon a saddle-cloth, and lying down close to him, fell into the broken sleep usual to horsemen on a solitary ride. During the night he woke occasionally, and watched his horse munching his corn, and later, standing sleeping, resting a leg, and with one ear laid back upon his neck.

Long before daylight he had saddled up, and joined a caravan to cross the river, which lay deep down below the village, a mere white ribbon in the mist. Slowly, the train of horses and of mules, followed by a long string of camels, slithered and stumbled down the slope. At first they crossed a tract of stones, on which grew tamarisks, stunted and broken by the browsing of the goats, then they passed several branches of the stream, and lastly entered the main channel, which, grey and cold, brawled through the stones, affording a precarious footing for the beasts.

Pressing in front, Bu Gidri passed the river with the water to his saddle-skirts, the current edging his horse sideways, until he reached the bank. The pony scaled it like a cat, just stopping at the top to shake the water from his coat, and as his rider turned to see the others cross, the dawn just lit up the encircling hills, making the tops float in the mist, mysterious, and looking like extinct volcanoes in the moon. It fell upon the rock from which the crossing takes its name, of Hájara Cherifa, and showed it standing gaunt, a natural obelisk upon the plain, a palm tree growing at its base, and giving it an air as of a temple, raised by nature to some strange deity, never yet known to man.

Leaving the caravan, Bu Gidri pushed on over the stony plain, crossing the Ardatz and the Wergha, high up in their course, where they present an infinity of little streams, meandering through sheets of pebbles, and came by noonday, with his horse still full of strength, to where a stream just issues from a ruined Roman wall. Fish played about the entrance of the pool, and, as the shadow of the horseman fell upon the water, they darted back into the dark recesses of the arch. There he passed the hottest hours, waiting for when the sun, the enemy of man in Africa, should fall a little — and once again pushed on.

The heat rose from the stones as from a lime-kiln heated to its extremest point, and with his head bowed in his haik he still pushed onwards, the sweat dripping from off his horse's belly, and drying white and saltish on his coat. At times Bu Gidri crooned a high-pitched Berber song, but always kept a watchful eye on the horizon, just as a sailor scans the sea, observing nothing near him, but on the watch for anything unusual on the limit of his view. The setting sun saw him just passing down the steep red track, from where, amongst the orange gardens, Alcázar just appears set in its woods and cultivated grounds, a league or two away. Fear fell upon him that he should find the gates all closed against him, for he knew well that raiding mountaineers from Gibel Zarzar and the adjoining hills made the outskirts of the town dangerous at night to him who sleeps alone. So he pressed on, after a good look at his horse, and after feeling him sharply in the mouth, to try his spirit, with the fixed look and constant shogging of the feet, which come upon a horseman, all unknown to him, towards the evening of a long march, when there is still a mile or two to do before the sun has set.

Nobly the pacing pony answered to his call, switching his scraggy tail, and scurrying along the road so smoothly that the little bundle scarcely moved, just kept in place by a light pressure of the rider's hand. He reached the Koos, which runs between high banks, and where the ford makes a great horseshoe bend, to avoid the fury of the stream. Putting its feet together in a bunch, the pony slithered down the muddy bank, and in a moment Bu Gidri found himself contending with the flood.

The men who hang about the ford to help the passers-by and to point out the passage, had returned to town, leaving the river desolate, grey, foaming, and broken into rapids here and there, the outer one of which was certain death to the unwary horseman who should essay to cross. Carefully fixing both his eyes upon a tree which stood out on the further bank, he spurred his pony into the deeper water, which in the twilight seemed about to overwhelm him as it banked up upon the weather side, and flowed across the saddle for a step or two. Then suddenly it shallowed, and entering the slack water Bu Gidri waded to the bank, and, coming out amongst the orange gardens on the top, set his horse galloping, and did not stop till he came to the gate, which he found almost about to close, and passed into the town just as the call to evening prayer rang out from the high towers cased in dark metallic tiles, which rise like lighthouses from the flat sea of yellow houses and the thatched negro huts. Only some sixty miles were left to ride, so he slept well, and rising early took his way across the black alluvial plain, where by the Wad M'hassen runs the long bridge which marks the battlefield on which the ill-fated King of Portugal was slain, although some look for him still to come back and claim his kingdom, after three hundred years. Knowing he now could reach his village in good time, Bu Gidri rode along less anxiously, his pony eating the road, as say the Arabs, like clockwork, pacing so steadily that his master never felt the pace, which seemed to skim the surface of the ground just as a sledge flies on the surface of the snow. Towards evening he crossed the Ackbal Hamara, leading his horse down the steep, craggy track that comes out on the plain. He passed Ain Dallia, and then in an hour more, upon a little hill, rode into the sea breeze, which seemed like coming into paradise, after a day or two in hell.

He reached his village outside Tangier, just at nightfall and dismounted at a house. Almost at daybreak he was afoot with one or two companions and an old woman whom he had hired to wail beside the grave. With hoes they hacked a hole in the rough stony village cemetery, and quite impassively Bu Gidri laid the bundle in the grave; the woman broke out into a shrill, ear-piercing lamentation, and the brief ceremony was at an end. All day he lounged about Tangier smoking a pipe or two of kief, and drinking tea occasionally, to show he was in town. Next morning saw him on the road, and on the eighth day after leaving Fez, the consul, going to his office, found him at his post seated at the front door, and with an air as of a man who has performed a duty, sheepish, self-satisfied, and just a little blackened by the sun.

Faith

An Arab Funeral

A sound of chanting filled the streets as a small white-clad group of men carrying a body, high on an open bier, passed through the town. The dusky haik that swathed the corpse, outlined its angles, making it look just like a sculptor's sketch in clay, covered with linen and damped to keep it wet.

The bearers, chosen at random, of all heights and ages, stumbled along, now trotting and again walking with the peculiar swing the flowing Arab clothes give to a mass of men upon the march. As the procession made its way through the streets, filthy with refuse, and past the market where the blood of animals left on the stones had formed a purple mud, the people whom it passed, scarcely appeared to notice it, as if the funeral merely were an incident in the long journey of the lives, so many of them pass upon the road. A casual European looked with interest, his hand rising involuntarily towards his hat, then stopped upon the way, feeling uncertain how his salutation might be received; but the compatriots and co-religionists of the dead man, lying so stiffly underneath his haik, bought, sold, and talked of money (their favourite theme) unmoved, trusting in God to stay His hand toward themselves, and give them a long day. Yellow and wolfish dogs ran in and out between the bearers' legs, and no one cursed them, as Europeans do on lesser provocation, and as the bier was borne into the open market-place, it found itself entangled in a crowd of people all dressed exactly in the same white rags that their dead brother wore. So thick the people swarmed that the procession halted several times, to let them separate. Long strings of camels, bearing bales covered up with brown and white striped rugs, swayed past it, their heads towering above the bier, at which they looked with the grave curiosity that seems to stamp them as inhabitants of a world older than is our own. Asses and mules carrying great nets packed hard with straw pressed on the mourners, and on the bier itself, as they passed by, and now and then the mass of human beings opened sullenly to let a horseman pass, who, upright in his saddle, appeared to kneel upon his horse, in his short stirrup-leathers. Huts made of sacking or of old blankets, lined the road which cut the market into two, and by them, squatted their owners selling charcoal, bundles of firewood, vegetables and fruit. Men carrying goat-skins full of water, and a brass cup in their left hands, tinkling a bell, trudged to and fro, now and then stopping to pour out a cupful and receive a copper coin infinitesimally small. Over the press there hung the scent as of wild beasts distinctive of crowds in the East, and dust and particles of horse-dung floated in the air, making it pungent and difficult to breathe.

The market passed *[sic=past]*, the funeral took its way through the town gates into the open country, which, when a belt of gardens had been crossed, stretched out a waste of stones. The cemetery, built by the fostering care of the French conquerors more than a mile beyond the walls, surrounded by a high white wall and set about with European trees which drooped in the fierce sun, stood out gaunt, modern, and as unlike as possible to an Arab burying-ground with its rough slabs of stones, crossed by innumerable footpaths and browsed upon by goats.

Emerging on the stony plain, from which the sun gave back its heat a hundredfold, the mourners halted and changed bearers, chanting the whole time in a minor key. Their flowing dusky clothes blended exactly with the landscape, on which the sun poured down a flood of light so white that every colour disappeared, and the corpse on its bier appeared suspended in the air, or left alone, as if it were the grave of some Araphoé or Apaché chief, left on four stakes to moulder, so absolutely the carrying figures melted into the stones.

Once more they started, and their chant in the thin air just reached the ear, fine and high-pitched as a mosquito's song. They seemed to fly, their feet just brushing on the road, in the half-mirage raised by the heat and rising from the ground. The bier swayed to and fro, but gently, just as a rider sways upon a pacing horse, and the procession, white and unearthly-looking, floated towards its goal, as if borne by the wind.

So, for a little space there came an air as of romance over the last act connected with a man who perhaps in life had been a petty shop-keeper, or perhaps one of those nameless brawling Arabs who in the market-place of any town in Barbary, jangle and shout the livelong day, sit in a café drinking green tea if by the merest chance they have a penny, and sleep at night upon the cobble stones at a street corner, or lie with other waifs in the "m'darsa" of the mosque.

Nature was making up to him, although he knew it not, and probably would not have cared even if he had known, for his life's sordidness and want. As you looked out upon the fleeting spectacle, so cloudlike and so similar to life itself, hurrying along the road towards the cemetery, the thought occurred, what if it is the last stage of the journey that some wandering tribesman is making through the world?

Then, as if confirmation of the idea was wanted and to make the simile complete, the bearers once more halted, laying the bier upon the ground and sitting down to rest. Only a fragmentary note or two of the wild chanting now reached the ear, deadened by passing through the semi-tropical belt of garden land planted with palm trees, apricots that grew as high as elms, and with bananas, and those so faint and so disjointed that they appeared as if they had been wafted from afar, and that the actual little group seated amidst the stone-strewn landscape had no reality and was an image of a scene projected on the sky, as by a mirage in the Sáhara.

Once more they took their burden up, and once again their drapery fluttered as they trotted on, but now all in a mass, and the high bier had faded out of sight against the stones. They passed between high rocks, and then once more came out upon the plain, always a little nearer to the cemetery. Then, as they neared it, once more they came into full view, their dusky clothes standing out clearly against its whitewashed walls. A green gate opened, and they entered and were lost to sight, leaving the gazer from the town walls uncertain whether they had really passed before his view, or had been but a figment of the brain, or a refraction on the retina accustomed to the various scenes of Arab life. Around the shallow grave no doubt they stood, after their custom, chanting their testimony of belief in the One God, which moulds their faith but does not influence their works. Lastly, the corpse was lowered from the bier, and lay, looking pathetically small in its white wrappings, in the hot sandy soil which had so often been its bed in life. Then, without waiting, whilst the others still intoned the versicle "No God, but God," the noblest, baldest statement of belief that man has yet devised, three or four took the mattocks with which the grave-diggers had wrought the grave, and filled it, shovelling down the sand and stones upon the corpse, which seemed to shiver as it felt their weight, and shrink into the ground. They shed no tears, for to have done so would have been to doubt of Allah's wisdom — Allah the merciful, the compassionate, He who had breathed the breath of life into the nostrils of the dead believer for a spell, and then withdrawn it, as it seemed good to Him. When all was done, and a small sandy mound was raised over the body, and then edged round with stones, they stood a moment silently gazing on the ground. Then sitting down, some on the bier and others on the sand, they once more raised their chant, wailing and long-drawn-out, sounding as if the soul of the dead man still fluttered round about the spot, bewailing its disseverance from the flesh, which alone gave it feeling and existence, if ever it had lived.

Long they sat singing, chiefly in verses from the Kóran; verses affirming their belief; belief in Him who chose the Praised One as His prophet, and let him in his youth guide camels, so that the experience thus gained would stand him in good stead, when it was time for him to guide mankind. Hours passed, and then in groups they sauntered back towards the town, emerging from the cemetery bathed in the evening light, glorious and statuesque in their white robes. Then as they neared the town, and as the setting sun fell on their backs, the halo which it had thrown upon them far away dispersed, they passed the gates, a group of dirty Arabs, carrying some boards and chattering loudly as they trotted through the sand.

Mektub

All Tangier knew the Rubio, the fair-haired blind man, who sat upon the mounting-block outside the stables of the principal hotel. His bright red hair and bleared blue eyes, together with his freckled face, looking just like a newly-scalded pig, had given him the name by which the Europeans knew him, although no doubt he was Mohammed, something or another, amongst his brethren in the faith.

He spoke indifferently well most European languages up to a point, and perfectly as far as blasphemy or as obscenity was concerned, and his quick ear enabled him as if by magic to ascertain the nationality of any European passer-by, if ever he had spoken to the man before, and to salute him in his mother-tongue.

All day he sat, amused and cheerful, in the sun. Half faun, half satyr, his blindness kept him from entire materialism, giving him sometimes a half-spiritual air, which possibly may have been but skin deep, and of the nature of the reflection of a sunset on a dunghill; or again, may possibly have been the true reflection of his soul as it peeped through the dunghill of the flesh.

As people passed along the road, their horses slithering and sliding on the sharp pitch of the paved road, which dips straight down from underneath the mounting-block of the hotel, between the tapia walls, over which bougainvilleas peep, down to the Soko Grande, El Rubio would hail them, as if he had been a dark lighthouse, set up to guide their steps.

Occasionally, but rarely, he mistook his mark, hailing some European lady with obscenity, or bawling to the English clergyman that he could tell him "where one fine girl live, not more than fifteen year"; but his contrition was so manifest, when he found his mistake, that no one bore him malice, and he remained an institution of the place and a perpetual rent-charge on all passers-by.

By one of the strange contradictions which Nature seems to take delight in just to confound us, when after a few thousand years of study we think we know her ways, the Rubio had a love of horses which in him replaced the usual love of music of the blind. No one could hold two or three fighting stallions better, and few Moors in all the place were bolder riders — that is, on roads he knew. Along the steep and twisting path that leads towards Spartel he used to ride full speed and shouting "Balak" when he was sent upon a message or with a horse from town out to the villas on the hill. All those who knew him left him a free road, and if he met a herd of cattle or of sheep, the horse would pick his way through them, twisting and turning of his own accord, whilst his blind rider left the reins upon his neck and galloped furiously. In what dark lane or evil-smelling hole he lived no European knew. Always well dressed and clean, he lived apart both from the Moors and from the Europeans, and in a way from all humanity, passing his time, as does a lizard, in the sun and in the evening dis-appearing to his den. The missions of the various true faiths, Catholic, Presbyterian, and Anglican, had tackled him in vain. Whether it was that none of them had anything to offer which he thought better than the cheerful optimism with which he was endowed by nature to fight the darkness of the world he lived in, is difficult to say. Still, they had all been worsted; not that the subject of their spiritual blandishments could have been termed a strict Mohammedan, for he drank any kind of spirits that was presented to him by Christians, anxious perhaps to make him break the spirit, if they were impotent to move him in the letter of his law. Still though he sat with nothing seemingly reflected on the retina of his opaque and porcelain-coloured eyes, his interior vision was as keen or keener than that of other men. He never seemed a man apart, or cut off from his fellows, but had his place in life, just as throughout the East the poorest and most miserable appear to have, not barred out from mankind by mere externals as are their brethren in the North, shut in the ice of charity, as bees are shut behind a plate of glass so that the rich may watch their movements in the hive.

Up from the Arab market over which he sat, as it were, presiding in his darkness, just as God seems to sit, presiding blindly, over a world which either mocks Him, or is mocked at by Him, there came a breath of Eastern life, bearing a scent compounded of the acrid sweat of men, dried camel's dung, of mouldering charcoal fires, of spices, gunpowder, and of a thousand simples, all brought together by mere chance or fate, a sort of incense burned in his honour, and agreeable to his soul. It seemed to bring him life, and put him into touch with all he could not see, but yet could feel, almost as well as if he saw, just as did other men.

Sniffing it up, his nostrils would dilate, and then occasionally a shadow crossed his face, and as he ran his hands down the legs of the horse left in his charge, marking acutely any splint or spavin they might have, he used to mutter, half in a resigned, half in an irritated way, "Mektub," the sole profession of his faith that he was ever heard to make, for if a thing is written down by fate, it follows naturally that there is somebody who writes, if only foolishly. Whether the mystic phrase of resignation referred to his condition or to the possible splint upon the horse's leg, no one could tell, but as the shadow passed away, as quickly as it came, he soon fell back again into the half-resigned good humour of the blind, which, like the dancer's lithographic smile, seems quite involuntary.

Years melted into one another, and time sauntered by, just as it always must have sauntered in the town where hours are weeks, weeks months, and months whole years, and still the hum of animals and men rose from the Arab market, and still the shadows in the evening creeping on the sand seemed something tangible to the blind watcher on his stone. Not that he cared for time, or even marked its flight, or would have cared to mark it, had it been pointed out to him, for life was pleasant, the springs of charity unfailing, wit ever present in his brain, and someone always had a horse to hold, to which he talked, as it stood blinking in the sun. His blindness did not seem to trouble him, and if he thought of it at all, he looked on it as part and parcel of the scheme of nature, against which it is impious to contend. Doctors had peered into his eyes with lenses, quarrelled with one another on their diagnoses of his case, and still the Rubio sat contented, questioning nothing, and enduring everything, sun, rain, wind, flies, and dust, as patiently as if he were a rock. Nothing was further from his thoughts than that he ever once again could see. Plainly, it had been written in the books of fate he should be blind, and so when European doctors talked to him of operations and the like, he smiled, not wishing to offend, and never doubting of their learning, for had not one of them cured a relation of his own of intermittent fever by the use of some white magic powder, when native doctors, after having burned him with a red-hot iron, and made him take texts of the Koran steeped in water, had ignominiously failed?

All that they said did not appeal to him, for all of them were serious men, who talked the matter over gravely, and looked on him as something curious on which to exercise their skill. All might have gone on in the same old way, and to this day the Rubio still sat upon his stone without a wish to see the horses that he held, the sunlight falling white upon the towers, or the red glare upon the Spanish coast at eventide, had not a German scientist appeared on the horizon of his life.

From the first day on which the Rubio held the doctor's horse a fellowship sprang up between them, not easy to explain. No single word of Arabic the doctor spoke, and all the German that the Rubio knew was either objurgatory or obscene, and yet the men were friends. Tall and uncouth and with a beard that looked as if it never had been combed, his trousers short and frayed and with an inch or two of dirty sock showing between them and his shoes, dressed in a yellowish alpaca jacket, and a white solar topee lined with green, the doctor peered out on the world through neutral-tinted glasses, for his own eyes were weak.

Whether this weakness drew him to the blind, or if he liked to hear the Rubio's tales about the Europeans he had known, to all of whom he gave the worst of characters, calling them drunkards and hinting at dark vices which he averred they practised to a man — not that he for a moment believed a single word he uttered, but thought apparently his statements gave a piquancy to conversation — the doctor never said. Soon Tangier knew him for a character, and as he stumbled on his horse about the town, curing the Arabs of ophthalmia and gathering facts for the enormous book he said he meant to write upon North Africa, his reputation grew. The natives christened him "Father of Blindness," which name appeared to him a compliment, and he would use it, speaking of himself, complacently, just as a Scotsman likes to be spoken of under the style and title of the land he owns, although it be all bog. Though in the little world of men in which he lived the doctor was a fool, in the large field of science he was competent enough, and when he proved to demonstration to the other doctors in the place that a slight operation would restore the Rubio's sight, they all fell in with it, and though for years the object of their care had held their horses and they had seen him every day, without observing him, he now became of interest, just as a moth becomes of interest when it is dead and put into a case with other specimens.

Whether the sympathy that certainly exists between wise men and those whose intellect is rudimentary, and which is rarely manifested between a learned and an ordinary man, prevailed upon the Rubio to submit himself to the ministrations of the German man of science, Allah alone can tell. A season saw the mounting-block deserted, and tourists gave their horses to be held by boys, who tied them by the reins to rings high in the wall, and fell asleep, leaving the animals to fight and break their bridles, and for a time no stream of cheerful blasphemy was heard, in any European tongue, upon the mounting-stone. In a clean unaccustomed bed in a dark corner of Hope House, the missionary hospital, the Rubio lay, his head bound up in bandages, silent, but cheerful, confident in the skill of his strange friend, but yet incredulous, after the Arab way.

During the long six weeks, what were his thoughts and expectations it is difficult to say. Perhaps they ran upon the wonders of the new world he would inherit with his sight, perhaps he rather dreaded to behold all that he knew so well and so familiarly by touch. He who, when like a lizard he had basked against his wall, had never for a moment ceased from talking, now was silent, and when the doctor visited him, to dress his eyes, and make his daily diagnosis of the case, answered to all the words of hope he heard, "It will be, as God wishes it to be," and turned uneasily between his unfamiliar sheets. At last the day arrived when doctors judged the necessary time had passed. No one in Tangier was more confident than was the "Father of Blindness," who went and came about the town buoyed high with expectation, for he was really a kind-hearted man, learned but simple, after the fashion of his kind.

At early morning all was ready, and in the presence of the assembled doctors of the place with infinite precaution the dressings were removed. Cautiously and by degrees, a little light was let into the room. Holding his patient's hand and visibly moved, the German asked him if he saw. "Not yet," the Rubio answered, and then, throwing the window open wide, the sunlight filled the room, falling upon the figure in the bed, and on the group of doctors standing by expectantly. It filled the room, and through the window showed the mountains standing out blue above Tarifa, and the strait, calm as a sheet of glass, except where the two "Calas" cut it into foam. It fell upon the cliffs which jut into the sea below Hope House; upon the hills of Anjera, and on the bird-like sails of the feluccas in the bay, filling the world with gladness that a new day was born. Still on his bed the Rubio lay, pale with his long confinement, and with his hands nervously feeling at his eyes. All saw that the experiment had failed, and with a groan the German man of science buried his head between his hands and sobbed aloud, the tears dimming his spectacles and running down upon his beard. With a grave smile the patient got out of his bed, and having felt his way to where he heard the sobs, laid his rough, freckled hand upon the shoulder of his friend, and said as unconcernedly, as if he had not suffered in the least, "Weep not; it was not written"; then, looking round, asked for a boy to lead him back again to his accustomed seat upon his stone.

Lochan Falloch

Brown billowing woods spring from the rising ground beyond the lake. The lake itself is set in fir woods on three sides, and on the other bounded by a wild moor.

Almost all round it stretches a pebbly beach, broken by beds of bulrushes, which now and then rise from a mossy patch between the stones. Islands with ruins of the past stud its smooth surface, and are reflected upside down, as in a looking-glass reversed. The woods, chiefly of beech, appear like outworks thrown before the hills to guard their mysteries. Rough, roaring burns here and there cut a passage to the lake and brawl between banks fringed with rowan trees and ash. After the woods are passed, a further outwork of wet boggy ground, in which grow willows and sweet-gale, extends.

This by degrees melts into a dull waste of ling, strewed with great boulders of rough pudding-stone. The heath grows sparser higher up, where the wind sweeps upon it all the year. Then it gives place to tracts of stones. Lastly, the hill rising up steep from the last slope is reached, and following a burn, until it issues from a green mossy "well," you stand upon the ridge.

There, a panorama stretches out, studded with lakes, with woods, and interspersed with farms towards the west. Towards the east lies the brown Flanders Moss, an ancient sea, which even yet appears to roll in the white mist of evening. The whole is framed in ranges of long undulating hills, which guard the south.

Northwards, the Grampians, still mysterious and wild, tower up, in peaks, in castles, and in serrated ridges, through which the passes, now disused, formerly penetrated.

Standing upon the topmost ridge, and quite invisible from any other point, quite unsuspected, lost, almost forgotten by the outer world, is hid a little lake.

It is indeed a little hidden loch, lying so deep and unsuspected in its hollow between hills, that the first Kelt or Pict who came upon it, ages ago, must straight have hit upon the name it bears. Nature seems, now and then, to have suspected that a time would come when all her secrets would lie bare and open to the prying eye of vulgar curiosity, and to have hid away some of her chiefest beauties in places where they are in sanctuary, hallowed from human gaze, which at the same time worships and violates them. So, she set this her little gem, remote, hiding it as a hind conceals her young, deep in the heather, underneath the tallest bracken, and in a wilderness of hills. They tower on every side, bare, bald, and wind-swept, whilst in a corrie nestles the little lake, upon whose surface the wind scarcely or never preys, leaving it calm, mysterious, and unruffled, as if it held some secret, too natural for us to understand. If fairies still exist, they come, no doubt, from the Sith Bruach which guards the Avon Dhu at Aberfoyle, and sail their boats of acorn-cups and leaves on the black lakelet. Upon the little beach they run their craft ashore and dance on the broad ribbon of smooth sand which rings the lake, as a black mezzotint is edged around with white. But if the fairies come, they come unseen, leaving no token of their passage but a few turned-up leaves which they have used for boats, and the mysterious circlet of white foam they churn, which hangs between the fringe of bulrushes and the mimic surf in which float flies that have ventured further than their wings can bear them, and now wash up and down, as in some distant island of the South Seas, drowned mariners may drift upon the beach. Sunk in its hollow far from the world, the tarn seems to have been left adrift, a derelict floated down to us from some older age, and with one's eyes closed one can see strange animals of monstrous size come down the steep hillsides and drink and play, throwing about the water as they stand knee-deep. Around its banks grows equisetum, as if to point back to a time when different vegetation, gigantic and distorted, towered by its edge, and in which harboured the strange beasts that must have been familiar to its shores.

Light-footed tribesmen, as they drove the "creagh" from the fat Lowlands to their hungry hills, must have stopped by the lake to slake their thirst, prone on their breasts their rough red beards floating like seaweed on the water as they drank. Even in summer, when bees hum in the heather, and the scent of peat fresh cast and left to dry perfumes the air, and little moss-trout bask in the tiny stream that issues from the lake, or dart amongst its stones, there broods an air as of aloofness from mankind. Over the corrie which the water fills, leaving but little ground between it and the hills except at one end, where a long-forgotten, perhaps Fingalian, mountain trail is still half visible on the stones which lie amongst the ling, the wind sweeps softly, and the water-spiders, with greater faith than Peter's, walk on the surface of the lake so lightly that they hardly leave a shadow as they pass.

In winter, when the wind laments aloud for the lost sun, and the dark water of the lochan turns to black ice, whilst the white foam congealed clings round the stalks of the dead bulrushes, and all the heather droops in the keen frost, the scene is wild and threatening, as if the spirits of the past kept watch over the last of their possessions that had remained untouched. Then, in spite of the keen cold, the birds and animals all venture out, certain that they are safe, at least from man, and leave strange tracks amongst the snow, which form a chart of them and of their habits, readable but to those whose eyes have not been rendered dim by poring upon print.

Even in snow and cold, and when the wind drives all the grass and heather crouching to the ground, and when the little fish rise to the air-holes in the translucent ice to breathe, and nature seems to wither in the frost, there yet remains over the lochan dhu an air as of content, amidst the desolation of the hills.

Whether the breeze just curls the water, or drives a dust of particles of frozen snow along the surface of the ice; whether the cotton-grass waves silkily and the bog-asphodels spring from the peat and the green "wells" are bright with mosses, or the field-mice play hide-and-seek between the stalks of the stiff frozen grasses, the lochlet seems to smile as enigmatically as does the Sphinx, showing itself in full communion with the past. It smiles, like a fair woman who hides a guilty secret — for knowledge, especially of happiness that is not shared with others, must be guilt, and to withhold it from us, who seek it all our lives, is surely criminal, that is, if the lake's secret were not beyond our reach, removed out of our ken, by its sheer innocence. As one looks down from the ridge, watching the black tarn sleeping in the heather, you see that what it holds is not for us, and that the sighing of the wind, which to it is a language comprehended, clear and sympathetic to its soul, to us serves but to stir the senses, and you turn away despairing, watching a heron or a gull enter at once into the fellowship, outside of which we stand.

It might be that at night, when the moon silvers all the waters, and mist enshrouds the hills, calling out from the grass and mosses their secret perfume; when roe steal from the copses browsing so timidly about the open patches of green herbage, scattered like islands through the heath; when dark grey moths flutter about the edges of the lake, that if a child dared venture up to the lone tarn, its eyes might open and behold a wondrous world of fairies, and it would understand all that the rustling of the wind amongst the heather really means. But if it did so, either it would turn rank poet and be damned amongst its fellows, or be snatched away to dwell for ever in some fairy hill, remote from man, seeing the world as in a camera obscura, with people running to and fro like ants, in a perpetual gloom. No child will venture; the spell will not be broken, and the black, little loch will remain hidden from men's hearts, lost in the mist, lost in forgetfulness, just as it was intended that it should be lost, by Nature, when she hid it in the hills.

At the Ward Toll

The mist had blotted out the moss, leaving the Easter Hill, Gartur, and the three fir trees above the Shanochil, rising like islands out of a dead sea. At times the waves of mist engulfed the islands, and then slowly fell back and left them clear, as if some tide, unseen and unsuspected, had ebbed and then had flowed again, or a volcano underneath the moss had been at first half doubtful of its work and shrouded it in steam till it had taken shape. Great drops of damp hung from the feathers of the larches in the long sheltering plantations on each side of the road. Damp filled up the interstices of spiders' webs that clung between the bents, stretching like fairy rigging between the stems, as a triatic-stay stretches between a schooner's masts. It settled on the heads of grasses, enveloping them as in a veil, making each individual stem look like a little ghost of what it had been in the summer, when it was green with life. Where banks of rushes, now turning brown, emerged out of the shroud of steam, they looked like frozen water weeds protruding from the ice, by a pond's side, during a winter's frost.

The perfume of the spruces and of the beds of moss and blae-berries hung in the moist atmosphere and filled the nostrils with a scent of something older than mankind, keen, subtle, vivifying, and which somehow connected man, by some unseen, uncomprehended essential oil or particle so small no microscope could make it manifest, with the whole universe.

Beyond the moss the five-fold hummocks of Ben Dhu ran out into the rolling waves of mist, as a great cape runs out into the sea. Far off, in the interior ocean of the mist Ben Ledi showed its topmost ridge, just as the Peak of Teneriffe rises among the fleecy clouds of the Trade Winds.

The approaching evening added to the gloom, and night appeared about to fall with double darkness on the wide valley of Menteith. My horse's feet fell with a muffled sound upon the road, as if it had been hollow underneath. Now and again out on the moor the crowing of a grouse was heard, and once an owl floated across the road as silently as thistledown is wafted through the air, like an enormous moth. All was so quiet and mysterious, one seemed to ride enveloped in a shroud which kept one from the world. The spirit of the north was in the air, intangible, haunting and vague, that makes the dwellers in the north vague and intangible, poetic and averse to face the facts of life, with a hard rind covering the softness of their hearts. Gigantic forms rode in the billowy vapours by my side, those Valkyrie which northern poets have discerned, either projected on the mist, as I did on that night, or else projected on the *pia mater*, of their brain, round which a mist of vapour always seemed to brood.

The shapes I seemed to see — or saw, for if a man sees visions with the interior sight he sees them, for himself at least, as surely as if he saw them with the outward eye — loomed lofty, and peopled once again Menteith with riders, as it was peopled in the past. The ill-starred earls, their armour always a decade out of fashion, and now and then surmounted by a Highland bonnet set with an eagle's feather, giving them an air half of the Saxon, half of the Kelt, their horses lank and ill-groomed, their followers talking in shrill Gaelic, seemed to defile along the road. Their blood was redder than the King's, their purses lighter than an empty bean-pod after harvest, and still they had an air of pride, but all looked "fey," as if misfortune had set its seal upon their race.

They passed and vanished into the mist they once had known so well, and it seemed to me that they all rode, just as if they knew the way as well as they had known it in their lives, towards their ruined castle in the low island of the rush-ringed lake. I did not turn and ride with them, though had I done so I feel sure, upon arriving at the ferry-keeper's hut thatched thick with heather, out of which sprouted corydalis and on whose ridge grew tufts of ragweed, there would have been a place empty and waiting in the decaying, insubstantial boat. Highlanders, driving the "creagh" towards Balquhidder, passed, their mocassin-shod feet leaving as little impress on the mist as they had left in life, upon the tussocks of bent-grass. They urged the phantom cattle with the points of their Lochaber axes; and, last of all, wrapped in his plaid, his thick hair curling close about his hard-lined features, passed one I knew at once by his great length of arm and the red beard, on which the damp shone in a frosty dew, just as it glistened on the coats of the West Highland kyloes that he drove before him on the road. Though for two hundred years he had slept well in the lone graveyard of the deserted church beside Loch Voil, he seemed to know the road as intimately as he had known it in his old foraying days. As he passed by he moved his target forward and his hand stole to his sword, as if he recognised one of his ancient foes. Then he was swallowed up by the same mist that had protected him so often in his life.

The gloom grew thicker, and in the clinging air fantastic noises surged, as if the spirits of the hills, so long oppressed and overcome by modern life and by man's dominance of nature, were abroad and had resumed their sway. All the old legends appeared natural, the second-sight a thing so evident, it seemed a madness to deny. The Bodach Glas would not have been surprising had he appeared, his head averted and his plaid twisted about him in the ancient fashion of the Isles. London was millions of miles off, lost in reality, and the true world was that I thought I saw on every side, in the grey pall of mist. It seemed that I had ridden miles through the dark, steamy woods. The damp chilled to the bones, and if I put my hand upon my horse I left the imprint of my fingers in the white dew that clustered on his coat. Emerging from the woods, at least upon one side, where the rough moorland pasture stretches out towards the moss, close to the toll-house at the cross-roads, four-square to all the winds, there is an island of old ash trees amongst the firs and spruces, which stands upon a knoll close to a gate. At all times the old trees look strange against the background of dark firs. Upon that evening they appeared gigantic, menacing, and magnified to twenty times their size. As I approached them, glad to have left the gloomy woods, my horse snorted and bounded half across the road. A voice in Spanish hailed me, and a figure moved from the shadow of the trees and stood, dew-damped and shivering, in his light southern clothes.

His olive face had turned an earthy colour with the cold, and it was rendered ghastly-looking by a red sash tied like a comforter about his neck. He told me that at a village which he thought was called Bocliva, or something of the sort, he had been informed there lived a gentleman hard by who could speak Christian, and he believed that I must be the man. He was, he said, "fasting from all but sin that day, and he esteemed his having come across me almost a miracle, for he felt saved as on a plank, when he had heard me speak."

He knew a "litel Inglis," which he would "spika so that I might hear." Then in that language he informed me that "he had lose the ship in Liz and walka Glasco"; and then, turning again to Spanish, thanked me, and in particular for some cigarettes I gave him, which he declared "were better far than bread when the heart is empty and the feet sore, and that the scent of them was sweeter than the orange flower or than the incense in a church."

He came from Vigo, so he said, and if I went there any time, I had my house in Teis, just past the blacksmith's, and he, though a poor man, was one who could appreciate. Then, after telling me that "Ildefonso Lopez was my servant, and God would pay me," he raised his battered hat and, starting off again upon the road to "walka Glasco," disappeared into the night, singing a tango in a high falsetto voice.

I rode into the open between the rough stone dykes that bound the road beyond the toll, passed the old-fashioned cast-iron mile-stone on which a hand is moulded pointing the way to Aberfoyle, and, riding cautiously down the stony brae, crossed the Ward bridge and came out on the moor.

White waves of vapour came surging up against the posts that marked the road, and foamed about them, as the surf surges round a rock. Through the thick air the scent of the bog-myrtle penetrated, acrid and comforting, and on the banks of peat the willows trembled as my horse passed them, as if they floated on the moss.

All was as lonely and as northern as before, but the spell had been broken by Ildefonso Lopez in his brief apparition out of the mist and gloom of the October evening, and though I knew I rode along the road towards the Kelty bridge, and marked unconsciously the junipers that grow just by the iron gate that opens on the path towards the Carse, it seemed somehow that I was entering Vigo, by the north channel between the Ciés and the high land on which a clump of pine trees overhangs the sea.

The noble bay spread out between the hills, which ran down sheer, right to the water's edge, leaving at intervals just ground enough for a white, little town with red-tiled roofs to lodge itself, half hidden amongst vines.

The fishing boats, brown and with sails as sharp as a shark's fins, dotted the water, and on a tongue of land the town of Bouzas seemed to rock upon the sea, as it lay basking in the sun.

Vigo itself, with its steep, winding streets, its dark-tree'd alameda, its mouldering fort, and the decaying hulk of an old ship left derelict upon the sand, appeared, just as I first had seen it thirty years ago. The castles, where the brass guns had sunk upon the ground beside their mouldering carriages, towered above the town.

Chestnut and pine woods almost met the houses, and from the beach the chattering of the fishwives, in their bright red and yellow petticoats, resounded in my ears. Beyond the town the harbour narrowed, and the white oratory of La Guia crowned the pine-clad hill that rises up from the black point of the Cabrón. Still narrowing till it seemed a lake, the harbour stretched towards the Lazaretto, where under piles of sand that clearly show on a still day, lie the galleons Drake hunted up the bay, until they sunk themselves to save the treasure that they held. It passed by Redondela, with its high bridge, and finished at San Payo, from whence as I looked backwards I seemed to see the islands at the harbour mouth float in a sunset, red and glorious, and crossed by bars of purple and of black.

It all appeared to hang outlined and visible upon the vapour rising from the moss, just as a wood appears, projected on the clouds, in the South Pampa on a misty morning, with its roots growing in the sky. Slowly it faded, and as I jogged along, passing the Kelty bridge and turning by the watering-trough into another belt of wood, I almost wondered whether Ildefonso Lopez had been a real man, or but an emanation from the mist from which he issued out so suddenly, and which had swallowed him again almost as suddenly, upon his lonely way.

Faith

An Idealist

The comrade who had lectured having sat down amidst applause, the chairman asked for questions on the speech. In the long narrow hall the audience sat like sardines in a box, so thickly packed that they had hardly room to shout. The greater part were workmen, but workmen of the London type, sallow and slight and dressed in cheap slop clothes. Some foreigners gave colour to the gathering, and showed up curiously against a sprinkling of middle-class inquirers after truth. The latter, mostly, were callow-looking, earnest young men from various provincial universities, dressed in grey flannel suits with green or yellow neckties, their fluffy hair looking as if it never had been brushed, and their long scraggy throats so thin, one wondered they contained the enormous Adam's apple which protruded over the low-cut collar of their shirts. One or two ladies, chiefly dressed in stuffs from Liberty's, sat half-constrainedly, and jotted down either impressions of the scene or notes of the more salient portions of the lecturer's remarks. Three or four comrades, of the kind whose daily life is Socialism, that is of course talking about it, and laying off what the world will be like at its glad advent, sat in front places, and now and then during the progress of the lecture had interjected an " 'Ear, 'ear" or "Let 'em 'ave it," meaning of course the Bourgeois, who certainly that evening must have trembled in his shoes, to hear his vices publicly unveiled. They had a kind of likeness to the men who in the Quartier Latin remain art-students all their lives, wearing wide peg-top trousers, flat-brimmed hats, and flapping neckties of black crêpe de Chine, and who in cafés spout continually of art, and in their way are comrades, thinking that everlasting talk is the best way to paint a picture or to revolutionise the world. In front at a deal table sat one or two reporters, dull and uninterested, to whom all creeds and faiths were equal, and any kind of lecture or of speech, so many hours of tedious work, which they, bound to work out their purgatory here on earth, lived by reporting at so much the column or the thousand words.

Over the hall there hung that odour of hot people, and stale scent, mixed with the fumes of coarse tobacco in the clothes, which is the true particular flavour of all meetings, Tory and Socialist alike, just as in times gone by extract of orange peel and sawdust marked a circus, or as in Catholic countries incense tones down the various smells which rise from off the faithful in a church.

No one responding to the chairman's call, he just had risen up to thank "our comrade for his eloquent, well thought out and delivered lecture, which all who 'eard it must allow was miles a'ead of all the frothy utterances of members of the two parties of boss frauds between 'oom laybour 'angs, as 'e might say upon the cross, the Liberals and Tories, 'ypocrites and Pharisees . . . If ever there was 'umbugs . . ." when a man arose and said "Excuse me, Mr. Chayrman, I 'aven't got a question, but seeing you was arsting for one, I'd like to say a word."

Boys seated in the gallery, to whom according to their philosophic state of boydom all meetings and all speeches simply were chances for diversion, shouted out " 'Ear, 'ear, I saay let Betterton 'ave 'arf a mo.' "

The chairman half-constrainedly resumed his seat, baulked like a fiery horse at yeomanry manoeuvres, in full career, and toying with the water-bottle, on which great drops of moisture hung condensed, called upon Comrade Betterton, with a request he would be brief. A little withered-looking man of about seventy stood up, yellow in colour as old parchment, and with some still remaining wisps of yellowish, grey hair hanging about his head, like seaweed on a rock. His clothes were rusty black, and neatly brushed, his faded eyes of porcelain blue, were set in rims of red, his knees were shaky, and his whole being was pervaded by an air of great benevolence. Clearing his throat and looking round the hall with the assurance of a practised speaker, he broke into a breathless sentence, fluent, unpunctuated, and evidently well known to the admiring boys, who cheered him to the fray.

"I've 'eard the speech," he said, "of the comrade who has addressed us at some length, I've heard and think it 'umbug. As Shakespeare says, whilst the grass grows, the 'orse is starving." At this quotation a boy yelled "Why the 'ell don't he eat it then?" The ladies coloured, fearing the social revolution had actually begun, and from the chairman came the hope that the audience would keep to parliamentary language "seein' that there was lydies in the 'all." Then having called upon our comrade to resume and not to take up too much time, and order being once again established, Betterton took up his interrupted speech, just as a phonograph, cut off, begins again exactly at the place where it was stopped. "What do I find? Nothing but all the means of livelihood monopolize *[sic]*, means of production in the 'ands of one set, land in the other, even the raw material all taken up by the capitalists. Things I say, comrades, is getting' daily worse, nothin' being left on which a man can exercise his lybour, without a tax to pay to somebody for doin' it. What is a man to do? Sometimes I think, all I can do is to go out and throw a bomb of dynamite involvin' in the sayme destruction all the blood-suckin' sweaters and land monopolists alike . . ." What more the speaker might have said. Providence only and the boys seated in the gallery knew, for a voice emanating from the body of the hall was heard to say in a sarcastic tone, "Why don't you go and throw it?" and in the shouts of laughter that ensued, the speaker discomfited, but still benevolent for all his fiery words, subsided in his seat, and with the usual compliments and the collection, without which no meeting, Socialist, Anarchist, Liberal, religious or Conservative, can ever end, the hall was emptied in a trice, the audience passing swiftly, with their eyes fixed on vacancy, before the comrades who at the door sat selling "literatoor."

This was the first occasion that Betterton revealed himself to my unworthy eyes. As time went on I knew him better, and became so to speak one of his intimates, for there are many kinds of intimates, besides the sort you eat and drink with and stand with in the club windows, to criticise the ladies' ankles as they pass. In the first place, he lived on bread and milk, thinking it wrong to take the life of anything (except of course a Bourgeois), so that the pleasures of the table were not exactly in his way.

The work of his profession, that of bill-sticker, took him far from my haunts, and caused him now and then some qualms of conscience, as when he had to cover hoardings, with the announcements of some stuff or other which he knew was made by sweated work. An atheist by choice and by conviction, he yet had texts of Scripture always in his mouth, and used to say, "Only I know you see the laybourer is worthy of his 'ire, or now and then I should just chuck it, it 'urts me to be covering up an 'oarding with a great picture of some 'arlot, for the advertisement of some bloodsucker's soap. An' badly drawn too, bad art" (for he was great on art) "and sweated stuff, not that I've anything to say against a 'arlot in herself, the most of them is driven to it by the rich."

As to why this should be, or how, he did not condescend to explanation, but still believed it firmly, holding as the chief axiom of his faith the wickedness of peers, who he apparently considered had as much power, for evil, as the French aristocracy before the Revolution, or as Beelzebub. But notwithstanding poverty and the whole hive of bees he carried in his bonnet, his life was happy and his faith so great it might have moved the House of Commons from its foundations in the mud, could he have found a lever ready to his hand. As it was, at his lodgings in a slum in Drury Lane, he used to issue broadsheets, printed and set up by himself, on yellow packing paper. The one on which he prided himself most was headed "Messalina," under which style and title he typified the Queen.

"Pause, brutal and licentious old queen," it opened, "and think, if you have time to think, in the wild orgies of your bestial career." It finished with an adjuration to the proletariat to unite, and the last line was "Blood, Blood, Blood, Heads off, Freedom and Liberty for all."

No larger than a sheet of notepaper, the little periodical was stuffed, so he averred, as full of facts as an egg is with meat, and naturally was never paid for, but placed by him upon his daily round in letter-boxes of houses of the rich. One of his pleasures (and they were few and innocent enough) was to depict the feelings of the lord into whose letter-box he had deposited his squib. "When he sits after dinner, drinking his port wine, with his boots off before the fire, it will go through him like a small-tooth comb, and maybe mayke 'im tremble, perhaps touch up his 'eart — who knows? — sometimes those kind of chaps is not all bad, only they eats and drinks too much, and 'as no time to think."

Not a dull day could Comrade Betterton remember in his whole life.

"Talk of the Greeks and Romans," he used to say, "of course the Romans mostly was bourgwaw, like ourselves, but the Greeks certainly 'ad opportunities. I mean in art and such-like, and seeing people go about without their clothes, thus getting' rid of all 'ypocrisy and that, but then as to an ideal for hewmanity, they was deficient. All art was for a class. Now we live in a glorious time, I wouldn't 'a missed it for a lot. But, as to art, exceptin' poor old Morris, most o' your painters and litteratoors and such is middle-class in their ideas, thinks that their kind of stuff is only for the cultivated classes, . . . and see your cultivated class, always at races and shootin' pheasants, . . . care as much about the arts as dockers down in Canning Town. What I mean is, a man like me 'as 'is ideal nowadays, and can look forward to a time, when all them Bastilles is pulled down, . . . it's figuratively I use the word. You needn't larf... It does a man's 'eart good to look forward to a time when all your middle-class ideals shall be swept away, and mankind let alone, to grow up beautiful, 'ealthy, artistic, and as unmoral as the Greeks. That 'ere morality has been the curse of men of my class, making 'em 'ypocrites and driving 'em to drink."

So he went on bill-sticking for his daily bread and moralising always, both in and out of season, and testifying to his faith, with all the unction of a martyr at the stake, as once, when at a public meeting, packed to the ceiling with religious folk, someone averred he spoke "as he hoped in the spirit of my master, Christ," Betterton, rising from his seat, remarked, "'E ain't my master, Sir."

Benevolent and yet ridiculous, kindly, half mad, and shrewd in all his speculations upon life, on things, on motives, and on men, most likely years ago his bills are covered over an inch thick with others, his pot of paste turned mouldy, his brushes worn down to the wood, and he himself safely enfeoffed in the possession of the inheritance to which he had been born, a pauper's funeral, and grave.

Still, when I sometimes look on his life's work in literature, the pamphlet *Messalina*, in which poor Queen Victoria is both so roundly and unjustly vilified, and think upon the pleasure that no doubt the writer had in its production in his one stuffy room in Drury Lane, it is not always easy to be sure, if one should laugh or cry.

Faith

In Christmas Week

The roar of London slackened, and those pterodactyls of the streets, the motor- omnibuses, seemed to disport themselves like great Behemoth or Leviathan, reducing their creators to an inferior place, as if they lived upon the sufferance of the great whirring beasts.

The white-faced, hurrying, furtive-looking crowds, which throng the pavements for the most part of the year, had given place to multitudes of comfortable folk on shopping bent, who walked less warily than the work-driven slaves, who move about the streets seeming as if they felt that everybody's hand was armed against them, and that to halt a moment in the race exposed them to its blow. A biting frost clad hydrants in steel mail where water dropped from them, and spread white blotches on the wooden pavement at which the cab-horses, inured to petrol patches on the stones, to mud, even to blood after an accident, to paper blowing in their eyes, and all the myriad night noises of the town, shied as at something menacing, so far away had Nature gone out of their lives, as if no vision of green fields in which they played and raced beside their mothers, so stiltily [sic] upon their giraffe-looking legs, ever returned to haunt their labour-deadened brains.

The electric light shone blue against the trunks of trees, and the sharp cold almost dispelled the scent of horse-dung which perfumes the air of London, as if to nullify all our attempts to set a bar between ourselves and other animals, and bring us face to face with their and our common necessities and origin, laughing at the refinements of material progress, and showing us that the one way by which we can escape the horrors of the world, lies through the portals of the mind.

Peace upon earth, goodwill towards all mankind, was the stock phrase in every church, as if to make the bitterness of life outside, more manifest, reducing as it did the preachers' words to a mere froth of wormwood on the air, or at the most a counsel of perfection, towards which it was not worth one's while to struggle, seeing it set so far out of our reach.

Holiday-making crowds filled Piccadilly, which looked quite unfamiliar without its strings of crawling cabs and prostitutes plying for hire upon its stones, as eventide drew near. One felt a sort of truce of God was in the air, and that the Stock Exchange, the sweating den, and the gigantic manufactory, in which a thousand toiled to make vast sums for some uninteresting and quite unnecessary man, were quiet, and that perhaps even the wretched negro in the india-rubber bush might have a day of rest.

The parks, under their canopy of white, turned fields again, and as the dusk came on, the sound of church bells in the air gave a false feeling of security, though one was well aware no tiger-haunted jungle held half the perils of the vast stucco solitude, in which we pass our lives. Day followed day, cold, miserable, and cheerless, and the town left deserted, by the myriads who make it look like some vast anthill, on which the ants all strive against each other, instead of helping one another after the fashion of their semi-reasonable prototypes, set one a-thinking on the Eastern legend, framed in a warm and sunny land, and therefore quite unfit for the chill north, which was the cause of such a change in life.

The frosty stars shone out, so cold and clear, they seemed but the reflections of some world extinct, which had preserved its light, but with the heat evaporated. The moon was more congenial to our northern blood, pale, passionless, and with an air of infinite yearning after something unexpressed, whilst the full yellow beam of light from Jupiter, recalled one to the plains, where in far Nabothéa the three kings sat gazing on the stars — a kingly occupation, and one which nowadays all their descendants have allowed to fall into disuse. Perhaps unwisely, for if they followed it, who knows if some particular, bright star might yet arise on their horizon to guide them upwards out of the realms of self?

It may be too that all of us are kings born blind, and that the guiding star is shining brightly in the sky, whilst we sit sightless, with our dim orbits fixed upon the mud. Or it may chance that motor-cars, arriving at the stable where the lowly Saviour babe was laid, would have affrighted all the humble company assembled to adore. The gulf that yawns between the millionaire and the poor man is wider far than that between the watchers by the ass and oxen's stall, and the three sheikhs, who lighted down from off their horses to reverence the babe.

Nor was the gulf between the sheikhs, and the animals stabled so snugly, with their warm breath making an aureole about the sleeping baby's head, so deep as that which yawns between the modern dweller in our stucco Babylon, and his selected breeds of animals rendered so bestial by improvement as scarce to move the pity of their owners for all their various pains.

In that old cosmos, with its simple, reasonable life, so like the life of plants and trees, as fixed and as immutable as are the seasons or the tides, there was a sympathy, unthought of, but all the same at hand, which though it did not spend itself in theories, redeemed mankind from many of its sins. Justice, one hears, is but of modern growth; but in its action on the lives of men it toils a thousand leagues behind the old brutality which, though it certainly denied all rights, admitted kinship, or at least was conscious of a link between all sentient things, just as some deity who had created man in his own image might feel ashamed when called upon to punish and destroy beings so like himself, though for all that he could not hold his hand.

So in the Christmas week, with its fierce cold and misery to thousands mocked by false protestations of the brotherhood of man, and pinched with hunger in the midst of wealth, it must have seemed that all the legend was but another of the corpse-candles lighted to set them running after its thin flame.

Then came a thaw, and all the iron-bound streets became Sloughs of Despond, in which a million horses, turned to machines, chained in their stables, and taken out, but to pound ceaselessly upon the cruel stones till it was time to be led back again and chained up for the night, toiled wretchedly, not comprehending that they were agents in the progress of the world. Still all the time the church bells pealed, and all the time the planets shone out soft and mellow, making one think involuntarily upon some old bright world which perhaps never has existed save in dreams, but which we now and then have to imagine for ourselves or else go mad at seeing ugliness revered as beauty, and wealth adored as wisdom, with all the meanest qualities of man enthroned as virtues, like a tin sky-sign setting forth some trash with its full-bodied lies. Frost, silence, traffic, all was the same to the vast vulgar town, the hugest monument of Philistinism that the world has seen, or ever will behold.

The blackened muddy snow, reminding one of something pure, defiled, then scorned and cast upon the mire, lay piled in heaps in the chief squares, left there by accident or by design, as if to give the magnates in their shapeless palaces the mumps, and render them as hideous as the

247

great cubes of masonry in which they lived. Misery seemed to reign triumphant in the wilderness of bricks, where dullness strove with smug hypocrisy to make life unendurable, whilst slowly the great city seemed to take up its usual course as the drear week drew out. Ladies in motor-cars, with the hard, uninviting air that wealth imparts so often even to youth and beauty, flitted about, scattering the mud on those whose toil paid for each article of dress they wore, as if they had conferred a favour on the world by deigning to exist. The chill and penetrating damp which rises from the London clay after a thaw, and makes its way into the bones and soul, to them was but another stimulus to life, and aid to appetite. Neither the look of wretchedness of men or animals seemed to say anything to them, although no doubt their minds were all alive with charitable schemes; for never in the history of the human race has charity, that most unhumanising virtue which has ever made mankind think itself better than its fellows, walked in our midst so blatantly, or justice hid itself more timidly, than at the present day.

Boys, cold and pinched, with voices rendered harsh by all the gin their parents had imbibed, ran shouting out the names of newspapers, flourishing broadsheets on which the headings told of murders, adulteries, cheating and robbery; and smug-faced citizens and prurient-minded girls, their pink-and-white complexions strangely at variance with the twinkle in their eyes, eagerly stopped and bought them, jostling the men as if by accident, pleased at the contact with them as they passed, and yet taking offence at once if but a word was said, saving their conscience in the national way, which finds all things permissible if but due silence is preserved.

So dull and strenuous was the life that it appeared impossible in other lands the sun was shining, and that the brown-faced men and merry black-haired women had time to love and be beloved.

That nothing might be wanting to set forth all aspects of our pomp and state, in a small, narrow street well strewn with offal from the stalls of costermongers' barrows, under the flaming light of naphtha lamps, a line of men stood waiting at the door of a soup-kitchen at which some charitable soul or council had provided refreshment for the body — that body which, we know, matters so little in a transitory life.

The mud had eaten holes into their clothes, and their pinched faces under the electric light, drink-swollen and blotched, looked corpse-like as they stood shivering in the snow, which, falling down like feathers on their hats, gave them a look as if they had been supers at the pantomime of life, and at some signal from the wing, would break into a dance.

The stream of passers-by watched them unmoved, thinking no doubt that idleness or drink had brought them to their present situation; and as they waited for their turn some coughed and others scratched themselves, or muttering it was " 'ellish cold" shuffled and stamped, as the snow melted on their hair and filtered through their rags.

On every side the current of the world flowed past them, leaving them stranded on the mud, with the safe shores of progress and of wealth slipping away from them, as a spent swimmer, struggling for his life, watches the banks of a swift-running stream, race past before his eyes.

Sometimes the line of men swayed like a wounded snake upon the road as one of them passed through the door, and as the others waited for their turn one muttered to a chum, "Blime me, cheer up! it'll be better under Socialism," and spat upon the stones.

Faith

Paja y Cielo

Now, the whole Pampa from the Romero Grande to Nahuel-Huapi and far Patagones is cut into innumerable chess-boards of wire fencing, and railways puff across it, taking up wool and corn and hides, and other merchandise, to send to Europe, that Europe from which once came all the few luxuries the dwellers on the Pampa ever knew.

But it was not so always, and where now wave interminable crops of corn, once waved the long brown virgin grasses, which made the Pampa a sort of ocean, to the eye.

Nothing but grass and sky and sky and grass, and then more grass and still more sky. Nothing, for Pampa means "the space" in Quichua. A vast and empty space, empty, that is, of man and all his works; but full of sun and light, and of the sweetest air imaginable, so sweet that merely to think of it keeps the lungs fresh amongst the reek of towns, and makes the soul rejoice, even when petrol-belching motor-cars fly past carrying their goggled freights.

It was the home of deer and ostriches, and of wild horses, dappled and pied, slate-coloured, roan, blood-bay, sorrel and dun, spotted like pudding-stone, calico, paint, buckskin, clay-bank, cream, and some the colour that the Arabs call Stones of the River, they all were there, tossing their manes and whinnying for joy, leading their lives in that great grassy space, where there was nothing to be seen but grass and sky.

Nothing but deer and ostriches were there, with swiftly whirling teru-teros, the mining tuco-tucos, and the mysterious matáco, the quiriquincho, the Patagonian hare, chajás with their great horny wings, flocks of flamingos, and marching columns of the black-headed Patagonian swans, with the wind ever rustling in the grass, sounding the dirge of the fair Eden so soon to be defiled. Wind waved the surges of the grass, lifting the loose hair on the necks of animals, and on the sandhills bending the plants, and making them draw patterns on the sand, just as in colder countries they trace figures in the snow.

Something there was about the Pampa, almost unearthly, so natural it was that in a world where all is artificial, and man appears a giant, controlling everything, it seemed impossible he should be relegated back to his position as but one of the many animals, with but a little more intelligence than theirs.

A grassy sea, in which the landmarks were the stars, so that a man rode straighter in the night than in full noontide, if he had lost his way. A green illimitable sea, in which the horse was ship; a desert without camels, but as terrible to wander in as is the Sáhara, in which the horseman who had lost his trail was swallowed up and never heard of, except some traveller chanced to find his skull, just sticking out of a dark tuft of grass, which had grown rank and vigorous, as his decaying flesh laid bare the bones.

This Pampa, that now seems to be a dream, so far away it is, and so defiled by pestilential and beneficent progress, was above all an insects' paradise. All day the hum of unseen wingéd things hung in the air, just as if millions of Eolian harps had been set everywhere — perhaps they were — and the long filaments that used to stretch from grass to grass, in a north wind, may have been good conductors of their song. All kinds of flies buzzed, hummed, and whirred, and made themselves a nuisance or a pleasure, just as you looked at them. Grasshoppers sprang into the air, just as a salmon springs up in a weir, and settled down again into the grass, in the same way the fish slips back into the water after leaping — even the splash was paralleled by the stirring of the grass the insect made and the sharp breaking noise his wings caused in the stems. Crickets sang ceaselessly, seeming to be just at your horse's feet, but if you stopped and looked for them chirruped again behind you, making a sort of will-o'-the-wisp of sound. Locusts in myriads used to pass, high up, in search of cultivated land making a noise as of an army in the air, darkening the sky, and followed by a multitude of birds, hanging upon their ranks.

The dwellers on the plains put all the tribe together under the name of "bichos," and only thought of them as dangerous to crops, or disagreeable to the skin, although no doubt they would have missed them vaguely had they disappeared, just as a man bred in the country, though born without imagination, still misses something in a town, that he can not describe.

Birds, from the ostrich, which the old Quichuas called the "Desert's Mirth," down to the little black and white "viudita," swarmed in their millions. Vultures and crows hung almost out of sight like specks, and yet, when a tired animal was left to die, appeared as if by magic and waited, just as an heir waits with resigned impatience for a rich uncle's death. Along the streams the pink flamingos fished, or rising in the sun looked like a flock which had strayed out of some old picture, lovely and yet unnatural to eyes accustomed to see birds, all grey or brown, flying through air as thick as blotting-paper.

All these were of the nature of exterior graces, but the interior vision of the Pampas as revealed to one who writes of it, as of some personal friend, lost, but still recollected vividly, always lamented, and to be called again to memory by an effort of the will, was something that enflamed the heart with joy. Mountains and woods, snows, sands, and the illimitable vision of the sea, all have their moments when they seem to smile. Green woods in spring, mountains at sunrise, the deceitful sea when on the beach of some fair island it ripples in, as innocently as if it never drowned a mariner, or beat a ship to matchwood in its destroying surge; even the desert sands, for the brief season when the camel-thorn turns green, or when the setting sun flushes the sand-hills, all seem to smile. The keynote of them all is sadness, sadness and melancholy, which spreads a sense of cloud over the heart — tightening its strings and turning back the soul upon itself.

In the wide ocean of the Pampa, where the waves seemed to roll without advancing or receding, tideless but for the ebb and flow of winter and of summer, all was joy. Even a storm obscured its smile but for a moment, and the wise saying that joy cometh in the morning — almost incomprehensible in other countries where each day brings care — might have been written by a Gaucho prophet, or a philosophising Manzanero chief, or skin-clad Patagonian seer, with the strange emblems that they used to paint upon their guillapices *[sic]* of guanáco skin. Perhaps the being near to nature made all lightsome, for looking down below the surface, all was as horrible as it is elsewhere, man preying on the animals, they on each other, Indian on Gaucho, and in the then small, isolated towns the conquering European was just setting out on his career to enslave them all and make them miserable.

That it was near to nature was seen at once, both by man's attitude to man, and to the animals. So ruthless was he in his dealings with them that he was scarcely cruel, that is unless a tiger be so when he strikes down an ox. Life was so joyous that it was taken without thought and rendered up without a tear; and when the taker, having wiped his knife upon a tuft of grass, sat down to smoke a cigarette, certain it is no qualm of conscience troubled him, more than it does a wolf. The little air that comes at sunset ruffled his hair as he pushed back his hat, and stirred the poncho of his victim lying huddled on the ground, and it may be he muttered, if indeed he thought at all about the matter, "pobrecito," as if he felt he had accomplished both their destinies, almost against his will.

In the thick montés fringing the river banks an air as of a temple in which to worship nature stole on you as you entered them on horseback, following strayed animals, whilst birds in their degree seemed to sing greetings as they sat about, too unaccustomed to man's presence even to move away. The ceaseless wind which either howled or rustled on the plains was broken, and animals were fatter and less wild than those outside the woods. They moved amongst the trees, just as they must have done in the dim Nabothéan Entre Rios where they all took their birth. The parrots chattered joyously, the monkeys howled, myriads of frogs raised their metallic note, and sitting sideways on your horse, rolling a black Brazilian cigarette, you saw at once that it was love of nature, not want of faith, that made the Israelites propose to rear two tabernacles for their own wandering chiefs.

Deeper within the monté flowed some stream, set thick with camaloté, as thick as is a piece of cloisonné enamel, with the same coloured flowers. Beneath them ran the water, and to cross you cut down branches, the horses treading gingerly along, their riders shouting when they gained the bank, out of the joy of life, and being answered back antiphonally by the sage cormorants seated upon the trees.

Over the plain and monté the same air of natural joy hung equally, making the darkest woods seem bright, and the wide Pampa brighter still, to the interior vision of the man attuned to them and their primæval air. Railways may cut the one into vast chess-boards, on which the pawns are human lives, and in the darksome glades of the thick woods of espinillo and of ñandubay, sawing-machines, fed by pale, sweating men, may whirr and clatter, giving a foretaste of a hell compounded of the simples we ourselves have deified; but the bright recollections of the days of ostriches and deer will still remain and become legendary. Perhaps at daylight, or better, just at the false dawn, when the white mist enshrouds the pajonáles making the ghostly heads of paja brava loom gigantic, all may be blotted out and purified, and the vast sea of grass and sky take for a moment its old aspect of a great inland ocean on which the ostriches appear just as a nautilus looks, blown by the north-east Trades.

That is the way in which I see it. . . . Adios Pampa . . . or perhaps, until so long.

"Los Peares, Un Minuto!"

The line ran close beside the Minho, which foamed and brawled in the deep channel it had cut between the hills. Along the banks thickets of oleanders grew, mixed here and there with tamarisks. Clouds of white mist, raised by the sun after a touch of frost, hung over everything, shrouding the chestnut forests, half-way up the trees, leaving their tops, as it were, detached and floating in the air.

It lingered in the stacks of maize, making them look like bee-hives. About the curious little hutches of rough stone, in which the peasants in Galicia store their Indian corn, it clung, leaving their squat stone crosses, suspended in the air without a base, as if, by a perpetual miracle, they were sustained, through some mysterious power. Then, the sun rose in all its glory, and as the train slowly crawled past, jangling and creaking like a bullock-cart, all the old agricultural life, such as that which Theocritus or Columella have described, was plain in all the beauty of its old-world simpleness and charm. Impassive men stood herding sheep, leaning upon their sticks.

Girls held sleek, coffee-coloured cows by a long rope to graze, and twirled their distaffs, as they watched them eat. Women washed clothes, at great stone tanks fed by a rill that issued from the rocks, conducted in a cane, and overarched with vines.

As they knelt in a row, dressed in bright red and yellow petticoats, with scarlet handkerchiefs upon their heads, their wooden shoes appearing like canoes behind their tucked-up skirts, they sang, a natural, harsh, wild song that penetrated to the marrow of the bones. Sometimes from other working places or from fields, other high voices answered them, and so a dialogue went on, just as it passes between birds unseen in a deep wood, all in a minor key. Primitive bullock-waggons, with solid wheels, and sides of wicker-work, like those on Roman coins, slowly crawled on the roads. The gentle oxen, swaying to and fro, just as a man walks, wrapped in a Spanish cloak, appeared to fabulate as they turned towards each other, when the driver touched them with his goad, or called them by their names, exhorting them to be themselves and pull. The wheels creaked with a jarring sound, and seemed to sing as if a swarm of bees had been imprisoned in the axle, making a noise which, as the peasants say, both stimulates the beasts and frightens wolves, and is agreeable to those who do not care for progress and modernity, or the sharp whiz of steam.

Under the brown-tiled eaves long rows of maize-cobs ripened in the sun, and on the bushes here and there red and blue rags, and petticoats were hung to dry, and stood out blotchily, like colours on a painter's palette, against the grass, and the metallic-looking scrub of arbutus.

In the minute and old-world gardens grew patches of cabbages, upon high stalks, like that which the old-fashioned Scotch knew as "long kale," and by the steps which led up to the houses plants of red salvia, and underneath the pollard oak trees, the autumn crocus spotted the grass like stars. Up many of the hills terraces of vines, all turning red and purple, mounted in tiers, and through the gorges now and then a distant bagpipe wailed like a soul in pain.

As the train wriggled like a snake through tunnels, the engine taking the short curves just as a bicyclist wheels in and out of heavy traffic in a street, creeping along the edge of precipices, and then emerging once again through woods into the cultivated fields, it passed a village, and drew up at a little station, near the river's bank. A crowd blocked all the place, and on the house-tops men stood watching for the train; boys seated in the trees looked down upon the scene; and as the porter, in a nasal voice, called "Los Peares, un Minuto," it was at once apparent that the cry was quite illusory, for piles of boxes, bags, and bedding crowded the platform, whilst the perspiring stationmaster struggled in vain to make a passage to the line. The crowd surged to and fro, and to the questions of the passengers, women in tears, and boys excited by the crush and noise, replied that the whole hamlet known as Val de Cabras was going to Buenos Ayres, taking their priest with them, to found another Val de Cabras, out on the southern plains. As always happens in a country such as Spain, where time is of no value, the people rushed about as if the Day of Judgment were at hand. The station-master, who, if no one had been in the train, would have allowed it minutes beyond its time, was sweating blood and water to get everyone on board. Old women hugged their sons, and men stood stifling down their tears, their patched and parti-coloured clothes looking in keeping with the scene.

Girls raised an almost Arab wail, and in the midst of the confusion stood the priest, a stalwart, red-cheeked countryman, surrounded by a group of people, who held him, some by his hands, some by the lappels [sic] of his coat, and all pressed round him as a swarming hive presses about its queen, conscious he was the centre of their little world, wrenched up from its foundations, and so soon to be absorbed in the mysterious continent beyond the seas, which either swallows up their fellows, just as a fish sucks down a fly, or else returns them, rich and unrecognisable, at the end of years. The people struggled round the priest, those who had elected to remain behind, kissing his clothes, the men grasping his hands in theirs — hard, horny, and deformed by toil — and asking to be blessed. Now and again he turned towards the gate, behind which stood a row of donkeys and of mules, tied up to posts, with coloured blankets on their saddles, and their heads nodding in the sun. Women, with coloured flannel petticoats, red, green, and yellow, like a bed of tulips, clattered across the platform in their wooden clogs, and boys raised the shrill cry they use in Portugal and in Galicia when excited, which sounds like a horse neighing, and from the crowd of hot, perspiring men and women there came a smell as of wild animals, mixed with the scent of bundles of salt fish, which almost all of them bore in their hands. Some dragged great parcels wrapped in striped blankets tied with innumerable knots, and others carried on their shoulders the little ark-shaped trunks, covered with cowskin with the hair on, that look as if they had been made upon the pattern of a mediæval coffin, which, on a platform, seem as if they mourned the bullock-waggon where they had passed their lives.

Hard, knotted hands reached out and grasped, for the last time, others as hard and toil-stained, which were thrust towards them through the palings, and men clasped one another with their heads looking over each other's shoulders, just as the patriarchs of Scripture embraced and wept upon each others' breasts, and quite as naturally. A universal sob shook the whole crowd, which billowed to and fro, like water agitated in a tank, resisting all the efforts of the station-master to get the train away at its appointed time.

At last, when all the bundles and the trunks, the water-bottles, and the poor household treasures, which the departing villagers, driven from their idyllic old-world life by weighing-down taxation, were taking with them, to wring and salve their hearts in the New World, were put on board, the priest was left alone, holding a bulky umbrella in his hand.

The porter clanged upon the bell, the futile horn, which hangs upon a nail in Spanish stations, tooted feebly, and deep down below, the Minho dashing through the rocks, roared a farewell to those who, in the future, would, from the rivers they would know, hear nothing but an oily gurgle, and the occasional hollow sound of the alluvial soil as it fell down into the deep and muddy stream, that undermined the banks.

The emigrants all climbed into the train, and from the crowd assembled rose a cry, "The blessing, father; bless us once more before you go"; but he, standing with one foot on the step, still looked towards the palings, when through the crowd a breathless boy came elbowing his way, and dragging by a string a white and liver-coloured pointer, which, when it saw the priest, rushed forward, and fawned upon his knees.

Handing his umbrella to a woman in the train, he drew his left hand hurriedly across his face, leaving a snuffy mark, where it had met the tear, and then, patting the dog upon his head, murmured, "Adios, Navarro," and with an effort and a gulp, steadily gave his blessing, as the companion of his rambles whined and strained upon the rope.

Rough, friendly hands stretched out and drew the priest into the train, which, after jolting heavily, began to wind about through the deep cuttings in the rocks, emerging now and then close to the road, on which stood groups of people, waving and shouting their farewells. Just as it passed the last house of the village, running close to the road, an olive-coloured man upon a mule, stood in his stirrups, and with uplifted hand made a cross in the air, as the train, gathering way, slipped past and, entering a tunnel, was swallowed up and lost to those who, standing on the platform, stood waving handkerchiefs, and gazed with yearning eyes at the last carriages as they vanished from their sight. Then it emerged again into the sun, and a girl washing by a stream, her donkey tied beside her, putting one arm across its neck, waved a red dripping petticoat, and the train, puffing and snorting, resolutely set its face towards that Buenos Ayres which was to make and mar its freight.

It bore them westward towards a land bare of traditions, of vegetation, of everything that hitherto had made their lives; a land in which their children would be educated men, not knowing good from evil, as their fathers in a rudimentary way had dimly comprehended them, where they would eat their fill and lose their individuality, becoming uncomprehending instruments of the greatness of a vast empire, and from whence they would regard Galicia with a mixed feeling of contempt and pity, after the fashion of self-educated men.

At every puff the wheezing engine made, it took the emigrants further away from their old, hungry, but idyllic life; further away from bee-hives, made from the section of a cork tree, and laid in rows amongst the lavender and thyme; further away from the sleek, mild-eyed oxen, and from the "romeria," where they had danced "muiñeiras" to the sound of "gaita" and of pipe.

No more the ploughman in the deserted Val de Cabras would return home at night, carrying his plough, after the fashion of the ploughmen of whom the Georgics treat, or girls at evening time gather round the steps of the stone fountains and gossip as their hooped wooden buckets automatically were filled through long tin pipes, fitted upon the iron nozzle, where the water flowed. Lovers would no more linger in the oak woods of an evening, and tell the tale that never wearies those who tell or listen to it, whether amongst the cistus-carpeted "robledos" of Galicia, or in the alleys of a town. Each jolt and jerk upon the coupling chain, and each white bellowing burst of steam, left the deserted village more deserted, more given over to the decay that soon would settle on it, when in the winter nights the snow would lodge unheeded on the roofs, and the wolves scamper through the streets.

As it went twisting on the track, winding and wheeling through the tunnels, and emerging now and then into the sunshine, the people, sitting hunched amongst their bundles, broke into a high-pitched song, which floated in the balmy, pine-scented air, and was taken up from one end to the other of the train. Cistus and lavender, thyme, burnet, and wild marjoram, germander, and the dead leaves of oak and chestnut, gave out their aromatic scent, and floating in the sun, white butterflies were borne across the Minho, skimming the streams, and soaring steadily across the linns.

Nature had put on all her charms, to make the parting bitter, and to fix more firmly an eternal, sad recollection in their minds, of their lost homes. Nothing was left of the departing village, but the name, and a few elders, who had remained behind to hunger and neglect; and in some other village, perhaps, Navarro, left to the care of some strange priest, sorrowed and wondered, for the great Power that chastens whom He cares for, extends a hand even upon the dogs of those He blesses with His love.

Faith

Transfigured

The winter sun, after a day of glory, was sinking gradually, though there was still an hour or two of light. The glare had blotted out the walls and fences; the relics of an older, pleasanter, more human civilisation rose like islands springing from a sea of burnt dry grass. Towers, castles, aqueducts, tombs, and piles of masonry, now shapeless, but which once had been well known to the inhabitants of Rome, who no doubt hailed them with joy on their return from foreign countries, just as we hail he gasworks by the bridge at Battersea, the Lambeth shot tower, and the church in Langham Place, stood up on every side. They stood like finger-posts upon the road of history to guide us backwards to an age of cruelty and of oppression, in some respects just like our own, but differing from it by the possession of the sense of beauty, and by the lack of cant, that fourth dimension of our state. The heat had raised a haze, which had turned everything to gold. The decaying piles of bricks, and the long lines of ruined aqueducts, the distant city, with the cross upon S. Peter's seeming to hang against the sky, as when it first was seen by Constantine, had lost their air of ruin and dejection, and appeared glorified, as if they waited for the triumph of some emperor, who should deliver man. The gold had tinged the snow upon the Sabine hills, turning them back again into volcanoes, with streams of molten lava running down their flanks. The towns perched on the rocky hills were glorified and shone refulgent, each looking like a little Athens, as it must have looked to Pericles, their churches each one turned to an Acropolis. The sleek cream-coloured oxen stood and chewed the cud, their limpid eyes looking like coal-tar heated and allowed to cool till it acquires a jetty and transparent glaze. They stood, conscious of their nobility, direct descendants from the time when Rome was noble and the centre of the world. The Gracchi must have loved their ancestors, tended and ploughed with them. Where shepherds dressed in brown herded their sheep, their great white dogs beside them, there rose an acrid scent, which took you back to a remote and tiny Rome, in which the flocks were folded every night.

At times a peasant on his rough black pony, holding an ox-goad balanced across the saddle like a lance, jogged past, wrapped in a tattered cloak. In the deserted Via Appia, once thronged with busy folk coming towards that Rome to which led every road, and now an avenue which somewhere must come out upon the Styx or on the banks of Periphlegethon, no one seemed to stir. The tourists had gone home, and the clear air no more resounded to the voices of the citizens of the great republic which no doubt one day will proclaim Rome and its Agro a territory, pending the time when it may qualify to be a State. The living seemed to be effaced and to have given place, as in fact they always must, to those who had become the real owners of the soil by mingling with it after death. Those who had paved the Appian Way, and built the tombs which fringe it, and who had ruled the world as confidently as does the Anglo-Saxon race today, appeared to smile derisively when from the neighbouring high road the hooter of a motor-car smothered the bleating of the sheep. They ruled so confidently that they could not have seen the figure of a man advancing slowly by a road at a right angle to the great thoroughfare which led from Rome to Brindisi in the days when Horace ambled out upon his mule. He tramped along slowly and doggedly, carrying a short, bright hedge-knife, with which he had been working, in his hand. Bent, dirty, and with the air of resignation that a hard life often imparts, he trudged along the road, just as he must have trudged through life, without complaint, and yet resentful as is an over-driven ox. The sun had burned his hair a rusty brown, his flesh a livid colour, and on his hands great freckles like the blotchings on a trout, showed he had once been fair, that is for an Italian, although his face was almost hidden in a week's growth of beard. A black tight-fitting jersey, stamped with half-moons in white, discoloured underneath the arms with sweat, and darned in places with a light-coloured thread, did duty for a shirt. It left his neck, scraggy and wrinkled as a vulture's, bare, and round it was a faded red silk handkerchief tied in a sailor's knot. A thick moustache covered his mouth, which when he spoke revealed his teeth, all stained and broken, looking like those of an old horse, yellow and long with age. Across his shoulders, dangling like a cloak he wore his jacket, made of a brown and shoddy-looking cloth, such as you see at a ship-chandler's in a little foreign port. A broad and greasy leather belt kept up his trousers, which time and wear had made as shiny as a piece of oil-cloth, rubbing the pattern out and laying bare the woof. His black felt hat was tilted at an angle, covering a hole, gaping and ugly, where his left eye had been, which seemed to have been taken out by an unskilful surgeon, who had gashed and scarred the cheek. Patience had given to his face an air of dignity, as of a Samson, blinded and in chains, peering about sightless and puzzled in the darkness of his life, and wondering why men laughed. He stopped to pass the time of day and make a cigarette, moistening the paper with a tongue as dry as a macaw's, and after lighting it, with a match rolled up in a bit of newspaper, drifted quite naturally into the story of his life. He told it fluently, with a good choice of words, but in a perfunctory way, neither commenting or extenuating anything, and yet when he began, something within him made him keep on and finish it, not that he knew it was a scripture, written for anybody's learning, but in the same way a volcano belches forth its flames, from its interior fires.

"Two francs a day, at forty-eight, for ten hours' work, and an hour to walk each way. Of course, the two hours should be paid for as I do not walk them for amusement, but what's the good of talking? Turn redeemer and you are crucified. Look at my hands at forty-eight, after a life of work. . . ."

He held them out. They certainly had been well crucified, and looked like roots of trees, but dirtier, gnarled, knotted, and not inviting to the eye. A finger, too, was missing from the left hand, leaving a stump, just like a candle-end.

He smiled, not the least bitterly, but as a man may smile in a picture gallery at an unpleasant martyrdom by Ribalta, Ribera, or other painters of the Valencian school, to show that he is human, and that the sight of suffering does not disgust, when it is masked by art. Spitting, in a philosophic way, not at the world, but merely on the ground, he broke again into his monologue, almost against his will, just as the prophets sometimes seemed to speak, in the Old Testament. "I ought, perhaps," he said, "to have gone to the Argentine Republic when I was young. A man can have a horse there — stand upright on his feet, and does not need to go about, as he does here in Italy, with his hat always in his hand.

"Besides, it was the land of Garibaldi in his youth — there he learned to be free. Now what is the use of talking? I am too old, and an old dog loves the house that he knows, even if he is beaten in it. My age too, and my finger make it impossible. They would not let me sail. Instead of that, when I was young I went up the Levánt, first to Greece, which I liked well enough, for the wages on the Corinth railway were good, the wine sound, cheap, and would be better, if they had not a cursed way of filling it with pitch. What can you expect, though, from a people who cross themselves like Turks, from right to left, when all the other Christians make the sign from left to right? Not that I often make it, or ever, except perhaps at night on a dark road, or when a master looks.

"In Greece I married. She was an Italian girl, not a bad housewife, and tidy — religious also; a little of it is good for women, just as a little wine is good for men. Well, that lasted only a year or two. When I got back from Corinth she was dead, and all my savings stolen.

"After that, Greece was black to me; I left my little boy with Sisters and off to Candia, an island of the Greeks, belonging also to the Turks, but under international control, why I don't know. There I worked for a year or two, I can't quite remember; but I do remember that I lost my finger there, working with a steam crane at Lárnaca. There was no compensation to be got, as the man I worked for was a consul, and I had no passport, so when I wanted to appeal . . . pay and appeal, eh? . . . he threatened to send me home to Italy. Repatriation was what he called it, but it is all the same, when a poor man has to do with rich men, especially if they are consuls or the like. Justice, but not in my house, as the proverb says. After that I took a passage in a pilgrim ship to Alexandria. She was packed as full of infidels as a basket is with fish. I hadn't anything to steal, so I was not robbed; not that the infidels are any worse than we are in that respect.

"Alexandria I found a place in which a man could live. Hot, but not too hot, except now and then, and wages good, upon the railway, until I lost my job: good sterling English money too, gold without fluctuation; there I saved seven pounds, all in the little sovereigns, two of which make one.

"So now I got my little boy across from Athens, for I had no wish he should become a clerical, and found a first-rate job, to clean the city sewers, four francs a day — that is chellini, better than francs, they are.

"A dirty job? Yes, but four chellini! sheelins, eh, you call them. A cursed illness overtook me — not fever, but another kind of bad air — and all my seven pounds soon vanished. Again I got no compensation. My employer was a Jew; but Jews and Christians are alike in such things. Then I went to Beyrout, paying my passage, and worked at making railroads as before in Greece, with hundreds of Italians, for we Italians are the beasts of burden of the world. From there I tramped on to

Damascus. Frightened? No, not the least; Christian and heathen poor are kind enough to one another, and when a man has nothing anyone can steal he is safe enough, almost in any country.

"Yes, they say Damascus is a pretty place, but I saw nothing of it but the electric-light works and the hospital. 'Twas there I lost my eye, owing to the sudden fusing of a wire, that and because the doctor in the hospital made a mistake and left a little piece of iron in the wound. To save my other eye I had to have the wounded one taken out, and saw the stars, I can tell you, during and after the affair.

"Then — this was two years ago — I got repatriated as unfit to work by our consul at Beyrout, and went to work again here in our own Campagna at cutting firewood, making drains, sheep-herding — anything a man of forty-eight, with one eye, and with a finger gone, is competent to do."

He stopped, and his cigarette having gone out, he put the stump behind his ear for future use, asked me the proper time, seeing that I had come from Rome; then, having stuck the broad, curved hedge-knife in his belt, from which it hung just like a legionary's sword, he struck into a track which led up towards Albano, for the recitation of his life had lasted for three miles.

The sun was almost sinking, red and glorious, and distant Rome appeared to rise from a great ocean, just as Cadiz rises from the sea. All was lit up and changed. The great sad plains turned to a sheet of silver, the hills to fire, the decaying relics of the past to palaces; and as the man, stopping a moment on the upland path to wave his hand, stood in the setting sun's full glare, he was transfigured, and appeared gigantic, outlined against the sky.

Then, as the gathering darkness seemed to bring the clouds close to him, he grew taller still, and as he vanished, seemed to be bearing the weight of the whole world, like Atlas, on his back.

Faith

Brutta Passeggiata

The sky was full of larks, and over all the great brown plain, just turning here and there to green, an air of gladness hung. Nature and Spring appeared to have awakened after their winter's sleep, and to be starting out once more, like maidens on their bridal morn, to court the kisses of the sun. A smell of warmth and growth gladdened the senses, and man seemed once again to have entered into full communion with the beasts, the flowers and trees, just as he once had done in the fair garden by the Chât-el-Arab, in which God by His last creative act received that human recognition which proclaimed Him God. Along the muddy streams the canes were bursting from their winter sheaths of brown. The water spiders timidly began to venture out, each one as bold a navigator into the unknown as was Columbus, endued with faith as great as his, and each one with his own magnetic needle, planted by instinct in his microscopic brain.

Myriads of the minutest flies swarmed with a gladsome hum about the edges of the pools, in which the water now and then was ringed by the round head of some exploring tortoise, after its winter sleep. All animals and insects seemed to have come into a glad new world, inherited by right divine from their remote and prehistoric ancestry, which in primæval times had long ago appeared as well equipped for their existence as their descendants of to-day, unlike mankind, that slowly has ascended by degrees. The sun itself shone, as it seemed with youth, refreshed by winter and a season of long nights. Nature rejoiced in its renewed exuberance, knowing exactly what it had to do, taking no thought either upon to-morrow or to-day.

Drops of green life congealed, hung at the ends of twigs, that soon should be unfolded into the glory of the leaves. Occasionally a lizard darted from the crevice of a wall, looked at the light a little timidly, and disappeared again, just as a timid bather dips his toes into the waves and runs back to the shore.

Calves frisked beside their mothers, and lambs skipped up and down, arching their backs like a wild horse first saddled, whilst lazy shepherd dogs lay basking, one eye upon the sheep and one upon the flies which buzzed close to their noses, as if the sense of danger gave a zest to play.

Even the peasants on the plain, yellow and ague-racked, and bound, almost as fast as trees, to the small district where they had been born, seemed less downtrodden, and shepherds minding sheep sang in a high falsetto voice songs which all ended in a long-drawn note struck on a minor key.

It was a day in which Pan and the nymphs, the hamadryads, and the rest of the humane and Pagan gods, whose worship still endures under another name in Italy, might have come forth like butterflies after their hibernation of a thousand years, and found all the Campagna, which they had once known covered with buildings, pulsating with life, still lovely in decay. In the brown solitude they had once known all peopled with their shrines, they might have danced, after a tear or two, to find themselves the sole survivors of their world, and sung, just as a man when he comes back after the lapse of years and finds his house deserted and in ruins, first weeps to ease the aching of the heart, then falls a-humming some old tune, almost involuntarily, as things forgotten well again into his mind. It seemed as if Death had forgotten for a space his work, and as if envy, hatred, poverty, suffering, and pain must have been banished, or held over for a spell; as if all gold had disappeared, except in poetry or on the domes of cities far away, just seen at sunset, but unattainable as those sunk in the sea, which now and then appear for a brief season, just before a storm. A veritable truce of God seemed to have been proclaimed, including every living thing in its provisions, and sealed and witnessed by the spring, God, Nature, and the world. Soracté stood out, blue and serrated to the east, rising sharp up from off the plain just as an island rises from the sea.

The Alban Hills, Horace, had he returned to life, would have known at a glance, with the wild ridge, underneath which the Speculum Dianæ sleeps, blue and unruffled, hiding beneath its depths the golden galley which lies rotting in the mud. All these he would have known, and portions of the Via Sacra where he used to walk, more by the inequalities of ground than by the sight of anything he saw; but all the rest would have been as a dream, horrible and unreal, except the plain itself, and the unchanging life that shepherds live, like that which he described. There seemed no reason that the apparent truce should ever have been broken judging by the eternal sense of quiet, which hung in the air, only disturbed by the metallic croaking of the frogs, the crickets' note, or the rustle of the wings of dragon-flies, which hovered round the flowers, as do the humming-birds, on the Tijuca, or round the orange trees run wild, in the deserted missions of the Paraná.

Sheep followed shepherds who walked in front of them, piping, some upon rude wooden pipes, such as their Etruscan ancestors had used, and some on penny whistles made of tin, but which they still attuned to old-world strains, proving that even progress bows its head to custom; and oxen, feeding in the long lush-grass, answered their names when called, by lifting up their heads.

Had one but gone into the Bosco Sacro with a modicum of faith, Egeria would have been there waiting, just as she sat and looked for Numa in the round clump of trees upon the shoulder of the slope above the Via Appia Nuova; but faith has paled before belief, and the nymph waits in vain.

Along the smooth-worn stones on which the legionaries tramped to civilise and to enslave the world, those round flat stones that once stretched right from Rome up to the Grampians, a ceaseless stream of traffic still poured on, as it has poured for nineteen hundred years. Brown peasants driving sheep, and rich Americans nursing their indigestion and their spleen in motor-cars; herders of buffaloes, on black and shaggy ponies, such as the Volsci rode; tourists on bicycles and ladies riding to the meet; and all those nameless nomads who in warm countries always seem on the move (true gypsies, either by blood or grace), succeeded one another, and each without the least connection with his fellow, just as motes dance about, seen in a sunbeam, on a hot summer's day.

The thick white dust hung in the air and covered everything. It blotted out the rags and changed the summer fabrics that the passing ladies wore into an indistinguishable and neutral tint; upon the coats of horses and of mules it clung congealed in sweat, and from its folds the passers-by emerged just as a steamer slips out from the fog and looms gigantic, abreast of Finisterre, or at the mouth of a slow river running like oil between the mangrove swamps, through which it filters to the sea.

A puff of wind cleared all the road, carrying the dust like a white cloud across the plain. The day wore on, and as the freshness died away, an air of sadness, born of the sunshine, which in hot countries seems as if it emanated from a sun wearied by his daily task for myriads of years, invaded everything. The unseen larks sang shrilly in the sky, their note just filtering to the ear; the lizards basked as if they had been glued down to the stones, and on the margins of the streams the new-born canes drooped in the scorching heat. The passers-by upon the road became more rare, then ceased, except for peasants who at long intervals appeared, seated high in their carts with nautilus-shaped canvas covering, a green bough flapping in their horses' head-stalls to keep away the flies. No songs were heard, except the crickets', which as the day closed in became intensified, sounding as shrill and as perpetual as the electric bell which twitters as a train stops at a southern station, in the full noonday glare.

Slowly the heat abated, and a freshness stole into the air, as the light breeze coming up from the sea at Ostia gently stirred the leaves. Along the edges of the road the peasant women sat and drank it in, combing their children's hair, and looking out across the plain, just as a sailor sits on the fore-bitts, and looks out on the sea, after a long spell at the wheel, under a baking sun.

When the whole road was bare of traffic, and the sadness of the night, taking the world out into the unknown, was near, a troop of oxen slowly came in sight. Gently they surged along, with the same movement that a man wrapped in a cloak assumes. Their limpid eyes belied the promise of their monstrous horns, and as they walked some of them munched a little grass, which left a greenish foam upon their lips. The noblest of their race, descended from the times when men and they had first combined to till the earth, their sleek cream-coloured flanks heaved gently, and it appeared as if they marched to victory, with the blind faith in man that centuries of service had encouraged them to hold.

Beside them frisked some calves, snow-white and innocent, and with their budding horns just showing black beneath the skin, as buds upon an elm show black before the leaves unfold. Behind them came the drovers on their black ponies, each with his goad across the saddlebow. Slowly they marched along, and as they passed before the crossing where the road breaks off towards the "Latin Tombs," a woman sitting by the road looked on the oxen and the young calves regretfully, and muttering "brutta passegglata, vanno alla morte," opened the gate to let the herd pass through.

They passed along unconsciously, towards the slaughter-house, and in a quarter of an hour the sun set in a sea of blood, crimson and violet, and breaking up like an Aurora Borealis into strange shapes, which seemed to chase each other through the sky, before they vanished in the night.

Dutch Smith

Painters all knew Dutch Smith and laughed at him, for a kind-hearted, ineffective soul, damned in the love of art.

His kindliness he had acquired from nature, his nickname from his love of the Dutch school.

Tall, gaunt, and with an air of having been an officer of volunteers, he looked out on the world through steel-grey eyes, which gazed far off, yet seemed to see nothing particular, in the horizon of their view.

Withal he had a subcutaneous humour, which now and then welled to the epidermis (just as the pitch suddenly bubbles in the lake of Trinidad), but never overflowed. Bred as a corn merchant, his attitude to art was that of the traditional hen to ducklings. He loved, but wondered at it, but still more wondered at himself for his great daring in having left so sure a calling to follow such an ignis fatuus, as art.

Thus it appeared that a continual debate went on between the objective corn merchant and the subjective painter, just as Maimonides averred the dual personality of Moses held converse with itself upon the mountain-top. Having embraced the artist's state and faith, he laboured at his self-imposed vocation with a persistency which would have made him great, that is, if greatness were attainable, merely by work alone.

With honest pride he used to tell how much his painting cost him every year: so much for brushes, canvases, and paint, but leaving out of all his calculations what he expended for his personal wear and tear, for any thought of self had never filtered to his mind. Each spring he went to Haarlem to paint a subject much painted by the school he loved, in which a red-brick church with a tall spire sheathed in corroded copper was the chief feature of the scene.

Seating himself before it on his stool, his paints and various accessories spread out before him as if he had been offering them for sale, most conscientiously he would reproduce each brick and all the pointing, even the stork's nest on the parapet, just where the spire sprung from the tower, together with the clock, on whose cracked face one hand did duty, so that you had to make a complicated calculation to find the time of day.

From year to year he migrated to Haarlem, appearing in the spring, just as the stork which built upon the tower came back from Africa at his appointed time; and with ten times more regularity than the one hand set forth the hour on the cracked dial of the clock. Had a bombardment or an earthquake tumbled down the church, it could have been built up again from any of his works without an item missing that the most long-lived burgher in the place could not recall from childhood, and the right tale of bricks.

His colouring was dirty and opaque, looking as if his pictures had been dropped into the mud, dried hastily, and varnished with a treacly kind of stuff, to which the dirt adhered.

Serious towards his art and towards life in general, and naturally a prey to anyone who chose to cheat him, he yet was a still greater prey to his good impulses, which pushed him now and then to acts bordering on idiocy, that is, if anyone can say where generosity and folly, mingle and overlap.

Virtue in peril moved him to step out and offer his assistance upon the smallest provocation, and no one ever came more readily to lead blind men across the street, even although to do so he was obliged to leave a timid lady shivering upon a refuge in the rain. Children who could not find their way, lost dogs, and every kind of waif and stray came to him like steel filings to a magnet and stuck as fixedly. They used him, even to the dogs, who generally after a meal or two made off, leaving his rooms like pigsties, and his heart bleeding at their ingratitude, all to no purpose, for he no sooner saw another cur without a master than he repeated the experience, never remembering that the man who gives his bread to a strange dog loses the dog and bread.

But most of all those who were slighted or neglected had his sympathy. His friends all loved and laughed at him. Even the children he led home, taking them by the way into the pastry-cook's to buy them sweetmeats, looked at him with contempt, for they discerned at once he did not know the kind of chocolate that was in fashion amongst their slobbering compeers. Good humour in his case was of the nature of a devouring passion, not of a virtue, and almost tended to become a vice, so much had he surrendered to its sway. Never in all his life had he been known to dance with a good-looking girl, for, as he stood crumpling his gloves up in his hand into a ball and making up his mind whom he should ask, someone was sure to bustle up to him and say, "Dear Mr. Smith, not one of the Miss Browns has had a partner; do you think that you would mind asking the eldest, and after that, taking her mother down to supper?" Then he would stumble forward and be introduced to some high-shouldered freckled damsel, who at first sight despised him, but used him as a makeshift till her own friends arrived, and then passed him on to her mother, who kept him busily employed fetching and carrying plates about till she had had her fill.

Still, he was popular with all who knew him, and not a fool, except upon the business of the world, about which he was ignorant to an incredible degree, though wise in theory, talking sententiously about all kinds of things which he had never seen but from afar. Though he was so minute a draughtsman that every edge of every brick he drew in Haarlem church was sharp as if it had been turned out from the kiln but yesterday, he yet would theorise as to the advisability of blending all the picture in a harmonious whole. "Nature," he used to say, as if he had enunciated some great unsuspected truth, "abhors a line, hence we impressionists" (for he believed himself a follower of Manet) "always endeavour to present things in the mass."

He either never could have seen one of his own paintings, that is, with the eye of observation, or else his retina was so constructed as to present a different image to that of other men. Women and wine he used to touch on with the air of one who, though no Puritan, could never see what led men to excess in either of them, pronouncing them quite natural tastes, just as he might have said a hoop is a fit toy for children, or a mail-coach or motor-car for those of riper years.

He might have gone on all his life succouring the unmeritorious, painting the church at Haarlem every spring, and moralising with a half-foolish wisdom upon all things sublunary, had it not been that he once made a trip to the Levánt. Having made friends with several of the passengers on board the ship, they went ashore to dine at a small Spanish port.

His friends, mostly young men and painters, having dined badly at a Spanish Fonda, consuming dishes yellow with saffron, or fiery red with cayenne pepper, a sort of culinary parody upon the national flag, sat drinking what the waiter called champán. Why, when the native wines were good, they should have thought it best to drink the essence of petroleum at a pound a bottle is only known to youthful travellers. Still it was so, and as they drank their sweet and nauseous mixture, and cursed the place for being so unlike either to London or to Paris, they fell a-talking as to what they could do to pass away the time. There was no theatre, and gypsy dancing does not usually appeal to Northerners, who look for rapid motion in a dance, and miss the lights of theatres, not being able to see beauty in anything with a poor setting, after the style of those who think that paste well set, exceeds a diamond in a silver hoop. An unfathomable gulf is fixed between the idealism of the north and the materialistic vision of the south, both of which qualities are best for those who have them, as they are quite as unattainable by either, as is a cubit to the stature, merely by taking thought.

So, after a long stumbling conversation with the waiter in bad Spanish, and many curses on a place without amusements, they sallied forth, led by a boy, to visit what they called "the ladies," carrying Dutch Smith along with them. He went half philosophically on the "humani nihil alienum puto" system, and half protesting, but still a little interested in spite of everything.

Their guide, accustomed to such errands, led them by devious paths, up alleys where at the corners lights burned before a virgin or a saint; past taverns where men played at cards, their jackets thrown on their shoulders like a cloak; across a solitary plaza, one end of which was filled up by a church, the space before it, paved like a chessboard with blocks of marble, which in the moonlight seemed to dance about like waves.

With all he met he exchanged witticisms, which luckily his followers did not understand, pointing them with expressive pantomime quite understandable of all. Then he plunged into a dark silent street, and coming to a house through the drawn wooden blinds of which lights shone, stopped furtively before an iron grated door. Twice he hissed sharply like a snake, and ran his fingers up and down the iron bars. The door was opened by a fat woman of about forty years of age, her sleek black hair shining with oil, white "cascarilla" on her face, and having as it were an air of an obscene prioress or abbess clinging about her, coming perhaps from the large bunch of keys she carried in her hand. She bade them welcome in a strange mixture of all languages, and following her they trooped in single file up the steep, badly lighted stair, leaving their guide smoking an evil-smelling cigarette, which he had taken from behind his ear and lighted from a dog-eared match-box hidden between his tattered trousers and his red greasy sash. As they passed up the stairs, stumbling and laughing, hearing the prioress call to her nuns to come down to the drawing-room, Smith reasoned with himself after the fashion of a man over-persuaded, but who knows he is a fool. He was quite sure, having been brought up as a Puritan, that to enter such a house was wrong, but then again, as a philosopher he felt half pleased to show his fortitude and his detachment from the things which rendered others fools.

Lighting a cigarette, to give him countenance, just as some ladies dare not for the world walk through a public promenade without a parasol, he followed his companions, who were waiting for the coming of the nymphs. The place appeared to him not so repulsive as he had thought it must have been. Over the red-brick floor matting was spread, clean, white, and with a picture of a Moor on horseback, carrying a hawk, run through it in coloured worsted work. Upon a black enamelled table with a marble top there stood a vase of flowers, and on the mantelpiece were waxwork fruits, brought from Madeira, under a glass shade. The clock, stopped at the hour of twelve, was French, and represented a lady riding on a goat: perhaps Europa, or perhaps merely a fantasy of art drawn from its maker's brain. Blue glass spittoons stood here and there, and round the room were sofas draped in brown holland, and on the walls hung coloured prints of Garibaldi entering Rome, Victor Emmanuel with a moustache a fathom long, and one, faintly in character with the genius of the place, displayed a German-looking Venus toying with a fat, curly-headed youth who struggled in her arms. Nothing in all of this could shock a saint; even the large and common looking-glasses, draped in pink muslin to keep away the flies, were not alarming, but for the crazy way that they were fastened to the wall.

A pattering of high heels and laughter on the stairs showed that the girls were coming down, and all the company, including Smith, greeted them in bad Spanish as they stood huddled in a heap, smiling, and pinching one another furtively, before the open door. Wrapped in their dressing-gowns, exhaling common scents, and painted heavily, with flowers in their hair, they filed into the room. Gravely they answered the salutations they received, and then sat down so quietly that it seemed to their northern visitors that they were seated at some evening party in some suburb, or that the girls were quite respectable. None of them asked for drink, and no one pushed herself forward beyond the others, being restrained by some invisible bond of etiquette, which seemed to keep them passive until their customers had chosen for themselves.

As conversation was impossible, and Esperanto, fortunately, had not then been invented, rather shamefacedly the visitors made their selection and trooped off up the stairs, the Oriental-looking girls, with their large lustrous eyes, appearing still less civilised and still more Oriental beside the tall and civilised barbarians, so infinitely less human than themselves, who followed in their train. When all had gone, Dutch Smith sat talking to the prioress, who "spik a leetle Inglis," and informed him that she "was call Anita Ramos, Inglis is calling me fat Anne," and that she "like the Inglis gentlemen who coming to her house."

Smith, who had sat with the air as of a member of Parliament at a committee, during the process of the natural selection, now unbent and found himself more interested. He learned the lady was the daughter of a general in Granada, and had received "regular education," but circumstances and hard necessity, for "we are all the slaves of destiny, my son," had brought her to the pass of "keeping house of how you call it . . . doves." All of the doves were as hard-hearted as a millstone, though she did everything she could to make them comfortable, looking at them, not as some women did, but just as if they were her flesh, and she had borne them with much pain. As for herself, time was, a colonel, now in glory and, she hoped, pardoned for his sins, had been the mainstay of her life. At times she hoped that he might marry her, and often prayed in church, for she was very Catholic, that he would do so, but who shall fight with death? Now she was old and ugly . . . "the Inglis gentleman was kind enough to say 'No, no,' but still it was so, and no one looked at her. Old and a sinful woman, but God knew her heart, and kindness touched her to the soul."

This was the kind of thing to appeal to the kind impulses and foolish sympathy of Smith, and, how he never knew, for certainly lust of the flesh was not a factor in the business, he let himself be led out of the drawing-room by the neglected fair.

The storks and swallows found him faithful at the spring tryst in Haarlem, painting his church industriously, and still the providence of everyone who chose to play upon his feelings; still a philosopher, though, as he said, even philosophy is not a certain guide, when human nature chooses to step in. Except for moralisings such as these, and now and then reflections, more or less bitter, which escaped him, on the female sex, the even tenor of his life ran on as it had done for the last twenty years, with the exception that he took a journey now and then to drink the highly smelling waters of a German bath, from which he would return, shamefaced and irritated, and swearing that the malarial fever he had caught in the Levánt would plague him to the last day of his life. Then sitting down to work, he would proceed to daub his canvas with a colour as opaque as glue, and paint for hours just as a man throws coal into a cart, as if he sought to expiate by work the slip from virtue that he had made, as it were, inadvertently, and which was costing him so dear.

Andorra

Andorra yet survives and flourishes, one of the last of the innumerable small States that once were set as thick upon the map of Europe as stars in heaven on a clear winter's night.

True, San Marino still crowns its rock, and is well known to philatelists for its postage stamps, and illustrious in history for having sheltered Garibaldi, the last of the heroic figures of the past.

Montenegro falls into another category, for it had strength enough to win its independence by the force of arms. Some say that Monaco still rears its head, but such a cloud of *poudre de riz*, and such a stench of *patchouli*, of *frangipane*, of *trefle* of white rose, *iris de Florence* and of *chypre*, and of the sweat of all the *cocottes* and the *rastas* of the whole world, obscure it, that reasonable men have doubted of its continued permanence upon the map. Andorra is different from all the rest in that she sells no stamps; has not a *cocotte or* a gambler in all her territory; has never known that such a thing as *poudre de riz ever* existed; never saved any patriot in his extremity; and all her battles were fought in the dark ages against the Counts of Foix and the no less intruding bishops of La Seo de Urgél. Happy the country that has no history, some unimaginative man has said in some book or another. How right the Arabs were to have begun so many of their histories with the phrase, "Says someone."

Andorra, though, has had a history, as those who take the trouble to read Froissart may find out; but who reads Froissart nowadays? Certainly she must have fought against the above-named potentates to keep her independence; but she has kept it, not by fighting but by electing to live quietly, just as her fathers lived a thousand years ago.

True, every citizen is bound to have a gun; but that seems to be all the duty, in a moral military sense, he has, for no one ever saw him with it, or still less heard him touch it off. "To touch it off" seems possibly the phrase to use, as probably it is, in the most of cases, a hereditary piece of ordnance. For all that and in spite of lack of training, and simple as they are, the people have a look as of a Puritan bull-terrier, uncouth and awkward, but not encouraging, should any person happen to tread upon its tail. Civil and courteous they are to a degree that seems extraordinary to those who live in countries which have emerged from patriarchal customs and not yet found their sea-legs in the new state of things. The greatest piece of fortune that has happened to this happy valley lost in the hills, is that up to the present time it has had no roads. Want of communication has kept out the tourist, under whose foot all ancient customs wither, as certainly as did the grass under the horse's hoof of Attila.

To reach the valley, one has to toil upon a mule over the mountain roads, stumbling and sliding, just as the Christian stumbles and slides upon the inconvenient path to Paradise. If though the latter traveller is repaid when he attains his goal, by visions of black eyes smiling upon him in eternal youth, and by supplies of sherbet cooled with snow (I fear that frequent communings with the Moors have caused me to confuse the persons and the substance of our paradise and theirs), so is the traveller re-paid when, after shivering on the Puerto de Saldeu, six thousand feet above sea-level, he gradually descends into a land of sunshine and of warmth.

Possibly in Juan Fernandez, or in some island in some sea or other, there may be valleys like Andorra; sometimes in dreams one sees (with the interior vision of the soul) a valley of the kind, hedged in with towering peaks to which cling pines, and with a little town set in a frame of gardens, from whence ascends the tinkle of a cow-bell or the faint wailing of a bagpipe made melodious by the distance that the sound travels through the air. Commonly in such cases the noise of a steam-hooter wakens one, as it once wakened William Morris after he had dreamed about John Ball, and of what England might have been without machinery, and the real world lies open, in its last incarnation of a dirty street, through which a shrieking motor runs like a car of Juggernaut.

In the deep valley of Andorra, down to which wind paths like beds of mountain burns, with lichened crosses standing at the corners, and at whose sides water is always plashing, led in a hollow tree or piped in canes, there is no need to rub the eyes (*el ojo con el codo*), or if you must, you rub them to send yourself to sleep, so that the vision may not fade and leave you waking in the world.

Once you have crossed El Puerto de Saldeu, a world within a world reveals itself; a view of Europe as it must have been a hundred years ago. In little terraced fields planted with ripening tobacco, with beans and maize, in which lie water-melons so intensely green they seem like something tropical, women and men are working in the way that people must have worked in Arcady or the Paumotas before the well-intentioned missionary with his fateful hymn-book, already charged with death, appeared to save their souls and to deliver up their bodies to consumption and to drink. From the steep fields in which the trailing vines hang over the rough walls there comes a singing, between the note of a wild bird and that of some rude pipe, which winds itself about the inmost recesses of the soul (that is, the soul of those to whom its drawn-out melody appeals) as does no other music in the world, and shows the Arabs, on their way to take the Pope of Rome, as said their General Muza, by the beard, must have passed by Andorra and left their trail. Long trains of mules with dangling trappings of red worsted, conveying bales of tobacco to the rough factory, where ten or a dozen women lazily work to make the nastiest cigars known to the world, pass to and fro; their drivers either sit sideways on their backs or pick their way upon the illusory roads beside them, their sticks stuck down between their ragged jackets and their shirts. In fact, a page of Borrow or of Ford, which some one has turned down and then forgotten, up to the present day. Now, when there are so few forgotten valleys and so few dog-eared pages worth the trouble to smooth out, I had half thought that to write this, is of the nature of a sacrilege, and that I had done better to have forgotten all about Andorra, or merely to have said the beds were verminous, the food abominable, and that the people spoke a dialect between the *patois* of Urgél and that of Foix, quite unintelligible to any reasonable man. Had but the valley been an island, I would certainly never have thought of telling its right bearings, or merely have reported it as a vigia or an atoll quite uninhabited, with brackish water and no landing-place for boats.

Withal, ten or eleven hours on muleback make the navigation difficult enough to keep the island free from contamination, and it lies far beyond the ordinary track, except of ships that pass by night and do not care to have their number known.

Before I take you over the steep-pitched, one-arched bridge which crosses the Valira, with its long trails of ivy swinging eternally backwards and forwards above the roaring stream, guarded by ancient crosses at each end and with a low stone parapet a foot in height, which makes one think upon the proverb, "He who on horseback crosses the bridge, looks death between the eyes," it may be that you would like to hear about the road. Thus did the ancient navigators entertain their readers with a discussion upon every subject under heaven, commonly describing in great detail the Cipango or Manoa they had not reached, and almost at the last, say in a perfunctory way, on December the 13th I left Cadiz or San Lucar, as the case may be, in the caravel *Marigalanté*, sailing with the Acapulco fleet, and as God willed it, had a good passage of about two hundred days, seeing the flying-fish and other wonders of the deep, and by the grace of the Almighty safely came to port in Acapulco of New Spain. Even Bernal Diaz, he of the Castle, the prince of chroniclers, so to speak, sandwiches in the date of his arrival between great slabs of facts and comments, terse, humorous and still pathetic, such as only he could make.

Well . . . two roads lie open to you. One by La Seo de Urgél and one by Ax-les-Thermes. The first is from the Spanish side and has its difficulties.

La Seo de Urgél, stronghold of Carlism, is situated — luckily for it — full eighty miles from any railway. You get off at Caláf (it sounds so Arabic, I had almost written El-Caláf), and get into the coach. That coach, a box, made of white pine and painted red and yellow, "Viva España!" conveys you in the short space of thirteen hours (but not including stoppages) up to La Seo de Urgél. Borrow and Ford and others have described the journey, not this particular journey, but others of the kind, so picturesquely that it is vain to try and emulate them. They both have told of the apocalyptic horse and the four mules; of the blaspheming *mayorál* and the *zagál* who now and then gets off and stimulates the team by throwing stones. Even the names (in Ford's case, some of the oaths) have been preserved, so that we know them when we hear the long-drawn syllables of Capitaana, Generaala, and the impersonal Aquella Otra who receives most stones and all the choicest flowers of speech of the attendant sprite. Well do we know the country-women with their baskets, the fat and jovial priest, the friar, the horsedealer, and the strange Turk, or Greek, or Jew whose family from the days of Ferdinand Isabella *[sic]* had secretly continued the customs of their race. We know the gipsy who gets in, and speak to him (having the gift of tongues) in Romany. We share our lunch with all the passengers, drink with the priest out of a leather *bota*, and leave the company delighted with us and our fast friends for life.

Those were the days, and certainly Ford and George Borrow were the men; but even now the journey has points of resemblance to those they wrote about. The painted box on wheels lands you at last in the strange, world-forgotten town, to which but little breath of modernism has penetrated, and leaves you there marooned. Then you must hire a mule from an *arriero*, some Tio Chinche, Tio Ponzoña, or the like, and make your way over five hours of mountain road, which leads along the banks of the Valira, until you come upon Andorra quite unexpectedly at the bottom of a pass. All things considered, I am doubtful whether this road is quite the best to take for those who pass their time in motor-cars and are accustomed to eat well at regular hours and sleep in comfortable beds; but as I never travelled it myself I do not describe it in great detail, though I am sure I could.

The other road, though not exactly what would be called luxurious, is yet a little easier than that by Seo de Urgél. A well-appointed railway (Baedeker says so) lands you at Ax-les-Thermes, passing by Foix and Pamiers, a name corrupted from the ancient Apamea (once more Baedeker). Then you take carriage for four hours to Hospitalet, a little goaty, sheepy town, Swiss-like and cold, and with its little inn facing the road and music of the ceaseless stream of motor-cars which come and go, as regularly as does the planetary system, from Ax to Puigcerdá. Once there, so that you turn your back on the high road and stop your ears after the fashion of Ulysses or the deaf adder of the Scriptures, you are in the wilds. Cows wander down the street; goats browse upon the broken walls; and round the rough stone cross, boys sit all day and criticise the women and the girls who go for water to the fountain at the corner of the square.

A road, like the dry track of a Highland burn, leads out towards Andorra, and on it, early in the morning, two horsemen, my guide and I, might have been seen some weeks ago making their way, just like the personages of some bygone novel, along the stony track. The trail led upwards through some Alpine pastures, in which men mowed the grass with scythes exactly like the scythe Time holds in ancient prints, immensely broad at the butt-end and tapering to a point. All wore blue *berets*, and all sang as they worked; but being on the French side of the Pyrenees, they sang the latest melodies from Paris music-halls instead of some wild *Jota fiera* as they would certainly have done upon the Spanish side.

We rode along, smoking and talking about "things and others," of the late war, for so it seemed to him, between the French and Prussians, and how he, with twelve youths from Hospitalet, had joined the army of the Loire, and he alone returned. We talked of literature, that is, he did, unpacking all his store, which in the main consisted of a history of the Punic Wars, with much of Scipio ("Un fameux lapin, va!") and of Canibal. Soon at a little hamlet with a fine old cross we passed the frontier of Andorra, that is, my guide averred we did, as there was nothing tangible to mark the line.

Still we went on along the Ariège, which boiled and tumbled far below our feet, the horses giving us plenty of opportunity to look into its depths by hugging, after the fashion of their kind, the outside limit of the path.

No houses were in view, and only rarely on the road did a man pass, driving before him a packed mule, or now and then a girl seated upon an ass. Horses and cows in hundreds fed along the slopes, their bells tinkling and jangling in the still air, a thousand feet below. Sometimes they stood, their bellies buried in the rushing stream, and now and then two bulls fought in a perfunctory way, as sword-and-buckler men fought in old times in Edinburgh, to keep the "croon o' the Causeway," that is, when anyone was there to look at them and cheer them to the fray.

"C'est un vrai paradis pour toutes nos vaches," the guide observed as he broke off explaining all about Regulus and "la mort douloureuse de ce brave Canibal." Four or five hours we rode along, passing the little lake in which the Ariège has its source, and talking of the fall of Carthage, which in some way had got itself connected in the commentator's brain with *les sales Prussiens*, until we reached the pass.

"This is El Puerto de Saldeu," said my guide, breaking out suddenly in Spanish, which he spoke well after the French fashion, sounding all syllables quite equally, taking the nerve and backbone out of it, although he knew the words. Standing upon the summit of the pass and looking down upon a sea of pine woods and right into another brawling river, the Valira (the cousin of the Ariège), cutting its way through a deep channel in the hills, forming a valley which, in the distance, broadened to a great amphitheatre of mountains, above which rose white peaks, you feel that you have come into a world apart. It is so seldom nowadays, even in Equatorial Africa, to which you carry tents and smokeless powder, quick-firing guns, sun-helmets, and are carried by subservient or rebellious porters (but in each case members of a subject race, with whom there can be naught in common save death or want of food), that made you feel cut off from the world.

Once or twice in the lifetime of most men they feel alone, and I remember years ago, in Paraguay, coming down from the Yerbales, a hundred miles from anywhere, uncertain of the way, I camped, not having eaten all the day, beside a wood. Looking about, I found a bed of the sweet fruit known there as *guavirami* (the sweetest in the world when you are parched with thirst and there is nothing else to eat), and having eaten well, unsaddled, and sitting down (it was just sunset) on my saddle-cloths, wrapped in my *poncho*, drew out tobacco, chopped it, and made a cigarette, then lit it with a flint and steel, striking the flint with care, not to alarm my horse. Just then a tiger roared, deep in the woods, and when, after a struggle, I had quieted my horse, for to have lost him would have been to lose my life, I felt I was alone.

Well, strange as it may seem, upon the Puerto de Saldeu, not forty miles from motor-cars, and with my garrulous and history-loving guide beside me, looking down on a valley which had been civilised for centuries, I felt the feeling I had felt in Paraguay. One rarely feels it in the East, for there, even in deserts, man has so stamped himself upon the world, nothing astonishes, and one is certain, beyond the mountains, or in the middle of the plains, that you will come upon some tribe of nomads who have not changed since Nimrod hunted, and the walls of Babylon were built.

It may be that the sudden change from modern life created the impression; but as we drove the horses down the hill-path before us, cutting off corners to rejoin them, by little trails worn in the stony soil, it seemed one was about to enter into an unknown land.

Sliding and stumbling down the hill, the guide shod with his hemp-soled *alpargatas*, going as lightly as a cat, we reached the hamlet of Saldeu, which, with its deep projecting eaves, looked Swiss-like, had it not been for the iron rings set in the walls of every house to tie the mules to, and for the knockers placed about six feet above ground, so that the passer-by could knock without dismounting from his beast. We passed a watering-trough made of a huge old tree, looking as if a tribe of Indians or negroes had left their dug-out high and dry, and riding through an archway, dismounted in a stable, in which some twenty mules, each with its pack beside it, stood munching at their corn.

Beside them, some sleeping on the packs and some upon the straw, lay men who, at first sight, I knew were smugglers, having seen many of them in the wild roadless country between Gibraltar and Gaucin, that is, the country that was wild and roadless thirty years ago. There in Saldeu they looked so much in place, the stables would have appeared as the stage would appear in *Carmen*, in the third act, without the turnpike Andaluces, who bear the mark of Saffron Hill writ large upon their backs.

Leaving our horses tied up, by the mules, we passed into a gallery which looked out on a maize-field, sloping down to a little burn, in which a row of women were washing clothes, their red and yellow petticoats giving them an air as of gigantic tulips, as they beat the linen on a board, or washed their stockings, filling them with sand and thumping on the stones.

In the long gallery, three or four men were lounging, whilst one of them thrummed a guitar, whose strings, mended with wire, sent forth a sound, when the player struck them with the back of his brown hand, like an old-fashioned jew's-harp or a hurdy-gurdy. The march of progress has probably now relegated both these instruments to the museum, unmercifully leaving us the gramophone, which, like the rich, is always with us, to remind us of our sins.

Following the example of George Borrow (Ford would have addressed himself to a black-haired girl who leaned out of a window humming a *Zorzico*), I entered into conversation with the breakers of the law, and found that most of them had once been soldiers, and had fought in Cuba, about which they knew as much as a returned Imperial Yeoman knows about the Orange Free State, that is, the inside of the hospitals and the long useless marches in the sun, Much did our conversation turn upon things technical, such as the dogs that in Gibraltar run the gauntlet of the carbineers, each with his little pack upon his back, and many were the tales about the heroes who in times past had earned a place in history by their bold smuggling deeds.

The seven of Ecija held them all spell-bound, as the Homeric heroes held the Greeks, and when I spoke about Jose Maria, and of the town of Casariche, where those who have a soul above mere smuggling take boldly to the road, they crowded round to hear. The fate of El Vivillo and the great fight he made in the *cortijo* stirred their enthusiasm, and when at last the *Guardia Civil* entered the burning farm, leaving five of their number stretched upon the field, they held their breath, and one of them, murmuring "He was a man, may God have pardoned him," held out a glass of *aguardiente* in which I drank his health. They looked upon the heroes of the South as prototypes, averring sadly that in the North the true *aficion* was getting lost, and thought the smugglers of to-day were weaklings compared to those of yore. So might a superannuated general in his club lament the days of purchase in the Army, or in the fens of Cambridgeshire a stableman strive hard to mould himself after the true West-Riding type and as Sir Thomas Overbury says, "speak Northern no matter in what part of England he was born."

I learned how one of them died of yellow fever, had been thrown out to wait the dead-cart, then come to life again when he had felt a land-crab nibbling at his toe, and so resuscitated. The word resuscitated evidently pleased him, for taking the guitar (after first passing it to me, in the fashion of Sir Philip Sidney, as if my need was more than his), when it came to his turn to play, struck into a *guajira*, to which, as he informed me, he had made the words and put a title, "El Resuscitao." Death had not staled the infinite variety of his arpeggios, nor had returning life altered the haunting melody of the half-negro air, nor blurred its semitones.

When he had finished, and as he hung the instrument upon a nail, a flower fluttered down from the window where the girl had leaned, and looking at the singer critically, I saw he was a handsome fellow and "properly deliver," which fact, no doubt, the giver of the flower had seen some time ago. After some talk about the badness of the government in Spain, a theme which, I believe, if one but chanced to meet him, so to speak, off duty, the Premier would join in with much zest, we passed into the dining-room, and sitting down at a long table, without a cloth, upon rough wooden stools, enjoyed a meal of salt cod *à la Vizcaina*, pork sausages made red with saffron, and beans stewed in an oil which might have served to lubricate a waggon-wheel. The women of the house stood in the doors and round the table, as it would not have been a fitting thing for them to sit down with the men, although they joined quite freely in the conversation, which now and then was spiced as hotly as the sausages, only exclaiming "Bárbaro," when the bounds were overpassed, just as a mother may reprove her son for swearing, in a half-hearted way.

Smoking as sententiously as an Indian chief, the owner of the house, a member of the Council of the Republic, sat like an idol in a josshouse, carved in walnut wood. Report averred him rich, and witty *(gracioso)*, an unusual compound, and his *gracia* consisted in his knack of giving nicknames, which form of wit is thought the highest in Andorra to which man can aspire. His fellow-humorists had countered heavily upon him by giving him the name of "Tio Alimentos," which he appeared to merit, for when the company had finished their repast, he sat down solemnly at his own hospitable board and fell to work like a half-starved coyoté on a dead buffalo.

The smugglers took their leave, quite openly, with each man carrying on his back his bundle of tobacco, all smoking their own wares. They crossed the stream upon a narrow plank and slowly disappeared amongst the pine-trees, on the rough path to Spain. When they had gone, across the river floated back in the still air the long-drawn notes of the *guajira*, sung by "the resuscitated one," and taken up, when he had spent his breath, by all the rest of his compeers. At last it melted into the thin air, just like a cricket's note, but leaving still a sense of sound upon the ear. When it was quite extinguished, a window shut down in an upper room, showing the giver of the flower had been upon the watch for its last quavering notes.

It was time for them to go, for hardly had they disappeared than two or three French frontier guards, under the protection of an Andorran peasant, who, because he had a gun, appeared to think he was some kind of soldier, appeared, and asked if anyone had seen *les contrebandiers*. They were assured that no one had and went their way contentedly, smoking cigars which had been purchased half an hour ago from our late fellow-guests.

Mounting our horses in the dark stables, and bending down to pass the door, we struck into the street, which ran about a hundred yards between low, deep-eaved houses, and then came out upon some stony fields, planted with what in Scotland used to be called long kale. The road was bounded by low walls of rough-piled stones, and at the top of a steep natural staircase of smooth rocks there stood a high stone crucifix, with something Gothic in the carving of the Christ, who, dumpy and too much foreshortened, looked like the figures on the Gloria door of Santiago de Campostela *[sic]*, and yet was human and even pathetic-looking on his grey granite cross.

My guide crossed himself rather in a furtive way, explaining that he did not do so as a "clerical," but because business took him often to Andorra, where every one was "black." The reason seemed to me sufficient in itself, although perhaps the act either was one of supererogation or of interior grace, as the place we were in was far from houses and no one was in sight.

Quaint little hamlets dotted the hillsides, with little churches in proportion to their needs, and tiny belfries formed of rough stone and innocent of mortar, the windows in their sides so sharp, they looked as if they had been built for archers in the tower to shoot down their foes.

From every village ran a mule-track to the main torrent-bed that served as a high road, showing the stones all whitened, where mules and men had passed for centuries, and still had left the way as rough and difficult to tread as when the first explorer, stumbling on his beast, had passed along the trail.

In a deep chasm far below the road the river roared and tumbled, sending up clouds of spray, which hung in a white mist upon the larches growing by its brink.

At all the cross-roads stood a Calvary, and before every church a massive crucifix cut roughly in grey stone. Another staircase of a league or so led to the village of Encamp, where we dismounted at a *venta* and drank some *aguardiente*, which turned the water in the glass a milky white, and sitting on a barrel under some bundles of salt cod-fish which dangled from the roof, exchanged a greeting with the owner of the house, a red-haired Catalán.

A pale-faced caitiff-looking man he was, who might have sat for Judas to an Italian master, and yet he looked civilised amongst the rough Andorrans, as perhaps did his prototype of old amongst the fishermen.

Whilst we discoursed on politics, and answered questions as to the health of the young Queen of Spain, the possible duration of the Ministry in France, the price of barley in La Seo de Urgél, and whether Machaquito or Bombita was the best master of his art, a crowd had gathered at the door. They stood expectantly, just as in lands more favoured men wait to buy the last edition of a newspaper, not that they think it may be interesting, but on the chance of something turning up to gratify their hopes. I hoped I answered to the full what was expected of me, and thought I did so, until I heard a man remark I was the agent of a circus which they were waiting for. Sadly I spurred my unwilling pony through the crowd, looking as like a ring-master as I was able, but in my heart conscious of failure, for to give pleasure to one's fellows should be one's chiefest aim, here in this transitory world.

By quick descents in which the ponies put their feet together and skated down the hill, just as a cowboy's horse in the Bad Lands slips down a "slide," we cut off half a league, saving some time, and proving the proverb, that there is never a short cut without some trouble, is not quite absolute.

Settling our hats upon our heads, and brushing off the dust with which the ponies' scramble on the slide had covered all our clothes, we struggled back into the road which led through groves of ilexes and chestnut trees and finally emerged into a rich and fertile valley, where little fields, fenced with flat pieces of grey stone stuck close together, encircled every house. Maize and tobacco showed the richness of the soil, and as we rode along, the mule-path melted by degrees into a modern road. A milestone bore upon its face "Andorra, 9 kilometros," but as upon the road itself there was no traffic, save for the passing of a mule-team now and then, or a stout farmer riding on his nag, with an old rusty gun tied to the cantle of his saddle, it seemed a work of supererogation, and my guide cursed it as an innovation which lamed the horses, and would, in his opinion, ruin the country, in the long run, for men who lived by mules. I felt by intuition he was right, for the stout mountain pony that I rode, active and hardy as a goat on the steep trails that we had left, stumbled perpetually and fell upon his nose. I hauled him up upon his feet, and getting off found that his knees were quite undamaged, whilst my guide, sitting on his horse, looked at me pleasantly, saying with pride, "He often falls upon this portion of the road, but never hurts himself."

I did not comment on the fact, knowing the horseman's grave is always open, and that the wayfarer may sometimes stumble on the road towards Andorra, even when not a fool.

The sun was sinking as we came to Las Escaldas, a little watering-place built in a gorge between the hills. The river rushes by the side of the main street, in which, hedged in by cottages with overhanging eaves, and set about with half-built little villas, stands the Bath House, in which the citizens of the Republic bathe and drink sulphuretted water of some kind, which, as I learned with pleasure, is nauseous to the taste and smells like rotten eggs.

All was in miniature and as if drawn to the scale of the Republic, of which it is the pride.

Cows sauntered up and down the street, and from the mills came the click-clack of hoppers, as the enormous wooden wheels, constructed to require the greatest possible amount of water-power to set them going, slowly revolved with a dull bellowing noise.

All was Arcadian, and from every side there came the noise of water which in a hundred rills ran everywhere, rills and more rills and still more rills, with water led in canes, in hollow trunks of trees, splashing down rocks and gurgling under the high-pitched little bridges, with an old millstone forming the keystone of the arch.

Burly Andorrans, who in the tranquil current of their lives could never have endured an ache or pain, but who were led to take the cure just as a millionaire at Aix-les-Bains, to drink its nauseating waters, in case at any future time he may be ill, lounged up and down and passed the time of day.

Women conversed across the street from balconies, informing those who cared to listen, of their domestic troubles, and of their children's health. A priest went down the street, and as he walked along, from every house a little boy or girl rushed up to him and raised his fingers to their lips, catching a blessing as it were upon the wing, and rushing back again.

In order that no jot or tittle of the Arcadian scene should be left wanting, just as I crossed the little Plaza of the town, a stout, broad-shouldered peasant passed, jogging upon his nag. His clothes were made of a two-carat kind of cloth, and on his head he wore an imitation Panama, set firmly on his brows. He sat upon his horse, a fine bay colt with four white feet and a white star upon its forehead and branded with a K, strongly and squarely, with something of the look of Colleone, on his immortal steed. On the high pommel of his old-fashioned Spanish saddle, of the kind called *albarda*, he rested his crossed hands, and as he slowly jogged along at the pace known as *el paso Castellano*, his horse's tail swung to each movement, and his forefeet now and then rang against the stirrups, in his high dishing gait.

Men nodded to him and the boys all seemed his friends, and from the windows women looked shyly but approvingly as he passed slowly down the street.

"Voici le Président!" exclaimed my guide, adding for my instruction in a low tone, "pas fier le bonhomme," and as he spoke he raised his hat and was saluted gravely in return by the chief magistrate. I, too, saluted, and was saluted in return, and then leaving the despot in the full glare of the fierce light which no doubt beats as fiercely on the presidential chair as on the throne, rode through the winding street, passing the time of day with the inhabitants all seated at their doors. Women sat twirling distaffs, and in the fields girls held their cows by a long cord; some combed their hair, and others seated on the ground held children on their knees, whose heads they searched as diligently as a man hunts a particle in a Greek lexicon, in spite of kicks and cries.

No one appeared to use the modern road, which took its course, remote, unfinished, and possibly slow, between some water meadows; but we, knowing the traditions, so to speak, struck into the old trail.

It wound about, through a small grove of ilexes, and though the capital was a short league away, had not been altered since the creation of the world, so that at times we skirted huge boulders, and again dodged the spray of waterfalls, picking our way, just as one picks it in the Atlas mountains, and taking care to step into the holes made by the traffic of the ages, by the mules' passing feet.

The oak wood passed, the valley broadened out into a fertile plain, to which tobacco gave an air as of the "Vuelta de Abajo," with its brown ripening leaves. Streams flecked the mountain sides with streaks of silver, making them seem alive with movement, and at the bottom of a cliff Andorra lay, grey, ancient, and an epitome in stone of what the greater part of European towns had been, in the long-vanished past.

We passed the roughly built tobacco factory, stopping a moment to buy a few cigars, so to speak, at the fountain head, finding them green and pungent and with a flavour something resembling the perfume of a weasel with a strong touch of goat.

Wrapped in a coarse brown paper with the mendacious legend "Tabaco Filipino" stamped upon it in faint lettering, they served to form the universal brotherhood of man, and show one plainly that a touch of commerce, even so slight a one as this, makes everybody kin.

Ten hours of riding on the mountain trails had brought us to our Mecca, into which we passed over the steep-pitched bridge on the Valira, just as the night closed in.

The Plaza with its tall old houses, frescoed with yellow arabesques, was quite deserted, save for a pig or two which lay about, right in the middle of the square, or dodged the efforts of a boy to drive it home. On one side rose the belfry above the body of the church, just as a lighthouse rises on a shoal.

Into its doors were passing women, veiled to the eyes in black, yellow and parchment-looking, and of a type that only Spain affords.

Their only home appears to be the church, where they squat motionless upon the floor, or, kneeling on a chair, remain for hours with their eyes fixed upon a saint.

The beggars at the door all know them and long have recognised they have no alms to give, and as they pass mutter to one another, "There goes old Doña Tecla," or "Doña Gertrudis," or simply, as they hold the leather curtain up, say "La Beata," in a resigned and hopeless way, knowing that the poor lady's need is probably as great as is their own, and then sink back again upon the moulding underneath the door, to wait what fate may bring.

Upon the other side was *El Commercio*, that is, the shops, which in this instance were represented by the apothecary and a large general store. I glanced inside as we passed by, and in them sat the usual *Tertulia*, that is, the gathering which in Spain repairs to shops at night to talk about the news.

I only caught a word or two, and passing by the other portion of the "Commerce" of the place, saw quiet women cheapening calicoes, and heard upon the counter the sharp ring of a large silver dollar and an expostulating voice exclaiming, "No, Señor, it is not false, nor yet from Seville as you say, but sound and of the law."

One narrow winding lane led us into another lane, as winding as the last, in which our horses, though they knew the way, stumbled and slithered and now and then stood snorting at a black object on the ground which, when we passed it, proved to be a pig asleep and snoring, and stretched out at his ease. One little square led to another little square, with houses all with long flights of steps in front of them, on which their owners sat, and in response to greeting, told us "to go with God," a form of salutation which in most other lands has fallen out of fashion, perhaps because God does not manifest himself so plainly as He does in Andorra, or from some other cause.

At the *posada* door we met the owner, a stout Andorran known as "El Tio Calounes," a burly, greasy-looking man, his head bound in a black silk handkerchief with the end dangling underneath his hat, and smoking pensively.

Travellers are not too frequent in these parts, but for all that he was not anxious in the least to welcome us, but seemed put out by our arrival, till I, getting abruptly off my horse, unpacked a budget of the news of the world, quickly and volubly and so distorted as to be palatable to almost everybody. The stern Republican unbent, and after greetings faithfully given and received upon both sides, said in an uncouth dialect, "Seeing you come with François here, I thought you were from France."

This difficulty over, we soon were friends, and talked till supper-time, upon all kinds of things, such as the spread of Carlism in La Seo de Urgél, and the new bishop, who it appeared was a friend of the King's, who Tio Calounes always called Alfonsito, either to show he was a democrat or in affection, for he averred that he had heard the King was one who gave himself no airs (*no se daba tono*) and could ride well and shoot. Accomplishments of that kind being exactly what men look for in emperors and kings, I instantly agreed with him, and ventured to predict a happy and prosperous reign for one who in his youth had risen to the sense of his responsibilities and made his people's welfare his first care and duty, above all other things.

When at last supper came, we took it in a room lighted by a petroleum lamp, which leaked, and on whose sides, stuck in the oil that daubed them, were carcases of moths and flies, which fell into the soup. Mosquitoes hummed, and now and then a rat ran through the room and bats flew in and out, circling about above our heads like swallows round a pool.

As for the meal itself, it was a replica of the lunch at Saldeu, though perhaps even more highly flavoured, and after it we sat and smoked the national cigars, during a thunder-storm.

The bedroom which I shared with a French cattle-dealer, who was drunk and snored as loudly as a gramophone, contained two iron beds, made for the Spanish market or in Barcelona, of a thin iron piping with pictures of the Annunciation in three colours set in a varnished oval at the head. They had the highest free-board, if the term free-board rightly applies to beds, that I have ever seen in all my wanderings.

Mosquitoes and a fair sprinkling of the pterodactyl that have remained in the Republic, rendered night one long conflict, so that I heard the long-drawn cry of the *sereno*, as he called every hour.

Early next morning I was afoot and found the owner of the house still at his post, smoking and drinking coffee, which he was stirring with a knife, as he sat tilted on a chair. The town was waking, and in the streets women drove goats to pasture, or led the horses down to water, or stood about the fountain in the square, waiting their turn to fill brass water-buckets, which they bore balanced on their heads. Men in the old Andorran dress, breeches and jacket of dark velveteen with sashes round their waists, red Phrygian caps upon their heads, their legs encased in woollen stockings of a grey-bluish hue, and on their feet white *alpargatas*, lounged smoking everywhere.

Under arcades, mule-drivers were packing mules, which, after the fashion of their kind the whole world over, squealed and kicked spitefully, now and then throwing off their load, just as the men were tugging at the ropes, with their feet stuck against the girths or twisting them with sticks.

The acrid reek of wood curled lazily into the sky and the dense smoke of charcoal braziers placed before the doors to "pass" as people say in Spanish, combined with the rank scent of goats and sheep, which here and there were folded in a deserted cottage, produced a pungent scent such as that which in markets in the East blends with the morning air.

At the south corner of the town, built of grey stone to which a yellow lichen clings and flanked by turrets at each angle of the tower, rises the "Valley House."*

Built, as some commentators say, in the tenth century, though others just as strongly hold the twelfth as the true date of its foundation, it serves as Council-chamber, prison, and archive, and as it looks toward the south over an ocean of tobacco-fields, with the Valira brawling underneath its walls, is the true centre of the microcosm which clusters at its gate.

For centuries, when throughout Europe liberty was dead, stifled in England by the nobles, and in Spain killed at Villalár, in Italy drugged by the Popes, and in the North chilled by the feudal system with its ideal of a humanity that commences with the baron, here it has flourished in a patriarchal way, just as a pine, which in a rich soil deteriorates and dies, springs vigorous from stones.

A woman summoned from her spinning and carrying in her hand a key ten inches long, fit for the gate of a great town or citadel, served as the janitress.

With pride she struggled with the lock, which only yielded to the united efforts of the guide and myself and of the faithful guardian of the key, and ushered us within.

In a great vaulted hall the Council meets, the members, twenty-five in number, chosen by universal suffrage, the test of voting being apparently the strength to bear a gun, assemble, and debate. When they have finished their deliberations, which, as the janitress informed me, rarely exceed an hour or two in length, they dine together at great tables, set in the Council-room.

The custom seems a good one and might be followed with advantage in other Parliaments, for it promotes good feeling and cannot be a hindrance to debate, judging at least from the way jurymen despatch their business, when dinner is in sight.

The robes and the three-cornered hats of all these simple representatives were hanging upon pegs, and a rough picture done from a photograph showed them assembled at the entrance to the place and in the midst of them their overlord, the Bishop of Urgél, who seemed a pleasing-looking prelate, neither too fat nor thin.

Below the Council-chamber is the State kitchen in which great cauldrons swung on weighty chains, and in them, so the janitress averred, are cooked whole kids and sucking-pigs and trifles of that kind which keep the fire of liberty alight in the stout stomachs of the Gargantuan Archons who batten on the cheer.

The stables where their horses and their mules, for many of the members have a long ride when they attend their parliamentary duties, are tied and munch their corn, what time their masters banquet and debate, are large and airy and perhaps rather dirtier than is a cattle-byre in the Long Island or Benbécula, but still seemed adequate enough for the rough horses and the mules I met upon the road.

A priest assured me that there is no written law in the community, but that in spite of this the folk are honest and God-fearing, and as there are no laws to break, they never break them, which piece of reasoning upon his part seemed to me quite conclusive, and taken into consideration with the fact that public functionaries have no fixed salaries, but serve their valley all for the honour and the glory of the thing, makes up a state of things almost ideal in this transitory world, that is if transitory can be applied to places like Andorra, which never can have suffered any change since God was God or the sun first commenced to shine upon the hills.

Next morning saw me early on the road, riding along and smoking, musing contentedly on this thing and on that, upon the fall of nations and of kings, creeds, principalities, and powers, and why it is that fate had spared Andorra when it had eaten up Greece, Rome, and Babylon, and also on the various ways in which men pass their lives struggling to do things quite impossible to do, when, after all, nothing is better than to jog along the road and to shout "Arré" loudly now and then when a mule lags behind.

El Pastor de Las Navas

Amongst the multitudinous figures above the high altar of the Cathedral of Toledo, there is one that I have often caught myself looking at with as great interest as if it were a work of art. It represents, roughly painted, carved in a warm yellow stone that seems to have congealed sunshine in it, the figure of a mediæval Spanish shepherd. His loose frock is secured by a belt, and falls to his knees, leaving the rest of his legs bare. On his feet are sandals. His head is bare, and shows a thick growth of curly black hair, clustering round his blunt, open face, in which are set two honest brown eyes, which look out upon the world so directly that you feel at once their owner is an Old Christian, on all four sides, as the saying is, and without a drop of either Jewish or Moorish blood.

A long and rough staff is in his hand, and round his waist is hung a gourd, just such a gourd as you can see growing to-day in the *cigarrales* outside the town. On every side of him stand in serried ranks the effigies of kings, of knights, of saints, of virgins, bishops, confessors, and on his left hand a statue of a converted Moorish *alfaqui*, who by the grace of God became a Christian to the greater glory of our faith, and perhaps to serve as an example of the unsearchable ways of the Creator of the world, who might have made him, if He had chosen so to do, a Christian, without attaching to him the stain of being a traitor to the faith in which he had been bred.

All the stone worthies look nobly out upon the world, with the exception of the poor *alfaqui*, who has a hangdog air as of a renegade.

They seem to feel that they will never die, whilst those they look at, all are transitory.

The shepherd has no look either of faith or of nobility, but leans upon his staff just as he must have leaned upon it in his life, when he stood, on the sunburnt plain, a mere dark spot, watching his black and yellow sheep, amongst grey plants of fennel and yellow flowering thistles, which in the clear Castilian air stand up so sharp against the sky that they appear as tall as trees.

Nothing in his appearance, as he stands so modestly, waiting apparently for the sun to strike upon some ridge or other of the hills, to know the time, to turn his flock towards home, suggests that he was other than a shepherd, such as a hundred others of his kind. Why he should be enshrined amongst so many noble lords and ladies above the altar, opposite the silver gates that shut the choir, in the same fane in which Don Alvaro de Luna sits headless in his vault; why he should be bejewelled when the sun streams through the glorious stained glass, as if he were a knight, a king, a bishop, or a saint; why he should have been counted worthy to appear in the long line of figures that ring about S. James himself, trampling a never-dying Moor to death under his horse's hoofs, the sacristan will tell those who expend a franc. Look at him well and mark his sturdy legs, his hands like roots of whin-bushes, his air of simple faith made manifest in all his carriage, and then turn to the encircling throng of knights and nobles, his bold compeers in stone, and see if in their eyes there is not to be found a look of gratitude and admiration for the squat figure who makes so strange a blot amongst their ranks. Why do they look at him, as you might look upon a man who had done you some great service, almost unconsciously, a service greater than it is possible to pay?

Hard by, beneath the altar of El Transito, are laid the bones of Juan Padilla and his heroic wife, those of Juan Bravo, and the rest of the illustrious band who died at Villalár. Kings, constables, an emperor, bishops, archbishops, emirs, sultans, and high-priests have helped to form the penetrating dust that makes the eyes smart in Toledo when the north wind blows, and which makes every church smell like a charnel-house. Scholars and queens and clerks, learned both in Arabic and Latin, and warriors skilled in both saddles, the high-peaked tree of Fez and the flat bur of Europe, as is set forth upon their tombs, lie thick on every side.

All round the church in which the shepherd stands so patiently, unmarked by those whose admiration only can be stirred up by high-sounding names, the wondrous city stretches out a very palimpsest of Gothic superposed on Moorish architecture, and that again reared on foundations dug by the Romans, set with innumerable gems, El Cristo de la Luz, the Alcázar, Santa Maria la Blanca, once a synagogue, a mosque, and now a church, the jewelled cloister of San Juan, the square known as the Zocodovér, the Puerta del Cambron, and all the myriad and tortuous lanes in which the marigolds grow from the walls, and where the red valerian attracts the cats, from Moorish ajimeces — all go to form a casket in which each house has something noble in it, even in decay. A noble city, set on a noble river and surrounded by a landscape resembling nothing more than that seen in the moon through a good telescope; and in it, in its chiefest gem, the incomparable church, in which the French once bivouacked, stabling their horses in the choir, unconscious that the heavy gates that shut it, then painted black, were solid plate, the simple figure stands.

He stands unconscious that the whole city, Spain and even Christendom itself perhaps, owes its existence to his fortunate appearance, and that without his knowledge of the passes in the hills, for at the time the Moorish host lay in Las Navas de Tolosa, and all the width of Sierra Morena intervened between them and Alfonso (he who rode his horse into the waves at Algeciras, brandishing his sword against the infidel across the straits), we all should now be rising in the night to testify to the existence of the one God and of his prophet, the immortal camel-driver.

In those days, whilst the shepherd, whose effigy now is sculptured in the church, kept sheep upon the slopes of the dark mountains that cut Castile off from the south, a wave of faith had stirred the souls of the veiled camel-riders, deep in the deserts far below Marrakesh, impelling them to move, just as the instinct stirs a swallow to take wing. Lost in the sand, owning no property but their swift camels, which drink only on the third morning after they have drunk, and a few horses foaled as they say by mares impregnated by the south wind, they cherished their belief in the one God, their God, made in their image, austere, patient of hardships, self-centred, individual, and impatient of restraint. They felt, there, in their thirsty land, in which not even an occasional great rock affords a shade; there, where the lizard's head is almost photographed upon the sand; where water is the chiefest gift that Allah gives, and that so sparingly he seems to know it is above all price, and therefore often impregnates it with salt, so that its drinkers shall not turn necessity to pleasure, that the time had arrived to testify.

They knew that far away in Spain their brethren had become degenerate, reading and writing, studying the Greek philosophers, eating and drinking, not to sustain life, but to gratify the senses, and that the land they lived in was a paradise, all ready to their hand. There, poets told them that the jasmine ever flowered, the roses bloomed, and that the sound of water always fell upon the ear, trickling in rills or plashing on the stones. Almost involuntarily, they found themselves upon the march. They poured across the Atlas, crossing its snowy passes (they who had never felt the cold, dressed in their unsubstantial desert blue), through the rich valleys of the Sus and to the north of the Oasis of the Palms, past Tafilet the sacred city, till they appeared like locusts on the wing, before Marrakesh, assaulted, conquered it, dethroned the king and placed one of themselves upon the throne, making him God's vicegerent upon earth, by the one right, the sword, they and their God could comprehend.

Saints, brown and ragged, sometimes illuminated folk, often mere madmen, preached to them as they lay camped in the palm woods that circle round Marrakesh, setting it in a ring of green enamel, and they, in their dark goatskin tents pursued the desert life, watching their camels, sitting for hours looking away at nothing, silent, and all veiled to the eyes. Their new-appointed Sultan, Yusuf-ibn-Tachfin, felt their fire in his veins, and passed his time between the mosque, the javelin-play on horseback, and in conferring with his wise magicians on the right time to start, and whether stars seemed favourable to those of the One God. From every side, as months slipped past, tribes and more tribes came to his standard, camping upon the stony plain, amongst the palm woods, and filling all the country round about with men all clamouring to be led against the foe.

All the wild Berbers of the Atlas came, on foot or riding shaggy ponies and rough mountain mules. In their shrill Shillah tongue they sang wild songs that sounded like the chattering of the cranes. They stalked about dressed in their orange-coloured cloaks, with the strange eye embroidered on the back, that makes a band of them appear like Argus, all composed of eyes.

Ait Atta came, the riders of the plains, skilled in the javelin, living like pirates by plundering caravans, just as the pirates of the sea plunder the ships both of the Faithful and of the Christian dogs.

From far Shingeit, close to the confines of the Slaves of Idols, came bands of holy men, each with his Koran in one hand and in the other a long spear. The hunters of El Jouf, who ride the wind-drinkers that gallop down the ostrich and the gazelle, their ragged-looking mares descended from the mares the Prophet rode, to one of which Yusuf-ibn-Tachfin owed his escape and life after the battle of Las Navas de Tolosa, marched in to join the last and greatest of the Arab raids. Tuaregs and men from Timbuctu, black as jinoun and only but a little while ago converted to the faith, arrived and camped beside the rest. Rehamna and Howara sent contingents, and from Glimim came men commanded by the Biruks, who claim descent from Hannibal and the great Barca clan. Then by degrees and without order, just as a flight of locusts starts upon the wing, the horde began to move. It struggled through Chawia, at every step receiving reinforcements, from Tafilet, from Fez, from Tlemcen, and taking with it all the tribes through which it passed upon its way. At Tangier and Hisnr-el-Mujaz, the Castle of the Crossing, was the tryst set, and there the ships were sent to ferry them across.

In Christendom news had been brought to King Alfonso at Toledo, where he held his court, of the great gathering across the straits. Horsemen came spurring in, telling the Andalos was all aflame, bringing reports that the army of the infidel numbered a million men. Fear fell upon the King, and he sent messages across the Pyrenees to France, Navarre, to Germany, to Rome, even to farthest England, to come and strike for Christ, for Christendom was in sore danger, from the number of the foe. Still as they mustered from the various kingdoms and principalities, their forces straggling through the Pyrenees, passing through miles of beech forests at Roncesválles, and over the Sompórt, following the course of the tumultuous Aragón, skirting the little town of Jaca, which rises from the plain just as Gibraltar rises from the sea, and coming out at length upon the brown Castilian plain, the infidels at Hisnr-el-Mujaz were crossing busily in galleys, feluccas, fishing-boats, and great barcazas, the strait they called the Gate of the Road, as by it they were wont to enter Christendom. At last on both sides they were ready, and from Toledo the Christian army, swollen by contingents from every European Power, advanced to meet the Moors, marching from Cordoba, up to the central plain. On the one side, the Christian host moved on under the banner of the Cross, its warriors, sheathed in mail, riding their ponderous Flemish war-horses, with crossbowmen from Genoa, archers from England, and Swiss battalions bristling with pikes, its ranks in order, and with a host of priests and bishops just behind the King; the Spaniards, almost as swarthy as the Moors, riding their semi-Moorish horses, fearing no heat nor cold, sober of diet, fierce as Indians, and northern knights, who in the unfamiliar climate and vegetation thought they already were in Africa. Upon the other, like an angry sea, the Infidel straggled and stormed along, their horses neighing and fighting with each other, keeping no order in their ranks, and more destructive to the country that they passed than is a band of wolves amongst a flock of sheep, the Sultan, dressed in white, riding in front under a crimson umbrella, with footmen trotting by his side. Each army must have seen the sullen mass of the great sierra that cuts the plain, barring the desert wind from Africa, tempering the piercing Christian northern air, and serving as a barrier to vegetation, so that the plants from Africa and Europe in neither instance venture to the further side.

Still they marched on, and, coming to the hills, both armies camped, for neither knew the passes and both were fearful of surprise. The Commander of the Faithful pitched his camp on the south side upon Las Navas de Tolosa, stretching a strong iron chain around his tents, and on the north the pavilion of the Christian King, conspicuous by the blood-and-orange standard fluttering at the door upon a lance, stood high above the rest. Long did they lie upon their arms, and each of them sent out their scouts to find a passage through the hills, and each without success. At last, as King Alfonso sat in his tent cursing and praying, and with his army almost about to separate, a shepherd came to him and, being brought into the tent, offered to show the King a path by which merino sheep descend to the rich plains, when on the northern side winter has burned the grass.

Chroniclers on both sides have told the battle, those of the Spaniards relating how the Christians smote the Moors, killing two hundred thousand of them, and how Don Sancho of Navarre, the strongest man in all the army, burst through the chains that ringed the Sultan's tent. They tell, with many pious saws, how great the slaughter was, and of the mighty spoil the Lord of Hosts vouchsafed to grant them, and they aver the blessed San Isidro, taking upon him (in his humility) the style and garments of a shepherd, appeared and led them on.

All this they say and much more of the same kind, all in the vein of men who know the Lord has chosen them to be His instruments. The Moors say less, and merely state Allah did not see fit to smile upon their arms, and how (no doubt to punish lack of faith) that he delivered them into the hands of the accursed King Alfonso; may God destroy him and consume his race in fire! Then they give praise to the One God, and say, in passing, that Yusuf-ibn-Tachfin, seeing his warriors flee and himself left alone, was sitting silently before his tent when there appeared an Arab from El Jouf, an aged man with a white beard, and leading in a rope of camel's hair a bright bay Arab mare.

Laying his hand upon the Emir's shoulder, he said: "Mount and ride; the mare is desert-bred, nurtured on camel's milk, and of the colour that the Prophet — may God have pardoned him — commends. When greys and chestnuts falter in the race and roans and blacks sink down and wallow in the sand, she will still pull upon her bridle. Mount and ride." The Emir mounted and escaped, and King Alfonso marched back to Toledo carrying the spoil and a long line of captives in his train. Bishops and archbishops celebrated solemn thanksgivings in the cathedral, thanking especially the blessed San Isidro for his protection of the host, and praising his humility for having left the celestial choirs and taken on him once again a humble shepherd's weeds. All Christendom heaved a sigh of satisfaction at its escape, and some one, perhaps a simple man to whose unlearned eyes the vision of the blessed San Isidro was not vouchsafed, employed a stonecutter to carve the figure of the man who, after God, had been the instrument of saving all the Christian world, and set it up on high.

Hope

R. B. Cunninghame Graham

To
Santiago Perez Triana
(Minister of Columbia)
Writer, Patriot and Friend

Introduction

Hope is the second of the three collections of short stories and sketches published by Robert Cunninghame Graham as a kind of notional trilogy between 1909 and 1912. *Faith* (1909) contained stories which seemed to touch on different kinds of trust or faith which might very well be misplaced. *Hope*, given Graham's habitual tone of unsentimental realism, can be expected to deal, in his hands, with expectations more likely to be disappointed than fulfilled. In the Preface to the collection, Graham considers the three elements of the pattern:

> *"Tyne hope, tyne a'!" the Scottish proverb says, and it is right, for hope is like a northern hawthorn bush, late flowering but continuing long in bloom.*
>
> *There is an element of speculation in it which faith quite lacks.*
>
> *Thus, faith is for youth, hope for middle life, and charity, which only comes when faith and hope are dead, for age.*
>
> *Sometimes, indeed, hope and her half-sister faith run almost into one another.*

Such an opening to the Preface might be expected to give rise to a more extended speculation about the nature of hope. At this period, Graham was in his later fifties, having lost his wife Gabriela, his ancestral home of Gartmore, his political career, and even his favourite horse Pampa, and yet he was becoming well-established as a writer with much to look forward to. If he was past the youthful stage of faith, which never in fact seemed to direct his earlier life, and in spite of many disappointed hopes, he was nevertheless committed hopefully to the causes of Socialism and, more dubiously, to Scottish Home Rule. The world was still wide and open for travel, if not for youthful exploration. And, as he said, charity would come when faith and hope were dead. Yet the rest of the Preface is taken up with an anecdote of his days in South America back in the 1870s, a story that he had told before in his long story, "Cruz Alta" (*Thirteen Stories*, 1900), about the loss of a mare through drowning in a river during his horse-driving venture from

Argentina to Brazil. Any moral that may be drawn from this story is not basically hopeful. Graham's youthful hopes were dashed by insuperable difficulties and the vagaries of chance. Yet hope can still persist. One of the riders with Graham says, "Life is a fandango", to which another replies, "Yes, but all do not dance." The final, more positive response is "Yes, but all hope to dance."

The title story, "Hope", displays this ambiguous attitude towards people's expectations of life and fortune. On Christmas Eve, an old married couple, German immigrants to Texas, who have been successful in ranching and rearing their family far from their homeland of Swabia, are thinking of the past and the old custom of putting shoes outside for Santa Claus to fill with gifts for the children. They put one of the wife's shoes, saved since her childhood, outside the door in the blizzard and hope for something wonderful to happen. Next morning they look to see if Santa Claus has come. In a material sense, their hope has been disappointed; in a symbolic way, however, it has been coldly fulfilled.

Two other stories deal more explicitly with the failure of hopes, despite the conviction with which these hopes are entertained. "A Sebastianist" describes the strange impractical hopes of an old Portuguese shopkeeper, Dom Jeremias, who is portrayed as the last surviving adherent of a now little-known belief, the hope that one day the sixteenth-century King Sebastian of Portugal will return from the legendary limbo into which he disappeared following his defeat (and probable death) at the hands of the Moors at the Battle of Ksar-el-Kebir (1578), and that he will save Portugal in its darkest hour. This belief is of the kind found in various nations through the centuries, most notably the belief in the British Isles that, at some time when he is most needed, King Arthur will return from his sleep in Avalon and save his people from disaster. In Portugal it was called Sebastianism and traces of it persist down to the twentieth century. In Brazil during the last years of the nineteenth century, Sebastianism was one of the elements underlying the anti-Government revolt by the mystic and rebel, Antonio Conselheiro, about whom Graham later wrote the book, *A Brazilian Mystic* (1920). In the short story Graham describes the emptiness and obsessive quality of Dom Jeremias' life, where the most vigorous aspect of his existence is his intense imagining of the progress of King Sebastian's last crusade against the Moors across the Straits of Gibraltar from Cadiz until his final crushing defeat. This device of the old man's imagination gives Graham the opportunity to counterpoint his narrative with a vivid account of the historical episode.

The other story of a seemingly explicit failure of hopes is "The Fourth Magus", in which Graham tells the story of the fourth Wise Man, King Nicanor, who is separated from his three companions and misses the encounter with the Infant Christ in Bethlehem, being constantly detained by his attempts along the way to help and succour an unending succession of poor, sick and desperate people. Nicanor is delayed for many years by his compulsion to do good wherever he sees the need, and it is more than thirty years before he reaches Jerusalem, just in time to see the adult Jesus die on the cross. His hopes of finding the mighty prophet who was foretold were seemingly frustrated, and yet Graham makes clear that, however long that frustration lasted, the hope was eventually fulfilled in a more significant and meaningful way.

South America does not figure greatly in this collection. *Hope* is dedicated to "Santiago Perez Triana (Minister of Columbia) Writer, Patriot and Friend)". Santiago Perez Triana was the son of a Liberal President of Colombia who was driven into exile after a civil war in the 1870s. Santiago also lived in exile for much of his life as a writer and diplomat, spending some years in London where he came to know many of the literary figures, including Graham. He was briefly the official envoy of Colombia to Great Britain. Graham deals with Colombia in one of the stories in *Hope*. "Mirahuano" tells of a negro peasant poet, Silvio Sanchez, whose nickname is ironical in that mirahuano, or miraguano, is kapok, a light white fibre used for stuffing pillows, etc. Mirahuano comes to prominence and fame as a poet in his native district of Antioquia despite his colour and poverty, ultimately winning the poetic laurel wreath in the Floral Games. He is crowned the winner by the most beautiful white maiden, Nieves Figueroa, with whom he falls deeply in love from a distance. Yet he comes to realise that he will never be accepted as an equal in society, and in a fit of anger and desperation he commits suicide by drowning. The peasant who finds his body strips it of its fine black suit to sell as the only thing he sees of value belonging to it. Graham's irony is bitter in this story. He loved South America and its people, but on the evidence of this story their racism and colour prejudice clearly appalled him.

The story that follows "Mirahuano" in *Hope* creates an interesting and relevant parallel. "The Captive" is also set in South America, this time on the pampas of Argentina in the province of Bahia Blanca, which

Graham himself knew from his ventures of the 1870s. A mixed group of ranchers and adventurers are camped for the night after trying to recover horses that have been stolen from them by Indians. Sleepless around the camp fire, they listen to one of their number tell a story, supposedly about a neighbouring rancher, but actually about himself, dealing with the capture of an Indian woman from a marauding band. She attaches herself to him, serving him faithfully at his ranch and eventually becoming his mistress. She reveals that in fact she is not Indian but pure Spanish, having been captured by Indians who had killed her family. She had suffered greatly at their hands and borne three sons to an Indian chief. Now she began to resume her white Spanish identity, taking her own former name, Nieves (meaning 'snows', the same name as the object of Mirahuano's hopeless adoration in the previous story). Yet eventually she becomes unhappy and has to return to the Indian way of life, to her sons and their father. In "The Captive", Graham has been exploring another aspect of race division and prejudice, and, as in "Mirahuano", the conclusions are not comforting to notions of white supremacy.

These two stories are the only ones in *Hope* that are located in South America. It is Morocco that claims more of Graham's attention as a story setting, in "The Grave of the Horseman", "Villa Florida", "A Repertory Theatre" and "Buta". The first of these is a grim piece describing how the chieftain of a Moroccan tribe, the Ait Yusi, meets his end suddenly. In the middle of musing over the power and success that he hopes is awaiting him in the future, Si Omar is thrown from his horse and, as he lies crushed and disabled on the ground, the men of his marauding band gather round and shoot him dead as being of no further use as a leader. The savage law of kill or be killed is seen in action, and Graham presents it unemotionally without any moral or humanitarian gloss. "Villa Florida" also deals with a fallen Moroccan leader. The narrator, undoubtedly representing Graham himself, visits the former Sultan of Morocco, Mulai Abd-el-Aziz IV, who was deposed in 1908. Graham describes the setting for the Sultan's place of exile, an ill-built modern house, Villa Florida, on the outskirts of Tangier, and the brief meeting the two men have, Graham ill at ease and embarrassed at seeing the decline in Mulai's fortunes and the loss of all his hopes, and the deposed ruler still conducting himself with dignity and nobility in adversity. By contrast, the story, "A Repertory Theatre", set in the little Spanish territory of Tetuan in Morocco, looks with ironic humour at the manners of the Spanish colonial establishment keeping up the standards of Spain in an alien setting, enjoying an amateur dramatic production of a classic play, "Don Juan Tenorio". The Moors in the audience are visibly uneasy and perturbed by the action and dialogue of the drama, the unreality of which they do not fully comprehend. One Moorish official indeed is convinced that an actor had actually been killed by a sword and is amazed to see him alive after the play.

Graham's sympathetic attitude towards women can be noted in many stories throughout the range of his collections. This sympathy is extended to women who have lapsed into prostitution to make a living, as several powerful stories testify. In *Hope*, there are two stories of this nature, "Buta" and "Un Monsieur". "Buta" is set in Morocco and employs the same narrative device as was seen in "The Captive", a group of men sitting in a circle by night listening to one of their number telling a story. Here it is Nazim, an Arab manager for a Scottish trading company, telling of an Arab woman, widowed with two children, who becomes a prostitute used by the British clerks and officials of the coastal trading post of Fort Juby. Her own name of Rahma, meaning 'merciful', was dropped in favour of Buta, which is the Arabic pronunciation of 'puta', the Spanish word for a prostitute. Graham is undoubtedly highly critical of his fellow-countrymen here, revealing their moral hypocrisy through the eloquent words of a cultivated and thoughtful Arab Moslem. Similarly, in "Un Monsieur," a cultivated and refined Parisian prostitute, Elise, living and working in London, recounts her dealings with one of her regular clients, a rich middle-aged Englishman, and how she came to meet his wife. There is an element of pathos in Graham's account of how, although she maintained a professional confidentiality about her connection with the 'monsieur' and he made many promises to her, she was well aware that she would never be of any significance to a man so secure in his respectable family life.

Death is never far away from a Graham story or sketch, as many of the pieces in *Hope* so far treated reveal. Two of the stories in the collection deal specifically with the rites of death, funerals in different strata of society. "At Dalmary" and "Ave Caesar" are respectively set in Scotland and Spain. Dalmary is in Menteith, Graham's home district, just a mile or so south of Gartmore. The sketch describes the location with its hills, moors and mosses, the mourners coming on foot from all over the district and greeting each other, and the simple funeral of a ploughman in his cottage before the body is taken off in a cart to the graveyard, leaving the widow excluded, mourning alone in the empty house. "Ave Caesar" on the other hand, is set in Madrid, where the funeral of a diplomat, probably the German Ambassador, is held in state with a military escort, a train of important mourners including the King of Spain himself, and a great crowd of people lining the street. It is like a Roman Imperial occasion, as the title suggests. However, the pomp of the occasion is undercut by two contrasting sights. Firstly, the cheap and sparse funeral of a poor man cuts through the state procession in a visual contradiction of its power and wealth. Secondly, after the funeral is over and the streets are empty again, a cart drawn by oxen carries past a great block of stone intended for some building project, seeming to emphasise the transitory nature of human life in the face of the permanence of the earth.

Five of the pieces in *Hope* are character sketches of men known to and in some cases related to Graham himself. "A Sailor (Old Style)" and "The Admiral" describe the two husbands of his grandmother, Doña Catalina. The first husband, the subject of "The Admiral", was Admiral Elphinstone Fleeming, who had made a name for himself in the Liberation Wars in South America. The second husband, whom Doña Catalina married after the death of Admiral Fleeming, was Commander (later Admiral) James Edward Katon, with whom at his home on the Isle of Wight Graham and his brother often stayed as a boy. "A Sailor (Old Style)" vividly presents Graham's personal memories of him. "My Uncle" deals with one of Graham's relations on his father's side, the Cunninghame Grahams. The picture of an eccentric gentleman of a bygone period is strikingly detailed with a blend of affection and humour. "The Colonel" was a old veteran of the Peninsular War who lived in a tower house in Graham's local district and occupied a prominent place in local affairs. Graham clearly knew him only from a distance, given their difference in ages, but writes of him with understanding if not with affection. The sketch, "A Retainer", treats a man bound to Graham by his employment and tenancy. Graham's consistent reference to him as 'my retainer' smacks of an ironical sense that this man has been a follower of the Graham family ever since the time of Bannockburn, rather than that he performs any personal services. A stern and stolid Lowlander, he follows his own personal road with a gritty integrity until the day he dies and is buried far from his own home territory. In these Scottish sketches, Graham comes close to home for his inspiration, making rather a welcome digression from his usually far-flung literary sources.

Two short pieces in *Hope* remain to be considered, "Appreciation" and "A Vigia". "Appreciation", the last piece in the collection, is a bitter observation of the shallowness and complacency of a prosperous social set, rich and vulgar people gathered together for supper in a fashionable hotel or restaurant, talking of their material and selfish concerns while a Hungarian band plays for their delectation. A particularly affecting rendition of music by Offenbach arouses them temporarily to some kind of appreciation of higher things, but they quickly relapse into discussion of their self-centred trivialities. Dawn comes and they disperse into the clear morning carrying the fug and staleness of the night's occasion with them. In "A Vigia", as a place of escape from such an oppressive and corrupted society, with its relentless pressures, Graham envisions an idyllic place, a visionary island of the mind, where one can walk and refresh oneself apart from the modern world for a space before returning to real life. Graham calls such a place a 'vigia' (literally in Spanish, a reef or uncharted low islet) and interprets it as an undiscovered haven apart from the well-mapped and known locations on the high seas. As one reads "A Vigia", however, it becomes clear that Graham's own personal vigia is the Isle of Iona, off the coast of Mull. Although he makes a pretence of keeping it a secret, this real place is his Isle of Dreams, his enchanted city, his mirage in the desert.

Hope is a collection of stories and sketches that reveal Graham's by now well-established versatility as a writer. He plays with his own wide experience of the world, his favourite places, his store of well-remembered real characters from the playhouse of his vigorous and retentive memory, to give the reader an ever-changing and satisfying involvement with his wide and fascinating world.

AMacG

Contents

Preface

To Horsemen and Others

"Tyne hope, tyne a'!" the Scottish proverb says, and it is right, for hope is like a northern hawthorn bush, late flowering but continuing long in bloom.

There is an element of speculation in it which faith quite lacks.

Thus, faith is for youth, hope for middle life, and charity, which only comes when faith and hope are dead, for age.

Sometimes, indeed, hope and her half-sister faith run almost into one another.

I remember once, in the Republic of the Banda Oriental del Uruguay, close to the frontier of Brazil, we came, my partner and myself, driving a troop of horses, to what in South America is called a "pass," that is, a ford. What was the river's name I cannot tell without an atlas, and that would be to put a slight upon my memory, so I refrain; but the ford was "El Paso de los Novillós," and to get to it you had to ride down through a wood of "espinillo de olór."

The trail that we followed to the pass was steep and sandy, and cut by the passage of the animals into deep ruts, leaving long hummocks here and there, called "albardones" (that is, pack-saddles) on which grew thorny shrubs. Great cactuses with their flat leaves, looking like gigantic seeds of honesty, white, gaunt, and sear [sere], stood here and there, and seemed to guard the road. They had an almost human look, and report said, not very long before we passed, a band of robbers had stripped themselves, and standing naked by the whitish stems, were so invisible that they were able quietly to kill some travellers, who rode right into them before they were aware. Therefore we rode with care, hitching our pistols now and then round nearer to our hands as we urged on the troop, swinging our whips about our heads, and pressing close upon the driven horses to prevent their cutting back or separating when they came to the "pass." Humming-birds fluttered like gigantic day-moths hung poised, with a thin whir of wings invisible, so that they seemed all body, then darted off so swiftly that no eye could follow them. In the hot air myriads of insects, seen and unseen, raised a shrill melody. Upon the trees black cormorants sat and discoursed, and herons, white, slate-coloured, and brown, stood fishing silently. Carpinchos, looking like little hippopotami, just showed their backs above the surface of the water as we came to the crossing of the stream. We closed upon the troop, Mansel, myself, Exaltacion Medina, Raimundo Barragán, and the two peons; one of them rode a white and dun piebald, whose coat was curly as a sheep's. It had a strip of hide tied round the lower jaw to which the reins were fixed, for it was still unbitted. I see them now just as I saw them then, through a thin cloud of dust. The horses — there were about two hundred — entered the water in a bunch. The stream flowed strongly, yellow and turbid, and in the middle rose a low island, almost awash, long and grass grown, and looking like one of those "albardones" in the road which I have spoken of before. The horses took the water well, and we stood back to give them space, so that they should not crowd upon each other and get choked.

How well I see them, their heads laid flat upon the stream, the lines made by their backs in the swift current, their tails spread out, and all of them swimming a little sideways, just as a carp swims sideways when he comes up for bread. Their eyes were fixed upon the bank, and in their wake a little wave as of a boat washed to the shore. We stood and gazed, watching a piebald mare, fat, strong, and wild, who led the troop. Her too I see and well remember, for she was barren and therefore just as good as is a horse. Moreover, though a natural pacer, she could bound forward like a deer when you but closed your legs upon her sides. *Linda la overa negra!* Well, just as we were thinking about entering the stream ourselves, having taken off our clothes and piled them on our heads, cinched up our saddles a little forward, and with our boots and pistols round our necks, the spurs inside the boots, one of the peons cried out the mare was drowning. I, sitting sideways in my saddle, saw that the current, which ran strongly just below the island, had swept her on her side; perhaps she was a trifle fat to swim. Little by little she appeared to sink, her quarters dropping perpendicularly and then the water creeping up round her neck. Once for a moment her fore feet emerged, battling for life, her eyes were blue with terror, and then with a loud snort she disappeared.

One of us, I think it was Medina, exclaimed, "It was a pity of the mare, and she a barren mare as good as any horse . . . but God is not a bad man after all, the rest have landed safe." We crossed, the water lapping up almost to our mouths at the first plunge. I rode a horse that swam a little low, and on the other side we drove the troop into an open glade, and then dismounting, spread our clothes to dry.

The horses, after rolling, began to feed, guarded by a man who rode naked but for a light vicuña poncho, and we sat in the shade and boiled a kettle to take maté, in the lee of a fire of smoky wood to keep the flies away.

It may have been Raimundo or Exaltacion, most certainly it was not either of the peons, who observed, "Life is a fandango," and received the answer, "Yes, but all do not dance."

This time I am almost sure it was Exaltacion Medina who replied, "Yes, but all hope to dance."

As we sat thinking on his dictum, and also on the poor mare's death, one of those sudden panics that at times befall a caballada, set our horses off.

When we had got them turned and we were riding slowly round them with the sun blistering our naked backs, I noticed that our feet were bleeding, for we had mounted barebacked in the hurry of the fright and ridden through the thorns.

R. B. Cunninghame Graham

Hope

Hope

Snow had fallen ceaselessly for hours, blotting out all the features of the landscape, but leaving here and there the red earth, bare, upon the trail that led from San Antonio to La Bandera as it wound about between the scrub of huisache and mesquite. It lay congealed upon the half-transparent twigs of the pinched redbuds that looked as miserable as does a ruffled parrot in a cage on a cold winter's day. In the deep hollows horses thrust their muzzles into the powdery snow, and now and then beat at it with their feet impatiently, as if they thought that Nature had played some joke upon them that they found out of place. The Helotés Creek, half frozen, formed the boundary between the post-oak country that stretched out like a natural park and the low plains thick with a scrub of thorny bush. Upon the mound, shaded by a thick grove of dark pecans, a low-eaved house surrounded by a low snake-fence looked down upon the creek.

The unfamiliar snow piled on the roof gave a false air of Northern Europe, which the wild howling of the prairie wolves intensified. Inside and blinking at the fire sat the old Swabian peasants, who had emigrated years ago, and now in their old age had become rich and owned the ranche [sic] and the wide range for cattle that ran from the Helotés, to the north fork of the Pipe Creek. Their children, born Americans, had left them when they grew up, and lived, some on the Rio Grande, others in Arizona, but all of them thousands of miles away in tastes, in sentiment, and in their view of life. Hard and unsentimental, they had all received that education which their parents lacked, but the old people had preserved their pristine ignorance of modern life and wonder at the world. Gretchen and Hans they had remained to everybody, and spoke a mixture of bad English and their native tongue. They sat and gazed into the fire, and the wreathed snow perhaps had set them thinking on their old home and life, for it was Christmas Eve, and memory stirred in their hearts.

After a silence the old man turned to his wife and said, "Gretchen, to-morrow will be Christmas Day. That Mexican who herd the sheep say it is Noche Puena, just as he saddled up his horse to go to town. It is the night of nights . . . dat night the Kings all come to Bethlehem ... it set one thinking, eh?"

Gretchen, after a long look in the fire, rejoined, "Yes, lieber Hans, I think of many things — of the old country, of you when you was young . . . myself too, mit my yellow hair, you say was like de gold, and of our life . . . where has it gone to, so long and yet so quick, it seems as yesterday?"

Hans drew his chair across the hearth, and, taking up her hand, patted it tremulously and said, "Ach, I think too of many things; but your hair, Gretchen, still is golden, for old Hans. . . . What a night, eh? How de coyotés howl, just like the wolves in Swabia in that long time ago you speak of."

They sat holding each other's hands, till Gretchen said, "To-night the children all put out their shoes for Santa Claus . . . you will laugh, but — no, I hardly like to say it — I still have one of the wooden shoes that little Gretchen mit de golden hair was wearing long ago in the old country. . . . What if we put him out?"

The old man ran his hand affectionately over his wife's grey, wiry hair, and pinched her withered, but still rosy cheek, just as he might have done in the far-off time towards which their thoughts were straying on that night.

Rising, he walked across the room and, throwing back the shutter, looked out into the dark. The clump of tall pecans formed a vast snowy dome; in the corral the horses huddled close together with their tails to the blast, owls hooted, and the wind roared amongst the trees. "It is still snowing, and the creek is rising; dat Mexican did well to start for town: in an hour more no one could cross," he said. "If the black schelm was a white man he'd lose the trail to San Antonio and die in the drifts; but, never fear, the devil knows his own. . . . Ah, yes, the shoe, you say — put him out then, little old fool; all we can hope for now is that Santa Claus take us for children and send us something; for what shall we hope for now, eh, little old fool? . . . Well, put him out."

All the time that he had been speaking, his wife had had her head bent over a great box, and now drew out, wrapped in a piece of flannel, an old wooden shoe. She held it tenderly, but half ashamed, just as a savage might have held some fetich in his hands, after conversion to the true faith, before a missionary. Clumsily, but artistically made, somehow, out there on the Helotés Creek, removed from all tradition, and face to face with Nature, it spoke of Europe and of an older world. The pebbles of the village street had dinted it and left impressions of themselves upon the sole, just as life leaves its wrinkles on the face. As the old couple looked at it, unbidden tears rose to their eyes, and Hans stretched out a bony finger and touched it timidly, just as a man touches the face of his first child, half proudly, half in alarm at the new fetter he has forged upon his life. He said, "Ach, Gretchen, your foot was not so big then, back in those days. I tink I hear you now run like a little pony on the street." Taking the shoe, he crossed the room and, opening the door, let in the driving snow with a cold blast that made the cheap petroleum lamp flicker and jump, and set it down outside.

Gretchen had thrown new logs upon the hearth, and, drawing up her chair, said to her husband, "Come and sit down, and let us drink glass beer. I always hope for something, something that come into our life even now and make us happy . . . not that we are not happy . . . but something wonderful."

Her husband, either impressed by her simplicity — the one thing in the world impressive — or to humour her, answered her with a smile, "Ja . . . yes, and Santa Claus, he send us something, maybe . . . at any rate, tomorrow, if the trails are passable, some of the children will be here." The glare of the great logs, of hard mesquite, fell on their wrinkled faces as they sat, married by Time, before the fire. Hans, in a suit of homespun clothes, his trousers tucked into his boots, with his bald head as shiny as a billiard ball, his grey and tangled beard, red cheeks, and hands like roots of trees, looked hale and prosperous. His wife, in her bed-ticking gown confined about the waist with a broad string of tape, her feet encased in slippers down at heel, and a white cap upon her head, was thin and angular; and as she sat holding her husband's rugged hand in hers, looked like a wooden toy, made in Thuringia, in an old-time Noah's ark.

Still there was something spiritual in her face, as if the world and all its trials, toil, disappointments, and the cares of a large family had left no mark upon her soul, and as if the wrinkles on her brow were but the work of Time and went no deeper than the skin.

A German clock, brought from their home across the sea, ticked on the wall, measuring out time, as it were, in an old-fashioned Swabian way, pausing a little every now and then and whirring wheezily before it struck the hour. An air of cleanliness almost unnatural was over everything. The plates and dishes shone as if they had been varnished, in the rough wooden rack above the dresser, and chairs and tables had been beeswaxed over till they appeared to glow. The air of comfort and of home contrasted strangely with the wild night and the position of the ranche on the north fork of the Helotés Creek out on the Texan plains.

Sleep fell upon the couple sitting by the fire, and as they slept the fire burned low upon the hearth. Outside nothing was heard but the wild seething of the wind, and now and then a rush as of an avalanche in miniature, as the snow slid down from the steep roof. An hour or two slipped past, and the storm moderated. The moon shone brightly, and in the snow the tracks of animals were seen — the small, round holes that the deer's feet had made, the footsteps of the wolves like those of a large dog, the bear's flat trail, as if a man had passed on snowshoes, revealed as on a chart their passage through the storm. The sleepers stirred uneasily, and then, awakened by the cold, sat up and looked at one another.

Hans piled fresh logs upon the fire, stamping them in position with his foot, and then, when they had warmed themselves at the red blaze, said, "Did you dream, Gretchen?" "Yes, Hans," she answered. "I dreamed a lovely dream. We were both young again and walking in a wood. You take my hand and say, 'Gretchen, I lofe you . . . your hair is golden, your lips so red, I want to kiss them.' . . . Oh, it was lovely. . . . Did you dream, Hans?"

A shadow ran across his face as he replied, "Yes, I dream too. I dream of all our struggles — we came to America without a heller, and how we starved and fought . . . of how we slaved, and then of how we build this house. Of our first son — the one the Indians killed . . . of all the rest; and then it seemed I saw us both sit sleeping here before the fire."

"Oh, Hans!" his wife rejoined, "what for a dream was that? You have not been asleep." She paused and saw her husband really had dreamed, and then, smiling a weary smile, said, "Go, liebling schatz — this is the way I used to speak to you in the old days — and bring the shoe you put outside the door. I hope that Santa Claus may have put something in it, something wonderful."

Her husband kissed her cheek, and, gained a little by her faith, opened the door and carried in the shoe. Something was in it of a truth, for Santa Claus, who never disappoints people who trust in him, had filled it up with snow. As they stood looking at it ruefully, the long-drawn howl of a coyoté sounded far out upon the plain.

The Grave of the Horseman

A little town just glimmered in the distance, lost in orange groves, with a few date palms waving above the saint's tomb near the gate, their ragged tops looking like seaweed in a pool left by the tide upon the beach. High mountains flanked the road, which ran between great boulders, with here and there flat slabs of whinstone cropping up, shiny and slippery with the heat. A grove of cork trees shadowed it on one side, and at the other the precipitous street of the strange mountain village called Bahallein, with the houses separated by a brawling stream which roared and foamed eternally, ran surging into caverns, and, again emerging into view, made a right angle to its course.

Smoke rose from many of the houses, and a wail of Arab women pierced the noise of the tumultuous stream. A band of horsemen, with a scout or two thrown out on either side, picked their way through the stones, their horses propping themselves on their forelegs, drawing their quarters after them when they had found a foothold, making their riders sway upon their saddles as when a camel rises to its feet. Some of them bore fresh-cut-off heads upon the muzzles of their guns, either stuck stiffly on, as boys stick turnips on a stick, or with a lap of skin left on the throat, through which the gun was thrust, leaving the head to hang down limply like a fish. They drove before them cattle, urging them onwards with their spear-like guns. Occasionally a man stood out upon a rock and fired his long and slender-barrelled gun, which went off sullenly as the rough, home-made powder, ill rammed home, ignited slowly, sending the bullet over the heads of the retiring band. Sometimes a woman stood close to their path, shaking a ragged haik and cursing, and when a horseman passed he turned a little out of his way and rode on with his eyes fixed far away, as if he had seen nothing, leaving her wailing by the road.

They closed their ranks and rode into the track that leads from Fez to Séfru, the scouts falling back on the main body when the last dropping shots of the harried villagers were spent. Horses neighed shrilly, and when they passed mares feeding by the outskirts of the cork wood, danced sideways or plunged into the air, their riders checking them so sharply with the curb that a red foam hung round their mouths as they fell back upon the bit. A cloud of dust hung over all the band, through which at times appeared a horse and rider, the man dressed all in white, save for a long, blue cloak which streamed out in the wind, and the horse saddled with the high-cantled Arab saddle covered with orange silk. Faces tanned to the colour of a boot or white as ivory and set in jet-black beards looked out from under hoods drawn up above their turbans, with here and there a flat-nosed negro, looking still blacker in the white clothes he wore. Black, grey, and chestnut, with roans and piebalds and the mixed colours that the Arabs call "stones of the river," their horses looked as if they had all stepped from pictures by Velazquez, with tails that swept the ground, manes reaching almost to their knees, and forelocks falling to their nostrils, covering their eyes like veils. Their riders, thin and wiry, were of those who live by "clashing of the spurs," as goes the Arab phrase, and their wild eyes appeared to be eternally fixed on the horizon and to see nothing nearer than a mile away. Except the love of blood and pillage, they had but one thing in common — the fear and hatred of their chief, who rode along behind them, swathed to the eyes in white, on which a spot or two of blood served as a sort of trademark of his interior grace.

Seated a little heavily upon a chestnut horse with a white tail and mane, Si Omar had returned his gun to its red flannel case, but held it still across the saddle, balanced against the pommel with an occasional motion of his hand. His horse reared and plunged forward now and then, fretting to join the others, but its rider took no notice except to slack his bridle hand a little, and when the animal came back upon the bit and gave its head, he threw the long red silken reins across his shoulder, where they remained, looking as if someone had drawn a bloody finger down his clothes. His spear-like, single-pointed spurs hung loosely from his red-and-yellow riding-boots, and just behind his heavy stirrups damascened with gold, had made a bloody patch upon his horse's flanks, which he spurred constantly, after the Arab fashion, to keep him to his pace. Dark, for a Berber, and marked a little here and there with smallpox, his spare black beard showing the skin between the hairs, Si Omar looked about forty-five, and had begun to put on flesh a little, after the fashion of his race when fortune smiles upon them, although he passed his life on horseback and in the open air. He wore the lock of hair, hanging down on his cheek, called by the Berbers "el kettaieh," that gave an air of fierceness to his face, which his wild eye and ever-twitching mouth accentuated. His hands were small with the nails clean and cared for, and when he raised his arm the loose sleeves of his selham left bare his wrist, slender and nervous, with something of the look as of a leopard's claw or of the leg of a gazelle. As he rode on he drew a fold of his selham about his mouth, covering his face, leaving his eyes, bloodshot and staring, alone exposed to view. Passing the cork wood, the horsemen, driving their "creagh" slowly in front of them, came out upon the plain and struck into a road which ran along the foothills of the mountains, from which the little, glistening town of Séfru appeared, a league or two away, buried in gardens and in woods. The sun was slanting towards the west and bathed the plain in a pale glow which blended everything together, making the pastoral Arab life a perfect illustration of the Old Testament as we conceive it, in the glow of the imagination of our faith. Herds lowed, and sheep drawn out in lines straggled towards the fold, preceded by a boy who piped upon a reed whose twittering notes hung in the air like the faint echo of a lark's song when it has soared into the clouds.

The women went and came about the wells dressed in the desert blue that makes their supple figures look even more slender than they are, with pointed amphoræ upon their shoulders or balanced on their heads. Foals frisked beside their mothers, and here and there camels stood up outlined against the sky or browsed upon the thorny bushes, their out-stretched necks writhing about like snakes. Elders sat at the doors of tents in groups, and the whole plain looked peaceful, happy, and exhaled an air as of eternity, so well the life fitted the scene and the scene sanctified the life. Above it, the marauding band passed, as a kite may pass above a dovecote, a wolf prowl past a fold, or as a train rushes at sixty miles an hour through some quiet valley in the hills. The horses neighed and passaged, and a cloud of dust covered the horsemen and the animals they drove, whilst in the rear the solitary chief rode silent and as if buried in a dream.

The world was going well with him, and the new sultan had confirmed him in his governorship both of the tribe and of the town. Indeed he was a man designed by nature to rule over such a tribe as was Ait Yusi, whose members passed their lives in fighting and in deeds of violence. His father had ruled them with a rod of iron, making himself so hated that at last the tribe had risen and burned him on a pile of hay. He knew himself detested, even by his horsemen, and for that reason always rode behind them to avoid an accidental shot, though at the same time they all feared him far too much to look him in the face. So he rode on, cursing his horse when it tripped on a stone, and muttering the proverb that declares the horseman's grave is always open when it stumbled in the mud, and keeping a keen eye on all the thickets for a chance shot from some of his own tribesmen and on his soldiers whenever they looked back. Still he had passed his life upon the watch, after the fashion of a tiger, and now he was content to muse upon the future as his horse paced along the road. The way seemed open for him to ascend, and the new sultan was on the look out for men on whom he could rely. Visions of larger governments rose in his mind, of the great kasbah he would build — for building is a passion with the Arabs — with courts that led from courts into more courts, with crenellated walls, a garden with its clump of cypresses, a mosque, rooms paved with tiles from Fez and Tetuan, a fishpond full of gold and silver fish, with water everywhere, gurgling in little rills of white cement beneath the orange trees. He saw himself all dressed in dazzling white, sitting upon a mattress in a room open to the court of orange trees, lulled by the murmuring of the water, drinking green tea flavoured with amber amongst his women, or talking with his friends, what time his secretary wrote his letters, in his guest-chamber.

Horses, of course, were plentiful, and all of lucky colours, so that a man when he set off upon a journey might be certain to return. Some should be pacers, for the road, and others for the powder-play, light as gazelles, and bitted so as to turn, just as a seagull turns upon the wing. He felt himself assured of fortune and safe to rise in the good graces of his lord, whilst the declining sun, which fell upon his face, blinding him to the difficulties of the rough track on which he rode, induced a feeling of contentment which perhaps threw him off his guard.

A mare and foal feeding close by had set Si Omar's horse neighing and plunging, and he, swaying a little to the plunges, may perhaps have touched it in the mouth too sharply with the bit. After a spring or two, the horse passaged and reared, and lighting on a flat slab of rock which cropped up in the middle of the road, slipped sideways and fell with a loud crash, its shoes, in the last struggle to maintain its balance, sending a shower of sparks into the air. All passed as if by magic, and the man who but an instant previously had ridden so contentedly lay a crushed mass of draggled white under the horse, which in a moment had regained its feet. He lay pale, but quite conscious, with his hand still clasped upon his rifle, looking up fiercely like a wounded animal awaiting the final stroke. His followers, hearing the noise, turned and surrounded him, glaring down at their wounded chief with hard, unsympathising eyes. Not a word passed on either side, and then a Berber, mounted upon a sorrel colt with four white feet and a large blaze upon its nose, exclaimed, "God wishes it; Si Omar's day is done." Then, slowly levelling his gun, he shot his fallen chieftain through the body at short range, and all the rest, crowding about him as he lay bleeding on the ground, fired into him, spurring their horses over the prostrate body on the ground. Whether Si Omar died of the first shot, or whether, seeing his day was done, he set his teeth and died as a wild boar dies, silently, without a sign, none of his slayers knew. A cloud of dust hung in the air above the spot where men rode furiously about firing their guns and shouting, and then it cleared away, leaving a small, white bundle of torn rags upon the ground stained here and there with blood.

The white-maned chestnut which the dead man had ridden stood grazing quietly a hundred yards away, and the declining sun fell on the stony hill beyond the road, flushing it with a tinge of pinkish yellow, between the colour of an old piece of ivory and a worn Roman brick. A league away Séfru lay sleeping in its orange groves, and from the plain below the road came up the bleating of the sheep as they were driven to the fold.

The slayers, pressing their Arab stirrups into their horses' sides, rode on a little, and as they passed an angle of the road, settling their flowing robes and loading up their rifles as they went, a Berber turned and, sitting sideways on his horse, fired a last shot at his dead chief, which struck the ground a little short and, flying upwards, flattened the bullet on a rock far up against the hill. The horsemen drew together, as if by instinct, just as a flight of birds collects after some incident which has broken up their ranks, and, swaying in their saddles easily, their long white selhams fluttering in the wind, they disappeared along the road.

Villa Florida

He who had been an emperor, and was the lineal descendant of the last prophet that the world has known, had been deserted and dethroned, and lived with the remainder of his household in three small villas on the hill beyond Tangier. In the same way that the whole world goes out to greet the conqueror — that is when he has conquered — so does it shrink from vanquished men as deer shrink from a wounded stag. "From the fallen tree all men cut firewood," as the proverb says; but when the wood is cut they leave the trunk to moss and rot, deserted in the woods. As fear guards vineyards more than do the walls, so sympathy really anoints a king more than the chrism oil, and usually it is more readily bestowed on kings in exile, dethroned, supplanted, or in some way or other fallen from their high estate, rather than on those monarchs who in their cotton-velvet robes and tinsel crowns sit in the full glare of the foot-lights on the stage.

So having known him in the heyday of prosperity in Fez, the Commander of the Faithful, a man so holy that the mere virtue of his presence brought a blessing, and when his will was law to millions, I took my horse to ride and visit him in the days when the silver cord of majesty was loosened, and when the golden bowl of popularity lay shattered by the puddle, and men shot out their lips.

The steep, paved road led upwards between gardens hedged round with cypresses. On every side houses of Europeans had crowded out the low thatched huts and the white cubes of masonry which a few years ago had been one of the chiefest features of the place. Jews perched on monstrous pack-saddles housed in red flannel, clattered and chattered on the path, followed by brawny Moors who trotted patiently behind, cursing them underneath their breath. Parties of tourists, seated on donkeys, their faces dyed bright scarlet with the sun, rode past, casting their patronising glances on the "pooah Moors" and yearning in their hearts to turn them into component parts of the great scheme of life, that makes us all adorers of accomplished facts, leaving us stripped and bare of all revolt against the meanness of our lives.

The cypresses beside the path gave out their spicy scent and shed their dry and withered cones upon the ground. The eucalyptus, with its balls of blossom, looking like clots of foam against the dark metallic leaves, stirred in the light west wind, making the strips of hanging bark rattle against their trunks. White poplars, just bursting into leaf, a maze of mystic white, so light and feathery that they appeared as if they must have been transferred straight from a screen made in Japan, replanted, and then by some botanic miracle endued with life, to bring the illusion of the north into the southern air in which they seemed to float, stood here and there in clumps. I passed the little saint house, which with its fluttering white flag and gnarled old olive trees stands at the roadside, and branching off into a muddy lane, whose mouth was guarded by a small thatched hut in which sat several dilapidated Moors in dingy rags, began to splash through pools of water and through mire so sticky that at each step my horse's feet sounded as if gigantic corks were being drawn from bottles, as he struggled through the mud. The track led up between high fences made of canes, with boughs of kermes-oak and of lentiscus thrust through the spaces where the canes were tied, forming an impenetrable screen and shutting off the household of the dethroned sultan from the gaze of infidel and faithful alike, as effectually as did the palace walls in Fez. As it ascended, the path grew narrower, and by its side, squatted on stones, sat groups of Moors, with their long white selhams all daubed with mud, waiting about upon the chance of being wanted to do something, just as they waited outside the palace doors at Fez or at Marakesh when their lord was king, and all apparently as insolent and as contented with themselves as when his word was law.

The stuccoed gateway of the ill-built modern house bore the legend "Villa Florida" on a slab of marble, which was stuck crooked on the pillar of the gate, and showed the same words painted underneath, in letters rather larger than the slab, in the same way as in certain pictures of Velazquez you see the drawing of a previous pair of horse's legs looming up through the paint, as if to show the painter of the horse was mortal after all. On each side of the gateway high tufts of canes waved in the wind, and a great clump of aloes stopped a hole where the fence ended and the masonry began. The mud, the wind, the scorching winter sun, the look as of a house in Arizona or in Western Texas, built by the Mexicans and left to be the incongruous dwelling of some incoming family from the north, produced an air of desolation, compared with which an Arab tent of camel's hair stuck down upon the sand might have looked homelike and an abode to which a man could have become attached.

The ill-fitting door, to which a Spanish knocker, formed like a hand in brass, was roughly nailed, though firmly locked, yet gave a vista through its cracks of a deserted garden, in which geraniums run to wood straggled about in beds of rosemary, and orange trees which never had been pruned sprang from great masses of white broom. The path which led up from the gate to the decaying villa through a wilderness of flowers was bordered on each side by peeling vases in red stucco, which stood dejectedly, like sentinels set up to guard a palace where the king was dead, and then forgotten on their post. It finished at a flight of stairs, broken and with great tufts of weeds springing out from the cracks between the steps.

Mysterious voices parleyed in whispers, and now and then an eye peered through the interstices between the planks, and a soft rustling in the path showed that the household of the sultan kept a close watch over the safety of their lord. As I stood holding to a bunch of canes to stop myself from slipping down into the mud, my eyes fixed on the gate, steps hurrying down the path behind me made me turn and almost fall into the arms of a fat, white-robed secretary, who came as delicately as did Agag, to ask me for my card. Long did he look at it, holding it upside down for greater ease in the deciphering. Then, asking me what my name was, he wrote it down in Arabic, asked me if that was right, again surveyed my card, the wrong side up, and quietly withdrew. Ten minutes passed, a quarter of an hour, and then the gate at which I stood was opened cautiously and once again the secretary appeared. This time he bore a European notebook bound in shiny cloth, and once again he inquired my name, asking me, when I had told him, if I was sure of it, and once again wrote it down carefully and once again withdrew. Two or three soldiers, with the long side-locks that the men about the sultan always wear, came down the lane, springing from stone to stone like cats, and every one of them inquired my business and my name. Half an hour passed, and, just as I had turned to go, the gate swung open suddenly, and three or four soldiers, rushing out, seized hold of my right hand, and all vociferating that Mulai Abd-el-Assiz waited for me, advanced at a quick walk.

Under a group of almond trees just bursting into flower there stood a figure robed in white, at sight of which the attendants all withdrew, leaving me to advance, bareheaded, and salute the man who once had been a king. He knew me instantly, motioned to me to be covered, with a gesture that the Tsar of Russia might have envied but never could have compassed, answered the usual formal compliments, and then stood silent, with a smile that showed his firm, white teeth, whilst I as delicately as I could touched on the mutability of fate, in Arabic quite destitute of grammar, saying not what I wished to say, but anything I could.

I floundered on, looking upon the ground, not to embarrass him with the recollection of himself in other times; and then, looking up for a moment, saw the tears standing in his eyes, and for the first time remarked adversity had set a seal as of nobility upon him, that he had aged, and lines had crept about the corners of his mouth. He met my eye a moment, thanked me, said "It was ordained," took my hand for a moment, carrying his own an instant to his breast, smiled again sadly, and withdrew towards the house. As I looked after the white gliding figure with its flowing robes I saw him as I had seen him first, in far Marakesh, riding before a cloud of horsemen, on a white horse, under the scarlet umbrella, revered by thousands both as an emperor and a saint; young, hopeful, the Commander of the Faithful; but not so noble as he had stood with the regality of adverse fortune on him, under the almond trees.

A Sebastianist

He must have been the very last of his extraordinary sect, and naturally all those who knew him tapped their foreheads or wagged their fingers to and fro before their faces when they spoke of him, and said that he was mad. For all that, in the ordinary affairs of life he did not seem much madder than are other people, but went about his usual avocations as if he thought that he would live for ever, just as they did themselves. Still, looked at without prejudice, his strange belief that Dom Sebastian was not dead, but by magician's art had been conveyed away to some mysterious middle region of the earth after the fateful battle of Alcázar-el-Kebir, and would return again to claim his throne, was not much stranger than are other faiths which we all take on trust. Men reasoned with him, and to all they said he merely answered, "He will return some day"; and fixed in that belief he took his evening walk, when the day's work was done, upon a terrace that looked out upon the sea, in the small town in Portugal in which he lived, to welcome home the king.

A little, wizen-looking man, with a large head to which a few scant locks of hair still clung, as mistletoe clings to an apple bough, and long grey whiskers like a fish's fins, Dom Jeremias always dressed in black, and his grave manners, with his waistcoat stained with snuff, gave him an air as if he was connected either with the Church or law. What heightened the illusion was the faint odour of stale incense that hung about his clothes, his frequent pious exclamations, and an air as if under no circumstance whatever could he have gained his livelihood at any business that required strict attention or needed much communication with mankind. Constant in church, after Our Lady, whom he adored with as much tender veneration as if he had been under personal obligation to her for the continual miracle of life, he was devoted most to S. Sebastian, the saint whose name the Cardinal Dom Enrique had given to the king for whose return he confidently looked, at the baptismal font.

Being as he was, a man more fit, as goes the saying (in the Spains), for God than man, his business could not have gone on for a year without his ruin, had not his sisters, Maria Agueda and Peregrina, looked after it, keeping the books and seeing into everything, whilst they pretended to consult him as to the smallest detail of the shop. His days he spent behind the counter, seated on a rush-bottomed chair, with his feet resting on an esparto mat, a cigarette, usually smoked down to the stump, between his lips, and with a wicker cage in which was an extremely plethoric decoy partridge, swinging above his head. Piles of rough plates made in Manizes stood in the corners of the shop upon the red-brick floor, and on rough, ill-planed shelves were ranged strange little bulgy mugs, earthenware pipkins, flower-pots, which looked as if they had been dug up from a Roman tomb, and jars of various sizes to hold oil, glazed a metallic green. His sisters jangled with customers and gossiped with their friends, whilst he occasionally cast his accounts in a long, narrow, dog-eared ledger, so thumbed that the soft cardboard of which the binding was composed, was bare about the edges and frayed into a pulp.

Flies buzzed in myriads about the shop, flying between the links of the long chain of coloured paper which dangled from the roof with a soft, rustling noise. The shop itself looked out upon a winding street paved with rough cobble-stones, the outside walls of many of the houses springing up from the summit of the cliffs which overhung the sea. The day would slip past imperceptibly, unless a neighbour chanced to look in and set him talking on his hobby, on which once mounted he became another man, and by degrees got heated with the argument, and set forth all the reasons that appeared valid to him, to account for his belief. "Nobody saw him die," he would exclaim, "for Mesa clearly is not worthy of belief, writing as he did in the Spanish interest after the crowns were joined. Now, if he did not die, and if the Lord of Heaven is omnipotent, is it not possible that for wise reasons of his own he may have chosen to preserve him, and will again, when the fit moment comes, let him return again to earth to manifest his might? Franchi, who wrote his life, is doubtful, and it is known that many persons of good fame swore on their death-beds they had seen the king, years after the great fight."

If, on the other hand, no one looked in but a chance customer or two, and nothing broke the languor of the day but the flies buzzing or the harsh cry of water-sellers in the street, late in the afternoon he made his preparations for a stroll. Standing a moment in front of the brown picture of a saint stuck in a corner and lighted by a lamp, he prayed a little, then after crossing himself elaborately, both on the breast and mouth, would take his hat from off the wall, where it hung dangling from a nail, and light a cigarette. This operation he performed from a brass chafing-dish in which a piece of charcoal always lay ready to be blown to a white heat. Next, calling for his cloak, which he wore all the year to keep out cold or to exclude the heat, according to the season, he turned towards his sisters, saying, "I think I shall just stroll towards the cliff, to look out for a sail." Then with a pious exclamation, or perhaps after quoting an old saw with the air of having lived through the experience himself, he stepped into the street.

Once there, he generally stopped for a moment as if he was about to take a resolution, though he had followed the same path for years, and then turned towards the sea. His friends who passed him on the way usually asked him, with a serious air, after the health of Dom Sebastian and when he was expected to return. To their inquiries he said nothing, but, smiling gravely, touched his hat punctiliously, passing along the street till it led out upon an open, grassy space that overlooked the sea. Then, sitting down and taking up his telescope, he looked out seaward, scanning the horizon till his eyeballs ached to catch a glimpse of the returning caravel which should bring back the king, still young and gallant, just as he was on John the Baptist's Day, when the fleet weighed on the full tide from Belem, three hundred years ago.

These were his happiest moments, for there was none to mock at him, and by degrees he generally passed off to that interior world of visions which men like Jeremias make for themselves out of the pia mater of their brains, as a retreat against the nullity of lives, in a world made from nothing. Dom Jeremias heard the cannons roar and saw the king upon the poop, bands played, and all the housetops looked like rose gardens with women, some joyful, seeing the king so confident, and others thinking that, as the historian wisely hath it, no battle ever yet was fought without blood flowing, and that the spawn of Mahomet was a stout foe to beard in his own territory. A great and lucid spectacle it was; at least Sebastian Mesa says so, and we can take him at his word, seeing that he was curate of the parish of S. Just and commissary of the Holy Office of the Inquisition in the most loyal, noble, and crowned city of Madrid, and capital of Spain.

All passed before the eyes of the man dozing on the cliff, just as things pass before the eyes of those who look into the camera obscura of the world and have no power to alter or to aid, by the least tittle, those whom they see upon the road to ruin, for all their willingness. He saw the ship that bore the standard of the king foul a great barque from Flanders, carrying away its figurehead and part of its jib-boom, and when a man was killed just by Sebastian's side by the chance bursting of a gun, Dom Jeremias held his breath, muttering that someone surely had the evil eye amongst his followers.

Galleons and galleasses, caravels, fly-boats, and galleys with the Moorish slaves all tugging at the oars, he saw, watching them till they disappeared down the round-sided world and vanished into space. He saw them anchor in the Bay of Lagos of the Algarvés, to take aboard Francisco de Tabora and the men that he had raised. There they remained four days, which seemed a little strange to Jeremias, knowing as he did the king's eagerness, and when they got to Cadiz, where they embarked the forces under the orders of the Ambassador of Spain, he longed to go ashore and help the preparations, for the delay but served to put spurs on his heels, as Mesa said it did on those of Dom Sebastian, as he lay idly in the port.

Tangier was reached successfully, and though he cursed him for a misbelieving dog, Dom Jeremias still was glad that the Sherif Mulai Mohamed was there and waiting for the king with a large force of Moors. Half waking and half sleeping, he would sit musing upon his visions, in his waking moments, and, when he dozed, seeing that which he thought about awake, unrolled before his eyes. Being a simple-minded man, he was not puffed up by the thought that he alone remained faithful to the delusion which had brought all the happiness he knew into his life, for faith, like virtue, is its own reward, though he may still have had a little pride in his sincerity. So may a Jesuit in the old times in Paraguay, in the recesses of the Tarumensian woods, meeting his unknown martyrdom alone, certain his death would be unchronicled and his bones moulder into dust without a hand to throw a little earth upon them, still have rejoiced that he had found the strength to stand his torture, and for a moment looked up with a smile, before the club descended or the swift arrow plunged into his heart.

Waking or sleeping, he still followed as he sat the fortunes of the expedition, seeing it disembark near the small, grassy knoll where now the saint-house nestles in its palms outside Arcila, knowing it was an error not to have gone on to Laraché and taken it at once. This saddened him, though he reflected that even kings are liable to err, a fact the Lord permits, no doubt, to show them they are human; and so fell musing on his hero's grace of person, his wit and gravity of bearing, his pleasantness in all his commerce with mankind, and boundless courtesy. Much did it please him to reflect, when he thought on the world in which he lived, that in Sebastian's heart no malice or suspicion ever found a place, that he was open in his dealings, patient in hardships to a miracle, looked kindly on the faults of others, and never once condemned a man to death, in his brief journey through his life of four-and-twenty years.

In everything proportioned like a king (as says Sebastian Mesa), he saw him, active, alert, short-waisted, legs long and bowed from riding in his youth, of middle height and fair, with a thin beard, and eyes large, blue, and open, which seemed to look beyond the man he spoke to, into the firmament. Still he gazed on the fated expedition, and saw it march towards Alcázar-el-Kebir, encamp upon the west bank of the Wad-el-M'hassen, and awake early on the fourth of August (S. Domingo's Day), to find the enemy in countless numbers blackening the plain. He saw the king, like an experienced captain, set his host in array; and then, when all was ready, Dom Jeremias seemed to hear him tell them to call to prayers, and see the Jesuit, Father Alexander, raise up a crucifix on high, so that it was in view of all the soldiery. When the king kneeled before his kneeling troops Dom Jeremias fervently crossed himself and prayed for his success. He saw him, still upon his knees, receive the message from his second in command, that they were waiting for the signal to advance, rise up and at a bound, armed as he was, spring on the back of a black horse of middle size, not gay to look at, but the best bitted and most fit for war of all the horses either in Portugal or Spain.

Long did the battle rage, with varying success, till about eventide, when everything was lost, he saw the king charge with a knight or two into the thickest of the enemy and battle furiously. Then losing sight of him, and when the sounds of warfare had grown dimmer in his ears, he seemed to find himself upon the ramparts of Arcila and listen to the voice of a mysterious stranger asking for shelter, and, when the guard refused, saw him turn away desperately and ride into the night. This vision strengthened his belief that the king had escaped alive; so when the evening breeze brought Jeremias back into a world in which he was the one Sebastianist alive he used to rise, and throwing back his cloak, walk homewards, his spirit shaken by the scene that he had conjured up, and his faith magnified.

He died as he had lived, and when they found his body seated on the cliff, his eyes wide open, staring out across the sea, his telescope was lying by his side, with the brass cap fixed firmly down with rust over the object-glass.

A Repertory Theatre

The red-haired Spaniard from Ceuta, who had been hired to keep the mules from eating up our horses' corn — for in a fondak an Arab never ties his mule — was a sententious man. After having thrown a stone which narrowly escaped knocking out a horse's eye, he said in answer to a question, "No, Tetuan is not a bad place on the whole. . . . I am a mason, and just now am working on a mosque — a nice job for a Christian, eh?" No one compassionating him, he continued: "The worst thing is that there are no amusements in the place. A man without amusements soon grows vicious." This he enunciated with so grave an air, some might have thought he had evolved and not inherited the phrase. "The infidel, of course" (he meant the Moors), "do not require amusement as we Christians do. Give them a cup of weak green tea, flavoured with mint, and they will sit for hours and talk about the price of barley or on the attributes of God, for all is one to them, and be as happy as a strolling player upon the evening of a holiday." He stopped and tried to light a cigarette with a flint and steel, and, failing, put the cigarette behind his ear, saying, "I'll leave it for the next bull-fight, as we say in Spain; not that they ever have a bull-fight in this benighted land. Why do we come here? I sometimes ask myself. True, here there are no taxes, and bread is cheaper than in Spain, but after all, it is a purgatory for us who come as pioneers of progress to this accursed land."

He did not look precisely like a pioneer of progress as he stood in the muddy fondak yard, his naked feet shoved into alpargatas, which he wore clown at heel like Moorish slippers, his jacket dangling from one shoulder like a cloak, and with a grey felt hat from Cordoba, battered and napless, kept on his head by a black ribbon tied underneath his chin. Still, we must take men as we find them, as we take bank-notes at their face value, and generally their estimate of themselves and of their worth is nearer to the truth than any we can form. So it may well have been he was a pioneer designed by fate to show the Moors all that is worst in European progress, and bound himself to suffer in the showing, debarred from bull-fights, gambling, and politics in what he styled "a cursed land of unwashed burnouses and of lice."

No one could say he was not civil in his manners, or fluent in his speech to a degree that would have made the future of a public speaker in the north. Then he was tall and strong and not bad-looking in a sort of villainous and cut-throat style, and certainly a good shot with a stone. For his abilities in his craft I cannot speak, not having had the curiosity to go and see the mosque where he was working, but he possessed a flow of ready and most idiomatic Arabic, an unusual thing for a Spaniard born in "Las Plazas Fuertes," that is Ceuta, Las Alhucemas, and all the rest of Spain's possessions on the coast.

He took his cigarette from behind his ear, just as a clerk resumes his pen, and looked at it regretfully, and, when I handed him a match, lighted it, perhaps as a concession to the progress he was introducing, and then began to smoke with that peculiar relish, drinking the smoke and then expelling it a minute after in the middle of a flood of words, which only Spaniards of his class can ever perfectly attain. His action somehow called to mind a certain Irishman who drove me to a meeting at a place, the name of which I have forgotten, somewhere near Lurgan. All that I can recall is that the meeting was in a gaunt, dilapidated hall, stuck in the middle of the fields, and had been built by an old clergyman who had lived a blameless life till sixty and then "renagered," as the people said, and turned an atheist. Such things happen infrequently except among the Kelto-Saxon race. Having "renagered," he had to testify. Just as the Moors will call in a loud voice to any European who has put on their clothes, saying, "Testify, O wearer of the haik!" so it seemed necessary to him to justify his creed.

Accordingly the quondam clergyman, now turned atheist, to show his faith in the nonentity of God, erected in the fields, a mile or two outside the village where he lived, a temple made with hands, and, having frescoed it inside with pictures of the pagan deities, called it the "Hall of Apollo," making, as it were, a sort of testimony of the bricks to his own idiocy.

The country people, more astute or more imaginative, called it the "Hall of Vanus," and to it I was bound.

Of course it rained, and as we passed by public-house or licensed premises the driver jerked his whip towards them, remarking, as a man talks in a dream, "Finucane keeps good spirits," or "Little Bob Coleary has nate whisky." Still I was obdurate, till he, drawing a green and freckled apple from his pocket, tendered it to me.

I asked him, "What is that for?" and he replied, "Sure it will keep down the drouth"; so we stopped at the first shebeen, and he drank whisky whilst I shivered in the rain.

Perhaps the remembrance of the episode softened my heart towards the red-haired dweller in "Las Plazas Fuertes," and so I tendered him the match.

It did not break the ice between us, for none existed; but it somehow drew us together, just as that acid-looking apple drew me towards the man upon the road in the Black North whilst shivering on his car.

My friend talked on, throwing a stone or two occasionally at a marauding mule, and telling me about the lives and habits of the Europeans in the town, by which I learned that Sodom and Gomorrah had been cleanly living places compared to Tetuan. As by an afterthought, he said, "Seeing that you speak Christian you might care to see *Don Juan Tenorio*, which is being played to-night at the dramatic circle in the consulate."

I did, and said that I would like to go, and he, calling loudly to a boy, "Oh Mojamito," after the fashion of his countrymen, who tack a Spanish termination on to an Arab name (perhaps for euphony), there and then constituted him his "caliph," as he explained to me, to keep away the mules. He added, "Now I am free to take you to the theatre, which in fact I had wished to see, but could not for want of necessary funds." Having hypothecated, as it were, some of his salary, which I advanced him on the spot, he dipped his hands into a drinking-trough for mules, sleeked down his hair with water, and having picked a marigold growing upon a wall, stuck it behind his ear, and so was ready to escort us to the play.

By devious ways he led us, through meandering lanes, talking quite at his ease to a young lady of the party, although she did not understand a word he said — which perhaps was well, considering the frankness of his speech. At last he led us to the place, having explained that in the dearth of all amusements the Spanish colony had organised theatricals to pass away the time, their idea being to give stock pieces, such as *Don Juan Tenorio* and the like, which everybody knew. "I see," I said, "a repertory theatre"; to which he answered, "Repertory — I rather like the name." We took the most expensive places, at a peseta each, and entered through a door at which just such another as our guide stood taking tickets, smoking a cigarette.

The hall, a long, low building off a narrow Moorish street, was lit by tin petroleum lamps, some hanging from the roof and others stuck against the wall. Most of them flared and smoked, and all of them gave out a rank, metallic smell. At one end of the room was a small stage, only a little larger than in a theatre of marionettes, but high above the floor. The walls were painted a pale yellow, something between the colour of a light montbretia and a canary bird. Upon them elongated vases, reminding one somehow of stained-glass figures by Jean Goujon, were drawn in a dull red. They held bouquets of what one might call superflowers, so violent were their colours and so difficult to tell the species to which they might belong. The audience was composed of almost all the Spanish colony in Tetuan and a few Moors and Riffs. In the front row the wives and daughters of the diplomatists and of the officers attached to the obsolescent military mission, and of the beef contractor, the doctor, and the interpreter were seated in a row. Most of them had a little run to fat, and nearly all wore white silk blouses over black silk skirts. Their fans were in their hands, and a light whir as of a locust's wings filled all the hall as they perpetually opened and shut them with the peculiar grace that only Spanish women ever attain to in the manipulation of this most potent instrument of war. Their faces were all white with powder, which in the case of those of lesser category (for all had brought their servants to the show) was carried up into the hair by natural instinct, so as to avoid a hard effect where the powder ended and the black hair began. Needless to say, their hair was done with taste, either piled high up on the head or, with the younger women, brought low about the ears and parted in the middle, looking a little like two waves upon the sides.

Though few of them were handsome seen alone, their great black eyes, long eyelashes, and the intense and jetty blackness of their hair setting their dead-white faces, as it were, in a frame, gave to them in the mass a beauty which threw the looks of women in more ambitious theatres into the shade by its look of wildness and intensity.

The men were, on the whole, inferior to them, as often happens in the South, where Nature seems to have put out her best effort in the women of the race. Still, they had most of them that air of nervous hardness which many Spaniards have, and from the superannuated colonel who filled an elusive post on the unnecessary and futile military mission, to the stout beef contractor they looked like men no one could venture to insult.

At one end of the room a group of Moors, looking like figures made out of snow wrapped in their fleecy haiks, and silent and impressive, sat on their chairs uneasily, just as a European sits uneasily when squatted on the ground. Now and then one of them furtively drew up a leg and tucked it under him upon his chair, and nearly all of them let the beads of their Mecca rosaries slip through the fingers of one hand, leaving the other free to make a movement now and then either of deprecation or assent. The play, *Don Juan Tenorio*, as was set forth upon the green and flimsy handbill, is one of the stock pieces of the Spanish stage, and all the actors and actresses were amateurs, drawn from the Spanish residents in Tetuan.

Nothing could possibly have been more democratic than the composition of the company. The receiver of the Customs was Don Juan; the corporal attached to the consulate, the comendador; his wife, the heroine; a tall, thin Spanish girl, the duenna; and yet they all looked, walked, and spoke as if they had been born upon the stage.

The poverty of the mounting of the piece, the common dresses made of cotton velvet, and the smallness of the stage, so far from spoiling, gave an air of such intense reality to the whole thing it would have been difficult to match in any theatre. Nothing could have been more intensely natural than the first scene, in which Don Juan Tenorio comes home from Italy. The naked stage, with a deal table in the middle of it round which were set two or three Austrian chairs, took one, incredible as it may seem, back to the Middle Ages, at the first words the actor spoke. Nothing apparently upon the stage seems harder to set forth than poverty. Here all was poverty; but for all that nothing was sordid, and it seemed natural to see a man dressed in trunk hose, with a long rapier by his side and an imperfect recollection of his part, swagger across the stage, because you did not think it was a stage, so strongly did the actors dominate the accessories and focus interest upon themselves. They came and went, spoke (when they could recollect their parts), exactly as they must have gone about and spoken at the epoch of the play. They quarrelled fiercely, so fiercely that sometimes the phlegmatic Moors moved on their chairs uneasily, although their movements may well have been caused by the novelty of their position and the cramp in their legs. Occasionally upon the stage swords flashed, and swarthy men attired in cotton tights which bagged a little at the knee, and yet did not in the least make them ridiculous, set on each other with such goodwill it was a marvel no one was maimed for life. The prompter was a man of genius, voluble, as one could plainly hear, but yet discreet, as his remarks, "Now, Don Luis, 'tis time to draw your sword," or "Brigida, don't let him press your hand till you have got the purse," most amply testified. At times I fancied by the sudden change of voice that when an actor had forgotten all he had to say the prompter boldly read it from the book in a loud key, although the actor still stamped about the stage like a demoniac. These were the blemishes upon the surface, but underneath the heterogeneous company of Spanish amateurs, ill-dressed, and acting on a stage scarce large enough for marionettes, defective in their parts, and playing to an audience a good half of which knew little of the language that the actors spoke, in some strange way brought mediæval Spain before one's eyes as I have never seen it done in the most ambitious theatre in Spain. It may have been because Spain always has been poor, for three parts of the gold from Potosi filtered to Antwerp and to Genoa; it may have been because things always have been done in Spain in a haphazard way, that the haphazard method of the actors really set forth her mediæval life as in a looking-glass. At any rate, an English lady sitting by my side, who knew but little Spanish, watched the whole play in rapt attention, her colour going and coming at each episode, and when the piece was over said she had never seen such acting in her life in any theatre.

When it was finished and everybody duly slain before our eyes, over the Spanish Consul's sweet champagne the actors wandered in and out, and a fat Moorish Custom House official involuntarily gave the measure of their unconscious art, for, seeing Don Luis Mejia still in his mediæval clothes, but smoking an anachronistic cigarette, he looked amazed, and said in halting Spanish, "By Allah, I thought that you were dead!" and wished to feel the place where he was sure the sword had run into his side.

A Vigia

When the old Spanish navigators, sailing in virgin seas, uncharted, undeflowered by keels, passed by some islet about which they were doubtful, seeing it dimly as the mist lifted for a moment, or in the uncertain light of the false dawn, they called it a Vigia, a place to be looked out for, and their old charts are dotted here and there with the Vigia of the Holy Spirit, the Trinity, the Immaculate Conception, or the Exaltation of the Cross.

Their followers, sailing with ampler knowledge, but less faith, kept a look out for the mysterious shoals or islets, not often finding them, unless they chanced to run upon them in the dark and perish with all hands. These were Vigias of the seas, but there exist Vigias of the mind, as shadowy and as illusive, to the full, as any that Magellan, Juan de la Cosa, or Sebastian Cabot marked upon their charts. We all know of such islands, low-lying, almost awash, as it were, in the currents of the mind. On them we make our land-fall when we choose, without a pilot, except memory, to guide us in the darkest night. We land and roam about alone, always alone, for those who once inhabited them and welcomed us whenever we sailed in, are now all harboured. Commonly we stay but little there, for though the men we knew are dead, their ghosts so jostle us that we are glad once more to re-embark and sail again into a world of noise, that modern anæsthetic of the mind, still knowing that one day we must return and swell the shadowy procession that walks along the shores of their dead, saltless seas. There is an island, whose whereabouts I do not care precisely to reveal, although only a little strait divides it from a land of mist, of money-making, a land of faiths harder by far than facts, yet there it rides swaying on the sea like some great prehistoric ship, looking out westward in the flesh, and with the interior vision straining its eyes to keep its recollection of the past, fresh and undimmed. Green grass, white sands, limpid blue seas, with windows here and there of palest green in them, through which you look into the depths and count the stones, watch sea anemones unfold like flowers, and follow the minutest fish at play fathoms below your boat; these keep it fresh, old, and uncontaminated. One likes to think of virgin souls, and so I like to think of this oasis in the desert of the sea, as virgin, in spite of tourists, steam-boats, and the stream of those who go to worship and defile. They have the power to trample down the grass, to leave their sandwich papers and their broken bottles in the ling, but the fresh wind coming across a thousand leagues of sea eludes them. That they can never trample down. So may a woman in a brothel be the mattress of the vilest of mankind and keep some corner of the soul still pure; for it is dull, befitting only to the spirit of the so-called wise, to say the age of miracles is dead. Those who have kept their minds unclogged with knowledge know that they never cease.

So old my island is that it seems young — that is, it still preserves an air as of an older world, in which men laboured naturally just as a bee makes honey; a world where the chief occupation of mankind was to look round them, as the Creator did in Eden and to find all things good. So they pass all the morning, meeting their fellows and saluting them, and in the afternoon repass and resalute, then work a little in the fields, lifting up hay upon a fork with as much effort as an athlete in a circus raises a cannon in his teeth, till it is time to sit down on a stone and watch the fishing-boats return upon the tides, the steersman sitting on the gunwale with his knee jammed against the tiller, and the sheet firmly knotted round a thwart. Just as of Avila, it might be said of my Vigia, that it is all made up of saints and stones, for not a stone is without its corresponding saint or saint without his stone. Thus in both places does the past so dwarf the present, that things which happened when the world was young seem just as probable as the incredible events we see before our eyes.

Upon a mound that looks out on a sand-locked bay the heathen crucified some of the new faith a thousand years ago, bringing, as we might think, their crosses with them ready made, or rigging up a jury cross, fashioned from spars and oars, for not a tree grows, or has ever grown, upon the island where now the sheep feed peacefully on the short, wiry grass broken with clumps of flags. A little further on fairies appeared the other day, not to a man herding his sheep and dazed with solitude, but to a company of men who all declare they saw the Little People seated upon a mound. Fairies and martyrs both seem as natural as does the steamer landing its daily batch of tourists to hurry through the street where the kings sleep under their sculptured stones, gaze at the

Keltic crosses and the grey, time-swept church which lies a little listed, as it were, to starboard, upon the grassy slope where once there stood the wattled temple of the Apostle of the Isles. The mud-built church, where the Apostle chanted his last Mass, is nearer to us than the cathedral, now being killed with care. We see the saint lie dying, and his white, faithful horse approach and make its moan and, bowing down its head, ask for his blessing, as is recorded by the chronicler, with that old, cheerful faith in the impossible that kept his world so young.

So standing on the Capitol, the Church, Popes, Cardinals, and Saints, the glory of the Middle Ages, the empire, the republic, and the kings, melt into mist and leave us, still holding, as our one sure possession, to the two children suckled by the wolf. Some men, like Ponce de Leon, have sailed to find the fountain of eternal youth, landed upon some flowery land, left it, and died still searching, all unaware the object of their quest, had it been found, would have left paradise a waste. There in my island, whose longitude and latitude, for reasons of my own, I keep a secret, there is, I think, some fountain in which those who bathe recover, not their youth, but the world's youth, and ever afterwards have their ears opened to the voices of the dead.

So, seated on the ground amongst the flowers that grow in miniature amongst the grass, bedstraw, and tormentil, upon the cairn-topped hill from which the saint of Gartan saw his vision, they see the history of the isle acted before them, as in an optic mirror of the mind. The setting still remains just as it was when the Summer Sailors from the north fell on the peaceful monks one day in June, twelve hundred years ago, and sacrificed them and their prior to their offended gods. The thin, white road which cuts the level machar into two has probably replaced an earlier sheep-track or a footpath of the monks. The dazzling white houses, with their thatched roofs secured against the wind by stones slung in a rope, only require a little more neglect to fall again into the low, black Pictish huts. The swarthy people, courteous and suave, in whom you see a vein of subcutaneous sarcasm as they lean up against a house, sizing the passing stranger up to the last tittle at a glance, would all look natural enough with glibs of matted hair, long saffron Keltic shirts, and the Isles kilt, made out of a long web of cloth, leaving the right arm bare.

Still in the Isle of Dreams remains the primitive familiarity between the animals and man, which only lingers on in islands or in the regions where no breath of modern life has set a bar between two branches of the same creation with talk about the soul. The still, soft rain yet blots the island from the world, just as it did of yore, and through its pall the mysterious voices of the sea sound just as menacing and hostile to mankind as they did when the saint preached to the seals upon the reef. Perhaps — who knows? — he preaches yet to those who have the gift of a right hearing of the soft, grating noise the pebbles make in a receding wave upon the beach. The wind continues its perpetual monsoon, blowing across the unpolluted ocean for a thousand leagues. In the white coves the black sea-purses which the tide throws up like necklaces of an antique and prehistoric pattern are spread upon the sands, waiting the evening, when the mermaids issue from the waves and clasp them round their necks. Soft wind and purple sea, red cliffs and greenest grass, the echoing caves and mouldering ruins, with the air of peace, all make the islet dreamlike, sweet, and satisfying.

To have seen it once is to have seen it to the last day of one's life. The horses waiting at the rough pierhead to swim a mile of channel with its fierce, sweeping tide, the little street in which the houses spring from the living rock which crops up here and there and forms a reef right in the middle of the road, are not a memory, but a possession, as real as if you held the title-deeds duly engrossed and sealed. When all is said and done, the one secure and lasting property a man can own is an enchanted city such as one sees loom in the sky, above the desert sands. That, when you once have seen it, is yours for ever, and next comes a Vigia, which but appears for a brief moment, in the mind, as you sail past on some imaginary sea.

At Dalmary

The road led out upon an open moor, on which heather and wiry grass strove for the mastery. Here and there mossy patches, on which waved cotton grass, broke the grey surface of the stony waste, and here and there tufts of dwarf willow, showing the silvery backs of their grey leaves, rustled and bent before the wind.

The road, one of those ancient trails on which cattle and ponies were driven in old times down to the Lowland trysts, was now half covered up with grass. It struggled through the moor as if it chose to do so of its own accord, now twisting, for no apparent reason, and again going straight up a hill, just as the ponies and the kyloes must have straggled before the drovers' dogs. It crossed a shallow ford, in which the dark brown moorland trout darted from stone to stone when the shadow of a passer-by startled them as they poised, their heads up stream, keeping themselves suspended as it were by an occasional wavering motion of their tails, just as a hawk hangs hovering in the air.

Beside the stream, a decaying wooden bridge, high-pitched and shaky, reminded one that in the winter the burn, now singing its metallic little song between the stones, brown and pellucid, with bubbles of white foam floating upon its tiny linns or racing down the stream, checking a little in an eddy, where a tuft of heavy ragweed dipped into the flood, was dangerous to cross.

The aromatic scent of the sweet gale came down the breeze, mixed with the acrid smoke of peats. Hairbells *[sic=harebells]* danced in the gentle breeze, and bumble-bees hummed noisily as they emerged, weighed down with honey, from the ling.

Across the moor, from farms and shielings, and from the grey and straggling village built on each side of the rough street, in which the living rock cropped up and ran in reefs across the road, came groups of men dressed in black clothes, creased and ill-fitting, with hats, grown brown with years of church-going and with following funerals in the rain; they walked along as if they missed the familiar spade or plough-handle to keep them straight, just as a sailor walks uneasily ashore.

As they trudged on they looked professionally on the standing crops, or passed their criticisms on the cattle in the fields. Root crops, they thought, were back, taties not just exactly right, a thocht short in the shaws, and every cow a wee bit heigh abune the tail, for praise was just as difficult a thing for them to give as blame was easy, for they were all aware their God was jealous, and it did not befit them to appear more generous than He. Hills towered and barred the north, and to the south the moors stretched till they met another range of hills, and all the space between them was filled with a great sea of moss, eyed here and there with dark, black pools on which a growth of water-lilies floated like fairies' boats. A wooded hill, which sloped down to a brawling river, was the fairies' court. Another to the south, steep, rising from the moss, the Hill of the Crown, received its name back in the times of Fingal and of Bran. Gaps in the hills showed where, in times gone by, marauders from the north had come to harry and to slay. The names of every hill, lake, wood, or stream were Gaelic, and the whole country exhaled an air of a romantic past.

In it the dour, black-coated men, although they thought themselves as much a part and parcel of the land as the grey rocks upon the moor, were strangers; holding their property but on sufferance from the old owners, who had named every stone, and left their impress even in the air.

It seemed the actual dwellers acted as it were a play, a sort of rough and clownish interlude, upon a stage set out for actors whom the surroundings would have graced.

Still, though they shared the land, just as we all do, by favour of the dead, they had set their mark upon it, running their rough stone walls across the moors and to the topmost ridges of the hills, planting their four-square, slate-roofed houses in places where a thatched and whitewashed cottage, with red tropæolum growing on the corner of the byre, a plant of mullein springing from a crevice in the wall, and flauchtered feals pegged to the thatch with birchen crockets, or kept down with stones, would have looked just as fitting as theirs looked out of place. A land in which the older dwellers had replaced the nymphs and hamadryads by the fairies, where, in the soft and ceaseless rain, the landscape wore a look of sadness, that the mist, creeping up on the shoulders of the hills, at times turned menacing, was now delivered over to a race of men who knew no shadows, either in life or in belief. If they believed, they held each letter of "The Book" inspired, and would have burned the man who sought to change a comma to a semicolon, and if they had rejected faith as an encumbrance they could do without, denied the very possibility of any god or power but mathematics, holding the world a mere gigantic counting-house in which they sat enthroned. The moaning birches and dark murmuring pines, the shaggy thickets by the streams, and the green hummocks under which tradition held Pictish or Keltic chiefs reposed, the embosomed corries over which the shadows ran, as imperceptibly as lizards run upon a wall, turning the brown hillside to gold, which melted into green as it stole on, until it faded into a pale amethyst, faint and impalpable as is a colour in a dream, seemed to demand a race of men more fitted to its moods than those who walked along the road chatting about the crops. Still it may be that though the outward visible sign was so repellent, the unexpected and interior softness of the black-clothed and tall-hatted men was bred in them by their surroundings, for certainly their hard, material lives, and their black, narrow, anti-human faith could not have given it.

The road led on until on the south side of it a path, worn in the heather and the wiry grass, and winding in and out between the hillocks, crossed here and there by bands of rocks, out-cropping, but smoothed down on the edge by the feet of centuries, broke off, not at right angles after the fashion of a modern road, but on the slant, just as a herd of driven animals slants off, stopping at intervals to graze.

The knots of black-clothed men, some followed by their dogs, slowly converged upon the path, and stood a minute talking, passing the time of day, exchanging bits of news and gossip in subdued voices, and mopping vigorously at their brows, oppressed with the unwonted weight of their tall hats.

"We've had a braw back end, McKerrachar," Borland remarked. The worthy he addressed, a gaunt, cadaverous man, so deeply wrinkled that you could fancy in wet weather the rain down the channels in his face, spat in contemplative fashion, rejoining in a non-committal way:

"No just sae bad . . . markets are back a wee." A nod of assent went round the group, and then another interjected:

"I dinna mind sae braw a back end for mony a year; aye, ou aye, I'll no deny markets are very conseederably back."

Having thus magnified his fellow, after the fashion of the stars, he looked a moment with apparent interest at his hat, which he held in his hand, and ventured the remark:

"A sair blow to the widow, Andra's death; he was a good man to her."
No one answering him, he qualified what he had said by adding:

"Aye, sort of middlin'," and glanced round warily, to see if he had
overstepped the bounds by the too indiscriminating nature of his praise.

The house towards which the various knots of men were all converging
stood at the foot of a green, grassy mound, which looked as if it might
have been the tumulus of some prehistoric chief. On it grew several wind-
bent ash trees, and within twenty yards or so of the front door of the grey
cottage, with its low thatched eaves, there ran a little burn. Two or three
mulleins, with flowers still clinging to their dying stalks, on which they
stuck like vegetable warts, sprung from the crevices between the stones
of the rough byre. A plant or two of ragweed grew on the midden on
which a hen was scratching, and out of it a green and oozy rivulet of
slush filtered down to the stream. On one side was a garden, without a
flower, and with a growth of straggling cabbage, gooseberry bushes, and
some neglected-looking raspberry canes, as the sole ornaments. In the
potato patch a broken spade was stuck into the ground. All round the
house some straggling plum trees, with their sour fruit half ripened and
their leaves already turning brown, looking as if they had struggled hard
for life against the blast, in the poor, stony soil, gave a peculiar air of
desolation, imparting to the place a look as of an oasis just as unfruitful
as the waste which stretched on every side. On one side of the door, but
drawn a little on the grass, not to obstruct the way, there stood a cart,
with a tall, white-faced and white-pasterned horse between the shafts,
held by a little boy. Peat smoke curled lazily out of the barrel stuck into
the thatch that served as chimney, and cocks and hens scratched in the
mud before the door, bees hummed amongst the heather, and once again
the groups of men in black struck a discordant note.

Inside the house, upon four wooden chairs was set the coffin of the
dead ploughman, cheap and made in haste, just as his life had been
lived cheaply and in haste, from the first day that he had stood between
the stilts, until the evening when he had loosed his horses from the
plough for the last time, his furrow finished and his cheek no more to
be exposed to the November rain. Now in the roughly put together kist
he lay, his toil-worn hands crossed on his breast, and with his wrinkled,
weather-beaten face turned waxen and ennobled, set in its frame of
wiry whisker, and his scant hair decently brushed forward on his brow.
The peats burned brightly in the grate and sent out a white ash which

covered everything inside the house, whitening the clothes of the black-coated men who stood about, munching great hunks of cake and slowly swallowing down the "speerits" which the afflicted widow pressed upon them, proud through her tears to say, "Tak' it up, Borland," or "It will no hurt ye, Knockinshanock; ye ken there's plenty more."

The white peat ash fell on the coffin-lid just as the summer's dust had fallen upon the hair of him who lay inside, and lay upon the polished surface of the thin brass plate, on which were superscribed the dates of the birth and of the death of the deceased, his only titles to the recollection of the race with whom his life had passed. Now and again the widow, snatching a moment from her hospitable cares, brushed off the dust abstractedly with her pocket-handkerchief, just as a man might stop upon the way to execution to put a chair straight or to do any of the trifling actions of which life is composed. As she paused by the coffin the assembled men exchanged that furtive look of sympathy which in the North is the equivalent of the wild wailings, tears, and self-abandonment of Southern folk, and perhaps stamps on the heart of the half-shame-faced sympathiser even a deeper line.

When all had drunk their "speerits" and drawn the backs of their rough hands across their mouths and shaken off the crumbs from their black clothes, the minister stood forth. Closing his eyes, he launched into his prayer with needless repetition, but with the feeling which the poor surroundings and the brave struggle against outward grief of the woman sitting by the fire in the old high-backed chair, in which her husband had sat so long, evoked, he dwelt upon man's passage through the world.

Life was a breath, only a little dust, a shadow on the hills. It had pleased the Lord, for reasons of His own, inscrutable, but against which 'twere impious to rebel, for a brief space to breathe life into the nostrils of this our brother, and here he made a motion of his hand towards the "kist," then to remove him to a better sphere after a spell of toil and trouble here on earth. Still we must not repine, as do the heathen, who gash themselves with knives, having no hope, whereas we who enjoy the blessings of being born to a sure faith in everlasting bliss should look on death as but a preparation for a better life. No doubt this hope consoled the speaker for all the ills humanity endures, for he proceeded to invoke a blessing on the widow, and as he prayed the rain beat on the narrow, bull's-eye window-panes. He called upon the Lord to bless her in her basket and her store, and to be with her in her outgoings and incomings, to strengthen her and send her resignation to His will. He finished with the defiance to humanity that must have wrung so many tears of blood from countless hearts, saying the Lord had given and that the Lord had taken, blessed be His Name.

All having thus been done that all our ingenuity can think of on such occasions, four stalwart neighbours, holding their hats, which tapped upon their legs, hoisted the coffin on to their shoulders and shuffled to the door. They stooped to let their burden pass beneath the eaves which overhung the entrance, and then emerging, dazed, into the light, their black clothes dusted over with the white ashes from the fire, set down the coffin on the cart. Once more the men gathered into a circle and listened to a prayer, some with their heads bare to the rain, and others with their hats held on the slant to fend it off as it came swirling down the blast. A workman in his ordinary clothes took the tall, white-faced horse close by the bit, and, with a jolt which made the kist shift up against the backboard, the cart set out, swaying amongst the ruts, with now and then a wheel running up high upon one side and now and then a jerk upon the trace-hooks, when the horse, cold with his long wait, strained wildly on the chains. The rain had blotted out the hills, the distant village with its rival kirks had disappeared, and the grey sky appeared to touch the surface of the moor. A whitish dew hung on the grass and made the seeded plants appear gigantic in the gloom. Nothing was to be heard except the roaring of the burn and the sharp ringing of the high caulkins of the horse as he struck fire amongst the stones on the steep, rocky road.

Leaning against the doorpost, the widow stood and gazed after the vanishing procession till it had disappeared into the mist, her tears, which she had fought so bravely to keep back, now running down her face.

When the last sound of the cart-wheels and of the horse's feet amongst the stones had vanished into the thick air, she turned away and, sitting down before the fire, began mechanically to smoor the peats and tidy up the hearth.

Ave Caesar!

The very loyal, noble, and crowned city of Madrid was all out in the streets. The sun poured down upon the just and the unjust, the rich and poor, making all feel alike the equalising gladness of his rays. Troops lined the Castellana, for a lucky fate had added, as it were, another day to Carnaval by taking off a foreign minister whose funeral the Government was celebrating with due pomp. Lightness of heart and not insensibility — for the dead minister had been a man whom all respected — had brought the people out, for life is short, food not abundant, and the streets are, as they were to the Romans and the Greeks, the general meeting-place whenever the sun shines. In the bright light the scene looked like a pageant on the stage. Generals, ablaze with orders, grey-bearded, their abdomens bulging a little on the pommel of their saddles, sitting up brown and immobile as if they had been Moors upon their high-nosed horses from the plains of Córdoba and of Jeréz, rode to their posts, followed by groups of officers looking like flocks of parrots or macaws, so harsh the colours of their uniforms and so metallic the crude blues and scarlets of their plumes. Batteries of horse artillery had unlimbered, and gave an air to the quiet streets as of a city in a siege. The short but lithe Castilian infantry, descendants of the "tercios" of Flanders who once shook the world, were grouped about in masses of dark blue, their grey-topped caps reflecting back the sun. The Judas trees were bursting into flower, and the confetti which had been thrown about during the previous days of Carnaval marbled the sandy footpaths as if a shower of blossoms had just fallen from the trees.

All was bright, hard, and scintillating in the keen white air, which in Castile is so translucent that it scarce throws a shadow, and acts on character and art just as a key upon a piano string, screwing them up to the intensest point. Men passed each other as if they had been enemies, glaring at one another in the way Strabo so many centuries ago depicts their ancestors, and still, in spite of railways and of time, chiefly arrayed in black. Girls heard without a blush remarks that if they had been said in other countries would have been answered by a blow or a revolver-shot from those accompanying them, and looked about a foot above the heads of those who uttered them, and passed upon their way. Horses neighed shrilly, stamping and tossing foam upon the passers-by, and through the sombre crowd girls, selling water carried in porous earthen jars supported on one hip, moved in and out, just as in Eastern towns, their harsh and Oriental voices resounding through the air.

The seats were thronged, and all the streets that led out on the Castellana, near the Embassy, blocked thick with people, all quiet and well behaved, with something Eastern in their restrained and compassed movements and their low tone of speech. In serried ranks they stood and gazed, not with loud exclamations like crowds of other nations, but silently and with unblinking eyes. Grave children stood beside their elders, held by black-haired and black-eyed women with unstable busts, who wore either black veils or else enormous hats which must have been rejected by the Paris shops as quite unfit for human use, or were of a special manufacture for countries such as Spain. The insubstantial house of mourning, with its cheap-looking palm trees and iron railings with the national emblem on the gate-posts, looked somehow meretricious, and the black blinds and banner at half-mast but half redeemed it, leaving an air of unreality about the ceremonial as if the owner was not really dead, but only setting out upon some journey from which he might return. The bursting trees and the fierce life of everything, people and vegetation, fostered the feeling that the ceremony was but the entry of some potentate into his kingdom rather than the extinction of a man who had played out his part.

Children played gravely, as only children in Castile can ever play, fitting themselves by their grave, compassed games for their grave, compassed lives; and yet beneath their quiet movements there was an air of an intense and almost savage life which linked them in an inexplicable way, bound as they were in the hats and hosen of the north, to the brown Arab children who sit about the doors of the black tents of some lost duar on the plains. Whilst the troops had been getting to their places in the streets a constant stream of cabs and carriages had driven up to the door, from which pale, fair-haired men, the members of the foreign colony of which the dead diplomatist had been the chief, descended, either to write their names in the great mourning-book which with due coronet was open in the hall, or else to leave a bouquet of immortelles, neatly tied up with crape, with the stout German porter at the gate. An hour or two of waiting in the dust had dimmed the helmets, dulled the steel scabbards of the swords, and made the horses hang their heads. Generals were sinking back into their ordinary look of sacks of flour upon their horses, and underneath the gun-carriages of the artillery the gunners sat and smoked, when, swinging and swaying to and fro, an enormous funeral car drawn by four horses made its way along the street. Hastily generals straightened themselves up, artillerymen got to their saddles, the infantry stood to attention, and an air as of a troop of schoolboys suddenly surprised by the apparition of an unexpected master pervaded all the line.

The groups of people in the streets pressed forward on the troops, but gravely, quietly, just as they gaze each Sunday at a bull-fight, silent but fascinated. Hours seemed to pass, and still the soldiers stood immobile in the fierce sun. At last, when even Spanish patience was almost exhausted, down the broad flight of steps the coffin, covered with a purple pall, was borne upon the shoulders of eight stalwart soldiers to the hearse. Amid a cloud of dust and glory the catafalque rolled down the street, an interminable line of cabs and carriages following stuffed full of black-clad men who sat upright and stifling, with the air that men assume at funerals, half of contentment that they are alive, and half as of a person who has seen a man fall from a scaffold, with eyes averted and with terror in his heart.

Thus the procession took its way right down the Castellana, with all Madrid afoot to watch the passage of the dead minister, plumes waving, horses passaging, soldiers with arms reversed, and all the pomp and ceremony of war tamed for a season and made subservient to death. It passed by streets guarded by mounted men, who, sitting gravely on their horses, saluted solemnly. Generals rode both in front and just behind the hearse. An endless line of mourning-coaches followed. The King, seated in a gorgeous carriage, his Austrian chin outlined against the glass and his retreating forehead disappearing under a plumed, three-cornered hat, was there to honour the dead man. Street after street the procession passed, and still the olive-coloured crowd stood silent, the men raising their hats, whilst now and then a woman of the older generation crossed herself.

The pageant slowly took its way towards the cemetery in all the glory of the sun, the spring, the bursting trees, and all the pomp of circumstance. Nothing was wanting but a human note to make the scene pathetic and as if someone really sorrowed for the man for whom so much was being done. It seemed as if, even in death, wealth, state, and rank had triumphed, and that there was a death we must all die, and yet another for the great, distinct in essence. Rank, wealth and state, science and progress, and all the gods that we have made and worship, and to whom we call for help in our necessity, oblivious they are all our own creation, appeared for this once only to have listened to our prayers and taken out death's sting, all was so glorious and so well arranged.

Just where the Calle de Olózaga runs down to Recoletos, in the full view of all Madrid, when the whole pageant was about to pass in all its majesty and pomp, a humble hearse, drawn by two shambling horses that looked as if they had originally been black, but had turned rusty-brown from want of food and care, coming out from a side street found its passage cut off by the troops. It stood forlornly waiting to go by, with the light wooden canopy above the open body of the hearse swaying a little on its four flimsy posts as the tired horses breathed. The cheaply put together coffin, with its great yellow cross upon the lid, appeared about to fall to pieces as it lay scorching in the sun, and the brown rug about the driver's knees was worn so threadbare that it would have been a mere mockery to put it upon one of the apocalyptic horses in the hearse to cover him at night. The little band of mourners in their ordinary clothes, most of them with their cloaks about them — the cloak hides everything — stood huddled round the hearse and horses as they waited, as if in parody of the rich funeral that had stopped them on their way to lay their brother in the ground, and to return to work.

The Civil Guards guarding the corners of the streets, perhaps as it were by intuition that the need of the humble dead, or at the least that of his mourning friends, was greater than that of those following the body of the minister, signed to them to pass on. The driver of the rusty hearse, who had been looking interestedly at the assembled troops, whipped up his horses, and, as the soldiers made an opening in their ranks, shambled and shuffled through the line. The ranks closed, swallowing the dilapidated hearse, and blotted out the straggling band of mourners, leaving their brief and humble passage through the street but a mere vision stamped for ever on the mind, just as when at a theatre a scene gets stuck during a moving passage on the stage and leaves a carpenter or two, bareheaded and perspiring at their work, full in the public gaze.

After the brief halt the procession once more started, winding about like a great boa-constrictor through the streets. Then it too disappeared, leaving a cloud of dust still floating in the air and powdering the fresh young leaves upon the trees. In the far distance a dull sound of muffled music now and then was heard, and the faint rumbling of the wheels of the artillery upon the ill-paved streets. The people slowly disappeared, and once again the very loyal, noble, and crowned city resumed its wonted air of a vast wind-swept steppe on which a town had grown by accident, still keeping recollections of the time when it was known but as a hunting-ground, good for both bears and swine. Lastly, when all the troops had slowly ridden and marched back, the soldiers sitting carelessly upon their horses and talking in the ranks, and when the last of the interminable string of cabs and carriages had left the Embassy, after having stopped a moment to let black-coated men descend and leave the all-healing card with a black edge, a creaking noise was heard. Up the now silent and deserted Castellana came a rough bullock-cart drawn by two dark Castilian oxen, bearing a block of stone. The oxen moved relentlessly as fate, swaying a little to one side and the other, each looking at his mate with his large, limpid eyes, either from love or else to see he pulled his fair amount upon the yoke. Slowly and imperturbably they passed, bearing their burden for some architect to go on building up a world from which the new-made equals had just departed, each having laid his stone.

Hope

A Sailor (Old Style)

He was, I think, my earliest recollection of the distinct personality of a man. No one, it appeared to me, could ever have been half as strong, or half as impervious to cold, as he was. I can still see him in my mind's eye, when I had to accompany him in a Sunday walk in the breezy little watering-place where we usually passed the winter — striding along, not with long steps, after the fashion of my other relations, who were mostly sportsmen before their Lord, but with a short, rapid, decided gait, as if he half expected the esplanade might pitch, under the influence of the perpetual northerly winds which swept across the strait.

My brother and I used to trot shivering beside him, and stand huddled up with misery, when he met and hailed some other old sea-going craft such as himself, who was now safely harboured. He never, as far as I can remember, wore a greatcoat, nor did his large, muscular, hairy but well-kept hands ever grow red with cold. On his fourth finger, above his wedding-ring, he wore a large, antique cornelian, with the head of a Roman emperor or Greek philosopher cut deeply in the stone.

Somehow or other this ring and his strong, hairy hands set one a-thinking (in those days) upon the Spanish Main; upon long, raking schooners with tapering masts and a mere rail for bulwarks; on barracoons and slaves; on the Blue Mountains and Port Royal; on Yellow Jack, and on enormous sharks that followed boats, their dorsal fins emerging now and then as a perpetual *memento mori* to the crew, who dressed in huge wide trousers and pigtails to a man. All had great, hairy hands, well set with heavy rings beaten out on a marlinespike from a doubloon. No ship could anchor at Spithead without his knowing it at once. Sometimes he would ask one of the longshoremen her name, and get the answer: "As far as I makes out, she be the *Warrior* the *Black Prince*, or one o' that class, admiral." He, after shutting up with a click the telescope which he had borrowed from the longshoreman, would hand it back to him with a "thankee," and perhaps remark, "Yes, yes, fine class of ships those are, better than that sea-coffin in which I saw poor Cooper Coles go off on his last cruise."

We, that is my brother and myself, who all the time had stood and shivered on the pier, our heels just fitting neatly into the cracks between the planks, assented cheerfully, for naturally we knew most of the ships of that remote, long-buried period, at least by name, and had heard often from the admiral the story of the ill-fated *Captain* and how she turned turtle in a stormy night outside Corcubión, on nearing Finisterre. The tale was ever fresh to us, and when it came to the episode of several men clambering upon her bottom, and there hearing the stifling stokers scream through the keelson valves, we felt we had been there.

The admiral had passed his twelfth or thirteenth birthday at sea (in the old *Barham*), and since that time, till he had made his final landfall in the Isle of Wight, had always been at sea. The suns and winds of forty years had tanned him a fine, clear brown, without a patch of red; nothing in after life altered the colour of his skin, neither the summer heat nor the winter cold had power either to deepen or to redden it, and looking at him you divined at once that he had walked hundreds of miles upon ships' decks, during the long commissions of his youth, when ships were months at sea. He used to tell us, how after three years, chiefly in Marmorice Bay, or just off Acre, he had anchored at Spithead on Sunday and "gone ashore, my boys, on Monday to see my mother, who lived at Gosport, and on Thursday night I was officer of the middle watch (in the old *Castor*) going down Channel on a three years' cruise. Not time to get my linen washed, and only managed to get my traps aboard, out of the old *Pyramus*, just as the *Castor* getting under weigh [sic]. Quick work! Oh, yes! Times have altered since those days. . . . I never saw my poor old mother after that, as I was transferred from the *Castor* stayed six years out in the West Indies. Sailors were sailors then." They were indeed, and when one looks back on their lives one does not wonder that they were a race apart, and certainly the admiral was as far removed from a mere landsman as it was possible to be. He had something of candour and simplicity, combined with a shrewd common sense, which showed itself in unexpected ways and which you half expected, when you looked at his sturdy build and his immense square head, thatched with perennial grey hair and set in bushy whiskers, which early in his life had turned snow white, but yet conveyed no look of age.

Born during the French War, in which his father fought, he touched with one hand, as it were, the fighting captains of an older age, having passed all his youth, as they had theirs, eating salt pork and junk, and biscuits which he tapped upon the gunroom table to knock the weevils out. So much of the old time he had, he never could endure to see fresh water wasted, but would exclaim: "I cannot bear to see it run away to waste, nor would you had you been like myself upon two pints a day down in low latitudes. Two pints a day, boys, for washing and cooking, and I had to hold my nose when I drank it without a dash of rum." With the other hand, so to speak, he touched not the present but the days of the transition navy. Not of course with his own goodwill, but by force of circumstances.

Standing beside him on a little undercliff which looks out over Spithead, thirty-five, or was it five-and-forty, years ago, I still can hear him say: "Yes, there lies my old ship the *Edgar*, a hulk like her old captain, and that little paddle-flopping thing" (pointing with his glass to an Admiralty tender) "is the tin-kettle sort of thing that takes her place." Why he brought up in the cramped, hilly, sandy, stucco-built watering-place in which he lived, with its long ranges of rubble walls stuck with glass bottles, its pill-box houses, shut in by hedges of dusty bay and laurestinus, I never understood. Time could not change its infinite vulgarity, nor has it changed it in the least, as I am told.

It still lies facing north, a veritable wind-trap with its two piers, one made of wood, the other fashioned, as I imagine, out of tin, stretching out far into the sea, and giving it an air as of a kind of ship. Perhaps he was attracted by that air as of a ship, perhaps it was because it offered an easy access to Portsmouth dockyard, to which the admiral used to gravitate occasionally to see new ships and to compare them disparagingly with the old, in the same way that farmers gravitate towards the nearest market-town to watch the price of corn.

Well can I see the place, looking down through a vista of long years, with rows and rows of invalid bath-chairs moored up outside the pier. The shops, now probably long altered, I could enter one by one, and ask for things that I remember as a boy, especially of the jeweller at the first corner of the chief street, on the left (going up from the pier), in which a red enamel watch, with a dog in rather brassy-looking gold, hung in the window, as it appeared, for all created time. The arcade, in which glass bottles filled with sand from Alum Bay jostled shell baskets, and boats constructed never to sail with any kind of wind, which fell helpless on their broadsides as soon as they were launched, must surely still be there. It had, as I remember, a mysterious annexe, behind the veil (of mystery) so to speak, in which displayed on a raised staging, such as one sees in an old-fashioned greenhouse now and then, were pincushions, cases for needles, and yard measures in which the tape was hidden in a shell. Over both "cades," such was the name we and our bold compeers had given to them, presided damsels with long ringlets, dressed in black gowns, with linen cuffs and collars, the latter fastened at their necks bv a neat artificial bow of ribbon either rose-pink or blue.

Churches, of course, abounded in the place, all very low as regards ritual, and in them admirals and generals galore repeated the responses fervidly in voices of command. In one of these the admiral was a churchwarden, why I could not make out, as he had generally something disparaging to say of clergymen; though, I believe, he held religious naval views, knowing the articles of war enjoined attention upon public worship, in a disciplinary way. So, neatly dressed in a well-cut frock-coat, which he referred to as a "jimmy-swinger," he would devoutly look into his hat for a few moments when he entered church, and then compose himself square by the lifts and braces in his seat, and opening his Prayer Book, which he took out of a hassock with practicable front, assume an air as of a criticising worship — that is of criticism towards the clergyman, but of devout belief in the church service, until the sermon time. This always irritated him, so when the time arrived to carry round the plate, he would step busily out into the aisle looking unfeignedly relieved, doing his duty like an officer and a gentleman, crossing his fellow-churchwarden in an elaborate sort of maze as they met at the lectern. There they fell into line, advancing bowing to the altar-rails, where they gave up their plates. When he came back and took his seat, he usually informed us underneath his breath as to the probable amount collected, commenting freely on the sums contributed in a low grumbling way.

This sort of Pyrrhic dance, in which the admiral took a part each Sunday morning, as it were half against his will, just as a rabbit lacks the power to run before a weasel, was a delight to us as boys, and sometimes during its execution, even in the sacred edifice, built as it was according to the canons of congregational Gothic, without a clerestory and with the roof jammed flat upon the walls, we used to pinch each other and murmur an absurd old negro song, with the refrain, "Cross over, Jonathan; figure in, Jemima," as the churchwardens waltzed through the aisle.

Most of the day the admiral sat painting in water-colours, an art which he had learned in youth, and been confirmed in by having taken the first prize at the old Naval College some fifty years ago. It gave him infinite enjoyment, and he filled sketch-book after sketch-book with ships and sailors, brigs, schooners, yawls, and *chasse-marées*, luggers, feluccas, and Bahama boats, barges, canoes, caïques, and anything that sailed. His colouring was muddy and his seas wooden and opaque, so that the craft appeared to sit upon blue boards, but still were life-like, each rope and every sail being depicted in its proper place, a fact he would remark upon with some complacency in talking of his work.

Nothing would please him better than to sit down and copy sea-pieces, which occupation often took him weeks, and when at last concluded, threw quite a novel look on the original, for he corrected any errors in the rigging, now and then putting the ship upon a different tack, and adding here and there a rock, or lighthouse, if it should come into his mind.

Landscape he seldom painted; but when he did, looked on himself apparently in the light of a pivot, for generally his pictures turned out panoramic and so minute that the first time I entered Lisbon I knew the harbour from the squat Tower of Bélem to the Ajuda Palace, with every street and a percentage of the houses, from plans that he had made. I believe that had I gone to any harbour in the Levant, starting at Malta and finishing in Marmorice, I might have, though a landsman, taken in a ship without a pilot, so well I knew the lighthouses, capes, rocks, and castles in each and every port.

The morning's work achieved and the great yellow goblet of Bohemian glass, in which he always dipped his brushes, emptied, and all his paints and apparatus safely bestowed in cupboards, like the lockers of a ship, that is the lockers of a ship of those days, and lunch over, the admiral generally went for a walk. If it was blowing fresh from the north-west, the prevailing wind of the delectable half seaport, half watering-place, he walked upon the pier. Young ladies in tarpaulin hats and blue serge jerseys promenaded up and down showing as much as was convenient of their ankles, and each one with her baronet in tow, for I should say, though peers were scarce, that baronets abounded in the town, each with his single eye-glass in his eye; for in those days all self-respecting men looked out upon their fellows, as it were, darkling, through a pane of glass. The admiral cared for none of these things, but only looked upon the pier as, in the summer, a good sketching-ground, and in the winter as a sort of deck on which to snuff into his frame the odour of the sea.

We looked upon a walk upon the pier in weather such as this with terror, for the admiral was sure to stop and say to some old mariner, one in especial, Josiah Southcote, a Plymouth Brother and the owner of a wherry called the *Pearl*: "Nice day for a sail, Southcote," and then we trembled in our shoes. Sometimes the owner of the abominable craft in which we passed so many hours limp and sea-green, as he leaned up against a sail, dressed in blue pilot-cloth as thick as a thin plank, a brownish duffel shirt, sea-booted to the knees, and with his loose blue trousers coming close to his armpits, supported by stout leather braces about a foot in length, would answer:

"Lor, admiral, it does blow a leetle fresh for the young gentlemen." This sometimes was a respite, and at others served but as an incentive, and we used to put to sea, seated down in a sort of well, where we saw nothing, but at the same time received plenty of salt water down our backs, shivering miserably. At times one or the other of us steered, jamming the *Pearl* about across the Solent, in the agonies of sea-sickness, till we relapsed upon the seat inert and miserable. Still I believe we liked it, and I am certain that the admiral enjoyed it hugely, saying it did us twice the good of any medicine; and as for Southcote, of course, it was his business, and so we all were pleased.

All these slight foibles and an infinity of tales he had about the "Nix Mangiare" stairs of Malta, Dignity Balls in Kingston, or Port Royal and the like, were but excrescences upon the bark. The tree was of the sort from which the Navy of old times was built — round, honest, and English to the core.

All novelties were his abomination, and so he hated double-"taupsles" from the bottom of his soul, and yet would frequently condemn Cunningham's reefing patent, which he declared was a mere lubberly affair more fitted to a blind than to a sail, which it was sure to wear to tatters at the bunt, and carry spars away.

Quite naturally he never could pronounce a single word in any foreign language so that any one could recognise it, with the exception of Portuguese, which he spoke pretty fluently, having acquired it, I suppose, in theatres and cafés about Lisbon during the days in which he laboured at the minute, ingenious plan in water-colours which had been so useful to me in making my first landfall on that coast. Treated as he had been, during the most part of his sea time, to all the rigours of the Admiralty, now freezing off Newfoundland, and again melting off St. Helena or

Port Royal; lacking advancement always, and seeing others younger than himself put over him, by intent or chance, he never grumbled at his luck. In fact, I think, he thought he was a lucky man always to have been employed, and to have been flag-captain in the Channel for a brief space of time. Of such as he was, is the kingdom of the sailor's heaven, that is, if single-mindedness and kindness, with a high sense of honour and a charity which though it naturally began at home extended to the limits of his world, entitle any man to a free pass.

No one whom I have met had such a large collection of "forebitters" in his repertory. Not that he ever sang, as far as I know; but on the other hand he whistled all the day, between his teeth, just like the wind between the hinges of a door, which habit made some people nervous, but to me seemed natural, as natural as it was to the longshore-men about the port to chew tobacco or to hitch up their slacks. When out of doors, especially when walking on the pier or seated in the abominable *Pearl* wherry, he hummed in a low voice such lyrics of the sea as "Tom's gone to 'ello!", or the adventures of poor Reuben Renzo, who, if I recollect, shipped in a whaler and underwent strange things. These "chanties," if he caught Mr. Southcote looking at him, or observed that we were dwelling on the words with interest, anxiously waiting for the verses which ended in an oath, he stopped at once and usually essayed to turn to ridicule, saying that no one sang them nowadays. This certainly was true; but still they photographed themselves upon my memory, one in especial, which told of something in the French wars and had a chorus, which I can hear occasionally (in my mind's ear) during the piano passages at an opera. It was as follows:—

> The little *Weazel* brought up the rear,
> Her guns and quarters being clear,
> The guns being primed ready for to discharge,
> She went through the fleet like a twelve-oared barge.

This song, in my opinion as a boy, went far to constitute a sort of apostolic succession from Sir Cloudesley Shovel, from Drake and Frobisher, and from the other worthies, who, as the old sea phrase goes, entered the services through the hawseholes and by degrees got aft. I do not think the fact of his full repertory of old sea songs was probably the reason of his being made a magistrate, the people of the place most likely never having heard of Fletcher of Saltoun and his dictum that he cared not who made a nation's laws as long as he could write its songs. Truth in the abstract (such as the above) seldom appeals to those who dwell in watering-places.

Thus I am forced to think (against my reason) that in some way or other the mere fact of the admiral's patent honesty had recommended him to the mysterious powers who appoint magistrates, for I am certain no one ever lived less capable of pushing himself to any kind of place. Once duly on the bench, "a beak" as he himself would say, he must have been rather a thorn in the sides of all his fellow-magistrates, who generally were dissenting tradesmen, with an occasional Low Church general of marked religious views. The admiral's view of law in general (with the exception of mutiny and piracy on the high seas) was that the culprit was a poor devil whom it was best to handle gently, remembering all are frail. Indeed, he gave great scandal, in the case of a woman whom he referred to as "a poor whore," charged with solicitation, or prostitution, or some one or another of the lesser misdemeanours of that sort, by saying, "After all, it took two people to commit the fault." Sound reasoning in its way, and human, and of a kind that law-givers often forget, having grown too old or become too circumspect for any cakes and ale.

About this time, for nothing, even in watering-places, succeeds so well as does success, certain fly-drivers and bath-chairmen began to trim their whiskers after the pattern of the admiral's. Whether they did it as a compliment to him for his humanity upon the bench, or only from the fact of his promotion to that elevated seat, is difficult to say. Perhaps it was as theologians tell us, that mankind must always worship something or another, and when we worship it is natural to wish to look as like as possible to those whom we adore. No speculation of that kind, I think, entered the admiral's head. In fact I am sure of it, remembering a story of a chaplain in a ship that he once sailed in, whose captain having heard a sermon upon Faith, in a disciplinary manner called the preacher into his cabin and commanded him next Sunday to hold forth on Works, or never preach again. "A damned good order," he was wont to say, after referring to the episode; not that in any way himself did he reject the spiritual side of things, as his assiduous carrying round of the plate went far to testify.

No oak could have been stauncher than he was, so that when first we noticed that he began to fail, it struck us with surprise, and when we saw that he was, so to speak, preparing to set sail, leaving each day some of the lumber that would have been of no use to him on his voyage, it seemed impossible. Clearly it was unjust that he must go and join the other admirals and generals whom he had seen drop off, as it were, naturally, leaving the watering-place as little altered as if they had but swaggered down the pier, and then forgotten to come back.

Time touched him tenderly. At first but shortening the area of his walks, intensifying gout; then by degrees forbidding his excursions in the *Pearl*, a deprivation which he endured with the more equanimity because Josiah Southcote had for some time rested in the churchyard, his sailings over, his ropes all flemished down, and with "affliction sore" inscribed upon the headstone, which bore a cable twisting round the rim.

What actually took him away I cannot recollect. The kind of man he was, ought to have died at sea and been committed to the deep, in the sure hope of joining Drake and Frobisher, upon some main where there is always a fair wind. I helped to lay him in his coffin and to cross the strong, brown, hairy hands upon his breast, and I remember wishing that he could just have waited long enough to see a red Aurora Borealis which lit the sky upon the night he died, for I am sure he would have said that it was most unusual to see the Northern Lights below some latitude or other, or something of the kind.

Hope

Mirahuano

Why Silvio Sanchez got the name of Mirahuano was difficult to say. Perhaps for the same reason that the Arabs call lead "the light," for certainly he was the blackest of his race, a tall, lop-sided negro, with elephantine ears, thick lips, teeth like a narwhal's tusks, and Mirahuano is a cottony, white stuff used to fill cushions, and light as thistledown. Although he was so black and so uncouth, he had the sweetest smile imaginable, and through his eyes, which at first sight looked hideous, with their saffron-coloured whites, there shone a light, as if a spirit chained in the dungeon of his flesh was struggling to be free. A citizen of a republic in which by theory all men were free and equal by the law, the stronger canon enacted by humanity, confirmed by prejudice, and enforced by centuries of use, had set a bar between him and his white brethren in the Lord which nothing, neither his talents, lovable nature, nor the esteem of everyone who knew him, could ever draw aside. Fate having doubly cursed him with a black skin and an aspiring intellect, he passed his life just as a fish might live in an aquarium, or a caged bird, if they had been brought up to think intelligently on their lost liberty.

The kindly customs of the republic, either derived from democratic Spain or taken unawares from the gentler races of the New World, admitted him, partly by virtue of his talents, for he was born a poet, in a land where all write verses, on almost equal terms to the society of men. Still there were little differences that they observed as if by instinct, almost involuntarily, due partly to the lack of human dignity conspicuous in his race; a lack which in his case, as if the very powers of nature were in league against him, seemed intensified, and made him, as it were, on one hand an archetype, so negroid that he almost seemed an ape, and yet in intellect superior to the majority of those who laughed at him. No one was ever heard to call him Don, and yet the roughest muleteer from Antióquia claimed and received the title as a right, as soon as he had made sufficient money to purchase a black coat.

In the interminable sessions in the *cafés*, where men sat talking politics by hours, or broached their theories at great length, on poetry, on international law, on government, on literature and art, with much gesticulation, and with their voices raised to their highest pitch — for arguments are twice as cogent when delivered shrilly and with much banging on the table — the uncouth negro did not suffer in his pride, for there he shouted with the rest, and plunged into a world of dialectics with the best of them. His Calvary came later, for when at last the apologetic Genoese who kept the *café* politely told his customers that it was time to close, and all strolled out together through the arcaded, silent streets built by the Conquerors, and stood about for a last wrangle in the plaza, under the China trees, as sometimes happened, one or two would go away together to finish off their talk at home. Then Mirahuano silently would walk away, watching the fireflies flash about the bushes, and with a friendly shout of "Buenas noches, Mirahuano" ringing in his ears from the last of his companions as they stood on the threshold of their houses, holding the door wide open by the huge iron knocker, screwed high up, so that a man upon his mule could lift it easily.

Beyond that threshold he was never asked except on business, for there dwelt the white women, who were at once his adoration and despair. With them no talents, no kindliness or generosity of character, had any weight. They treated him, upon the rare occasions when he recited verses of his own composition at some function, with grave courtesy, for it was due to their own self-respect to do so, but as a being of another generation to themselves, who had, for so their priests informed them, an immortal soul, which after death might be as worthy of salvation as their own, in its Creator's eyes.

He, though he knew exactly his position, midway between that of the higher animals and man, was yet unable to resist the peculiar fascination that a white woman seems to have for those of coloured blood. Those of his friends who had his interests at heart, and were admirers of his talents, argued in vain, and pointed out that he was certain to bring trouble on his head if he attempted to presume upon his education and tried to be accepted as a man.

His means permitted him to live a relatively idle life, and as he read all kinds of books in French and Spanish, his intellect always expanded, and it was natural enough that he should think himself the equal of the best, unless he happened to take up a looking-glass and saw the injustice which from his birth both God and man had wrought upon him. As now and then he published poems, which, in a country where all write, were still above the average of those his brethren in the Muses penned (for all the whiteness of their skins), his name was noised abroad, and he was styled in newspapers the Black Alcæus, the Lute of Africa, and a variety of other epithets, according to the lack of taste of those who make all things ridiculous which their fell pens approach.

The Floral Games were due. On such occasions poets write on themes such as "To the Immortal Memory of the Liberator," or dedicate their lyrics to the "Souls of those who fell at Mancavélica," or simply head their stuff "Dolores," "Una Flor Marchita," or something of the sort. Poets of all dimensions leave their counting-houses, banks, regiments, and public offices, and with their brows all "wreathed in roses," as the local papers say, flock to the "flowery strife." All are attired in black, all wear tall hats, and all bear white kid gloves, sticky with heat, and generally a size or two too large for those who carry them.

Each poet in the breast-pocket of his long frock-coat has a large roll of paper in which in a clear hand are written out the verses that are to make his name immortal and crown his brow with flowers.

Now and again their hands steal furtively to touch the precious scrolls, just as a man riding at night in dangerous country now and then feels at the butt of his revolver to assure himself that it is there, when his horse pricks his ears or any of the inexplicable, mysterious noises of the night perplex and startle him. On this occasion, after the other sports, the running at the ring, the feats of horsemanship, in which men stopped their horses short before a wall, making them rear and place their feet upon the top, the tailing of the bulls, and all the other feats which Spanish Americans love to train their horses to perform, were over, the poets all advanced. In the fierce sun they marched, looking a little like a band of undertaker's mutes at an old-fashioned funeral, and stood in line before the jury, and each man in his turn read out his verses, swelling his voice, and rolling all the adjectives, like a delicious morsel, on his tongue. The audience now and then burst out into applause, when some well-worn and well-remembered tag treating of liberty, calling upon the Muses for their help, or speaking of the crimson glow, like blood of the oppressor, which tinged the Andean snows, making them blush incarnadine, or when a stanza dwelling on alabaster bosoms, teeth white as pearls, and eyes as black as those the Houris flash in Paradise, struck their delighted ears. All read and stood aside to wait, looking a little sourly on their fellow-competitors, or with their eyes fixed on a girl, the daughter of a Senator, who, dressed in white, sat in a box beside her father, ready to crown the successful poet with a limp wreath of flowers. The last to read was Mirahuano, and the Master of the Ceremonies, after due clearing of his throat, read out his title, "Movements of the Soul." Holding his hat in his left hand, and with the perspiration, which in a negro looks white and revolting to our eyes, standing in beads upon his face, and in the thick and guttural tones of all his race, the poet nervously began.

At first the audience maintained that hostile air which every audience puts on to those it does not know. This gradually gave place to one of interest, as it appeared the verses all ran smoothly; and this again altered to interest as the figure of the uncouth negro grew familiar to them. As he read on, tracing the movements of the soul, confined and fettered in the flesh, lacking advancement in its due development owing to circumstances affecting not itself, but the mere prison of the body, a prison that it must endure perforce, so that it may be born, and which it leaves unwillingly at last, so strong is habit, even to the soul, the listeners recognised that they were listening to a poet, and gazed upon him in astonishment, just as the men of Athens may have gazed on the mean-looking little Jew, who, beckoning with his head, after the manner of the natural orator, compelled their silence in the Agora. The poet finished in a blaze of rhetoric after the fashion that the Latin race in the republics of America demands, depicting a free soul, freed from the bonds that race, sex, or conditions have imposed on it, free to enjoy, to dare, to plan, free to work out its own salvation, free to soar upwards and to love.

He ceased, and a loud "Viva!" rent the air, and though some of the men of property were evidently shocked at the implied intrusion of a mere negro soul into an Empyrean where their own would soon have atrophied, the poor and all the younger generation — for in America, whatever men become in after life, in youth they are all red republicans — broke out into applause.

Long did the jury talk the poems over, weighing judiciously the pros and cons, but from the first it was quite clear that Mirahuano's composition would receive most votes.

Again the Master of the Ceremonies stood up, and in dead silence proclaimed the prize had been adjudged to Señor Sanchez, and that he was requested to step forward and be crowned.

Shoving his papers hastily into his pocket, and clinging to his hat, just as a drowning sailor clutches fast a plank, the poet shuffled up towards the box in which the jury sat, and stood half proudly, half shamefacedly, to listen to the set oration which the President of the Floral Games stood ready to pronounce. Clearing his throat, he welcomed to Parnassus' heights another poet. He was proud that one of their own town had won the prize. The Muses all rejoiced; Apollo had restrung his lyre and now stretched out his hand to welcome in the son of Africa. The eternal verities stood once more justified; liberty, poetry, and peace had their true home in the Republic. Europe might boast its Dantes and Shakkispers, its Lopes, Ariostos, and the rest, but Costaguano need not fear their rivalry whilst poets such as Mira — he should say as Silvio Sanchez — still raised their pæans to the great and indivisible.

He could say more, much more, but words, what were they in the face of genius? — so he would bring his discourse to a close by welcoming again the youngest brother of the lyre into the Muses' court. Now he would call upon the fairest of the fair, the Señorita Nieves Figueroa, to place the laurel on the poet's brow.

Applause broke out rather constrainedly, and chiefly amongst those who by the virtue of their station were able to express their feelings easily, really liked Mirahuano, and possibly admired the poem they had heard, that is as much of it as they had understood.

Dressed all in white, with a mantilla of white lace upon her head, fastened high on her hair to a tall comb, shy and yet self-possessed, the Señorita Nieves Figueroa advanced, holding a crown of laurel leaves, with a large silver ornament, shaped like a lyre, in front of it, and with long ribbons of the national colours hanging down behind. Her jet-black hair was glossy as a raven's wing. Her olive skin and almond eyes were thrown into relief by her white clothes, and gave her somewhat of the air of a fly dropped in milk, or a blackbird in snow. Clearly she was embarrassed by the appearance of the man she had to crown, who, on his side, stood quivering with excitement at his victory and the approach of the young girl.

Raising the crown, she placed it on the negro's head, where it hung awkwardly, half covering his eyes, and giving him the look as of a bull when a skilled bull-fighter has placed a pair of banderillas in his neck. Murmuring something about the Muses, poetry, and a lyre, she gracefully stepped back, and Mirahuano shuffled off, having received, as he himself observed, "besides the wreath, an arrow in his heart."

From that day forth he was her slave, that is, in theory, for naturally he never had the chance to speak to her, although no doubt she heard about his passion, and perhaps laughed with her friends about the ungainly figure she had crowned. Debarred from all chance of speech with her he called the "objective of his soul," dressed in his best, he called each Thursday morning at Señor Figueroa's house to deliver personally a copy of his verses tied with blue ribbons at the door. The door was duly opened and the verses handed in for months, and all the town knew and talked of the infatuation of the negro poet, who for his part could have had no illusions on the subject, for from the moment of the Floral Games he had never spoken to the girl except, as he said, "by the road of Parnassus," which after all is a path circuitous enough in matters of the heart.

His life was passed between the little house, buried in orange and banana trees, where his old mother, with her head wrapped in a coloured pocket-handkerchief, sat all the day, balanced against the wall in an old, high-backed chair, watching his sisters pounding maize in a high, hardwood mortar, with their chemises slipping off their shoulders, and the Café del Siglo, where all the poets used to spend their time.

Poets and verse-makers were as much jumbled up in people's minds in the republic as they are here, and anyone who had a rhyming dictionary and the sufficient strength of wrist to wield a pen, wrote reams of stuff about the pangs of love, the moon, water, and flashing eyes, with much of liberty and dying for their native land. When once they fell into the habit, it was as hard of cure as drinking, especially as most of them had comfortable homes, though they all talked of what they underwent in the Bohemia to which they were condemned. For hours they used to sit and talk, reading their verses out to one another or with their hats drawn down upon their brows to signify their state.

To these reunions of the soul, for so they styled them, Mirahuano came, sitting a little diffidently upon his chair, and now and then reciting his own verse, which, to speak truth, was far above the rest of the weak, wordy trash produced so lavishly. As it cost nothing to be kind to him, for he would never take even a cup of coffee, unless he paid for it himself, they used him kindly, letting him sit and read when they were tired, help them to consonants, and generally behave as a light porter to the Muses, as he defined it in his half-melancholy, half-philosophising vein.

One night as they sat late compassionating one another on their past luck, and all declaiming against envy and the indifference of a commercial world, whilst the tired waiters dozed, seated before the tables with their heads resting on the marble tops, and as the flies, mosquitoes, and the "vinchucas" made life miserable, their talk drew round towards the hypothetical Bohemia in which they dreamed they lived. Poor Mirahuano, who had sat silently wiping his face at intervals with a red pocket-handkerchief — for in common with the highest and the lowest of his kind he loved bright colours — drew hear, and sitting down among the poets, listened to their talk. The heavy air outside was filled with the rank perfume of the tropic vegetation. The fireflies flashed among the thickets of bamboos, and now and then a night-jar uttered its harsh note.

In the bright moonlight men slept on the stucco benches in the plaza, with their faces downwards, and the whole town was silent except where now and then some traveller upon his mule passed by, the tick-tack of the footfalls of his beast clattering rhythmically in its artificial pace, and sending up a trail of sparks as it paced through the silent streets. Nature appeared perturbed, as she does sometimes in the tropics, and as if just about to be convulsed in the throes of a catastrophe. Inside the *café* men felt the strain, and it seemed natural to them, when Mirahuano, rising to his feet, his lips blue, and his face livid with emotion, exclaimed, "Talk of Bohemia, what is yours to mine! Mine is threefold. A poet, poor, and black. The last eats up the rest, includes them, stultifies you and your lives." He paused, and, no one answering, unconscious that the waiters, awakened by his tones, were looking at him, half in alarm, half in amazement, broke out again. "Bohemia! Think of my life; my very God is white, made in your image, imposed upon my race by yours. His menacing pale face has haunted me from childhood, hard and unsympathetic, and looking just as if He scorned us whom you call His children, although we know it is untrue. Your laws are all a lie. His too, unless it is that you have falsified them in your own interests and to keep us slaves."

Seizing his hat, he walked out of the *café* without a salutation, leaving the company dumb with amazement, looking upon each other as the inhabitants of some village built on the slopes of a volcano long quiescent may look, when from the bowels of the sleeping mountain a stream of lava shoots into the sky. His brothers in the Muses missed him from his accustomed haunts for two or three days, and then a countryman reported he had seen in the backwater of a stream an object which he had thought was a dead bullock or a cow. Wishing to secure the hide, he had lassoed it, and to his great astonishment he found it was the body of a negro, dressed in black clothes, as he said, just as good as those worn by the President. Being of a thrifty turn of mind, he had stripped them off and sold them at a pulperia, when he had dried them in the sun.

It seemed to him fortuitous that a black rascal who in all his life had never done a stroke of work, but walked about just like a gentleman, making a lot of silly rhymes, at last should be of use to a white Christian such as he was himself, white, as the proverb says, on all four sides.

He added, as he stood beside his half-wild colt, keeping a watchful eye upon its eye, and a firm hand upon his raw-hide halter, that as a negro's skin was of no value, he pushed the body back into the stream, and had no doubt that it would soon be eaten up by the caimáns.

The Captive

Somehow or other none of the camp could sleep that night. It may have been that they were hungry, for they were just returning from a bootless attempt to overtake a band of Indians who had carried off the horses from an *estancia* on the Napostá. Night had fallen on them just by the crossing of a river, where a small grove of willows had given them sufficient wood to make a fire, for nothing is more cheerless than the fierce transient flame ("like a nun's love") that cow-dung and dry thistle-stems afford. Although they had not eaten since the morning, when they had finished their last strips of *charqui*, they had a little *yerba*, and so sat by the fire passing the *maté* round and smoking black Brazilian cigarettes.

The stream, either a fork of the Mostazas or the head waters of the Napostá itself, ran sluggishly between its banks of rich alluvial soil. Just at the crossing it was poached into thick mud by half-wild cattle and by herds of mares, for no one rode where they were camped in those days but the Indians, and only they when they came in to burn the settlements. A cow or two which had gone in to drink and remained in the mud to die, their eyes picked out by the *caranchos*, lay swelled to an enormous size, and with their legs sticking out grotesquely, just as a soldier's dead legs stick out upon a battlefield.

From the still, starry night the mysterious noises of the desert rose, cattle coughed dryly as they stood on rising ground, and now and then a stallion whinnied as he rounded up his mares. Vizcachas uttered their sharp bark and tuco-tucos sounded their metallic chirp deep underneath the ground. The flowers of the chañar gave out their spicy scent in the night air, and out beyond the clumps of piquillin and molle, the pampa grass upon the river-bank looked like a troop of ostriches in the moon's dazzling rays.

The Southern Cross was hung above their heads, Capella was just rising, and from a planet a yellow beam of light seemed to fall into the rolling waves of grass, which the light wind just stirred, sending a ghostly murmur through it, as if the sound of surf upon some sea which had evaporated thousands of years ago was echoing in the breeze.

A line of sand-hills ran beside the stream. Below their white and silvery sides the horses, herded by a man who now and then rode slowly to the fire to light a cigarette, grazed on the wiry grass. The tinkling bells of the madrinas had been muffled, as there was still a chance the Indians might have cut the trail, and now and then the horse guard cautiously crawled up the yielding bank and gazed out on the plain, which in the moonlight looked like a frozen lake.

Grouped round the fire were most of the chief settlers on the Sauce Grande, Mostazas, and the Napostá.

The brothers Milburn, who had been merchant sailors, dressed in cord breeches and brown riding-boots, but keeping, as it were, a link with ships in their serge coats, were there, sitting up squarely, smoking and spitting in the fire.

Next to them sat Martin Villalba, a wealthy cattle-farmer and major in the militia of Bahia Blanca. No one had ever seen him in his uniform, although he always wore a sword stuck underneath the girth of his *recao*. The light shone on his Indian features and was reflected back from his long hair, which hung upon his shoulders as black and glossy as the feathers of a crow. As he sat glaring at the blaze he now and then put up his hand and listened, and as he did so, all the rest of those assembled listened as well, the man who had the *maté* in his hand holding it in suspense until Villalba silently shook his head, or, murmuring, "It is nothing," began to talk again. Spaniards and Frenchmen sat side by side with an Italian, one Enrique Clerici, who had served with Garibaldi in his youth, but now was owner of a *pulperia* that he had named "The Rose of the South," and in it hung a picture of his quondam leader, which he referred to as "my saint."

Claraz, the tall, black-bearded Swiss, was there. He had lost one finger by a tiger's bite in Paraguay, and was a quiet, meditative man who had roamed all the continent, from Acapulco down to Punta Arenas, and hoped some day to publish an exhaustive work upon the flora of the Pampa, when, as he said, he found a philanthropic publisher to undertake the loss.

The German, Friedrich Vögel, was book-keeper at an *estancia* called La Casa de Fierro, but being young and a good horseman had joined the others, making a contrast to them as he sat beside the fire in his town clothes, which, though they were all dusty and his trouser-legs coated thick with mud, yet gave him the appearance of being on a picnic, which a small telescope that dangled from a strap greatly accentuated. Since he had started on the trail eight or nine days ago, he had Hispaniolised his name to Pancho Pajaro, which form, as fortune willed it, stuck to him for the remainder of his life in South America. Two cattle-farmers, English by nationality, known as El Facon Grande and El Facon Chico from the respective size of the knives they carried, talked quietly, just as they would have talked in the bow-window of a club, whilst a tall, grey-haired Belgian, handsome and taciturn, was drawing horses' brands with a charred mutton-bone as he sat gazing in the fire. Of all the company he alone kept himself apart, speaking but seldom, and though he had passed a lifetime on the plains, he never adventured his opinion except men asked for it, when it was taken usually as final, for everybody knew that he had served upon the frontier under old General Mancilla in the Indian wars.

A tall, fair, English boy, whose hair, as curly as the wool of a merino sheep, hung round his face and on his neck after the fashion of a Charles II wig, was nodding sleepily.

Exaltacion Medina, tall, thin, and wiry, tapped with his whip upon his boot-leg, on which an eagle was embroidered in red silk.

He and his friend, Florencio Freites, who sat and picked his teeth abstractedly with his long silver-handled knife, were gauchos of the kind who always rode good horses and wore good clothes, though no one ever saw them work, except occasionally at cattle-markings. They both were Badilleros, that is, men from Bahia Blanca, and both spoke Araucano, having been prisoners amongst the Infidel, for their misfortunes as they said, although there were not wanting people who averred that their connection with the Indians had been in the capacity of renegades by reason of their crimes.

Some squatted cross-legged like a Turk, and some lay resting on their elbows, whilst others, propped against their saddles, sat with their eyes closed, but opened them if the wind stirred the trees, just as a sleeping cat peers through its eyelids at an unusual noise.

When the last *maté* had been drunk and the last cigarette end flung into the blazing brands and yet a universal sleeplessness seemed to hang in the air, which came in fierce, hot gusts out of the north, carrying with it a thousand cottony filaments which clung upon the hair and beards of the assembled band, Claraz suggested that it might be as well if someone would tell a story, for it was plain that, situated as they were, no one could sing a song. Silence fell on the group, for most of those assembled there had stories that they did not care to tell. Then the mysterious impulse that invariably directs men's gaze towards the object of their thoughts turned every eye upon the Belgian, who still was drawing brands on the white ashes of the fire with the burnt mutton-bone. Raising his head he said: "I see I am the man you wish to tell the story, and as I cannot sleep an atom better than the rest, and as the story I will tell you lies on my heart like lead, but in the telling may perhaps grow lighter, I will begin at once."

He paused, and taking off his hat, ran his hands through his thick, dark hair, flecked here and there with grey, hitched round his pistol so that it should not stick into his side as he leaned on his elbow, and turning to the fire, which shone upon his face, set in a close-cut, dark-brown beard, slowly began to speak.

"Fifteen — no, wasn't it almost sixteen years ago — just at the time of the great Indian, Malon — invasion, eh? the time they got as far as Tapalquén and burned the *chacras* just outside Tandil, I was living on the Sauce Chico, quite on the frontier. . . . I used to drive my horses into the corral at night and sleep with a Winchester on either side of me. My nearest neighbour was a countryman of mine, young . . . yes, I think you would have called him a young man then. An educated man, quiet and well-mannered, yes, I think that was so . . . his manners were not bad.

"It is his story I shall tell you, not mine, you know. Somehow or other I think it was upon an expedition after the Indians, such as ours to-day, he came upon an Indian woman driving some horses. She had got separated from her husband after some fight or other, and was returning to the tents. She might have got away, as she was riding a good horse . . . piebald it was, with both its ears slit, and the cartilage between the nose divided to give it better wind. Curious the superstitions that they have." Florencio Freites looked at the speaker, nodded and interjected, "If you had lived with them as long as I have you would say so, my friend. I would give something to slit the cartilage of some of their Indian snouts. . . ." No one taking up what he had said, he settled down to listen, and the narrator once again began.

"Yes, a fine horse that piebald, I knew him well, a little quick to mount, but then that woman rode like a gaucho — as well as any man. As I was saying, she might have got away — so said my friend — only the mare of her *tropilla* had not long foaled, and either she was hard to drive or the maternal instinct in the woman was too strong for her to leave the foal behind . . . or she had lost her head or something — you can never tell. When my friend took her prisoner, she did not fight or try to get away, but looked at him and said in halting Spanish, 'Bueno, I am take prisoner, do what you like.' My friend looked at her and saw that she was young and pretty, and that her hair was brown and curly, and fell down to her waist. Perhaps he thought — God knows what he did think. For one thing, he had no woman in his house, for the last, an Italian girl from Buenos Aires had run off with a countryman of her own, who came round selling saints — a *santero*, eh? As he looked at her, her eyes fell, and he could have sworn he saw the colour rise under the paint daubed on her face, but he said nothing as they rode back towards his rancho, apart from all the rest. They camped upon the head waters of the Quequén Salado, and to my friend's astonishment, when he had staked out his horse and hers and put the hobbles on her mare, so that her *tropilla* might not stray, she had lit the fire and put a little kettle on to boil. When they had eaten some tough *charqui*, moistened in warm water, she handed him a *maté* and stood submissively filling it for him till he had had enough. Two or three times he looked at her, but mastered his desire to ask her how it was that she spoke Spanish and why her hair was brown.

"As they sat looking at the fire, it seemed somehow as if he had known her all his life, and when a voice came from another fire, 'You had better put the hobbles on that Indian mare, or she'll be back to the *querencia* before the moon is down,' it jarred on him, for somehow he vaguely knew his captive would not try to run away.

"So with a shout of 'All right, I'll look out,' to the other fires, he took his saddle and his ponchos, and saying to the Indian woman, 'Sleep well, we start at daybreak,' left her wrapped up in saddle-cloths, with her feet towards the fire. An hour before the dawn the camp was all astir, but my friend, though an early riser, found his captive ready, and waiting with a *maté* for him, as soon as he got up and shook the dew out of his hair, and buckled on his spurs.

"All that day they rode homewards, companions leaving them at intervals, as when they struck the Saucecito, crossed the Mostazas, just as it rises at the foot of the Sierra de la Ventana, or at the ruined rancho at the head waters of the Napostá. Generally, as the various neighbours drove their *tropillas* off, they turned and shouted farewell to the Indian woman and my friend, wishing them a happy honeymoon or something of the kind. He answered shortly, and she never appeared to hear, although he saw that she had understood. Before they reached his rancho he had learned a little of the history of the woman riding by his side. She told him, as Spanish slowly seemed to make its way back to her brain, that she was eight-and-twenty, and her father had been an *estanciero* in the province of San Luis; who with her mother and her brothers had been killed in an invasion of the Indians eight years ago, and from that time she had lived with them, and had been taken by a chief whose name was Huinchan, by whom she had three sons. All this she told my friend mechanically, as if she had been speaking of another, adding, 'The Christian women pass through hell amongst the *Infidel*.' " The narrator paused to take a *maté*, and Anastasio sententiously remarked,

"Hell, yes, double-heated hell: do you remember Ché, that Chilian girl you bought from that Araucan whose eye one of the Indian girls gouged out?" His friend Florencio showed his teeth like a wolf and answered, "Caspita, yes; do you remember how I got even with her? Eye for an eye, tooth for a tooth, as I once heard a priest say was God's law!" The *maté* finished, the Belgian once again took up his tale.

"When my friend reached his home he helped his captive off her horse, hobbled her mare, and taking her hand led her into the house and told her it was hers.

"She was the least embarrassed of the two, and from the first took up her duties as if she had never known another life.

"Little by little she laid aside her Indian dress and ways, although she folded carefully and laid by her *chamál*, with the great silver pin shaped like a sun that holds it tight across the breast. Her ear-rings, shaped like an inverted pyramid, she put aside with the scarlet *vichu* that had bound her hair, which when she was first taken hung down her back in a thick mass of curls that had resisted all the efforts of the Indian women, aided by copious dressings of melted ostrich fat, to make straight like their own. Timidly she had asked for Christian clothes, and by degrees became again a Spanish woman, careful about her hair, which she wore high upon her head, careful about her shoes, and by degrees her walk became again the walk she had practised in her youth, when with her mother she had sauntered in the evening through the plaza of her native town, with a light swinging of her hips.

"Her Indian name of Lincomilla gave place once more to Nievés, and in a week or two some of the sunburn vanished from her cheeks.

"All the time of her transformation my friend watched the process as a man may watch the hour-hand on a clock, knowing it moves, but yet unable to discern the movement with his eyes.

"Just as it seems a miracle when on a fine spring morning one wakes and sees a tree which overnight was bare, now crowned with green, so did it seem a miracle to him that the half-naked Indian whom he had captured, swinging her whip about her head and shouting to her horses, had turned into the Señorita Nievés, whilst he had barely seen the change. Something intangible seemed to have grown up between them, invisible, but quite impossible to pass, and now and then he caught himself regretting vaguely that he had let his captive slip out of his hands. Little by little their positions were reversed, and he who had been waited on by Lincomilla found himself treating the Señorita Nievés with all the . . . how you say . . . '*égards*' that a man uses to a lady in ordinary life.

"When his hand accidentally touched hers he shivered, and then cursed himself for a fool for not having taken advantage of the right of conquest the first day that he led the Indian girl into his home. All would have then seemed natural, and he would have only had another girl to serve his *maté*, a link in the long line of women who had succeeded one another since he first drove his cattle into the south camps and built his rancho on the creek. Then came a time when something seemed to blot out all the world, and nothing mattered but the Señorita Nievés, whom he desired so fiercely that his heart stood still when she brushed past him in her household duties; yet he refrained from speaking, kept back by pride, for he knew that, after all, she was in his power in that lone rancho on the plains. Sleeping and waking she was always there. If he rode out upon the *boleada* she seemed to go with him; on his return there she was standing, waiting for him with her enigmatic smile when he came home at night.

"She on her side was quite aware of all he suffered, suffering herself just as acutely, but being able better to conceal her feelings he never noticed it, or saw the shadowy look that long-suppressed desire brings in a woman's eyes. Their neighbours, ordinary men and women, had no idea things were on such an exalted footing, and openly congratulated him on his good luck in having caught an Indian who had turned to a white girl. When he had heard these rough congratulations on his luck, he used to answer shortly, and catching his horse by the head, would gallop out upon the plain and come home tired, but with the same pain gnawing at his heart. How long they might have gone on in that way is hard to say, had not the woman — for it is generally they who take the first step in such things — suddenly put an end to it. Seeing him sitting by the fire one evening, and having watched him follow her with his eyes as she came in and out, she walked up to him and laid her hand upon his shoulder, and as he started and a thrill ran through his veins, bent down her face and pressing her dry lips to his, said, 'Take me,' and slid into his arms.

"That was their courtship. From that time, all up and down the Sauce Chico, the settlers, who looked on love as a thing men wrote about in books, or as the accomplishment of a necessary function without which no society could possibly endure, took a proprietary interest in the lovers, whom they called 'Los de Teruel,' after the lovers in the old Spanish play, who loved so constantly.

"Most certainly they loved as if they had invented love and meant to keep it to themselves. Foolish, of course they were, and primitive, he liking to rush off into Bahia Blanca to buy up all the jewellery that he could find to give her, and she, forgetting all the horrors of her life amongst the Indians, gave herself up to happiness as unrestrained as that of our first mother, when the whole world contained no other man but the one she adored.

"As in a day out on the southern plains, when all is still and the wild horses play, and from the lakes long lines of pink flamingoes rise into the air and seem translucent in the sun, when the whole sky becomes intensest purple, throwing a shadow on the grass that looks as if the very essence of the clouds was falling like a dew, the Indians say that a Pampero must be brewing, and will soon burst with devastating force upon the happy world, so did their love presage misfortune by its intensity."

"A strong north wind is sure to bring a Pampero," interpolated one of the listeners round the fire.

"Yes, that is so, and the Pampero came accordingly," rejoined the story-teller.

"Months passed and still the neighbours talked of them with amazement, being used to see the force of passion burn itself out, just as a fire burns out in straw, and never having heard of any other kind of love except the sort they and their animals enjoyed.

"Then by degrees Nievés became a little melancholy, and used to sit for hours looking out on the Pampa, and then come in and hide her head beneath her black Manila shawl, that shawl my friend had galloped to Bahia Blanca to procure, and had returned within two days, doing the forty leagues at a round gallop all the way.

"Little by little he became alarmed, and feared, having been a man whose own affections in the past had often strayed, that she was tired of him. To all his questions she invariably replied that she had been supremely happy, and for the first time had known love, which she had always thought was but a myth invented by the poets to pass the time away. Then she would cry and say that he was idiotic to doubt her for a moment, then catching him to her, crush him against her heart. For days together she was cheerful, but he, after the fashion of a man who thinks he has detected a slight lameness in his horse, but is not certain where, was always on the watch to try and find out what it was that ailed her, till gradually a sort of armed neutrality took the place of their love. Neither would speak, although both suffered almost as much as they had loved, until one evening as they stood looking out upon the Pampa yearning for one another, but kept apart by something that they felt, rather than knew was there, the woman with a cry threw herself into her lover's arms. Then with an effort she withdrew herself, and choking down her tears, said, 'I have been happy, dearest, happier by far than you can understand, happier than I think it is ever possible to be for any man. Think of my life, my father and my mother killed before my eyes, myself thrown to an Indian whom my soul loathed, then made by force the mother of his children — his and mine. Think what my life has been there in the Tolderias, exposed to the jealousy of all the Indian women, always in danger till my sons were born, and even then obliged to live for years amongst those savages and become as themselves.

" 'Then you came, and it seemed to me as if God had tired of persecuting me; but now I find that He or nature has something worse in store. I am happy here, but then there is no happiness on earth, I think. My children — his and mine — never cease calling me. I must return to them and see, my horses all are fat, the foal can travel, and . . . you must think it has been all a dream, and let me go back to my master — husband — bear him more children, and at last be left to die when I am old, beside some river, like other Indian wives.' She dried her eyes, and gently touching him upon the shoulder, looked at him sadly, saying, 'Now you know, dearest, why it is I have been so sad and made you suffer, though you have loaded me with love. Now that you know I love you more a hundred times than the first day, when, as you used to say, I took you for my own, you can let me go back to my duties and my misery, and perhaps understand.'

"Her lover saw her mind was fixed, and with an effort stammered, 'Bueno, you were my prisoner, but ever since I took you captive I have been your slave. . . . When will you go?'

"Let it be to-morrow, *sangre mia*, and at daybreak, for you must take me to the place where you first saw me; it has become to me as it were a birthplace, seeing that there I first began to live.' Once more he answered, 'Bueno,' like a man in a dream, and led her sadly back into their house.

"Just as the first red streaks of the false dawn had tinged the sky they saddled up without a word.

"Weary and miserable, with great black circles round their eyes, they stood a moment, holding their horses by their *cabrestos*, till the rising sun just fell upon the doorway of the poor rancho where they had been so happy in their love.

"Without a word they mounted, the captive once more turned to Lincomilla, dressed in her Indian clothes, swinging herself as lightly to the saddle as a man. Then gathering the horses all together, with the foal, now strong and fat, running behind its mother, they struck into the plains.

"Three or four hours of steady galloping brought them close to the place where Lincomilla had been taken captive by him who now rode silently beside her, with his eyes fixed on the horizon, like a man in a dream.

" 'It should be here,' she said, 'close to that tuft of sarandis . . . yes, there it is, for I remember it was there you took my horse by the bridle, as if you thought that I was sure to run away, back to the Indians.'

"Dismounting, they talked long and sadly, till Lincomilla tore herself from her lover's arms and once more swung herself upon her horse. The piebald Pingo with the split ears neighed shrilly to the other horses feeding a little distance off upon the plain, then, just as she raised her hand to touch his mouth, the man she was about to leave for ever stooped down and kissed her foot, which rested naked on the stirrup, after the Indian style. 'May the God of the Araucans, to whom you go, bless and encompass you' he cried; 'my God has failed me,' and as he spoke she touched her horse lightly with the long Indian reins. The piebald plunged and wheeled round, and then struck into a measured gallop, as his rider, gathering her horses up before her, set her face westward, without once looking back.

"I . . . that is my friend, stood gazing at her, watching the driven horses first sink below the horizon into the waves of grass, the foal last disappearing as it brought up the rear, and then the horse that Lincomilla rode, inch by inch fade from sight, just as a ship slips down the round edge of the world. Her feet went first, then the *caronas* of her saddle, and by degrees her body, wrapped in the brown *chamál*.

"Lastly, the glory of her floating hair hung for a moment in his sight upon the sky, then vanished, just as a piece of seaweed is sucked into the tide by a receding wave.

"That's all," the story-teller said, and once again began to paint his horses' brands in the wood ashes with his mutton-bone, as he sat gazing at the fire.

Silence fell on the camp, and in the still, clear night the sound of the staked-out horses cropping the grass was almost a relief. None spoke, for nearly all had lost some kind of captive, in some way or other, till Claraz, rising, walked round and laid his hand upon the story-teller's shoulder. "I fear," he said, "the telling of the tale has not done anything to make the weight upon the heart any the lighter.

"All down the coast, as I remember, from Mazatlán to Acapulco, pearl-fishers used to say, unless a man made up his mind to stay below the water till his ears burst, that he would never be a first-rate pearl-diver.

"Some men could never summon up the courage, and remained indifferent pearl-divers, suffering great pain, and able to remain only a short time down in the depths, as their ears never burst. It seems to me that you are one of those . . . but, I know I am a fool, I like you better as you are."

He ceased, and the grey light of dawn fell on the sleepless camp on the north fork of the Mostazas (or perhaps the Napostá); it fell upon the smouldering fire, with Lincomilla's lover still drawing horses' marks in the damp ashes, and on the group of men wrapped in their ponchos shivering and restless with the first breath of day.

Out on the plain, some of the horses were lying down beside their bell-mares. Others stood hanging their heads low between their feet, with their coats ruffled by the dew.

The Fourth Magus

Some ancient writer or another — the Arabs frequently begin a tale "Says somebody" — relates the story of his life and miracles. Balthasar, Gaspar, and Melchior were, as he tells us, kings in Babylon. How Babylon came to be supplied with such a superfluity of kings he does not say, even if he knew why. Still, it was so, for all of them had crowns; rich mantles trimmed with ermine; fine Arab horses with legs as slim as a gazelle's, tails floating in the air, heads like a peacock's, eyes that shot fire, and with a general air as of a hippogriff. In fact these kings had myrrh, frankincense, jewels, furs, scimitars, vessels of richest plate, and everything befitting to their state.

All this I know, for I have seen it all in pictures, and have rejoiced to learn their horses were of a pale sea-green or else of a rich cinnamon, colours quite natural in royal steeds, and blending well into the faint blue landscape of the Umbrian School of painters, who alone had the true vision of these kings. The circumstance that one of them was black was not the least bit disconcerting to the painters (no colour line exists in art), but on the contrary it helped them in their work, by furnishing a contrast to the pale, yellow faces of the other two. As they sat in their palaces, following the usual avocations of their kind, either being occupied in administering injustice or else in watching dancing-girls gyrate, strange news was brought into the town.

Shepherds, all seated on the ground, watching their sheep folded inside a net of ropes, their dogs beside them, and their thoughts fixed on the heavens — as often happens with people of their kind, which in itself accounts why they so often lose their sheep — had seen a wondrous star.

Lustrous and bright as Sirius, redder than Aldebáran, and far more luminous than Zuben-el-Chamali or Altair, it lighted all the sky. Around it was a space as if the other stars had all agreed they were not worthy even to feel its radiance fall upon them, and it appeared to beckon, as the shepherds thought, and move a little towards the West, as if inviting them to follow in its wake.

Night after night the star appeared in the same place, just up above their heads. At last, seeing, as shepherds will, something miraculous in the affair, they left their flocks — for, after all, what is a sheep or two beside so bright a star — and sought out a Wise Man. After consideration and due examination of the case, he solved the mystery, telling them that a mighty prophet would be born, who should raise up the lowly, redress injustices, cast down the powerful, make rough places smooth, and be the champion of the weak the whole world over; and all they had to do was but to follow in the way the star directed them, and it would take them to the place.

Such things not being for the kind of men they were, they went to Babylon, and, walking up and down about the streets, began to tell what they had seen and heard to everyone they met. Little by little the fame of what they said filled all men's minds, and in bazaars and markets, in fondaks, stores, and caravanserais, the wondrous rumour grew.

Lastly, as happens in such cases, now, as in Babylon, it passed the palace gates. The kings were fired with it at once, either being filled with faith and hatred of injustice, things natural to men of their estate, or else impelled by that desire of movement which in kings plays the part imagination plays in poets and sets their blood astir.

So taking horse, and followed by a fitting retinue carrying the presents which the painters of the Umbrian School have seen so well, and have depicted for us in the middle distance of their canvases, they set out on their quest. All the world knows the story of their ride, and how, following the star over the plains, through the defiles of mountains, and across rivers, at last it stopped above the stable in which the ox and ass were feeding, making a nimbus with their warm clover-scented breath round the child's head as it lay sleeping in the crib. Their reward was instant, for they beheld their faith made patent by their work, a thing that few attain, however firmly they believe, and whilst men read the simple story of their brief passage through the scene of history, they still will love them, as long as faith and stars continue and shepherds watch their sheep upon the plains. They saw the birth of God made man, and, after having seen it and adored, became immortal; but the fourth Magus, he who lingered on the road, saw man made God, and is forgotten and unknown to anyone except to those who, like some diving negro, seek their pearls in the unnavigated creeks of ancient chroniclers.

That Nicanor hangs out of fashion on his rusty nail, and Gaspar, Balthasar, and Melchior still are household words, is perhaps natural, for they by faith were justified, and faith is the true royal road to fame. King Nicanor followed the path along which man from the beginning of the world has worn out countless million pairs of shoes, blistered infinities of feet, and quite as naturally has been forgotten by his kind.

This, then, is how the thing fell out.

When the three kings had ridden off upon their quest, King Nicanor was left behind, owing to his horse having cast a shoe. When the Chaldean smith had shod the horse, after considerable delay — for then as now in black-smiths' shops, nothing was ready, and not a single shoe in the whole place would fit — Balthasar, Melchior, and Gaspar had vanished on the plain, and it was almost night. Determining to make at least a start, for being a Wise Man and from the East, where people know the benefit of camping even a league outside the city walls upon the first day of a journey, Nicanor got on his horse and sallied forth, passing the horseshoe arch of the great gate in the town wall towards the west, about an hour before the sun had set.

The camp was pitched just by the side of a wide crossing of a river edged by palm trees and broken into several channels by beds of sand and stones. Right at the crossing the feet of camels and of mules, passing for centuries, had made a well-defined deep track, in which the riders' feet were almost on the ground as they rode through to reach the stream, their horses stumbling occasionally as they struck their feet against the sides. Young date palms springing from the sand struggled against the nibbling of the camels and the mules that snatched a mouthful as they passed. A haze of orange fading into pink outlined the palms upon the farther bank, showing each knot upon their trunks. In the light air the leaves just stirred and made a creaking sound, unlike the whispering of the oaks and beeches of the north. White bones, and here and there a skull, showed where a baggage animal had been released from toil, and round them the sparse grass grew just a little greener, and myriads of the minutest flies crawled in and out between the vertebrae of the dry backbone that would never more bend underneath a pack.

Sitting upon his horse, with one leg crossed upon its neck, the long reins dangling almost to the ground as it hung down its head a little to snatch a mouthful of the grass, the Magus gave directions to his men to pitch his tents.

Quickly the packs were lifted off the mules' and camels' backs, and the tents rose as if by magic from the sandy grass, flecked here and there with tiny jonquils: a sky of flowery stars spread or reflected on the ground.

The evening call to prayer, which Mahomet must have perpetuated, for it could not have sprung into his brain unaided, being in itself a necessary action after the daily battle with the sun, rang out, and for a moment all the camp was prostrate, thanking some god or other for the evening breeze.

Slowly King Nicanor got off his horse, and a black slave tied it up to the rope of camel's hair which, stretched between two stakes, was set before his tent. Its lofty saddle stood up like an island outlined against the deep blue clouds, for nothing broke the horizon to the south but the tents and the feeding animals. As Nicanor sat on a saddle-cloth before his tent thinking upon the wondrous star of which the shepherds had brought tidings, and inwardly determining to push on at the first light of day to catch up his companions, three or four figures came out of the palm grove, and dragging themselves slowly across the sand and grass, stood in a row before him and pointed upwards to the sky with a mute gesture of despair. Famine had wasted them almost beyond the semblance of mankind. Their sunken stomachs and protruding ribs made them look something like a fossil fish embedded in the coal-measures, whilst their thin arms and legs hardly sustained their feet and hands, which looked enormous in comparison to their shrunk, wasted limbs. Save for a wisp of dirty cotton rags about their loins they were as naked as a skeleton, and their parched tongues were rough and horny, like a parrot's, within their parchment-looking mouths.

The Magus gazed at them fascinated, and in a moment the wondrous star and the new prophet to be born into the world were both forgotten in the horror of the scene. As he stood petrified, from every side, from hollows scooped out of the sand, from tufts of thorny shrubs, thin tottering figures rose and staggered to his tent. Women held children by the hand, and miserable boys supported aged men, whilst an old crone crawled on her hands and knees close to his feet, and then, raising herself a little, pointed a skinny finger to the sky. None of them spoke, but the mute glance of their beseeching eyes struck horror to his soul. When he could speak he called for bread, and with his men cut it in slices, then moistening it in water passed it along the ranks. It vanished as by magic, but still the line grew longer, and in the moonlight the famine-stricken people looked like a troop of wolves that had surrounded some belated traveller on the plain. Some of the people snatched the barley from the horses and the mules as they stood feeding, whilst others struggled for the crumbs, fighting like starving dogs. King Nicanor called to his men and sent back two of them to bring a mule laden with bread from town, as the throng seemed to grow as if the people sprang up from the sand. The mule-load disappeared almost as quickly as if it had been thrown into the sea. Night waned and the first flush of dawn still found the Magus and his camp besieged with famine-stricken folk. Several days passed, and then the starvelings, having eaten, vanished as speedily as they had come, leaving no trace of their appearance except upon the Wise Man's soul. Then, after resting for a day, he once more set out on his way. The sun was rising as he struck his camp, and as he started once again towards the west his thoughts reverted to the birth of the great prophet, the wondrous star, and to his friends, whom he supposed would now be almost at their journey's end.

He caught himself at times almost regretting the delay the starving folk had brought about, and then again thought that if the prophet to be born had come to heal the sorrows of the world, to clothe the naked, heal the sick, and feed the hungry, that at least he had tried humbly to do likewise, though not himself inspired; and that there still was left good work to do on earth during the childhood of the great one, whose birth he hoped to see.

So he rode on, finding upon his path here a blind man and there some wayfarer sitting dejectedly beside his dying horse. Each case delayed him, and when he reached a town his fame had gone before him, and halt and sick, those who had had their eyes burned out for theft, and others who had lost a hand or foot, lopped off to show that justice was as deaf to pity as she is blind to facts, swarmed round him and implored his alms.

Sometimes when passing a lone duar on the plains, just at the saint's house, with its tuft of feathery palms, some wretch would sally forth and, rushing to his side, clutch fast his stirrup, exclaiming, "I take refuge with you," and he would stop and look into his case.

Still, though he knew the prophet must by this time be a youth and growing to a man, when he escaped from the accumulating cares his pilgrimage had brought upon him he pressed on towards the west. Across the heated plains at times he toiled, mocked by the mirage, and with the heat reflected from some stony tract burning his face, and sometimes through some mountain pass where the frost froze his stirrups to his boots, he kept upon his way, just as men labour towards a goal they know it is impossible to reach, unconscious that they carry it within themselves from the first day on which they had set out.

Years passed, and not an animal which he had brought from Babylon remained alive, some having died upon the road, and others of old age, in the long halts he made in cities where some injustice or another had detained him on his way. Still, as he lingered, endeavouring to do good, news reached him now and then about the doings of the prophet whose birth he once had hoped to see, and when he got the news a sort of fever would come over him, making him long to see him ere he died.

The flight of time had not left Nicanor unaltered, and from the sleek and prosperous king who had left Babylon so many years ago, young, careless, and with hope springing in his heart, he had become a weather-beaten man, grizzled and careworn, and in his eyes had come that look of watchfulness that comes to those who pass their lives upon the road.

The horse he rode, a darkish bay of the Keheilan breed, he had received from an old Bedouin chief near Baalbec, whose son he nursed when stricken with the plague. No other horse throughout Irak could be compared with it, either for shape or blood. His full round eyes, and ears lean as a lynx's, his round and flinty feet, broad forehead, silky mane, and tail he carried like a flag, with the sunk channel running down his spine, which, as the Arabs say, could carry off the dew, showed him an archetype of the breed which alone amongst all the horses of the world is truly noble and fit for kings to ride. Years had fallen lightly on King Nicanor himself, leaving him upright, though they had flecked his hair with grey upon the temples, and given him that gravity which many Orientals seem to acquire in middle life, as it were, by an effort of the mind. Most of his followers had returned home or died, except a man or two who, by long converse with their master, had imbibed some of his ideas, or else found life upon the road too pleasant to desert and dwell again in the dull round of cities, seeing the sun rise from behind the selfsame mountain range and sink into the plain, at evening, leaving no sign to mark its passage through the sky, just as a stone sinks out of sight into a pond.

Now and again strange rumours reached the wandering Mage of what was going on in the far country he had left home to visit, and how the prophet who had come had gathered to himself a rout of fishermen, of outcasts, publicans, and women, who, it appeared, all followed him about, striving to found no kingdom, but listening to his words in desert places and on the tops of hills. Much did he ponder on the tidings, thinking at first the prophet must be mad, and then, as he thought more upon the case, seeing a half-resemblance to his own way of life, that is, of course, with that due difference of their respective standings in the world, taken into account.

At last, for even in the East all things draw to an end, he found himself close to Jerusalem. Halting upon a hill which overlooked the town, he pitched his camp near to a well, close to which grew a grove of olive trees. As he sat, after so many years, gazing down on the city where he had heard the prophet lived, whose wondrous birth, heralded by the bright star, had induced him in his early manhood to set forth from Babylon, he looked back on his life. The city lay beneath him, bathed in the golden haze that in the East hides mouldering palaces and tottering weed-grown walls into whose chinks dart lizards in their play, blots out the dirt and squalor and gilds the broken potsherds on the great dunghills by the gates, setting all floating in a sea of glory, above whose waters float the feathery palms.

After the custom, which in his case was now well sanctified by time, the camp of the Wise Man — for now at last, being in Jerusalem, he was a Wise Man of the East —was overrun by beggars, halt and blind. From them he learned that on the morrow the Romans, who had become the masters of the place since he set out upon his travels from the East, were going to execute two thieves, and one who, as they said, was to be put to death for having called himself a king.

After the beggars had been supplied with bread, a wandering fakir came to the camp, and sitting down before the tent entered into one of those long conversations which in the East supply the place of newspapers, filling exactly the same use even to the extent of tinging all the news with the narrator's sympathies, just as a newspaper is but the mirror of the mind of those who write in it.

Long did the dervish talk about the state of Palestine, the price of bread and barley, the raids the tribes had made on one another's herds, and lastly, of the execution which was going to be held.

The thieves he touched on lightly, saying they both were sons of mothers who had never yet said no. He thought the name of one of them was Dimas, the other Gestas, but was not sure of their identity. Of the third sufferer, the one who had been called a king, he had more details, and remarked, by the sun's light, he is a man.

Little by little he unfolded all he knew about the man who was to pay the penalty of being called a king. It seemed that prodigies had happened at his birth. A star had heralded it, and three Wise Men had come out of the East . . . wisdom is in the East, the stranger said, with the air of one who enunciates a fact that none can controvert. King Nicanor, who all the time had listened patiently, broke in upon the tale, exclaiming: "These Wise Men, I know them well, their names are Gaspar, Melchior, and Balthasar. They are my kinsmen; are they still in the town?"

The dervish looked at him, as people look upon a man who, without rhyme or reason, suddenly has a lapse of memory, and answered: "In the town! . . . Why, they were here, as I heard tell, some three-and-thirty years ago, and only stayed a night."

Drawing his hand across his eyes the Magus muttered: "Three-and-thirty years ago — it seems but yesterday when I set out. This prophet then of whom you speak, who dies to-morrow, is the wondrous babe of whom the shepherds told of yesterday — that is, three-and-thirty years ago; but he was to redress men's wrongs, lift up the down-trodden, to heal the halt, make the blind see, fight the oppressor, and be a shield unto the weak. Can it be then that in Jerusalem they execute a man for striving for such ends?"

If the fakir had thought the speaker mad at first, he now looked on him as a lunatic.

"Where have you lived," he said, "and do not know that such a man since the beginning of the world can have but such a fate?"

King Nicanor, after a pause, said: "I have lived, as I now see, upon the road, never remaining very long in any place; but I remember now and then it has amazed me, that when I fed the hungry, as you say this man who is to die has done, that many hated me, saying I did it, all for the love of praise."

Hours came and hours passed as they sat talking, and by degrees King Nicanor heard all the prophet's life, his love of liberty, his truth, his justice, charity, and how the people loved him, especially the lowly and the meek, and of the special charm he had for women, the sweetness of his nature, and how no one who ever heard him but fell beneath his spell.

At last, as dawn began to creep into the sky with a pale milky whiteness that gradually extended through the deep, blue eastern night, just as a drop or two of mastic tinges the water in a glass, King Nicanor rose to his feet and said: "It is now time to rest. Fate has deprived me of the joy of being present at the birth of him the star announced; I can at least be present at his death . . . and birth and death are not so very different, after all."

Fate, though, that mocks our resolutions, making us but the creatures of itself, had almost made him miss the chance, for in the morning he found his camp besieged with a great horde of beggars and of folk who had heard that one who, some said, was a fool and others a Wise Man, but who in any case gave bread away to all who asked for it, had come into the town.

All day he sat and gave his alms and listened to their plaints, until the seventh hour or the eighth, and then mounting his horse, rode up to Golgotha. Darkness was spread upon the land as he toiled up the rocky path, making his way with difficulty through the press.

Right at the top, in the half-light he saw three figures set on high. Two of them hung inert; the third just stirred and asked for drink, and Nicanor observed that his long hair hung down upon one side and half obscured his face.

Just at that moment a young man came running with a sponge of vinegar upon a reed, and, holding it up to the middle figure, pushed it into his mouth. He drank, and after a long shiver had run through his body, he gave a cry so wild and terrible that the dark bay Kehlani that the king rode reared up and snorted, pawing the air with his fore feet, and as he struck the ground King Nicanor saw that the middle figure hung limp upon the cross.

Un Monsieur

It may be the desire for sympathy that makes us yearn to pour our troubles into another's ear — how wise was the first Pope who hit upon auricular confession and made it sacred — that impelled Elise to tell the tale.

"He was," she said, "un Monsieur, about fifty years of age, rich, dull, and only wanting wings to fly, so much he was puffed up with his position in the world and with his wealth.

"No, he did not treat me badly for some time, that is to say, after the visits that he used to pay me, he generally put a ten-pound note upon the mantelpiece and got into his motor with an air as of a Jupiter who had just parted from a Danae. After he went I usually took a bath, and then sat down to read Hérédia or Verlaine, some author or another of a kind that took me off into a world shut to such men as was my wealthy friend.

"He did not talk much; you see he was an Englishman, and seemed as if he was ashamed of speaking much to me, although of course that did not stop his visits to my house. I fancy that he regulated them on hygienic grounds, and rather thought he was a virtuous man in not allowing a full rein to what I feel assured he called the baser appetites . . . baser, eh? . . . the only ones he knew. He looked upon me, I am well aware, but as an instrument of pleasure, a sort of musical-box which he could set in motion with a ten-pound note.

"Upon my side I thought of him but as un Monsieur, a man, that is, who, neither good nor bad, yet pushed by sensuality came to me at his stated intervals and went away appeased. His kisses bothered me, and all his efforts of what he perhaps called love were of a maladroit, that used to make me laugh . . . but then, in my profession, one gets to know what to expect of men.

"Of course he was quite unintellectual. The arts of every nature . . . love is an art" — and here she smiled and fluffed her hair out at the sides with conscious pride — "were but so many pastimes served up to him by men who lived by them. They all appeared to him a sort of intellectual *saltimbanques*, I verily believe, and he must surely have referred to them as painters, poets, fiddlers, and all that kind of thing."

She paused, and the light falling on her fair wavy hair and on her well-kept hands gave her an air of such refinement that it was hard to think of her as the wage-slave of such a man as she had just described. Tall, slight, and well proportioned, blessed with the taste that seems the birthright of the women of her race, the little jewellery she wore appeared as much a portion of herself as the faint, half-professional smile that played about her lips, from the teeth outward, when she was talking to a man.

"You must not think," she said, "that I have laid the colour on too thickly; that would be inartistic. No, he was simply, as I said, un Monsieur . . . not to use a vulgar word, which perhaps would have been better in his case.

"Ridiculous, of course — *cocasse*; I am not sure if there is any word in English that quite is the equivalent of that.

"Ludicrous, preposterous, no. . . . I mean he was absurd and had what we call *une vraie tête de mari* . . . need I say more than that?

"All fat, rich men of fifty, when they make visits to such girls as me must of necessity be . . . *ah yes*, odd. To me the fact of being rich has something in it of itself that seems preposterous. Fancy how I must feel, who look on love as one of the fine arts, to have to *singer* it with a dull, fat, old man, simply because he has a big account at some bank or another! Apart from morals, to which I make no claim, it is an insult to the God who, I suppose, created both of us."

As she said this she drew herself up to her full height, hollowed her back a little like a gymnast on the horizontal bar, and then went on again.

"I had not seen my Monsieur for a week or two and wondered what had happened to him, when a brougham with a pair of chestnut horses drew up at the door. Out of it got a lady, tall, dark, and with a sable cloak that must have cost an eye out of her head, elegant, *svelte*, well dressed and . . . beautiful. She did not give her name, but sent a message saying that she would like to see me, and when my maid had showed *[sic]* her up into the room she came forward and addressed me by my name . . . but charmingly, not stiffly in the least, and without any air of patronage. I asked her to be seated, and she sat down as naturally as if she had been on a visit to a woman of her own world, and after looking at me for a moment curiously, said in good French, 'I have come about a business matter.' I did not ask her how she knew my name, but merely smiled at her, with a slight inclination of the head, wondering internally what kind of business could have brought her, and as she paused a little as if she were debating what to say, I ran my eye over her, trying to recollect if I had seen her anywhere, but all to no avail. As we say, I undressed her, mentally, divining, as it were, she wore good stays and linen underneath. Her feet, of course, I saw, and her well-made French shoes and open-work silk stockings, and from her person generally there floated a faint odour of discreet perfume such as a woman of her world, who does not have to make men turn and look at her, can afford to wear.

"She certainly was beautiful and of my type, that is, the type that I admire, with dark and glossy hair in which you might have seen your face as in a looking-glass. All she had on I inwardly commended, her clothes and jewellery, though there was nothing in especial in the latter except a string of pearls, not large, like those in which a banker's wife or rich American, so to speak, hangs in chains, but finely shaped and dazzlingly white. All this review, of course, took but a minute, and as she did not speak a strange suspicion crossed my mind why she had come to see me, but as if she herself had read what thought was passing in my mind she blushed a little, making her look divine, and saying, 'It was on business that I came,' took from her muff a photograph, and holding it towards me asked me if I had ever seen the man.

"To my amazement, on looking at it I saw the man I have been telling you about, in all in his commonness. His ears, just like an elephant's, his mottled face, and above all that air of thinking he was somebody only because he happened to be rich, all shouted at me.

"Still, every *métier* has its etiquette, and mine, just like a lawyer's or a priest's, is, or should be, discreet. I did not like the man, and on the other hand the lady was quite charming; but I stood firm, and, after looking at the thing indifferently, answered, 'I never saw the man,' and sat expectantly. A shadow of annoyance crossed the lady's face, and once again she came back to the charge.

" 'Are you quite sure?' she said, 'for I am told he is a friend of yours, and let me tell you I am rich.'

"This got my back up just a little, for it appeared as if I never should get clear of riches, and it amazed me, as it annoys me now, to see rich people go about trampling on honour and on everything by the mere weight of gold. Still, she was far too nice to quarrel with, so I sat quietly and smiled, and happening to catch her eye, we both stopped a half-laugh, and I, divining that she was my Monsieur's wife, wondered what her next move would be to try and make me tell. After a word or two she got up from her chair, and going to the door paused for a minute as she held it in her hand, then, turning to me smiling, said:

"I respect your honesty; but, after all, what does it matter whose money that it is you take? I will pay you anything up to a thousand pounds if you but choose to recollect.

"Once more I thanked her, knowing, of course, that I was acting like a fool, but pleased to show her that I held honour above money — in spite of what I was. As she was going out she turned, and said again, 'Name your conditions'; and when I smiled and shook my head, she looked at me just for a moment, half with regret, half with approval, so that when finally she closed the door I felt, although she had not got her way, that she respected me for having made a stand against my interest.

"Three or four days had passed and the impression of the lady's visit had almost worn away, when who should come to see me but my friend.

"He looked so prosperous, and had so great an air as if the world might have belonged to him had he not been too lazy to write out a cheque . . . an oversight which, no doubt, when he had time enough, he still would rectify . . . I hardly found it in my heart at first to tell him what had passed. As soon, however, as he began what he perhaps called love-making and tried to draw me on to his knee, I, of course, seeing that he looked on the whole thing but as a hygienic visit, determined not to lose the chance.

"Therefore instead of letting, as I generally did, my head fall on his shoulder, closing my eyes, and thinking I was in the Calais steamer on a rough day, I pushed him off, and standing up, looked at him steadily between the eyes.

"He, for his part, knowing that he was going to pay for my complaisance, and having not an inkling of what was passing in my head, looked at me, half amazed, half puzzled, and exclaimed: 'Elise, old girl, what's up that you behave in this way to a pal?'

"Whether it was his confidence, a confidence that neither God nor Nature had given him the right to exercise with any woman upon earth, or whether I was revolted at my '*sale métier . . . car c'est un vrai métier de chien, tu sais,*' I do not understand. When I had my hand free, for he tried to pull me to him and treat my attitude as a good joke, I said without a prelude: "Your wife was here the other day.'

"He did not think I was in earnest and answered me in French, which he spoke fluently: '*Elle est bonne, celle-là.*'

"However, when I had told him how his wife was dressed and named a bracelet that she wore he got more serious. I rather liked to tease him, and for a moment thought of saying something that would throw doubt upon his wife, but being also curious to find out what had been the real reason of her call, I merely said: 'She took your photograph out of her muff and showed it to me.'

"You never saw a man change quicker than my friend.

"What did you say, Elise?' he muttered; and when I told him that I had quite disclaimed all knowledge of him, he took my hand in his and kissed it, exclaiming: 'Elise, you are a splendid girl. . . . My wife wants to divorce me, but we have a child, a girl of ten, old enough to appreciate the disgrace of the Divorce Court, and I would give the world to spare her.'

"For the first time I rather liked him, for he spoke feelingly, and really seemed a man and not a money-bag. He drew me to him, and for the first time in my life I let him do so without repulsion, and holding both my hands he swore I had saved him, that he would do anything in the world for me, and if I wished to lead a different life and go back home to France that he would settle money on me to help me either to learn painting, which had always been my dream, or to get married to a decent man. When I had thanked him and he had kissed me several times, but quite as a man kisses a real woman and not as he had done before upon his visits, he went away, assuring me of his eternal gratitude, and turning at the door, just as his wife had done a day or two ago, to thank me once again. This time I was *bouleversée* and sat down and cried, thinking what I would do, and came to the conclusion to go to Paris and begin work in some *atelier* some painter of repute. I thought of all that I should do and for the life of art cannot, of course, be quite devoid of love — determined to choose some young painter or another, whom I should live with . . . quite *en bourgeois*, and darn his socks and be as good to, for I am *très bonne fille*, as I have told you, as was possible.

"That was a happy afternoon, and my task, when in the evening business sent me out to the Alhambra or some other music-hall, comparatively light. Days passed and weeks, then months, and still my grateful friend was silent, until one day, walking beside the Serpentine, I met him with his wife. He paled, and she looked at me quickly, and clutching at his arm, said: '*Tiens! C'est elle.*"

"I made no sign, but fixed my eyes upon a child sailing his boat and passed on my way. That's all," said Elise; "and for the man, at first, I thought he was a *lâche* and then a scoundrel; but now I know he was but a rich man — 'un Monsieur' — and probably to-day, if he thinks of the matter now and then, promptly dismisses it, and says as he lights up a big cigar: 'She was a prostitute.' "

A Retainer

"Laird, ye ken ane o' my forbears gaed to Bannockburn wi' the Graemes." Though my retainer always insisted that this forbear was "nigh upon seven feet high," and used to add, "men nowadays run awfie small," he would himself with his inadequate six feet and four or five inches have wielded a good spear.

Indeed, no man could possibly have had a better spearsman at his back in the old days.

Tall, dark, and with a fell of hair that grew down low upon his forehead and met his curling beard, which grew so thick upon his face, if you had dropped a pin upon it, it would have never touched the skin, his twinkling grey eyes looked out suspiciously and yet with humour on the world. His upper lip was always shaved, that is to say, upon the "Sabbath morn," and bore throughout the week a crop of stubble on it, so that, had it not been an article of faith with him to shave it on the Sunday, he might as well have thrown away his razor, though I can never fancy him with a moustache. He had, I think, a vague idea that to have grown it would have been a sort of poaching on the customs of the "gentry," though if a long descent can make a gentleman, surely the fact of the grim forbear who had gone to Bannockburn should have entitled him to be so styled, even although the warrior ancestor may have been legendary. Most ancestors do not bear looking at too closely, not only for their moral worth, but for their authenticity, and my retainer's had done as much for him, as if he had, after the manner of most Scottish worthies, hall-marked his passage through the world by witnessing a charter, for he lived up to him, according to his lights.

Born just before the railway penetrated the remoter districts, he had, although he never knew it, preserved a flavour of an older world.

His speech was harsh and dialectic, but yet not vulgar, and in his voice you heard that cadence, as of a Gaelic song, natural to those born near the Highland line. Whether he ever knew it I know not, but he appeared to me a little wasted in a world which had no special function for such men as he was, to perform. Walking beside a cart, towering above the horse, or sitting on the cramped iron seat of some new reaper, cutting the corn upon his boggy fields, he seemed a little out of place, too fine a figure for the work, not that he was especially intelligent, beyond a certain "pawky" humour, the inheritance of nearly everyone who tills the soil in our bleak, kindly North, but because a manhood such as his imparts a dignity to its possessor quite as impossible to explain as humour, but seen at the first glance.

Huge and athletic as he seemed to me in later life, in childhood he loomed gigantic, and illness, death, or age appeared in his case as impossible as they would have been to a mountain or to the world itself.

Seated beside his father, his very counterpart, but bent and grey, he used to keep my eyes focussed upon him, half against my will, during long hours in church. It seemed a miracle how his great hands, in which the soil had entered, as it were, below the skin and dyed them dark as peat, could "whummle o'er" the pages in the "Book," and as I sat desperately waiting for "saxteenthly and seventeenthly," and often cheated by the preacher, who always seemed to have a "few words in conclusion," extending over twenty minutes, in reserve, I used to envy his composure as he sat as little moved as is a rock upon a moor during a shower of rain. As I look back through the long vista of the years, it does not strike me that he was religious to a great degree, though such a constant worshipper in church. In fact, I think he was one of the class of commentators who would not give "five minutes of the clash of the kirkyard for all the sermons in the world." It may be that in this I am unjust, for in things spiritual he did not venture an opinion, although on politics he thought he was a Radical, that is, with reservations, as are most of us, for I remember that on one occasion he remarked he "was na sure ould Wully Gladstane had done richt when he gave votes to the farm labourers". . . for, as he said, "yon class o' cattle is not eddicated up to it." It would have been a work of supererogation to have told him, that what he had just said was what was urged against his own class once upon a time, for he would certainly have answered: "Aye ou aye, prejudice juist dies hard," or something of the sort, with the assurance of a man who knows that he is right.

His house, just on the edge of a wild moss, was suited to him, for certainly it had no outward sign of any inward grace, as it stood gaunt and square, its grey stone walls and green-grey slates gave it that air of self-assertion which I suppose it had to have to face the climate, just as a Scotchman who is lacking in it is a Scotchman lost.

Needless to say, no flowers climbed up the porch, no garden broke the look of sternness of the place.

The only sacrifice, that is, if sacrifice it could be called, upon the altar of æstheticism were two small rowan trees which grew on each side of the iron gate which opened on the gravel path that led up to the house, and had been made to form an arch. I think that in his heart of hearts my retainer looked upon this as foolishness and waste of time, for once when I directed his attention to it, he muttered "havers of the wife's," and turned the conversation with a remark that sheep "were back at the October Tryst," or something of the sort.

Though not a grumbler, or a man who ever asked for a reduction of his rent, my retainer never would allow that any season could be a good one for the crops. Markets were always "back," during the many years I knew him; potatoes always either were diseased or just were sickening for it; the "neeps" had tae-and-finger, and the hogs wintering upon his farm either had foot-rot or the fluke.

None of these statements did he advance with an ulterior object, but simply threw them out for what they might be worth, either as pleasant subjects to discourse upon, or as a sort of formula with which to enter into conversation in an agreeable way.

This habit, and his enormous hands, and feet encased in boots like barges, heavily soled and tacketed, his homespun clothes and soft black hat (he lived before the age of caps), were but one side of him, the side that he turned outward to the world.

Not having Gaelic, he had lost the gift of picturesque expression, the birthright, as it seems, of every Highlander, even the dullest of his race. Deep in his mind, however, there seemed to seethe a mixture of hard Lowland Scotch ideas and a half Celtic spirit of revolt, not against powers that be, but against life as we all know it, striving for mastery.

This made him ever in hot water with his fellows, but, on the other hand, took him off into a fantastic world, not that of elves and fairies, of wraiths and second sight, but to a sphere in which all the occurrences of daily life were magnified till they became as interesting as they might well be, or perhaps really are, if we could see them in his way.

During the whole course of his life he was, as he said, "sair ta'en up wi' horse," and yet had the worst horses in the district on his farm.

Floods, frosts, and snows were deeper, fiercer, and more intense when he recounted them, than anyone had ever known them, and yet in all his dealings with his fellows he was honest to a fault, so that it may have been he either was a poet without the gift of words, or that the spirit of the strange, wild district where he lived worked in his soul, whilst the affairs of life, sordid and commonplace, but yet compelling, influenced his mind.

The village, close to where he lived, was rent asunder by feuds between the churches, which, as the difference between them was infinitesimal, rendered their quarrels almost as bitter as those between the Spaniards and the Moors.

Often the battle raged on little matters, such as the appointment of a school-teacher, or the like, and my retainer, having taken as it were the shilling of the Free Kirk, duly embroiled himself with almost everybody, offending just as much his co-religionists by too great violence as he outraged his enemies by his attacks.

At last he found himself left all alone, the one sincere and honest man in the whole district branded as an intriguer and a liar.

So he retired to his marshy fields, and passed his time between the plough-stilts and his own ingle-neuk, but never missing kirk on Sundays, where he sat silently, his hair a little greyer, and his hands a little more like roots of trees, turning the criticising gaze of the old-fashioned members of his race upon the preacher, and ostentatiously looking up all the texts he quoted, with a loud rustle of pages, reminding one of dry leaves falling in a wood.

All the strange waifs and strays, goin'-aboot bodies and the like, who forty years ago travelled the upland districts in the North, drifted up to his farm in the same way steel filings jump to a magnet, and he, although he bitterly complained about their presence and the small depredations that they made, was always ready to throw open barns and out-houses for them to pass the night.

Perhaps the district, with its wide mosses and enshrouding mists, its mouldering ruins of the past, mysterious-looking tarns lost in the hills, and its slow-flowing black-streamed river, upon whose bosom bubbles that seemed to rise up from the centre of the earth were ever bursting, was his chief friend, for no one could have pictured him in any other place. The great iron gin he dug out of the moss, and which he called a wolf-trap, and the claymore he found when casting peats, and which by a quite natural process soon became Rob Roy's, were his chief treasures. The one I have inherited, and the other, which he sold to a travelling antiquary, was perhaps the sole occasion in which he got the best of a bargain in his life. His all-embracing feuds, extending from his nearest neighbours, with every one of whom he had some question either of "marches" or of "trespass," did not exclude the humblest from his wrath.

The parish gravedigger, he declared, should never bury him, for as he had not been consulted over his appointment, he used to say, "Yon Ramsey canna howk a grave; he mak's them mair like tattie pits, no like a Christian's grave."

Happening to meet him on the road one day long years ago, I asked him whether he had made it up with Ramsey, and received the answer, "Aye ou aye, time is a sort o' healer. Aye ou aye . . . when I dee, Ramsey wull just hae to sort me . . . though he is sure to mak' a bummle o' the job!"

Fate, as it happened, was not willing that his grave should be bungled in the way he feared, for, dying in the North, a snowstorm caught the mourners and he was shoughed, as he himself would certainly have said, in a churchyard by a lake, where to this day his rough-hewn headstone moulders in the mist. All round him lie McFarlanes and McGregors, most of whose tombstones simply bear a sword upon them, thus setting forth the manner of their lives.

What he will think when he "spangs up" amongst them at the day of judgment I cannot say, for in the days gone by they were sworn foes . . . but, as he said himself, "time is a healer" . . . and in the meanwhile the little wavelets of the lake break up against the wall of the wild graveyard where he lies, with a faint gurgling sound.

No one, I know, is left in the whole world the least resembling him, so strange a mixture of the present and the past; on the one side a representative of the rough-footed Scots who harried and who reived, and, on the other, of the laborious race of ploughmen (loved of the sea-gulls) who have made Scotland what she is.

Roughness and kindliness so struggled for the mastery in him that they seemed after the fashion of the spirit and the flesh to fight an everlasting battle for the predominance, leaving the struggle fortunately undetermined, so that he still appeared a man, weak and uncertain in his strength, an infant grafted on a giant, such as, no doubt, was his fell ancestor, who gaed to Bannockburn.

Buta

We waded through the shallow tidal river in the moonlight, and getting off our horses sat down on a sandbank on which grew sea-pinks, a little woody ragweed, and some dwarf sea-hollies, and began to smoke.

The river in the moonlight seemed a sheet of quicksilver, the little wavelets of the rising tide scarce breaking its calm surface, and in the still night air was heard the occasional flight of sea-birds, of passing cranes, and now and then from the low scrub which fringed the river-banks a jackal yelped.

The tortuous valley flanked by rocky hills seemed to lead into infinite space, so lovely it appeared, twisting and lengthening out in the mysterious light. The ruined Roman town, massive, and built apparently to show, even in its ruin, that the builders built for all time, half filled the lower end. The docks for the galleys, now long crumbled to shapeless mounds of bricks, and used for saltpans, served to remind one that a power great as is our own had once possessed the land. Silent and beautiful the moon shone out on stunted palm tree and on lentiscus scrub; on the deserted gardens, fenced about with cactus, in which grew pomegranate, orange, and fig trees; and in the distance the white walls of the old Arab town gleamed bright along the sea. No human being was stirring, and as we smoked the horses now and then lifted their heads, pricked up their ears, and looked as horses will at night, as if they saw something invisible to human eyes.

We sat and smoked, and Nazim then broke silence, and took up the conversation which we had left unfinished an hour ago in town. "How strange you English are!" he said. "We never know whether it is you that deceive the world and God, or if it is yourselves that you deceive. When I was manager down at Cape Juby I knew an Arab girl. Her name I think, was Rahma, but that matters little to my theory or my tale. So if you like I'll tell you what I know of her, and why her name was changed from Rahma, which means 'merciful,' to Buta, which, as you know, is how the Arabs pronounce a certain Spanish word." The horses settled down to wait, hanging their heads with the resigned, self-sacrificing air which horses as well as men adopt when they are constrained to do something that pleases them. We, after a protest as to Anglo-Saxon *bona fides* both towards God and man, settled ourselves to listen, whilst from the river came the murmur of the flowing tide lapping against the banks, and carrying little promontories of sand into the stream. Then Nazim, with the look round at his audience which bespeaks the story-teller, launched into his tale.

"Sometimes I think that the four years I spent at Juby in the factory (where we sold nothing) were the best of all my life. The desert and the sea, the one flat and broken, but by the 'suddra,' what you call camel-thorn bushes, eh? the other shipless and stretching to nowhere, or perhaps to somewhere; but somewhere is all the same as nowhere if you know not where it is. Hot? no, not too hot; rather too cold sometimes, with the perpetual trade wind. Dull? no, not too dull either, for the affairs of the tribes are just as interesting, if you speak their tongue and know their ways, as are the matters of the larger tribes, French, German, and the *bona fides*, what is it you call it, Englishmen. In the morning I used to mount my horse and ride about, my rifle in my hand, sometimes alone and sometimes with the Arabs, cantering along the shore or through the bushes, hunting gazelles, and now and then firing at wandering Arabs and being fired upon by them. Scarcely a day passes in the desert without some powder, as the Arabs say. Rahma? ah yes, I'm coming to her. Well, inside the fort and factory there were packed fifteen or twenty clerks, almost all Scotchmen, chosen for their good morals and their book-keeping. Now I shall tell you why it is that we say all you English try to deceive both God, man, and the whole world; why I think sometimes that you deceive yourselves, but seldom one another. You know that God (Allah, I mean) made man pretty much all the same, no matter if he be Turk or Jew, Frenchman or German, Spaniard, and all of him. All these men, now, when they see pretty woman, look at her and say she pretty; they smack their lips and they look at her as if they like to take her for themself. Englishman he just like the rest, but he act differently; when he see pretty woman he pretend not see her, he look right through her as if she made of air. He say, 'Yaas, I think I see, but I'm not so sure,' but at the night he send a little boy to ask her come and speak with him. That why I say Englishman is a man different to all the rest, quite *bona fides*, as I hear you say."

"But Rahma, Nazim, when is she coming on the scene?" we said, as the tide was flowing, and we did not want to ride two or three miles upstream to find another ford. Not that anything in particular stopped us from mounting and crossing then, but that the moon was bright, and the melancholy of the night was on us, and we knew Nazim was a good story-teller, and having been brought up speaking English and with Englishmen, though liking us, knew all our weaknesses.

So he began again, "Ah, Rahma! yes, I see her now, sitting at the black tent door facing the sea; not many hundred yards from the factory; handy, you know, for your *bona-fide* clerks to talk to her, as they took their walk after what they called the labours of the day were done. Hers was a little, low, black camel's-hair tent running up to a peak, and pegged in the summer about a foot above the ground, so that you saw all that was going on inside. Her husband had been killed by the bursting of his own gun whilst fighting with another tribe, and she lived all alone with her two children. One was her husband's and the other sent from God, but she loved both of them (especially God's child), and dyed their hair with henna, and hung necklaces of beads around their necks. Her property was a few goats, a sheep or two, and an old loom like those they use in the Hauran — not that she worked at it too frequently, or worked at all, except to carry water in the evening from the well back to the tent. The people of the tribe were kind to her, and gave her what they did not want themselves, after the fashion of all kindly souls who have enough to eat.

"How paint a palm tree or describe an ostrich running on the sand, a serpent on the rocks, or a fair woman as she walks taking men's eyes into her net? The pen, eh; what, mightier than the sword? You say so, but then no one believes it; it is a saying made for serious fools, whose brains are in their bellies; but wise men shake their heads; so I will try, you must not laugh, eh?

"A palm tree with its head in fire, its roots in water, rustling with every breeze, turning its leaves towards the sun that looks at it, or looking at the sun, as you best like; just as a woman turns her head towards the eyes of those who look at her.

"Tall, brown, with velvet eyes, long fingers, slender feet, her nails stained orange-coloured with the henna, and when she walked a lengthening of the joints as when a desert mare canters along the sand. No, no, nothing of that sort. I never cared for her but as a picture, but as a type of the race that says so much to me, for its traditions, its literature, and above all the carriage of its sons."

And daughters, someone said.

"Yes, daughters too, but again only as pictures, for the infection of your civilisation has spoiled me for simple things, and what should I say, even in my own tongue, to a daughter of the tents? Yes, thrice accursed is your civilisation in its effect on men of other races, not born within its smoke. What has it done for me? What has it done for the young Syrians on whom your missionaries impose their hands, and teach them English, French, book-keeping, and Scripture history? as if an Englishman or an American could teach a Syrian the history of Christ, who was born amongst ourselves.

"True, true, you civilise us, and we drift into your proletariat, and perhaps may prove as dangerous to you as did our ancestors to Rome; but I will not philosophise after your fashion, but go on with my tale.

" 'Not too fat, not too thin,' the poet says, and adds, 'look not upon a woman or a fine horse, for looking leads to lust; and lust' — but you, as Englishmen, know well that subjects of that sort are not discussed. That which you cannot see does not exist, that which you do not hear has never been. The ostrich is the wisest of all birds, not that he has more sense than all the rest, but that he knows when he conceals his head beneath the sand that he is hidden from himself.

"Rahma, the merciful; it is an attribute of God (Allah, I mean); we call him merciful; and in a man it is good to follow God, to be like him as far as man may be, but for a woman, mercy is not so safe. Accursed be all men and women born from mothers who never yet said no. How it first happened I am not quite sure, but by degrees Rahma became acquainted with several of the clerks. They said they took an interest in her; some hinted that she would become a Christian if she were handled well, but none of them talked with her openly, but went by night to show their interest and their zeal for her soul's welfare — after the English way. Welfare of the soul, that is the trade-mark of you English. No, no, I do not mean to offend; but then, you see, you are, above all things, a commercial nation, and the soul is cheap, whereas the body is a costly thing to help. Buy in the cheapest, and sell, eh — well to anyone who wants to buy, that's how you look at it, I think?" He ceased a moment, and one Anglo-Saxon (there were three of us, two Britons and a Yankee) looked aghast, being convinced of the superiority of our race, our faith, our principles, and everything that appertained to us. A cormorant skimmed up the river, its neck outstretched, its wings just dipping in the stream; it saw us motionless, our horses standing listlessly, resting a hind leg and swinging their tails sleepily, and swerved across the water, uttering its hoarse cry. Then once again the story-teller took up his reminiscence of the Arab girl.

"The end of the swimmer is to be taken by the sea, we say; and so it was with Rahma; not that she ever swam. You know the Arabs on the coast look on the sea, the black, the mysterious, the unfathomable, with horror; but she was taken sure enough.

"Why taken though? I should not say taken, perhaps, for she lives yet; and when a stranger, coming to the place, inquires, they tell him, 'Yes, Rahma (that is, "El Buta," as we call her) lives in that tent close to the tamarisk bushes by the well. There, friend, you have your house; and she has drink, too, drink of the Christians. Accursed be the sons and daughters of the mothers who never yet said no."

He ceased, and we, having listened to his story, did not protest, but sat a little, silently watching the rising of the three Maries just behind the hill. Mounting, we crossed the river, which now was almost full, and struggling through the stream, our knees bent backwards, and our feet tucked up upon the horses' backs, emerged on to the hard, sandy beach; then, having caught our stirrups, shouted in the moonlight to our horses and galloped back into the town.

Hope

418

My Uncle

The folly of a fond mother had warped his life. No career was good enough for him, so he, like a good son, remained without one to the last day of his existence. Report had it that when young he was a personable man, though whether from modesty or from the difficulty of finding a painter skilled enough to depict him, no record came down to my time of his appearance in the heyday of his youth. When first I recollect him personal beauty was not what suggested itself to the impartial observer of his countenance. "A lang-backit, sort o' bandy-leggit, duck-footed body, wi' a' his duds in rags, and wi' his waistcoat hangin' a' in threads, I thocht he had been ane o' they burglars frae up aboot England," was the way in which a servant-girl described him to her mistress, upon whom my relative had called. She added: "He was aya [sic=aye] keekin' at the window, and when I turned awa' he took me round the waist and ettled to kiss me, a dirty, snuffy loon. Ca' ye yon man a gentleman? I just ca' him naething better than a tink."

Certainly few were the sacrifices he made to outward grace. A pair of hunting-breeches, loose at the knees, grey worsted socks and high-lows, a tartan waistcoat (hangin' a' in threads), and round his neck, summer and winter, he wore a worsted comforter. An ancient Scottish chronicler relates that the spearmen of Upper Annandale wore round their necks a similar adornment, and adds mysteriously that they thus wore it "not so much for cold as cutting." This latter reason could have weighed but little with my uncle, for history does not relate he ever engaged in any wars, or ran much risk of cutting, but from the finger-nails of some west-country servant-lass whose cap he had pulled off as she was carrying coals or water up a stair.

Summer and winter, year in and out, he wore a tall silk hat, brushed the wrong way, so that by accident or by design it looked like beaver. He kept it in its place by a piece of common twine, and seemed contented with the effect it produced on all and sundry who beheld and marvelled at it. Most commonly his shirt was scarlet flannel (which he called flannin'), and sometimes when the rare northern sun peeped out for a week or two in August or July he wore a smock-frock over all, and walked about, a cross between an old-time southern counties hedger and a scarecrow, but still a gentleman. Both in and out of season he took snuff, daubing it on his face and clothes, carrying a supply of it loose in his pocket as well as in a well-filled silver box, dropping it into tea and coffee, or in the soup, mixing it with the yolk of eggs, and turning tender stomachs by its omnipresence whilst he was in the house. Man doth not live by snuff alone, but yet my uncle would, I believe, have given up his food rather than stint himself in this ingredient to his happiness.

Sent by his loving parents to a university, he certainly learned Greek, which to the astonishment of those who did not know him well he quoted freely, especially when drunk. A horseman from his youth, although he looked more like a sack of coals upon his horse than like a man, he yet had hands of silk. Leaning well back upon the saddle, his broken high-lows jammed into the stirrups as he had been in irons, he rode in the first flight, sticking at nothing, or on a four-year-old would ride him through the streets, laughing and talking to himself as the unmade colt stumbled and slithered on the stones.

If his exterior was strange and wonderful, his inward spiritual graces were no less whimsical. Most people at first sight would have set down my uncle as stark mad. Often in Scotland, where personal originality is pushed to the verge of lunacy, where people cherish and cultivate those tricks of manner, gesture, and deportment which in most other countries men fight against, and though knowing they possess them deny them with an oath, it is not always safe to judge. Certain it is my uncle, for the possessor of a shrewd brain and mordant wit, went as near to madness as was possible. A calculated madness though, and near allied to that of those malevolent fools of history who, when the world laughed at them, returned the compliment by mocking at humanity. It seemed as if humanity itself was what my relative had set up as his target; not that he was a misanthrope, still less a woman-hater, for he liked company and sitting drinking at the dinner-table after the antique Scottish fashion; and as for women, any created thing that wore a petticoat he turned the light of his snuffy countenance upon with satyr-like content.

Few ever knew him guilty either of a kind or cruel action, but yet his humour was to offend, disgust, and above all revolt. So in his sister's house, where he would pay long visits, he used to come dressed as I have described, or for a change, in what we call in Scotland "a stan o' black," with frilled white shirt and collar, the ends of which stuck up like gills, the whole surmounted by a hideous soft hat of the species known as a wideawake, thirty or forty years ago, and made of tweed, sewn into many ridges, and lined with green or scarlet silk. In the poor maiden lady's drawing-room he sat, reading *Bell's Life*, his feet stuck into slippers of a kind which in those days, I think, were made in Paisley, and in Paisley only, and called "bauchles," all down at heel, and the cheap leather cracked. All round him was a rampart made of snuff, which befouled everything, and so he sat talking and singing to himself, retailing Rabelaisian anecdotes, or singing songs half jocular and half indecent, for his own edification, and to pass the time. No one seemed to him half so good an audience as he was himself; at times he had long conversations *sotto voce*, in which he held his best friends up to ridicule, or sometimes passed remarks on all and sundry before their faces, being half conscious, half unconscious of what he said, and if remonstrated with, chuckling and laughing, and saying, "Eh, did I though? Well, well, where's the snuff-box? Have any of ye seen my box?" His *sotto voce* psalmody was not much varied, and consisted chiefly of "Joseph Muggins' Party" (all his friends he did invite), and an old Scottish lyric, "Jack and his Master," quite democratic in its sympathy with Jack, which he gave in a crooning minor key, like that adopted by old Highland women spinning, or by a seaman keeping the anchor watch aboard a tramp.

Mysterious business used to take him into Glasgow now and then, when he would lunch at a good club, and then sink out of sight no one knew where or why. His relations and his friends, after the manner of their kind, attributed all kinds of vices to him, though, if the truth were known, I fancy there was nothing more awful than a left-handed wife, perhaps some country girl, and a knock-kneed, "short-backit" family, in the dim regions of his private life. In spring, about the month of April, he regularly appeared in Leamington to drink the waters of that ineffable stucco resort of Irish colonels and Scotch generals, partly because his sisters lived there, and partly on account of the fame the waters had enjoyed in Dr. Jephson's time. Although he spoke the English language with nothing of his native country in the accent but that faint intonation which reminds one of the air escaping from the chanter of a bagpipe, yet generally at Leamington, and with all those he looked on as stuck up, he discoursed in broadest Scotch. An English lady being displeased with the genial showers of our northern summer, remarked to him, "It always seems to rain whenever I come to Scotland"; to which he answered, "Yes, but it whiles rains when you do not come, mem." It was his humour usually to address a man as "mem," a lady by the style of "sir," and end his sentences no matter what the sex of anyone with whom he talked, "No, sir; yes, mem"; thus showing his contempt or his respect for both the sexes quite impartially. At breakfast-time he sat with his teacup making a ring upon the newspaper, silent but comminative, upon the extracts which he read, raising his snuff-smeared face at times to say, "I'll take aw egg. Yes, sir, no, mem, I think I will take aw."

And so he passed his life in alternation between Leamington and the West of Scotland, growing each day more snuffy, more untidy, and more cynical. Then came a period of nomadism, and to his friends' amazement, they heard he had attached himself to a travelling circus; whether from love of some young lady who in short petticoats and tights danced on a barebacked horse, from pleasure in the society of horses or the clown, or simply from the amusement he derived from scandalising everyone he knew, no one could tell. But with the circus for a year or two he roamed about, appearing now and then, when it chanced, either in Yorkshire or in Scotland, to perform near to a country house where he was known, and dropping in to lunch. On such occasions his sharp wit and knowledge of the world atoned for his strange dress, his dirty habits, and the trail of snuff which, as a snail leaves slime upon a window-pane, he left where'er he went.

This phase, after the fashion of the others, had its turn, and tired of his nomadic life he settled down at Largs. There in the semi-fishing-village semi-watering-place he passed his time, sauntering about artistically draped in his white smock-frock or pinafore, worn over white duck trousers, muttering to himself, and cracking jests alone upon the beach.

A terror to the unprotected nursery-maids, a frequent visitor in church, where he sat critically scanning the preacher with disfavour, putting a halfpenny into the plate, which in old-fashioned Scottish churches used to stand at the church door upon a pine or maple pillar simulating a stick of barley-sugar, he focussed every eye upon himself by his loud criticisms.

But as the most of us have in our heart of hearts some person or another before whom our cynicism melts, our knowledge of the world becomes of no avail, and kindness, love, or custom makes us regard them as perhaps a wayward dog regards its master whom it runs off from but returns to when it is hungry, so had my relative, hidden below the crust of snuff and whimsicality, with which he was well pitched inside and out, a feeling of regard, respect, or something for the elder of his sisters, with whom he sometimes lived. No sentimental feeling seemed to unite them; in fact, his sister criticised with frank outspokenness, reproved him for his sloth, for dirtiness, and for other matters about which modern ladies do not often reprehend their brothers, in good set Scottish terms. He seldom ventured to indulge in any of his coarse sallies in her presence, whether restrained by fear or by affection no one knew. Towards his other sister he had no such scruples, and when she talked of hunting, being like himself a rider from her youth up, he used to say, "To hear my sister talk you would think there never was a woman who could ride, and hardly any men."

Death in its foolish, blundering, inexorable way first took the hunting sister, who with her last breath enjoined upon her heirs not to allow a spavined horse to take her to the grave. Her brother bore her loss quite philosophically, and as the hearse came to the door, exclaimed that the near leader had a thoroughpin, and that his sister could never bear to see a hearse horse decked in petticoats.

After a year or two, which my uncle mostly spent between his snuff and newspapers, the other sister went. He gave no sign of grief, unless by taking a double dose of snuff, and at the funeral behaved himself more decently than was his wont. All through the lines of stucco villas, semi-detached, each with its garden plot and araucaria, its air of desolate respectability, and with its tent in summer on its little lawn, the cortège took its way. My uncle was more subdued than usual, but took his snuff at proper intervals, and talked a little with himself of horses he had known, and dogs which in their day had drawn more badgers than the degenerate dogs of modern times.

Under the elm trees in the corner of the quiet English churchyard, the rooks' nests swinging in the March east wind, the tardy buds of the late spring forming themselves like drops of amber on the twigs, the hard, old, upright, kindly Scottish lady's grave was dug. On the one side a cheap Carrara monument, commemorating all the virtues of some prosperous citizen, reared its head. Upon the other, a mouldering elm board with "affliction sore" marked out the grave of some poor cottager. In his canonicals the clergyman mumbled his prayer, and on the coffin fell the Warwickshire red loam. To say my uncle was affected outwardly would be untrue, for he took snuff with regularity. Just as I turned to go he drew from the recesses of his "stan o' black" a rose all smeared with snuff, holding it in his hand as a man holds a bird caught in a window, half cautiously as though he feared it might escape. Then stooping forward he laid it on the grass, and turning round said, "Did you spot the gurrl with the pink flowers in her hat?"

Fortune did not arrange I was to see his funeral, therefore I cannot say if in his coffin his relations had sense enough to place his snuff-box by his side. If they omitted so to do, or if a spavined horse was in his hearse, their sin was great. For me he is a memory of childhood, so quaint, at times I think that I evolved him from my own brain, could I not swear I saw him in the flesh, and testify to his strange mutterings, his singing to himself, his quips, his cranks, his quiddities, and to his snuffy rose.

The Colonel

The railway, that sworn enemy of old-world types, has done more in the last fifty years to make the whole world common than all the international pilgrimages of all past times. So that search England, Scotland, and Ireland all through, to-day you scarce shall find a man differing in any aspect of his mind or body from the next. But, as a wounded bird or animal sometimes seeks concealment in some place made difficult to find by obviousness, so chiefly is the eccentric to be sought in London and its purlieus. Still fifty years ago in wind-swept, ragged Scotch country houses not a few remnants of pre-railroad days still lingered on.

Scotland alone could have produced, and perhaps only Scotch people could have appreciated, such a survival of the youth of the nineteenth century, as was the veteran. He bore his eighty years as lightly as an oak tree bears its centuries, and used to tell with a twinkle in his fierce, brown, bloodshot eye that an old gamekeeper had said "the Colonel was born in the same year in which the saughs were planted in the West Park, and that they were maistly a' deid at the tap." Tall and broad-shouldered, he seemed as if his fell of thick white hair had bowed his shoulders, as the snow bends down the topmost branches of an aged fir. Otherwise time had but little touched him. Years had not blunted the intensity of his hatred for a Free Churchman, a Tory, or a Highlander. Experience had not taught him to tone down his restrictions on all who disagreed with him. The snows of eighty winters had not dimmed the fire of his glance. The very country people said the "ould Colonel had an eye intil him like a hawk."

No eccentricity of dress betrayed the man born in the eighteenth century. Either the tailors of his youth had mildewed off or become bankrupt, as their patrons one by one preceded them to that land in which their craft will presumably not be required, or the Colonel's own good sense had impelled him to conform, ostensibly at least, to the degeneracy of the times in which he lingered. His collars may perhaps have been a trifle higher than those of the time in which he lived; the skirts of his heather-mixture shooting-coat a trifle fuller than those worn in the sixties. So that except the fact of his large silver snuff-box, snuff-stained shirt, and red silk handkerchief, usually drying at the fire when not in active service, these were his only outward protests against the flight of time.

Lost in a corrie of the hills, miles from a railway, surrounded on all sides by moors and still more moors, looking out upon a little loch, on which grew yellow and white water-lilies and in which fed tench, stood his ancestral tower. Hills towered at the back of it, and the tall firs of the "pinetum" kept out such little light as the small deep-set windows, all built in a recess, might have admitted. Its thick "harled" walls, its "corby steps," the low hall door, opening without a porch upon the ground, the high-pitched roof, and air of gauntness over all, impressed the stranger sadly at first sight, as the house loomed greyly through the constant rain. Inside, three or four large and curly, but cross-tempered, dogs greeted the visitor, showing their teeth at him, and walking up the stairs beside him, holding their tails out stiffly, as the Arab says a lion does when in a forest in South Algeria he comes upon a man. The Kingwood furniture, the jars of rose-leaves in china basins on the stairs, the apples in a cupboard by the hall, mixed with the snuff, which lay like a brown dew on all the furniture, produced an atmosphere which only practice rendered tolerable. An old grey parrot in a bright, brass cage which bit at everyone as fiercely as an otter, and two green parroquets which flew about the rooms, rendered life livelier than was the wont of other country houses in the days of which I write. Few houses of the kind are left in these degenerate days, and men like the old Colonel have long since disappeared.

The long campaign of the Peninsula had softened off his angles towards both French and Spaniards, but the longer warfare of his life had left him still militant towards an Irishman or Kelt of any kind. Episcopalians were his detestation; on Catholics he looked with toleration, knowing that at the time he lived their power beyond the Tweed was small; but all the shades and little differences of Presbyterian dissent he lumped and damned in one fell swoop as hypocritical, giving no reason for his faith, but holding it and acting on it, after the fashion of his kind. Born when the echoes of the '45 were ringing (though faintly) through the land, he held the Stuarts in abhorrence, but yet hated the Hanoverians, whom he termed German Boors, and would, I fancy, have stood by Fletcher of Saltoun (he who let fools make laws so long as he made rhymes), had that illustrious Scoto-Roman flourished in his time. Nobody nowadays descants as he did on the divine right of monarchs to be hanged, dwells upon Robespierre's virtues, worships the Iron Duke, or swears by Ebenezer Elliott as did my ancient friend.

These incongruities of faith, these whimsicalities of creed, the penny logic of the daily press has quite obliterated, whether to the greater glory of the Lord 'tis hard to say. But, no such speculation came into the Colonel's mind, bothered his brain, or lost him for a single evening his after-dinner nap. Wine put upon the board, the great arm-chair wheeled to the fire, the red silk handkerchief duly set out to dry, his nostrils both well charged with snuff, the Colonel commonly embarked upon the tale of the French wars. The siege of Badajoz, the marches and the counter-marches in the Castilian and La Manchan plains, the bivouac in the wild mountains of Leon, the tales of straying Frenchmen dipped in oil and set on fire, his meeting with the guerrilla chief called the "Empecinado," the lines of Torres Vedras, all were brought out, together with some Val de Peñas, which, though he always said it was sour stuff, he never was without, since his campaigning days. Strange facts in natural history and in botany, lore about horses, odd reminiscences about the Capra Hispanica which he had seen in the Estrella Mountains, curious remarks about the bustard which he remembered in the Norfolk broads — the hotch-potch of a fertile brain, helped by his eyes, sharp as a lynx's, and trained by eighty years of practice to pick up the trail of anything unusual, as an Indian's eyes pick up the footprints of a strange horse, he would unpack with some prolixity.

Fortune, which smiles but seldom upon interesting folk, had treated him but scurvily. Some speculator had induced him to set up a mill. Right in the middle of his rushy ragweed and thistle ornamented park the monster stood. Failure, which waits upon all excursions of gentlemen into the serious affairs of life, had from the outset marked it as its own. Now long deserted by its crowd of blear-eyed operatives, it stood a skeleton, the marauding boy having shattered all its windows, and the fierce winter gales removed the slates. Still the walls stood four square, a monument of folly and of ugliness, and in his walks abroad the Colonel, stopping and leaning on his thistle spud, would curse it from the bottom of his heart, with so much unction as to show that our forces in the Peninsula must have maintained all the traditions of the Flemish wars.

Radical member for Paisley in his youth, convener of his county in his riper years, he lived a stirring, stormy life, endeavouring without success to pay off debts incurred by his luckless venture in the mill.

Friends he had many, but his relations, as a rule, were as anathema to him, especially his heirs. Tradition, that useful entity upon whose shoulders (as upon those of Providence) the humorist can throw so many of his griefs, some of his quiddities, and all his cranks, avers that for ten years before the Colonel's death he never mended fence, repaired a building, or laid out anything to benefit those who by inheritance should occupy his place. Sometimes (again tradition) he was heard to say, if God would only tell him the precise hour of his death, he would burn down the house the night before he died.

Up to the end he rode his chestnut hack at a slow canter up and down his avenue, attended county meetings, and preserved his senses to the last hour of his life. Death took him with his snuff-box in his hand, grim and prepared, although not pleased to go. He left the world the poorer by a type, and when I pass the lonely tower in the glen, and skirt the policies, in which no longer either ragweed, docks, or thistles bloom, I look at the tall saughs in the West Park, and remark sadly that nowadays not only are they all "deid at the tap," but most of them are rotten, and not a few lie bald and sere, their bark all peeling off in ribbons upon the upland grass.

The Admiral

There is a personality about some men which, even if they never get the chance to excel, still makes them in themselves superior to their fellows. Sometimes a man who neither writes, nor speaks, nor has excelled in his profession, yet in himself excels. Such sort of men amongst their fellows are recognised, and seldom create jealousy, that is, of course, amongst those able to appreciate them, for the mere herd of clever men see no superiority but when hall-marked by success.

The man whose personality has haunted me from my youth up did not succeed, nor did he fail, for everywhere he went his great abilities were recognised, and man can want no more. His picture, as he sat in the Reform Parliament, dressed in a high-necked coat, a black silk stock enveloping his throat, his curly, snow-white hair, in his youth so like a wig that a fopling of the day went into Truefit's and asked for a wig "of the same kind as those you make for Captain Elphinstone," hung in my bedroom. Born in 1773, he just remembered swords in general wear, and lived to finish *Pickwick*. His wife, a Spanish lady, whom he married when she was just fourteen and he was forty, long after he was dead, in speaking of him, said: "He lived an active life, and to the last was young." Of such men is the kingdom of the earth. A midshipman between eleven and twelve, at four-and-twenty a post-captain, a general in the Spanish army, friend of Bolivar and of Paez, and yet a welcome guest of Ferdinand the Seventh, he wanted but a Boswell to preserve his name. But it is best, perhaps, that a man who differed from the ordinary successful herd remains without a memoir; for soon a memoir and a knighthood will be entailed on everyone who rises to be a county councillor, and the few really distinguished men an age produces will die unwritten of, as they have lived misunderstood. Sometimes the lives of men whom one has never seen, but heard much talked of, seem more real than the lives we see around us, which, semi-vegetable and semi-human, appear unreal in their actual but unconvincing course.

So step by step from his tenth birthday in a ten-gun brig to Waterloo, where, after having danced at the famous ball the night before the fight, he saw the battle as a spectator, till I find him on the Peruvian coast in command of a two-decker which would neither sail nor stay, I follow the footsteps of the man I never saw. Becoming bored with the frequency with which his old two-decker missed stays, or perhaps wishing to make the Admiralty stare, he took her into Talcahuano and cut her down to a frigate, and being called upon to pay for his experiment, retorted by writing for his pay, which, since he entered as a midshipman, he had never drawn, serving for nothing, either through carelessness, or some punctilio, or from not having called to mind the scriptural commercial apothegm that the labourer is worthy of his hire. Tradition says that "My Lords" were glad to compromise the matter, which, if it was the case, shows them more reasonable than usual, for compromise is the soul of all administration, naval and military alike.

Besides his feats in naval construction whilst on the western coast of South America, he had, as it appears, a pretty taste in equipage, leaving a curricle in Lima, which long afterwards I heard a Peruvian talk of as "the strange carriage with a silver bar upon the horses' necks left by the Milord-Captain who altered all the ships." From Lima, too, he first brought dahlias, giving them to his friend Lord Holland, who of course figures as their introducer, as befits a peer. But, I forgive him, and may the glory still be his, as this same worthy peer repented, so to say, of all his errors, and with his friend who brought the dahlias drove in Hyde Park with Spanish mules and muleteers, with, let us hope, their sashes filled with stones to throw at the leaders, after the fashion of their prototypes in Spain.

Back again, married (his peace made with "My Lords"), having arrived in London the day before the Derby, and finding not a horse to be had for love or money, he hired an undertaker's team and drove them down in state, to the delight of all the road, and to the admiration of his wife, who, coming straight from Spain, was taken with the team of long-tailed blacks, and thought their stately steps and waving manes fit for the carriage of a prince. In fact they were so, for when a dead man passes down the street, stretched out so quiet in his hearse, he is a prince, having attained to the last pitch to which a man can come. Ideas of death and hearses did not, I think, much trouble him of whom I write, for as I take it, he must have looked on life as everlasting, after the fashion of the strong and occupied, who pass their time so quickly that when Death comes they think his presence an intrusion, almost an error, but, still smiling, take their way.

Married at forty (the ideal age), his hair quite white, not having turned so in a night or in some deadly climate, but as he told a lady, "here in this town of London"; after an adventurous youth, during the course of which he carried off a Spanish nun, who died on board his ship during an action with a Sallee rover, he started for a second lease of life and fresh adventures. Appointed admiral on the West Indian station, he sailed, taking a favourite horse or two and thirteen midshipmen on board his ship. Those were the days before the telegraph made admirals and generals the mere slaves of newspapers, of admiralties and war offices, and of the heterogeneous unintelligent expressions of the folly of mankind that we call public opinion and pretend to reverence, though each one in his heart reviles and laughs at it, not thinking that his individual folly is but a fraction of the universal folly of mankind.

In the West Indies, in those days, diplomacy seems to have been as much a part of an admiral's duty as manoeuvring a fleet. Perhaps it is so still; but if it is, most probably the admiral has to pass some sort of humiliating fifth or sixth standard examination, and report himself by telegraph, before he makes a move. None of these things existed at the time of which I write; so I find the Admiral travelling quite unconcernedly in Venezuela, accompanied by his wife and child, his flag-lieutenant, and a midshipman. At that time Paez and Bolivar, having expelled the Spaniards, after the fashion of true patriots, had come to loggerheads as to which of them should rule. In some mysterious way I find him established at Caracas as adviser and general mediator between the two. Then, friendship made, hands shaken, and Bolivar back at Bogata [*sic*], he is hailed by Paez at a banquet as "el nuevo Nelson," a title to which he had no claim and would in fact have repudiated with an oath, as he held Lord Cochrane as a much greater man than Nelson, with his common saying of "hate a Frenchman as the devil," his beautiful and vulgar mistress, and his perpetual good luck. A local poet at the banquet was ready with a complimentary song, which after heralding the advent of the "new Nelson" to this "sententrion," soared into the empyrean with a chorus, "Viva, viva, viva Bolivar, viva el nuevo Nelson, recibiendo de Paez esta demostracion."

Who would not like to have received from Paez or Bolivar a "demostracion," and to have seen the siege of Maracaibo, the last place that the Spaniards held on terra firma in America, and to have been a British admiral *in partibus* before the days of steam?

After the banquet, which took place at ten o'clock a.m., there came a bull-fight, and the flag-lieutenant, either fired with emulation or with wine, after endeavouring in the "llanero" way to throw a bull down by the tail, fell from his horse himself, and remained prostrate in the middle of the ring. The bull advanced, smelt at him, and turned him over with his horn, he lying motionless in agony; then, like a bovine good Samaritan, passed by quite unconcernedly upon the other side. The people in their simple faith espied a Lutheran, and shouted, "Heretic! Even the animals perceive his heresy." On such occasions the worst heresy may be preferred even to faith capable of removing mountains. Things being in solution at the time, it is extraordinary that the people of Caracas did not lay hands upon the Admiral suddenly and make a king of him, but the opportunity seems to have been lost. Either disgusted at their lack of apprehension, or being tardily recalled home, he sailed, taking a veritable menagerie with him aboard his ship. As passengers he had two pacing ponies, a tapir, parrots and peccaries, some boa-constrictors, and a small marvel of the animal creation locally known as a "chirhuiri," which used to eat off ladies' petticoats as they sat at meals, making them subjects for the sport of fools as they rose with their raiment shorn to the knees behind, like David's messengers. After an interregnum in his history, I find him at Gibraltar, where in the intervals of duty he became the founder of the Calpe Hunt, chasing a wolf through Almoraima with his hounds, and being first in at the death himself, by the veracious testimony of the *Gibraltar Guide*.

At Malaga, upon a visit to the Governor of the town, the season Easter, and the times not being so much out of joint with ancient customs as in these modern days, the Governor took him to the port to free a criminal. As in its most relenting moods justice must needs be at the best capricious, working its wonders after the fashion of the wind, just where it listeth, and according to no rules which reasonable men can claim to understand, the choice was made at random, so that the miserable men who in those days rowed in the galleys of the king must have passed agonies of expectation and suspense.

Turning towards the Admiral, the Governor invited him to choose a man, and he, quite in the manner of the man who at a venture drew a bow and had the luck to make a bull's-eye of a king, said, "This is the man I choose." The man, no doubt, made his acknowledgments as best he could, and when despair had settled down again upon the nine-

and-ninety poor "bezonians" left in their fetters and their misery, as the papers say in reports of parliamentary debates, the incident was closed. Neither the Admiral nor the Governor most probably thought of the affair again.

"Long live the King! Give me your cloak!" was a true saying in those days throughout the realms to which the King Ferdinand VII, of blessed memory, had been called to reign.

"Los siete Niños," they of Ecija, José Maria, and other rascals, whose pictures figure in startling, coloured prints in many a faded Spanish almanac, done in the days when Spain was fashionable, made all the roads unsafe. Humorists in their way, as were these merry men, stripping recalcitrant travellers to the skin, but always leaving them at least a newspaper with which to make their entry into the next town, they yet were perilous to meet, for not infrequently they fired a blunderbuss, well charged with slugs, without a word, taking their chance whether the traveller was in a state to answer to their call to stop, after the shot was fired.

Journeying towards Madrid, passing from "tierra baja," through the Sierra to Castile, the Admiral, with his wife and servants, all duly armed with blunderbusses, was one day upon the road. Between la Carolina and Almuradiel, Vilches left well behind, La Venta de Cardenas not quite in sight, whilst the party toiled up the rocky road which, edged with ferns and thicketed with smilax, leads to Los Organos, a troop of seven mounted men appeared upon the road. Terror assailed the travellers, their servants trembling till their blunderbusses almost fell from their hands, the Admiral no doubt cursing the day on which he started, and his wife, being young and lively, looking at the robbers half amused. The chief advanced, and greeting the Admiral with his hat in hand, said, "Admiral, these roads are dangerous. I and my followers have come to be your escort through the hills." Making perhaps what Spaniards call "la risa del conejo," the Admiral thanked him, feared to trespass on this kindness, said that no escort was required, and generally made that soft answer which those who are not strong enough to speak their mind, resort to at a pinch. The day wore on, and still the chief rode chatting by their side, talking of many things: of those strange ships which the mad English were reported to have made, which run upon the water without sails; of the great London, dark all the year, but light on Christmas Day; of the mysterious crimes of Luther, who like an evil spirit in those days haunted uneducated Spaniards' minds; and generally giving his views upon the world and things at large, confirming what he said with proverbs, which he enunciated gravely, as if they were personal experiences of his own. Evening began to fall, and the red, mud walls of Almuradiel appeared a league away; the storks' nests on the housetops of the town looking like clumps of bushes growing from the roofs, the "norias" cracking as the donkeys slowly walked round the elevated track, and the cracked pots revolving one by one, pouring their water down the irrigation rills, giving an Eastern air of peace and quietness, save for the jangling bells. Then suddenly the chief called to his men, who wheeled their horses round and cantered along the road. Riding up close to the Admiral he said, "I am the man you took out of the galleys upon that Easter Day. I knew you at first sight, though you no doubt had long forgotten me. The road across the sierras is beset by petty thieves, mere peddling scoundrels, who had they met you might have been troublesome. Whilst I was with you, and my men, you were safer than had the king's own guards escorted you. We are the seven of Ecija, and so . . . with God." He turned his horse and galloped down the road after his fellows, and the Admiral saw him no more; but his wife used to relate the story to the last day of her life.

Even the lives of interesting men are not all spent in crossing the Despeñaperros, in meeting with the "Siete Niños," and in releasing criminals; so home commands and the honours of a dockyard town at length descended on my personality. Needless to say, "My Lords" at the Admiralty distrusted my admiral ambulant, as it is befitting that the men who wear out acres of cloth on office stools should look askance at men of genius. In the same way the selfsame Lords distrusted and thwarted Lord Dundonald, perhaps the greatest sailor whom Britain ever has produced. They who have wit, and soon no microscope will have a lens sufficiently achromatic to detect their whereabouts, seem to be able to call forth wit in others, as steel strikes fire from flint, or as a witless person seems to render others dull. The solitary recorded witticism of a king is precious and in no wise should be lost, and so it may be fitting that I, unworthy, record the single instance in which our "Sailor King," William IV, was known to fall from the paths of regal seriousness and condescend to nod. At a breakfast at the dockyard on the occasion of the launching of some ship, His Majesty having taken his poor disjune, seeing the Admiral, and remarking that his hair was white, was pleased to say, "Ha, Admiral, white at the main, I see," those being days when admirals were of the red, the white, or blue, according to their rank. His Majesty did not, as he might well have done, on learning that the white hair was not surmounted by a white pennant, exclaim, "Gad Zookers, this will never do, we hereupon promote thee," but no doubt the courtiers, if there were any on the spot, went into "visibilio" at the royal wit.

Portsmouth by nice degrees led up to Greenwich, and there again the Admiral and the King came into contact, but this time without wit. In those days, which now seem almost coeval with Sir Walter Raleigh, so changed they are from ours, on the occasion of a royal visit to the Nore, the midshipman who steered the barge which conveyed the King from the royal yacht to land was always promoted, for having had the fortune to be there. Most admirals naturally took some scion of nobility, some friend of their wife's mother, or in fact some youth who stood in not the smallest need of patronage. But, in the flagship there was, as fortune willed it, an old mate, stricken in years, grey-headed, nurtured in misfortunes, a seaman, if there were such, who had seen, for five-and-twenty years, boy after boy pass over him whilst he remained a mate. Seated abaft the backboard of the Admiral's barge the mate must have appeared ridiculous enough; but the end sanctifies the means, so when the royal eye fell on the curious figure seated in the stern, it twinkled, and the royal voice exclaimed, "Eh what, eh, Admiral, one of your damned jokes! Well, well, he looks a little old still to remain a mate."

The end of men like him whom I describe generally comes without much preparation. Death takes them as a mower cuts ripe hay, leaving their friends almost astounded by their sudden absence from their place.

After a life of happiness and work, grief fell upon him unprepared for it in his old age, and he, not thinking it worth while to struggle, put out to sea at once, after a few days of a feverish cold, which was the name that people gave the influenza, in those quite unsophisticated days.

Hope

Appreciation

The supper-room was full of Jews, of Rastas, of demi-mondaines, of company promoters and adventurers from the five quarters of the globe. The clash of tongues rose high, forcing the most unscientific to admit man's near descent from monkeys, and his relationship to parrots, and macaws. Obsequious and yet half-insolent Swiss and German waiters poured out champagne, the only wine the goodly company of internationalists thought good enough to drink. Palm trees, bred, as it were, to stand tobacco smoke and to resist the artificial light, were stuck about at intervals in great gilt tubs, and their leaves when the draught stirred them were reflected in the enormous looking-glasses with which the walls were lined. Here sat an elderly financier, in his vast, white waistcoat, escorting a slight chorus-girl; a little further on a lady *sur le retour*, her gown cut open almost to her waist, her eyes touched up with kohl, and her hair dyed with henna, was seated with the lover of her pocket, a young man with his dark hair brushed back and plastered to his head. Americans sang like the bagpipes, i' the nose, and Germans grunted; and over all the heady, false, and artificial tones of the imperial race struck one as being used for fun.

Riches and vulgarity kissed one another, each recognising the other's worth, and understanding that the whole world was theirs by right of conquest as long as they combined.

It seemed, as one looked round, that the green fields, the sky, the trees, the songs of birds, the joy of horses, the dawn, the tides, the rhythmical and murmurous motion of the spheres, night, day, the twilight, and all the rest of the mere natural miracles, which nobody can imitate, so few appreciate, and none of us can alter, stay, quicken, or retard, were but mere common things which the assembled company either had never seen or comprehended, or, if they had, imagined they could buy, or set on some inventive, but unpractical poor man to counterfeit. None ate to gratify their hunger or drank because they thirsted, but merely for the sake of spending money, except perhaps one or two of the younger demi-mondaines, whose palates were not surfeited with gold. The guests looked meaner than the men who served them in appearance, and those who served them meaner still than they, for serving any man, when there were stones to break, waste lands to plough, or even a good drain or two to cleanse and purify.

An air of self-contentment, specious and quite impenetrable to pity or to sentiment, exuded from the pores of everyone. Their world was the best world their God could make, and on their seventh day, if they had thought about the matter, they would have called on him complacently, to rest, for it was clear that he could do no more to satisfy their minds. Men slouched into the hall, their hands plunged in their trousers-pockets, with the shamefaced and shambling gait that modern life seems to impart, and women swaggered or sailed in, conscious that wealth and luxury had done as much for them as it had failed to do for the male sex. Nothing in the whole place was human, but the Hungarian band, which, though disguised like monkeys on an organ, in red tail-coats and tight plush shorts, still played as carefully amongst the hum of talk — for music sets off people talking, just as talk starts canaries in a cage to sing — as they had played in rags in their own villages at home.

Their pale, thin faces, peering through glasses at the music, their concentrated air, and the quick glances which they shot at the first violin, who now and then ceased playing for a bar or two and beat the time with his bow hand, placed them in quite another world from the guests seated round the tables, one and all of whom were Semites, either by adoption or by race. In fact, the real Semites were superior in type to those of other races, whose noses had grown high, cheeks reddened, and stomachs swollen in the pursuit of wealth. Few listened to the music, till food and drink had done their work. Then they sat dulled like vultures after a meal of carrion, and their tongues ceased to clatter for a while. Some of them deigned to listen and applaud, but in a patronising way, as if not only the mere music wage-slaves, but the composers, had been called into being by some subconscious action of their own.

Czardas succeeded czardas, the violinist playing like a man inspired, his face illuminated, his black, turned-up moustache twitching and separating like the whiskers of a cat, his agile fingers sliding up the diapason of his fiddle just as a skipjack slips about the surface of a pool, in darts the eye can see, but never follow in their speed. Then, tapping on his music-stand, the leader with a gesture of his bow launched his musicians into the barcarole of "Les Contes d'Hoffmann," with its dreamy rhythm and its air of holding in its notes, suspended betwixt earth and heaven, the soul of him who sacrificed fifteen whole years of life to the work which was to show that he had something better in him than the mere jingling melodies that linked his name to those of Schneider, Elise Tautin, and the rest of their compeers.

It floated through the hall, rising and falling just as a gondola sways at the mouth of a canal, then faded by degrees till it ceased imperceptibly, as does the whirring of the wings of some great insect passing overhead as it flies on beneath the trees. A qualified applause, such as the rich bestow on a mere fiddler, broke out fitfully. Heads nodded, and fat, common hands that never in their lives had handled pick, spade, brush, or pencil, or anything but gold, tapped on the tables with a fleshy sound.

"Beautiful thing, 'Le Comte der Hoffmann,'" an Englishman exclaimed. "The fellow was a count. Offenbach had it all from Hortense Schneider, . . . you know, the gurl who used to dance the kanne-kanne when Louey Napoleon was emperor. Paree was never really Paree since those days. Louey was just the fellow for the French. He understood them. If he had lived, my boy, we never should have had the republic, and all that kind of thing." The women at his table admired his knowledge, and hummed the refrain a little out of tune, one of them who attended concerts remarking it was a little like, what she called "Singe d'Amour," to which a friend rejoined: "How strange! Why, Offenbach died years ago, and yet his music is quite modern." Music of course began to be an art about the time electric light came into use.

A Frenchman drew his wit to the finest thread to make a point about the writer having been a little German *dans le fond*, and then, when a stout German looked at him coldly and insolently, flushed up a little, pretending he had not quite understood what he had wished to say. For nearly half a minute the matter occupied the people in the supper-room, and then, after someone or other had delivered himself to the effect that "music had a soothing sort of effect on the digestive organs," they all forgot about it, and turned to discuss the important things of life — adultery, divorce, the stock exchange, and the last "aviator"dashed to pieces in his fall.

The writer, who in the coulisses of his theatre for years had kept a bright spot in his soul, working and polishing at his ewe lamb, that he was fated never to see born, at last had been appreciated. All had been done that man can do to wipe away a stain, and all the years of struggle and neglect to-day were as they never had been; for, after all, applause is what men work for, and not gold, and so that the applause be given, it does not matter in the least from whence it comes. The public crowns the artist, and if occasionally it puts the crown on just a little bit awry, no one need hold himself offended, for its great heart is sound.

Replete with food at last, the suppers slowly began to leave their seats, and as the function of a band is to add noise to noise, the leader tapped sharply on his music-stand, and as by inspiration recommenced just where he had left off. Once more the cadence of the barcarole quavered and floated through the hall, rose, fell, and finally melted away like the faint threnody of a dragon-fly heard in imagination by a mad musician in a dream. Then the good company definitely rose, exhaling fumes of scent and perspiration, whilst through the windows came the first flush of dawn, but smoke-ridden and grey, with the air sullied by the exhalations of a million pairs of lungs.

Appendix 1

Four Women in *Faith* (1909) and *Hope* (1910)

Mention of Robert Bontine Cunninghame Graham (1852-1936) usually raises very varied images: a Scottish nobleman with socialist beliefs; a fine horseman; an excellent speaker of Spanish; an adventurous traveller; a South American gaucho; a failed rancher in Texas; a fencing tutor in Mexico City; and a Liberal Member of Parliament (1886-1892) who argued against colonialism and imperialism and for radical socialist-style changes in British society. He campaigned hard, for example, to achieve true social and economic freedom for women, writing in 1908 in his usual combative style that

> "... the present political system is a potent engine for the subjection of women..." and that "... it has taken nineteen hundred years for women to gain the same equality before the law as they enjoyed in the time of Hadrian..." [1]

Graham began writing seriously in the 1890s, publishing fourteen collections of sketches and tales between 1896 and 1936. The collections *Faith* (1909) and *Hope* (1910) appear in the middle of his most productive period of writing. What evidence is there in *Faith* and *Hope* of Graham engaging in literary terms with significant female characters?

"Sor Candida and the Bird", the opening sketch or tale in *Faith* (1909), is set in the northern Spanish meseta town of Ávila. Ávila is forever associated with Saint Teresa of Ávila (1515-1582), the great nun, mystic, writer, reformer of the Carmelite Order and founder of the Discalced (sandal-wearing) Carmelites. A few details of nineteenth-century modernity barely diminish the aura of timelessness often associated with Ávila.

The fabric of the story is slight: a nun saves a dying bird, for a time all is well, the bird dies, and the nun accuses herself - and Saint Teresa. The nun's name - Sor (Sister) Candida - is intriguing. Whereas 'candid' in English means 'frank and outspoken; unbiased; white; clean and pure', Graham, fluent speaker of Spanish, would know that 'cándido, cándida' in Spanish means 'naïve; innocent; simple, ingenuous'. For most of the tale Graham deploys this Spanish value of innocence.

Interestingly, Graham shows Sor Candida and her closest colleagues infringing convent rules by keeping the bird to enjoy its singing. The mother superior, having caught them listening to the bird, allows the bird to remain till she can get a ruling from higher authority. As time passes, the bird is allowed to sing in the chapel, and all seems happy.

The following year, amidst the suffocating heat and hectic activity on Saint Teresa's feast day, the bird is forgotten about and dies of thirst. Whilst Sor Candida recognises her own responsibility for the bird's death, she also asks why the saint had not reminded her of the bird. In the nun's momentary quasi-rebellion Graham is perhaps playing mischievously with the 'frank and outspoken' English values of 'candid'. This apparent criticism of Saint Teresa is immediately followed by Sor Candida accepting the death as a punishment and a warning that nuns should not attach themselves to anyone but Christ.

Graham presents an enclosed order of nuns devoted to prayer in a benign light. He counterbalances this, however, with a series of sharp observations that deepen and sometimes darken the reader's understanding of the scenario. Sor Candida "made a little cage..., not thinking for a moment that after giving life she thus would take away life's chiefest treasure - liberty; but all in tender heart." Sor Candida "had left the world and all its vanities, losing her liberty, perhaps to save herself from want": poverty and hunger in old Spain drove many to join religious communities. The prioress, appointed to maintain obedience to the rules of the order, yet succumbs to very human sympathy. The visiting provincial much enjoys snuff, cigars, chocolate and sweetmeats. He also enjoys keeping the prioress as a mere woman in her subservient place as a lower-order agent of faith rather than as an enquiring intelligence. The tenderness of Graham's careful evocation of a kindly nun and her very traditional community is undercut somewhat by a slightly acid dimension in the vision of the opinionated external narrator.

"The Captive", in *Hope* (1910), is set on the open grasslands or pampa in the southern area of the huge province of Buenos Aires, very probably in the eighteen-seventies. This tale is dense with cultural reverberations.

Graham's wide readings probably included the popular novel of the early North-American frontier, *The Last of the Mohicans* (1826) by James Fenimore Cooper. In early Argentine literature Graham was almost certainly familiar with the works of Esteban Echeverría (1805-1851). Echeverría, after five years in France (1825-1830), introduced Romanticism into Argentina, penning the short story "El matadero"

("The Slaughteryard"), the first significant piece of prose fiction in independent Argentina; the political pamphlet "Dogma socialista"; and a long narrative poem entitled *La cautiva* ("The Captive") based on the abduction of a white woman by wild pampa Indians. Graham very likely also studied Sarmiento's treatise *Facundo* (1845), where the sub-title offered the young republic of Argentina a choice between "civilización y barbarie" ("civilisation and barbarism"). Graham like all the gauchos loved the *Martín Fierro*, José Hernández's long narrative poem of 1872 and 1879 devoted to the prototypical gaucho caught between the white and Indian worlds. These works by Echeverría, Sarmiento and Hernández set the framework for the long-term debate about the future direction of Argentina. Graham, though, does not allow these extensive readings in key Spanish-language texts to interfere with his telling of a fascinating story.

In Graham's usual long introduction - roughly one quarter of the tale - a group of white settlers of different nationalities of origin camp at night on the pampa: they have failed to find a band of Indians who had stolen horses from a ranch on the river Napostá. The night camp is fluently rendered. Graham often deploys a single speaker addressing a group of listeners and here, a Belgian offers to recount the experience fifteen or so years previously of a former neighbour.

One day out on the pampa the Belgian's neighbour took as a prisoner a young, pretty and seemingly Indian woman who was driving a bunch of ponies. The woman had brown hair rather than Indian black, and at first spoke faltering Spanish. In fact white, she had been abducted eight years previously by Indians and had borne three sons to an Indian chief. Settled into her white captor's *rancho* (hut), she gradually recovers her Hispanic identity, dropping her Indian name of Lincomilla to become once again Nieves ('Snows'). The man falls in love with the woman and - as with Sor Candida and the bird - for a time they are blissfully happy, till a melancholy Nieves reveals to her lover that she is desperately missing her half-Indian children. The man accepts her decision to return to the desert, to the wilderness, to the Indians.

Graham by 1910 had already often castigated the white man's view of himself as a superior civilising force for economic development and for Christian good, dutifully battling against the primitive savagery and paganism of native peoples and cultures. There is no attempt in "The Captive" - either by Graham or by the woman - to present pampa Indian society as anything other than brutal and savage, especially in its treatment of white women captives. Yet in the first encounter Lincomilla had not tried to escape - not because she feared returning to the Indians - but because she cared for her mare and its new foal, the latter unable to keep up with its mother in any attempt at flight. This same maternal impulse in Nieves leads her to surrender her new-found happiness with the white man to seek out her half-Indian children. Given the opportunity to re-adjust back into white society, Lincomilla/Nieves abandons white Hispanic civilisation as offered on the pampa: Nieves returns to being Lincomilla. The Belgian narrating supposedly on behalf of his old neighbour has of course told his own story.

The drama of the person caught between conflicting worlds is taken up two generations later in two tales by the Argentinian writer Jorge Luis Borges (1899-1986). In "Historia del guerrero y de la cautiva" [2] ("Story of the warrior and the female captive") from 1949, Borges first tells of the barbarian Droctulft who decides to defend the city of Ravenna against his own people: the barbarian opts to defend civilisation. Borges next recalls his grandmother seeing a blonde-haired blue-eyed 'Indian' girl in Junín, on the then frontier, in 1872 and trying to convince this English lass to return to white society. When "The other woman answered her that she was happy and she returned, that night, to the wilderness", the civilised person opts for barbarism. In Borges' "El sur" ("The South") from 1953 Juan Dahlmann, grandchild on the father's side of European immigrants and on the mother's side of long-established Hispano-Argentine stock, is provoked in a remote rural restaurant by three drunken ranch workers. When a knife is brandished, Dahlmann - a man of the European-style city and working in a library - accepts the challenge, picks up a knife for himself and steps out on to the prairie. Dahlmann knows that he is going to die in a classic Argentine scenario, the pampa knife-fight, but with such a death Dahlmann will achieve his heart's desire - Argentine authenticity. Graham's Lincomilla/Nieves and Borges' Yorkshire lass and Juan Dahlmann all abandon European-style civilisation to commit to an American barbarism.

In "The Captive" Graham - a Scotsman - makes a very early and very stylish contribution to the furious debate as to whether Argentina should adopt the native rural American cultural model or the white urban culture imported from Europe. Graham will return - powerfully so - to the same debate in "Charlie the Gaucho" in his last volume in 1936.

"Un Monsieur", in *Hope* (1910), is set in London perhaps around 1900. There are initially two characters - a listener (Graham) and a speaker, a woman called Elise. The tale is essentially a monologue by Elise, though her monologue reports on a series of encounters: between Elise and Monsieur; between Elise and Monsieur's wife; between Elise again and Monsieur; and finally Elise briefly encountering Monsieur and his wife together.

Elise describes regular visits by a fifty-year-old Monsieur who at the end of each visit leaves a ten-pound note on the mantelpiece and goes off in his car. Elise is a high-class French prostitute working in turn-of-the-century London. Elise is intelligent and cultured, much more so than the Englishman. She is for the Englishman nothing more than an instrument of physical pleasure. She has to tolerate "a dull, fat, old man, simply because he has a big account at some bank or other."

One day Elise is visited by a beautiful lady who produces a photograph of a man - Elise's customer. Elise, loyal to her code of professional etiquette, denies ever seeing the man. She guesses that her visitor is the man's wife, when the latter offers Elise a thousand pounds if she chooses to recollect the man. Elise again declines. On the man's next visit, Elise reveals that his wife had come to call. His wife is seeking a divorce, and with a daughter aged ten, the man desperately wants to avoid the highly public disgrace - c. 1900 - of the Divorce Court. Given this sign of paternal love, Elise for the first time likes the man. He offers to do anything for Elise if she will maintain her silence. He kisses her, now "quite as a man kisses a real woman", and leaves. Thoroughly upset, Elise cries. Months pass with no further word from the man. One day Elise encounters the couple in a London park. The couple, who seem to have come to some accommodation, recognise her. Elise passes on. She concludes: "... at first I thought he was a *lâche* and then a scoundrel, but now I know that he was but a rich man - 'un Monsieur' - and probably today, if he thinks of the matter now and then, promptly dismisses it, and says as he lights up a cigar: 'She was a prostitute'".

The contrast between Elise and her customer is stark: he wealthy, she a working prostitute; he somewhat old and fat, she much younger and very attractive; he views her in merely physical terms, whereas she is an artist in love-making; he lacks culture whereas she enjoys poetry and modern painting; his code of values is money-based, hers is one of professional honour. She despises him and his wealth-dictated values - till he shows paternal care for his ten-year-old daughter.

The encounter between the man's wife and Elise is well handled. The man's wife is tall, dark, well dressed and beautiful, and she addresses Elise unpatronisingly in good French. Her elegance contrasts sharply with the photograph of her husband showing his elephantine ears and an air of self-contentment based on his money. The lady visitor, Elise's equal in beauty and intelligence, makes the same mistake as her husband: she thinks that being rich she can buy Elise's compliance. This emphasis on wealth annoys Elise and over and over again she refuses to help the divorce-seeking wife.

Elise finally recognises that her customer is not quite an absolute scoundrel but simply a rich man. Yet Elise has shown her listener (Graham) and the reader that she has a higher standard of moral behaviour than the alleged pillar of society - the rich man who buys time with high-class prostitutes. The reader may have a smidgeon of sympathy with the rich man's wife, caught in a loveless marriage and aware that her husband has recourse to prostitutes. Yet the prostitute stands higher morally than even the misused wife. Graham presents the French prostitute almost as a guardian of moral rectitude in upper-class London.

"Buta", in *Hope* (1910), opens on a sandbank in a tidal river near a ruined Roman town and an old Arab town. The setting is North Africa, the time fairly recent. Several riders rest and smoke, until Nazim begins to speak. Nazim delivers the tale in a virtual monologue: his listeners (including Graham) hardly speak.

Nazim recalls working as manager for English commercial interests at Cape Juby on Morocco's southern coast. This remark recalls the nineteenth-century scramble amongst the European powers hungry for coaling-stations, warehousing facilities and monopoly trading rights throughout Africa and Asia. Unable to discern whether the English deceive the world and God, or whether they deceive themselves, he decides to tell his companions the tale of an Arab girl called Rahma.

Rahma's name, meaning 'merciful' in Arabic, has been changed to 'Buta' "which, as you know, is how the Arabs pronounce a certain Spanish word." The Spanish word not given is 'puta' meaning 'prostitute, whore', slightly modified in Arab pronunciation. Graham's sketch titles, especially personal or place-names in Latin, Gaelic, Spanish, Arabic and even Guaraní and Maori, can challenge the reader, as in "Salvagia", "A Pakeha", "Gualeguaychú", "Ha Til Mi Tuliadh" and "Bopicuá".

The Cape Juby factory managed by Nazim for four years sold nothing: its purpose was to establish a physical presence and create a basis for being awarded monopoly trading 'rights'. Scottish clerks kept the books. In Nazim's view all men on seeing a pretty woman smack their lips, whereas the Englishman at first looks through her but later sends a boy to ask her to come to him.

Rahma was a widow with two children, one fathered by the late husband, the other "sent from God". Her tent near the factory allowed the clerks to talk to her on evening strolls. She owned only a few animals and an old loom, and was given surplus food by local tribespeople. She was tall, brown, with velvet eyes. As "… by degrees Rahma became acquainted with several of the clerks", some of them claimed that they were interested in her soul's welfare. Nazim's opinion that English commercial values view the soul as cheap appals the three listeners, two British and one Yankee, his listeners "being convinced of the superiority of our race, our faith, our principles, and everything that appertained to us". Rahma is recognised openly by the local Arabs as a prostitute serving the Christians.

Rahma does not speak in the tale and is not interiorised in any way. She is a very poor and vulnerable woman, lacking a husband and having two children to care for. Graham highlights the hypocrisy of very junior agents of a foreign power who claim to be seeking to save the soul of a vulnerable native of a different faith while they use her for their sexual satisfaction. Rahma is an almost helpless victim of colonial exploitation: her being used sexually is perhaps for Graham a symbol of an even greater and more loathsome economic and political exploitation.

In hugely varied physical settings, Graham explores the different levels of moral, economic and social status in four women. The Moroccan Rahma/Buta is very passive and barely sketched in, perhaps because Graham was aiming rather at the small, local mechanisms involved in white European colonial exploitation of other races and cultures. The Spanish nun Sor Candida and the Argentine Lincomilla/Nieves do speak and act in their own cause. Sor Candida commits three small acts of independent behaviour (stepping outside the convent to rescue the bird, harbouring the bird in her cell and criticising Saint Teresa) before re-submitting to convent discipline. Lincomilla/ Nieves has to make a desperate choice between remaining with her caring lover or seeking out her three half-Indian children in the wilderness. Elise's monologue unveils a formidable lady capable, though a prostitute, of greater social insight and moral rectitude than either her ultra-respectable customer or her customer's ultra-respectable wife. With the exception perhaps of the Belgian settler in "The Captive", the men in these tales can all be found lacking. In contrast, the women display usually quite admirable behaviour and character.

Significant female characters are a minority in Graham's work, but they do exist and Graham through them explores a rich range of physical, social and moral scenarios, displaying a considerable understanding of and sympathy with women in the widely different situations - often male-dominated and oppressive - in which they have to function and survive.

[1]   "The Real Equality of the Sexes", in *The New Age*, July 11, 1908, page 207. Available on the Internet.

[2]   Jorge Luis Borges: *El Aleph* (Alianza Editorial, Madrid, decimonovena reimpresión en "Libro de Bolsillo", 1991)

[3]   *idem*, page 53.

(JMcI)

Appendix 2

Cunninghame Graham: Editing His Spanish

The material is taken from *Faith* (1909), especially from "Sor Candida and the Bird", "A Silhouette", "A Saint", "Paja y cielo", "Los Peares, un minuto!", "Andorra" and "El Pastor de Las Navas".

RBCG uses great quantities of Spanish in his tales and sketches. A very high percentage of his usages are appropriate in terms of the context and accurate in their rendition, including the stress marks in Spanish. This correctness is seen in four examples from each of the above tales: Virgen del Pilar, turrón, Sáhara and Andújar (SC); facón, Villaguay, chiripá and ñandubay (ASi); Las Puercas, La Mano Negra, Indulto and alameda (ASa); chajá, "bichos", pobrecito and espinillo (PyC); Galicia, Val de Cabras, gaita and robledos (LP); Viva España, cortijo, Guardia Civil and aguardiente (A); and cigarrales, Alcázar, ajimeces and Aragón (EP).

Graham in English favours some older spellings, as in Buenos Ayres, Teneriffe and possibly Santa Fé.

RBCG loves Bernal Díaz's chronicle of the Spanish subjection of the Aztecs in 1519-1521, yet his beloved Díaz is never given his written stress mark. The written stress mark is also omitted in many other common place-names and personal names: Cándida, Ávila, María, Entre Ríos, sí, López, Cádiz, Peñón, romería, Fernández, San Lúcar, Bernal Díaz, Gaucín, Écija, José, afición, Vizcaína, Tío, kilómetros, alfaquí, Tránsito and Córdoba.

Many words are given a written stress mark that they do not need: 'Arré' ('Gee up!'), monté, maté (the Paraguayan tea favoured by gauchos), Pampéro, Fuláno, Gualeguáy, Villaguáy, Jeréz, matáco, guanáco, camaloté, pajonáles, Urgél (nine times over), *Marigalanté*, mayorál, zagál, coyoté, Villalár, Roncesválles and Sompórt. Note that in "A Silhouette" Villaguay is delivered correctly, Villaguáy is not.

Graham usually places the tilde correctly, as in España, (Tio) Ponzoña, Doña Tecla, Doña Gertrudis, Señor and in the sup-tropical hardwood tree known as ñandubay.

Some of these confusions may be the hand of the printer. The ultimate responsibility is Graham's. His very subtle use in "A Silhouette" of 'ño Gregorio' - 'ño' being a term of respect used to older men in rural areas - suggests the depth of Graham's knowledge. He must have known that very high-frequency units like José, Díaz, López and Fernández should always carry the written stress mark. So whence all the flaws and errors?

By all accounts he loathed proof-reading. The Villaguay case suggests that he could not always achieve consistent presentation of an item within the same tale or sketch. In the second-last sketch in the collection, "Andorra", there is a sudden eruption of italics: *mayorál, zagál, bota, arriero, poncho, alpargatas, cortijo, Guardia Civil, aguardiente, guajira, gracioso, gracia, venta, albarda, tertulia* and *sereno*. Why in the same sketch are italics not also applied to yerbales, andaluces, el resucitao, bárbaro, kilometros and plaza?

An editor thinking to emend all Graham's flawed presentations of Hispanic units faces a considerable task. These editors prefer to signal their awareness of the problem and leave Graham's original texts unemended.

(JMcI)

Index to Stories in Volume 3